Edmond de Pressensé

Rome and Italy

at the opening of the cumenical council

Edmond de Pressensé

Rome and Italy
at the opening of the cumenical council

ISBN/EAN: 9783337381875

Printed in Europe, USA, Canada, Australia, Japan

Cover: Foto ©Andreas Hilbeck / pixelio.de

More available books at **www.hansebooks.com**

ROME AND ITALY

OPENING OF THE ŒCUMENICAL COUNCIL,

DEPICTED IN TWELVE LETTERS

WRITTEN FROM ROME TO A GENTLEMAN IN AMERICA,

By EDMOND DE PRESSENSE, D.D.,

PASTOR OF THE EVANGELICAL CHURCH IN PARIS,

And author of " l'histoire des trois premiers siècles de l'Eglise Chretiénne,"
" Jésus Christ, son temps, son oevre et sa vie," etc.

TRANSLATED BY

REV. GEORGE PRENTICE, A.M.

——— —

NEW YORK:

CARLTON & LANAHAN.

SAN FRANCISCO: E. THOMAS.

CINCINNATI: HITCHCOCK & WALDEN.

1870.

Per lor maledizion sì non si perde,
Che non possa tornar l'eterno amore.

DANTE.

INTRODUCTORY NOTE
BY THE AMERICAN PUBLISHERS.

The following Letters, furnishing a rapid pen photograph of the first impressions of a distinguished traveler on visiting Italy and Rome at the opening of the Council, are received by the American publishers immediately from the author's hands. As fast as received they have been committed to type, and the earliest possible publication has succeeded the reception of the last Letter. They are not to be republished in Europe within several months after the present issue. The American reader, therefore, has the first view, presented by the author's artistic hand, of the varied scenes through which he passes.

Pressensé has attained a noble and growing reputation in both Europe and America as the leader of the conservative-progressive branch of French Protestantism, as well as by several valuable productions ; particularly his " Life of Christ," his " Religion and the Reign of Terror," and his " Early Days of Christianity," the two former published, and the latter in process of publication, in both England and America. The first volume of the latter will appear in a few days from our own press. His principles and predilections, being on the side of freedom and progress, but averse to either political or religious destructivism, are in peculiar sympathy with the spirit of soundhearted American Protestantism. We cheerfully anticipate, therefore, that there are thousands in our country who will delight to survey from his standpoint the objects, characters, and events which he passingly portrays.

TRANSLATOR'S NOTE.

WHEN the dogma of the Immaculate Conception was proclaimed by the sole authority of the Pope, M. de Pressensé declared that a formidable crisis was inevitable in the bosom of the Catholic Church. He affirmed that an act which so deliberately trampled on the rights of the entire Church, could not fail to awaken great alarm, and provoke obstinate resistance. This prediction was soon fulfilled. The most enlightened members of the Catholic communion have never accepted that dogma. But as they did not resist its promulgation with sufficient energy, their bearing invited the Romish party to perfect its victory. This would be done if a General Council could be induced to decree that infallibility of the Pope which is plainly implied in the proclamation of the Immaculate Conception. The Council of the Vatican has it as its special mission, then, to surrender the rights and powers of the Episcopacy into the hands of the Sovereign Pontiff. It is pleasant and instructive to watch the preliminary movements and opening scenes of such a Council in the company of an observer so well informed and sagacious as M. de Pressensé.

His book will possess a permanent value as a record of events and impressions on the eve of the Council, and also from the interesting discussions which he has interwoven with them.

I have sought to render my version faithful to the original. That it always reflects the exact meaning of the author I am sure; whether it fairly represents the vigor and sparkle of his style I leave others to judge.

GEORGE PRENTICE.

HYDE PARK, MASS., *Feb.* 16, 1870.

CONTENTS.

LETTER I.

LETTER II.

LETTER III.

8   Contents.

LETTER VII.

LETTER VIII.

LETTER IX.

LETTER X.

RECENT EXCAVATIONS AT ROME — THE PALACE OF THE CÆSARS AND THE CATACOMBS.

LETTER XI.

LETTER XII.

ROME, ITALY;

AND THE

ŒCUMENICAL COUNCIL.

LETTER I.

Hints to the Reader—Reflections on leaving France: her Political Condition; her Interest in the Council—Father Hyacinthe—The Abbe Maret on the Infallibility of the Pope—A Sunday in the Alps —Lombardy: her Past and Present; her Artistic Jewels—Umbria: her Type of Piety in the Middle Ages; Scenery; Political State and Art—Perugino and Raphael—Assisi and St. Francis: his Spirit; Order; Errors; Lessons to us; Legend; Tomb and its Treasures—Goethe's Fanaticism—Hesitation of the Ultramontanists —The *Invito Sacro* with Comments.

ROME, *Nov.* 6, 1869.

DEAR SIR:—Permit me to remind you that I am to send you *letters;* that is, the lively, spontaneous expression of my impressions concerning this land of Italy, whose bare name suffices to arouse the imagination, and which has not lost the incomparable charm with which she has intoxicated all her visitors, and, on the eve of the Council which awakens so much disquietude, curiosity, and also hope. It is a solemn moment in the history of the Catholic Church, which may well sound the hour of her mortal agony, or at least put her in grave peril; for so great an effort issuing in a check, so formidable a sword-stroke ending in the rippling of water, would be a discomfiture unexampled in her history. But

one thing could be more dangerous to her—the insolent triumph of the frantic party which would truly
make the Pope a God to march before mankind,
according to the wish of the idolatrous Israelites. In
every respect, then, a visit at Rome in these excep-
tional circumstances has its peculiar interest. I shall
give you my conclusions with the most entire sincerity,
in all the vivacity of their primal gush. Do not expect in these pages the carefully carved chapters of a
controversial treatise, or of a Traveler's Guide for
Italy. No, you will here find in all their medley the
emotions experienced in the presence of marvels of
art, in the presence of the melancholy splendors of a
natural scenery which adorns with enchanting grace
the mourning array of a ruined world, and the not
less vivacious ones inspired by that modern Pharisaism which here has only the wit to whiten a magnificent sepulcher in which it would shut up the religion
of the Risen, and with it an enslaved world, under
the same sealed and well-guarded stone.

I left France, herself, too, in a dark hour of her
history, agitated, feverish, starting up from the long
despotism which she has undergone and almost deserved, as one starts with convulsive bounds from a
nightmare—divided between distrust of her governors,
whose concessions are blended with imprudent regrets
and insane recoilings, and the dread of socialist dema-
gogues, who hasten to transform the little freedom we
have regained into license, and speak every evening
of the approaching division of all possessions, or what
they call *the great social liquidation.*

Let us hope that the true liberal party will be able
to find its way between these two extreme sections,
and save us from a bloody catastrophe which would

lead to new Cæsars. Forgive my uneasy and sad-
dened patriotism these painful reflections, which occupy my mind at the moment of leaving my country
for a few weeks.

From a religious stand-point, the Council is naturally the great affair in France, as every-where; while
people expect it to produce universal harmony, it is
producing the most noisy divisions in the bosom of
the Church of Unity. I shall be told that these are
the discordant notes of musical instruments preparing to perform their part in a symphony. I doubt
whether they can be brought into unison, skillful as
the leader of the orchestra may be, at least without
breaking a few. The reason is very simple; the
principal cause of division among the symphonists
of the Catholic Church is precisely the authority of
the leader of the orchestra. Some think his baton
should be obeyed like the rod of Moses, or the scep-
ter of Judah. Others would have it tempered and
restrained. What, then, are the means of agreement?
Evidently, the Papacy can triumph only by imposing
silence on the recalcitrant; but to suppress discordant voices is not to melt them into harmony. Read
the circular letters of our Bishops, the articles of our
Catholic journals of various shades! On the one
hand, anathema is hurled at all who do not bow before the personal infallibility of the Holy Father—
that is the dogma of dogmas, for it is authority in
its supreme, palpable manifestation. On the other
hand, appeal is made to the history of the Church, to
the ancient Councils, and to the Gallican Church.
There is a discord of tumultuous and irritated voices.
Such is the preface to the Council in France. When
I left Paris two religious manifestations chiefly occu-

pied public attention. The first was the striking rupture of Father Hyacinthe with Rome. It is vain to talk; this is a terrible blow for Catholicism. Sarcasms and condemnations will not enfeeble the effect of this act, which reveals to all men the conscious inability of sincere and liberal minds to remain in the bonds of Romanism. This utterance of conscience, which is no seditious outcry, but an appeal to the tribunal of Jesus Christ, has had a deep reverberation among our people. It will have a more salutary effect than his most eloquent discourses in that pulpit of Nôtre Dame, where that mighty voice will resound no more—the most eloquent voice our generation has heard, and which was privileged beyond any other to attract and thrill thousands of listeners. The momentary silence of Father Hyacinthe is the most energetic of protestations against religious servitude; and of this silent preaching we may say that it is heard in the very depths of the consciences of men. I shall come back to Father Hyacinthe when I shall have to attest the effect produced at Rome by this courageous deed.

The second event of which I would speak is the book of the Abbé Maret, Bishop of Sura, against the infallibility of the Pope. This grave and solid work asserts the periodicity of the Councils, which alone, in union with the Papacy, have the privileges of infallibility. Doubtless we can no more accept this conclusion than that of the Ultramontanes—we who admit no other infallibility than that which comes from the Holy Spirit. But for the Romish party the book of the Abbé Maret, which is the standard of Gallican, and more or less liberal Catholicism, is the abomination of desolation. His colleagues in the episcopacy, too, feel no scruple in anathematizing it to their hearts' content. I mention this book because it sums up, in some sort, the pith of the most embarrassing question for the Council, and because, with the resolutions, so distinct under their respectful form, of the Bishops at Fulda, it presents the programme of what may be called the left wing of the great Œcumenical Council. I shall strive to learn here what its chances are, and whether it will succeed at least in preventing the follies to which the Coryphæi of the party of Rome would gladly push things. At any rate, there prevails, for these various reasons, a great anxiety concerning the Council and its issue. Do not these words, which express an incontestably true feeling, suffice for the condemnation of the entire Catholic system. What! you affirm that the Holy Spirit will speak through the Council! You indeed say the Holy Spirit, the very Spirit of God—and you are inquiet about what he shall say—you are not very sure that he will conclude on what is good and desirable for the Church! You are anxious—as if you had to do with fallible and ignorant beings—as though you had to do with yourselves! This is because you are dealing with yourselves, and yourselves alone. You feel this at bottom, and that is why you are perfectly right in being alarmed: the sequel will show how well-founded are these fears.

Such, sir, were my thoughts as I departed from my own country and approached this city, to which so many eyes now turn as toward the Zion of the Lord. My last pause on Protestant soil, before approaching the proper domain of Catholicism, was well-suited to make the contrast salient to me between the religion of the Spirit and that of the Letter. I spent Sunday,

October 30, in an Evangelical Church belonging to the
Free Church of the Canton de Vaud, which is situated on the heights of the Alps among the Ormonts.
Very modest is the humble chapel where these pious
mountaineers, zealous and decided members of a
Church which has known the baptism of persecution,
were assembled. And yet, in presence of the lofty
and snowy summits which surround it, and that were
illuminated by the most radiant sunshine, it rears before the eyes a still loftier summit, even of that worship in spirit and in truth which is solemnized neither
on the mountain of Jerusalem nor on that of Gerizim,
but wherever Jesus Christ has true adorers. It was
a fine and touching thing to see these sturdy shep-
herds of the Alps journeying along prematurely
snowy roads toward their chapel, to rest from their
rude toil as they sang the praises of the Lord in their
natal tongue. Their manly and weary features were
kindled up with the pure light of inward piety.
These were truly priests of the New Covenant, declaring " in their own tongue the wonderful works
of God." The Sistine Chapel, with its cardinals in
scarlet robes and its strangely delicate harmonies, will
offer me no spectacle comparable with that which I
witnessed with deep joy in a remote corner of the
mighty Alps.

Let us rapidly cross the Simplon, despite the magnificence of the Bernese Alps, which appear from the
rugged and narrow gorges, in all their glory, under
the splendor of a beautiful autumnal sun. Behold
Italy! behold the rich and monotonous region of
Lombardy—then the low and fertile valleys watered
by the Po! Every thing has indeed changed since
my first visit to this region fifteen years ago. The

traveler notes this agreeably in the greater facility of
public conveyances. He no longer has to suffer from
the infinite division of Italy into petty principalities,
each of which extended to him a hand eager for the
price of his passage. But especially, his eye is no
longer offended by the white coat of the Austrian
soldier, who appeared on this soil that detested him
like a consuming worm on a rose. It is all over with
those petty tyrants of Parma and Modena, who had
not even wit enough to keep their thrones, and needed
a German saber to preserve them. I know all the
faults with which the new Italian kingdom may be
reproached; the medley of intrigue and violence
which it has employed in swallowing the peninsular
artichoke. I shall beware of calling evil good; but it
still remains true that the new kingdom has responded to the deepest and most legitimate national aspirations, and that finally it has delivered the country
from an abominable clerical oppression which, had it
lasted, would have dried up the springs of all higher
life. The partisans of absolutism cast stones at the
New Italy, and laugh at her difficulties; they are
pitiless toward her eccentricities, toward the trouble
she finds in giving a solid and reasonable basis to her
public life. They forget that she contracted her defects under their tuition, and that the freedman long
retains the marks of his chains. These considerations
came back to my memory the other day as I roamed
through the city of Parma, which particularly suffered
under the most abject tyranny. She has not yet fully
awakened; the shadow of her past enfolds her. Her
population still seems given up to the listlessness of
enslaved nations; the flagstones of her streets are
worn by the lazy tramp of her numberless abbés and

her idle youth. Patience! All this is changing from
day to day—modern life with its severe exactions is
invading the ancient ducal residence. At any rate,
the town has incomparable artistic jewels in the
paintings of her Correggio. There must we learn to
know this genius who conceived a purely modern
type of beauty, full of intelligence and passion, whose
finest shades he was skilled to reproduce through the
infinite gradations of his *chiaro-oscuro*. The Virgin,
in his picture of St. Jerome, strikes you as a fresh
and more penetrating intuition of eternal beauty
than any other. I pass Florence, where I may pause
with you on my return, and I transport you
into marvelous Umbria, so long bowed under the
yoke of Rome, but which has ardently desired and
paid for its enfranchisement. It was here that the
Catholicism of the Middle Ages had its finest development, and that it created a truly Christian art,
which gave expression to a high ideal that we should
be able to admire, even though for us it has been in
many respects transformed. It is impossible not to
be struck with the singular relation existing between
the aspect of these beautiful scenes and the works of
the great masters who were born or developed here.
Nature is not at all oppressive in its grandeur, as
among lofty mountains, nor seductive, as on the coasts
of the Mediterranean. It is full of sweetness, calmness, and harmony, though along its horizon appear
the gentle peaks of the Apennines. The outlines of
the landscape stand forth in exquisite purity and grace;
they seem to undulate in light curves, following the
sinuosities of the innumerable little mountains which
cut up the plain, and are covered with the elegant
vegetation of the South. Fling over this lovely

scenery a golden light which imparts to every object the most perfect transparency, and you will understand that Umbria is admirably fitted to inspire an ingenuous and profound style of art. She does not stifle its flights beneath a startling magnificence; she gently stimulates it, and furnishes its palette with that pleasant coloring which suits purely ideal painting, whose contours should be firm and fixed as those of the horizon. There truly ought that fair blossom of artistic mysticism to spring up and unfold which preceded the splendid works of the Renaissance. Let us add that the appearance of the great Umbrian school coincides with one of the finest religious movements of humanity, of which, in some sort, it bears the burning impress. Before speaking of this movement, which is very interesting through the contrast it offers with the character of contemporary Catholic piety, let us pause a moment at Perugia, which was the center and focus of the Umbrian school. It overlooks the whole country that I have just described, and is stamped with that inimitable seal of Old Italy which the railways themselves will hardly destroy. Besides, it largely escapes the impetuous movement of civilization; for the trains that pass at its foot set down few travelers tempted to pause. Those who ascend its hill are true art-pilgrims, and not merely curious people. Yet patriotic feeling has awakened great agitations here. Before the hour of her deliverance, Perugia simply bore with indignation the dominion of the Holy See, which paralyzed all her national life, and would make her a mere museum, while beside her echoed mightily the cry of emancipation. On occasion of the war of 1859, she revolted.

Unhappily for her, the treaty of Villafranca came

to cut short for a time all hopes of the enfranchisement of Southern Italy. Before this time she had
been recaptured by the pontifical troops, who had
given themselves up to the most frightful excesses,
as worthy servants of the Vicar of the Prince of
Peace. This event produced a very lively impression
of indignation even in the bosom of French Catholicism, at least in its enlightened section. I remember
meeting at that period, in Paris, some of the most
eminent of her clergy. I dared not whisper a word
before them about the sacking of Perugia. But it
was quite needless prudence, for they loudly condemned the odious act. Not only, said they, do we
believe all the abominations imputed to the Swiss
troops of the Holy Father, but we believe even
worse things. In his service he has the vilest rascals
in Europe, and the best thing that could happen to him
would be to have his army soundly whipped, so that he
might escape the deplorable consequences to which his
temporal power leads. When priests hold such language we can imagine how disinterested laymen felt.
It is worth while, truly, to reconquer a wretched strip
of land by the ruin of thousands of souls! Paris is
well worth a mass, said Henry IV., to explain his
abjuration. It is an unworthy saying, even in the
mouth of such a prince as he. The Papacy of our
day seems to say, " My temporal dominion is worth
more to me than my spiritual dominion ; Rome is
well worth all the masses in the world." It is, indeed, certain that the more tyrannical the sacerdotal
yoke becomes in civil things, the less do men believe
in the mass, that is, in the spiritual pontificate. We
shall have more than one occasion to resume these
considerations. Let us return to the Perugia of

ancient times. From the stand-point of history and art it is immensely interesting; for it is there that we grasp the transition from the priestly and immobile Byzantine style of painting to the living and animated style of modern times. In place of a conventional type constantly reproduced on a golden ground, we have works of individuality. Life begins to break forth from the eyes; the glance grows suddenly animated, because that is the most direct organ of the soul, and because the focus of man's life is in his heart. In Cimabue we find precisely that radiance, that flame which was lacking in the Byzantine artists, who were rather vestry artisans. In Fra Angelico the human form is still somewhat swaddled, or buried in a conventional immobility. But its movements are more varied—picturesqueness crops out in the accessories. In Perugino, who is the king of ancient Perugia, we see veritable life still somewhat enchained, but it grows more and more free, especially in his admirable frescos, where simply human subjects take their place beside the consecrated subjects of the evangelical story.

The school of Perugia uttered its last word in Perugino, and this last word is still one of tender and lofty mysticism, all the more remarkable since the master himself seems to have been a stranger to it in his sentiments; but the atmosphere he breathed was so saturated with it that he could not escape it. After all, art is a great Æolian harp, shivering with the breezes that pass over it. The breeze in the time of Perugino came from the hights of the soul, and it was mighty enough to impose itself on the great master.

It is also at Perugia that we see the early works

of Raphael, when he followed with docility the inspiration of Perugino. But here we perceive a broader style and a serener grace. Moreover, Perugia possesses a Virgin from his hand which is a ravishing masterpiece, and which may be placed toward the close of his first manner. We might call it the swan-song of the Umbrian school; but this song is only the prelude of a sublimer harmony, for Raphael already stands in his completeness on this canvas. He leaves, as a farewell to the school of his tender youth, an immortal masterpiece wherein it again lives forever in a type which reproduces its most admirable qualities in an idealized form, and having thus paid his debt, he goes speeding to the conquest of new worlds.

Assisi, whither the railway brings us in an hour from Perugia, is altogether a great artistic and religious sanctuary. Thence proceeded one of those mighty impulses which mark a new phase in the history of humanity. To comprehend it, we who have been reared in reformed Churches, we must be able to rise above all that is external, for we have some difficulty in finding true Christianity under the robe of a monk. And yet it is certain that Saint Francis, the founder of the order of Capuchins, was a great Christian. What strikes us in the religious movement, of which he was the leader, is precisely what distinguishes it from the forms of Catholic piety preferred in our day. He was no knight of the Holy Church like Dominic, his sole aim to crush heresy. He was quite unconcerned about the Pontifical authority to which, in the candor of his soul, he easily submitted. The idolatry of the Virgin, too, was quite foreign to him. No, it is love for Jesus Christ that completely swayed him; that was the inmost basis of his moral life, not a love that had merely its fervid impulses, and plunged itself into idle contemplation. He recognized Jesus Christ in the poor; it was truly He who wandered naked and hungry in the cities and rural districts of his country. He received in its full seriousness the divine word, whatever you shall do for him is done unto me. It is to me that you break bread when you shall appease his hunger; it is to me that you give a cup of water when you shall quench his thirst. I am he and he I. This is what moved the heart of Saint Francis when he was yet a brilliant and wealthy young man, much more wonted to presiding in gay feasts than to attending church; that is what impelled him to strip himself of his cloak for a pauper. This first impulse of a self-despoiling charity paints his entire life. Observe carefully that he did not seek expiation in self-denial, but only to afford solace to that human suffering which had appeared to him in all its tragic reality. When we see this unvailed, we must either die for sorrow or devote ourselves wholly to its assistance. This is the eternal foolishness of the cross. I know well that Saint Francis went beyond all bounds in making almsgiving the condition of true religious life, as understood by him. Self-denial is only valuable and useful so far as it ends in an efficacious succor of the needy. Putting himself in a position to receive gifts, he made himself useless, for he did but add to the total poverty that was to be relieved. This was the mistake of Saint Francis—he might have given himself up to productive toil, and yet have practiced the heroism of charity. But how heroic and sublime he is! He triumphs over every difficulty; in his way he bends the rules of that ecclesiastical authority to his holy follies, which distrusted such vehemence, and feared it could not restrain the overflowing stream within its banks. It communicated from soul to soul like an irresistible contagion—it swept away in its impetuous current thousands of men till then sunken in worldly life; and this movement of a great soul became the starting-point of a considerable influence which renewed the Church. Saint Francis indeed displaced the center of influence; he caused it to pass from the superb hierarchy of Gregory VII. and Innocent III. to the humble fervor of a popular order, which was open even to laymen in its third order, for one of its most remarkable characteristics was, that it was in no respect sacerdotal. Saint Francis had accomplished the better part of his work before taking orders. Though submitting to the harshest privations, it was not as a stern fakir, who can only curse the world; he felt, on the contrary, a tender sympathy for all nature; he not only heard the sublime chant of the starry heavens like the Psalmist, but the lark and the cricket murmured in his ear a song of thanksgiving, and he calls the swallows his sisters. He gave the first impulse to a species of popular poesy full of freshness. The only hymn of his that has been preserved is a holy convocation of all nature to worship its author.

"Praised be my Lord! with all his creatures, and especially our brother the sun, who brings us light and the day; he is fair and bright with great splendor, and, O Lord, he signifies thee to us.

"Praised be my Lord for our sister, the moon, and for the stars which thou hast formed in the clear, fine sky.

"Praised be my Lord for our mother, the earth,

who sustains and nourishes us, and produces all kinds of fruit, the many-tinted flowers, and the grasses.

" Praised be my Lord for those who forgive for thy love's sake, and who patiently bear tribulation and infirmity. Blessed are they who persevere in peace, for by thee, Supreme God, shall they be crowned. Praise and bless my Lord, and give thanks to him, and serve him in great humility."

Surely this is a frankly Christian tone, and fixes a great gulf between St. Francis and the disciple of Buddha, who sees in nature only a perfidious enchantress, and compares earthly existence to an accursed forest, where the five senses await us like brigands at the turn of the most flowery paths. It is unnecessary to circle the brow of the Saint of Assisi with the halo of the marvelous. The famous legend of the wounds of Christ imprinted on his limbs has no satisfactory proof, and will not endure historico-critical examination. It has, nevertheless, a very fine and deep meaning. What is it to be a Christian but to be, as St. Paul says, crucified with Christ? Can true charity be any thing but an immolation? *Charitas est passio*, said Origen. Charity is a renewal of the passion, minus its expiation. To compassionate is to take upon one's heart the burden of those who suffer—to have the same feelings that Jesus Christ had ; to drink a few drops from his cup.

This legend of Saint Francis awakens another in my memory, which has just been very vividly recalled to me at a little chapel in the Appian Way, that I entered this afternoon. It is called the *Quo Vadis* Church, because, according to tradition, it was on this precise spot of the Appian Way that Jesus met Peter fleeing from the persecutions of Nero. *Quo Vadis?*

"Whither goest thou?" the disciple asked his Master.
"I am going to Rome," replied Jesus, "again to be
crucified." Peter perceived that the Master wished
to suffer in his servant, and he turned fearlessly back
to confront his punishment. Thus some of these ancient legends contain a profound meaning that might
well rebuke our barren orthodoxy, which has too far
forgotten that we are only Christian by becoming
truly members of Christ. But the Church to which
Saint Francis belonged, needs especially to learn from
him a living, loving piety, clear of the miserable superstitions and the frightful Mariolatry which now
stain her. There would truly be much to rebuke in
his exaggerations, and we would not transport them
as they are into our Churches, but at least they
would trench on that servile and idolatrous religi-
osity which now knows only two divinities, the Virgin
Mother in heaven and the Pope on earth. It seemed
to me interesting to evoke this type of the purest
Catholic piety of the Middle Ages face to face with
the pitiful deviations to which she allows herself to
be drawn away to-day. In speaking of Saint Francis
I have not departed from Assisi, for the little city
lives on his memory; she preserves it as the Vestal
guarded her sacred fire. Isolated on her mountain,
overlooking the entire plain, without blending in the
tumult of contemporary life, she is one of those grand
asylums where humanity one day approached so near
God that she could never more forget him. After
these glories of holiness, it seems that nothing further
can be attempted. The city is a vast, silent cloister.
The true sanctuary of Saint Francis is at the summit of
the hill. It consists of three superimposed churches.
The crypt contains the tomb of Saint Francis. There,

it is pretended he remained constantly on his knees
in prayer. The uppermost church is not used
for worship; the intermediate church is alone devoted to that. Dark and narrow, it contains admirable
frescos; among the rest, those of Giotto, showing the
espousals of St. Francis with virginity, obedience, and
especially poverty, then his glorification. These
frescos constitute a great page in the history of art;
they mark one of its most important stages. Saint
Francis also inspired Dante, and thus he would
vainly conceal his life; he could not help its becoming fruitful in every direction. It is related that
Goethe, in his Italian journey, took the trouble to
climb the hill of Assisi; but the superb Olympian did
not deign to cast a glance at the sanctuary of Saint
Francis; he had eyes only for three Corinthian columns to be seen in the market. Yet we have seen
that, even from the artistic stand-point, holiness is
fruitful. But any fanaticism is narrow, and the great
poet of Germany reserved all his worship for the
serenities of Grecian paganism; we have caught him
in the very act of narrowness of mind.

As yet I can give you no great information on
Rome, for I have but just arrived; but fear not lest
I should conduct you through churches and museums.
I shall only converse incidentally with you on matters of art, yet I shall not pass them by in silence,
since my letters would then lack sincerity. I desire
to cleave especially to subjects of present interest
—the moral state of the people, particularly of the
clergy, and every thing relating to the Council. It is
not the Rome that all travelers see which I would
wish to depict to you, but more particularly the
Rome of the year of grace 1869, which will mark so

important a date in the history of Catholicism. For
the moment, by what I hear, they are not so sure of
triumph in the ultramontane camp as they were
some months since; a certain hesitation betrays itself
in many members of the clergy. Germany now plays
the part that France played in the Council of Trent.
She is dreaded as being able to make serious opposition, while the English prelates are considered as the
elect of ultramontanism, who might rebuke the Roman monseigneurs. But we shall return to these characteristics of the various fractions of the episcopacy
when their positions shall be more distinctly defined.
Yesterday, Sunday, November 7, the Cardinal Vicar
Apostolic caused the following invitation to be
posted up on all the walls of Rome. I reproduce it as
one of the most important documents of the preliminary history of the Council, which perfectly shows
in what spirit the Roman *curia* would urge it on,
and under what auspices they desire to place it.

Invito Sacro.

" In a few days Rome will receive within her walls
pastors coming from all the countries of the world,
and the solemn day consecrated to the Immaculate
Conception of Mary draws near—a day which will be
more memorable in the future, since it will witness
the opening of the Council. Therefore, all true sons
of the Mother of God address themselves with the
greatest affection to her whom St. Cyril called *norma
rectæ fidei*, the norm or rule of the true faith, and
they address themselves to her, in order that just as
she was personally at Jerusalem the teacher of the
Apostles and their companions in prayer, to call down

the sanctifying Spirit from heaven upon the Council, so she may preside to-day over the new assembly gathered under her maternal protection, and that by her mediation she may obtain all the favors of which God has made her the arbiter and dispenser. Hasten all to the *Triduo* of the Church of the reverend Capuchin Fathers.

" We also exhort you to attend in the same church the *Triduo* of Jesus of Nazareth. We feel assured, O Romans, that you will second our paternal desire, and that, prostrate before the venerated image of Immaculate Mary, you will invoke her as your hope, and as the hope of the Catholic Church, and Mary will once more prove to the enemies of the truth how justly the sacred liturgy speaks thus of her: *Cunctas hæreses sola interemisti in universo mundo.*"

This official document appears to me of the highest interest, as an ingenuous revelation of ultramontane Neo-Catholicism. It especially brings into clear light the intention of the Pope in choosing the 8th of December for the opening of the Council. The 8th of December is, in fact, the day on which he alone promulgated the dogma of the Immaculate Conception of Mary, contrary to all the ancient rules of the Church. Is not this saying, in the clearest, most precise manner, that the Council is only an accessory wheel, since it is possible to dispense with it in the proclamation of an article of the creed, the most considerable innovation that can be imagined?

Convoking the Council on the anniversary of this most fearful usurpation which, three centuries ago, would have stirred up the whole Catholic world, the Pope does what Napoleon III. would do,

should he convoke the renewed parliament on the
2d of December, the festival of his *coup d'état*.
The Pope has thus found the most ingenious means
of consecrating his personal power with splendor, and
teaching the world that there is no means of limiting
it.   After this, what matters it whether the Council
decrees his personal infallibility or not, since it is certain that in no case will it be set aside by a formal
canon?   His infallibility would be truly rejected only
in case the Council protested against the proclamation
of the Immaculate Conception by the Pope; but the
boldest of the opposition would not dare hope for
any such thing.   The infallibility of the Holy Father
has been affirmed in fact; he has proved it as the
Greek philosopher demonstrated motion by walking,
and he has walked over the most indisputable traditions of the Church to attain his ends.   Consequently.
the debates of the high assembly can only possess a
theoretic interest; the practice is regulated, and very
conclusively regulated.

What is very striking, further, in the *Invito Sacro*,
is the audacity with which the Cardinal Vicar, speaking in name of the Holy See, draws the consequences
of the Immaculate Conception, in reality a true
apotheosis of Mary.   She, she alone is invoked at the
moment when the Church is to prepare for these
solemn sessions.   Of the Holy Spirit, who, however,
is canonically the inspiration of the Council, not a
word!   As to Jesus Christ, you have remarked the little
notice inserted in a parenthesis that he might not be
entirely neglected, but he is treated as a personage
of secondary importance.   The Cardinal Vicar, after
his effusions over the Immaculate Virgin, seems to
check himself, and say, " I forgot to mention to you

a certain Jesus of Nazareth, whom you would do
well to invoke, but in his turn, after our chief divinity. Great is Diana of the Ephesians!" This
benevolent attention, transitorily bestowed on the
Saviour of the world, is one of those luminous touches
which clearly define the whole situation. Mary is
set up not only as the merciful Mother, who procures
the forgiveness of sin by her intercession, but as the
morning star which sheds on the Church the pure
light of heaven. The *Invito Sacro* boldly proclaims
her *the norm of truth*. I think I never read such a
thing before; at any rate, never was any other
Council inaugurated in this fashion. The Cardinal
Vicar has private information on the part Mary
played in the Council of Jerusalem; he forgets, unhappily, to make this known to us, for, according to
the Acts of the Apostles, she shone there by her
silence; and it is this very silence, humility, the vail
in which she constantly wrapped herself, which is
her true greatness. Finally, to crown this masterpiece, the Cardinal Vicar ascribes to her the honor of
banishing all heresy from the world. It is often
said that we must seek the true idea of a letter in the
postscript. Do the latter words, then, signify that
the entire preceding *tit-bit* is an exquisitely delicate
irony? For, finally, we need but open our eyes to
see that Mary has very badly succeeded in suppressing
the heresies of the world. It seems, on the contrary,
as though the world more and more belonged to
them. Witness the immense expansion of the Anglo-
Saxon race, and the triumphs of Protestant Germany.
Catholicism can no longer say, like Philip II., that
the sun never sets on her empire; for all the Occident
is escaping her power. Let us confess that Mary is

just as much *the norm of truth* as she is the subduer
of heresies, and we shall agree with the *Invito Sacro*.
It is here that we must find the preface to the Council.
You see that it commences well.

This morning the ceremonies of the *Triduo* began in
the beautiful Ara-Cœli Church, whither the Franciscans daily ascend in throngs, sweeping the dust of
the Capitol with their robes—a striking contrast which
inspired in Gibbon the first idea of his work on the
decline of Rome.   E. DE PRESSENSÉ.

LETTER II.

A Glimpse at Rome: Like City like Citizens—A Chapter of Contrasts:
1. The City and the Surrounding Desert; 2. The Ancient Church of
St. Clement and the Modern Churches; 3. The Contrast of Quarters
in Rome; 4. The Contrast in Costumes: 5. Pagan and Christian Art;
6. The Capuchins and the Scipios; 7. Spiritual and Formal Religion; 8. Rome and the Coming Change.

ROME, *November* 9, 1869.

DEAR SIR:—And yet I must give you a rapid
glimpse at the city which is to be the theater of this
great religious event, not surely a description such
as you may find in books of travel, but a summary
of the impressions which the Eternal City makes
upon me.   After all, there is nothing new under the
sun, and if we merely sought novelty, it would be
well to keep silent.   Yet the sun is always new; it
awakens as much joy when it appears on the horizon
after so many centuries, as when the first daybreak
dissipated night.   And then emotion is an incessant
spring of novelty; it rejuvenates whatever seems
most wasted.   What is it but the peculiar tint which
light, ever identical with itself, takes on in traversing a new medium, and coloring itself with truly
fresh hues?   Is not this the charm which we find in
the landscapes of the masters?   What they reproduce is commonly well known to us; we have enjoyed
the shade of those trees in the neighboring forest;
we have often gazed on those mountains or the foam
of those waves.   But what strikes and ravishes us in
their pictures is their own way of looking at these
things, their individuality manifested in their propor-

3

tioning of light and shade; we see in the illumination of the picture what chiefly touched them; it is man that we seek in nature; and man, a changeful and individual being, always escapes monotony. Thus it is with those great landscapes which are successively depicted in our minds, and are kindled up in our imagination with the most brilliant colors. They may have been a thousand times described; it suffices that they inspire in us a sincere emotion which is truly our own; we need no longer fear wearisome repetitions. This is why I have the audacity to devote a few pages to that ancient Rome reproduced by so many painters, and sung by so many poets.

Besides, I have an excellent reason for speaking of the city; never shall we understand the duration of its worm-eaten institutions, unless we give heed to the proper and unique character of this strange city, where every thing combines to plunge the soul into an indefinable languor, in which time has an inexpressibly senile gait that keeps us from noting its flight. It marches with measured steps along that Road of the Tombs which has seen so much grandeur disappear. The present and the past are confounded. We might call it immobile duration. We should, doubtless, guard against those abject theories which are in favor in the materialistic philosophy of history, according to which man is absolutely like a vegetable in depending on the soil that bears him and the air he breathes. The history of this great and illustrious city itself suffices to give the lie to that system which forgets but one thing in the life of humanity, liberty, that is the soul and inward spring of that life. Has not Rome been, as her very name indicates, the image of power carried to its highest pitch, of the most indomitable vigor, of an energy without truce or rest, that conquered and then devoured the world? Yet the heavens are the same, and the sun. Let us admit, however, that the climate has been modified in consequence of the abandonment of the Campagna, which has become a vast and marshy desert; but this very change is due completely to moral causes. Man changed first; having suffered himself to be cast down beneath the task of a vast demolition, he then fell asleep under the shadow of a religion of servitude. He no more had the strength to hold the plowshare than to wield the sword of his fathers. Briars have taken the place of sheaves in once fertile fields, and the outward conditions of existence have changed, but not till after the moral conditions were transformed. Still it remains true that the Roman of to-day lives in a heavy atmosphere, made up of malaria and incense; and we do not entirely comprehend the condition of this people till we are acquainted with its circumstances. It is this that authorizes me to dwell on them a little, before devoting myself to the religious and social drama now progressing here, and which is drawing near one of its decisive crises.

Should I try to explain to myself the special character of the impressions that Rome inspires in me, from the wholly outside stand-point I now assume, I should sum them up in one word—*contrast*. It is this that seizes on the mind and the imagination, that prevents emotion from falling off; it is incessantly solicited and excited by a perpetual contrast which combines the most discordant things every moment under our eyes, yet without opposing them in an offensive manner. Nay, this singular city has a softening power which nothing resists; it is like

those persons of honied amiability whose mere presence hinders divergent opinions from coming to open
rupture, and who tone down all voices. This softening power comes largely from the grand poesy of the
place. The esthetic stand-point gets insensibly substituted for the moral stand-point, which alone dictates absolute judgments. Thus the sharp points are blunted;
what would elsewhere excite indignation or pity
glides easily over the charmed mind, and the most
diverse objects melt and blend in that broad and
purple light which is the glory and the ornament of this
country. Beginning with the most external of these
contrasts, let us rapidly pass over the whole series in
order to justify my conclusion.

The first, which most easily impresses one, is
that of an immense and magnificent city, with the
desert that circles it. You pass without any transition from the brilliant and tumultuous Corso, with its
palaces—each of which is an exquisite work of art—
its profusely gilded churches and its rich stores, to
the severe sadness of the Forum, which, without more
ado, conducts you into the dull and barren plain.
Thus civilization and desolation, the present and the
past, touch. This limitless plain produces the effect
of a sea whose destroying wave is ever advancing,
and which yet leaves afloat a few great fragments of
the ships it has swallowed up. But it is a voiceless
and unmurmuring sea, which silently destroys all that
it embraces; it is the Dead Sea of the Occident. But
let us not slander it; the sadness of the Roman
plain has an unequaled beauty. For myself, who
have visited the Orient—who have admired the mutilated but immortal marbles of the Parthenon—I set
nothing above a promenade along the Appian Way

at sunset.   The Road of the Tombs still retains but
two or three of its monuments, but what matters that!
You trample the dust of the most glorious past, and
the grand sepulcher is there beneath your eyes ! This
is the plain itself.   It spreads out, covered with a
luxuriant yet sterile vegetation, which is its green
shroud ; the ruined arches of the aqueducts of Claudius alone break the monotonous desolation ; while
along the horizon the Albanian hills mingle a little
grace with the oppressive sadness.   Behind you Rome
rears its spires and domes.   You looked for a Pal-
myra or Baalbec, and it is one of the capitals of the
world that presses upon you.   The same spectacle,
perhaps even more striking, presents itself to us at
Saint John de Lateran.   At the foot of the splendid
basilica which lifts its front, crowned with colossal
statues of popes and saints against a flaming sky, the
plain begins ; you find fragments of the aqueducts of
Nero and of the ancient walls ; the blue mountains
of Latium alone give repose to the eye.   All the
poets who have visited these places have celebrated
the supreme beauty of this contrast.   This inspired
in Byron some of the sublimest strophes of his Childe
Harold, those where he represents Rome as the Niobe
of nations, seeing in the wrinkles and folds of the
plain her widow's vail.   Châteaubriand has also
magnificently described this unequaled desolation.
Well then, vainly do you have in mind these pearls
of modern poetry ; the beauty of the spectacle is so
great that you seem the first to discover it.   This
feeling is oppressive in its intensity if one does not
react against it.   Taking possession of an entire
nation, which undergoes it without reasoning, it insensibly unnerves its men ; and they say in presence

of all that lies buried at their feet, that it is hardly
worth while to begin life afresh: and unless they undergo new influences they easily yield, in this region
of decline, to a government of old men.

The Forum remains the most imposing wreck of
ancient Rome. Every thing has been said, and said
again, on that incomparable street which, starting from
the Capitol, extends to the Lateran, passing under
triumphal arches that no longer triumph over any
thing, and which rise from amid the broken ruins of
edifices where the majesty of the Roman people was
enthroned between those columns that lift their elegant capitals amid decay. A few circular stones
alone remind us of the tribune where the voice of
Cicero resounded. Vegetation, with its green mantle,
covers the remnants of the imperial basilicas, as if to
attest the immortal youth of nature before the piled-
up ruins of human grandeur. The remains of those
pagan temples which fronted on the Forum have
been incased in Christian basilicas, which confined
themselves to surmounting with a cross edifices
reared for pagan divinities—another double-edged
irony, for if it displays the defeat of the proud religion of the Cesars so contemptuous toward those obscure Nazarenes who seemed in its eyes all that was
lowest in Judaism. It also suggests at what small
expense the degenerate Christianity of the Byzantine
emperors effected the renewal of the pagan world.
It was an entirely outward renewal, which fixes a
sign, and nothing more, on the past, and leaves it
at bottom identically the same, just like that great
neophyte called Constantine, who extends over the
Church a protecting hand stained with the blood of
his son and his wife.

Along the road that leads from the Forum to the Lateran we follow the entire drama of Christian persecution. Here is the basilica where the disciple of Christ was tried, and where he contented himself with the sublime response that sent him to death, *Christianus sum.* Two steps away is found the famous Mamertine prison, hollowed out in the bowels of the earth, a somber den, into which the confessor was plunged before being flung to the lions. It is probable that St. Paul spent his last days there, after the bonds of his captivity were tightened. Nothing can be more mournful and gloomy than this subterranean dungeon. We can imagine the confessor laid on the cold stones, plunged in a gloom somber as that of the sepulcher, and yet full of joy, because he saw appearing in the darkness which envelopes him the bleeding head of the Crucified, as some martyrs report in the *Acts* wherein their sorrows and their joys have been deposited. They are ready, according to the touching and sublime expression of the young virgin of Lyons, to follow the Lamb wheresoever he may lead them. He most commonly led them to the Circus.

Behold in its savage grandeur and gigantic proportions that famous Colosseum, still standing, though it has served as a quarry for the buildings of a part of the city. Nothing can give a better idea of material power in its inexorability. There the people thronged, drunk with blood, but never sated with it, even when the arena had been repeatedly reddened, and lifting up a more furious clamor than that of the ferocious beasts which howled behind their iron gratings. How many thousands of humble believers, both men and women, perished on this spot with the

name of Christ on their lips! Feeble and humble,
they nevertheless conquered amid their opprobrium,
and this immense Circus is nothing but the attesta-
tion of their pacific triumph.

Allow me to use the freedom given by the episto-
lary style, which has a right to multiply episodes, to
lead you a few steps from the Colosseum to the
Church of St. Clement. This is another contrast. I
visited it this afternoon with profound interest. It
presents us a faithful image of the basilica of the
early times of the peace of the Church ; even though
it should have been repeatedly rebuilt, the plan is
still unmodified. It perhaps furnishes us some information on places of worship toward the close of
the third century, for it is quite probable that they
had an analogous form. The church was so arranged
as to harmonize with the ancient discipline, of which
not a vestige remains in Catholicism. It was characterized by the eminently Christian idea that the
people of God should not be confounded with the
nation, which did not by right of birth belong to it
but by right of conversion ; that, consequently, a separation should exist between those without and those
within its pale. We find this idea expressed with
great energy in ancient liturgic fragments, particularly in those of the Church of Alexandria in the
time of Clement and Origen. That primitive liturgy
was summed up in these strong words, " Holy things
to the holy." Every thing was arranged so that the
spectator should understand that to participate in
the life of the Church a new heart, a new life, was
required. Hence the serious arrangements which
were made for the instruction of the *catechumen*,
which demanded that he should break with all the

habits of heathen life. Hence the division of religious services into two distinct and well-marked por-
tions, the first for all who desired to hear the divine
word, the second for those only who were entitled to
receive the eucharistic sacrament. Read the Alex-
andrian Liturgy and the Apostolic Constitutions in
Coptic, discovered some years ago, which go back
quite positively to the second century, and you will
obtain an idea of the rigor with which this separation between the converted and the unconverted was
established.

That most fatal revolution wrought by the union
of the Church and the Empire was precisely the confusion of the populace of the city with the members
of the religious society, and the bringing pell-mell
into the indefinitely enlarged framework of the house
of God the unconverted multitudes who brought
with them their ignorance, their vices, and had to be
now threatened with an iron rod for the advantage
of the hierarchy, and now abandoned to their passions and superstitions in consideration of a few
gross forms by which they acquitted themselves toward Heaven. Thus a degenerate Christianity, which
unites oppressive authority with the most dangerous
indulgence toward the natural heart, was formed and
grew up, very tyrannical toward the mind and
lenient toward the life; which substitutes the broad
for the narrow way; and promises to lead to the
gates of heaven by an easy path all who will bow to
its yoke, and let themselves be blindly guided by its
crook. We are well acquainted with such Christianity. It is Catholicism in its full development, as
displayed under our eyes at Rome. Well, is it not
remarkable to find in the very capital of this abased

Christianity, an undeniable monument of the ancient
constitution of the Church, which enables us to lay
our finger on the remarkable institutions of the Alex-
andrian Liturgy? The Church of St. Clement is indeed the architectural translation of this invaluable
document. The bare arrangement reveals the great
principle of the separation between the faithful and
the profane, which was carried out to the great advantage of both. St. Clement's has the form of a basilica
with three naves. It is entered by a porch of simple
style, the only one of its kind existing at Rome.

Between this portal and the church itself extends
a square court, bordered with columns; in its center
is the font which was used for baptism. The church
is preceded by a portico, or *atrium*, of small dimensions, called the *nacthea*. Here were placed, in various positions, penitent backsliders and catechumens;
the former could not cross the threshold of the church
before their restoration, nor the latter before profess-
ing their faith and receiving holy baptism. There
they listened to the preaching. They were dismissed
at the moment when the eucharistic cup was passed
among the faithful. It was impossible to draw in a
more striking manner the line of demarkation between the Church and the world, since those who
aspired to become Christians were thus retained on
the threshold of the temple. The interior arrangement of the Church of Saint Clement is likewise
very interesting. The three naves end in an *apsis*, at
once beautiful and simple, where was the episcopal
seat surrounded by the seats of the presbyters. This
shows that the times of early Christian liberty had
passed, and that the episcopal system was in full
vigor. The "Pastor of Hermas," written in the middle

of the second century, already anticipated its triumph, and indicated the cause with rare sagacity. " Why," we read in one of the more or less apocalyptical visions of which this singular book is composed, " Why does the Church wish to sit in the *cathedra*, the episcopal throne ? " The reply is, " Because he who is fatigued loves to sit down." Thus the cathedra, the sign of episcopal authority, is represented as a proof of the moral lassitude of the Church—a profound thought, which recalls the saying of the Apostle, " Stand fast in the liberty wherewith Christ hath made you free." These words of the " Pastor of Hermas" recur to my memory whenever I have before my eyes an ancient *cathedra*. It is true that the episcopal power was strangely restrained when it had before it, not an ignorant flock, but a truly Christian people interested in public matters, and sharing in them, especially by election and moral participation. In the center of the church is an inclosure, surrounded by a balustrade, which served as the pulpit. Right and left are two marble desks, called *ambons*, for the reading of the Holy Scriptures. The *ambon* of the gospels is higher than that of the epistles, as if to mark the incomparable character of the Master's word. Tradition assigns no pulpits to the hierarchy. The word of God alone bears sovereign authority. On this point, too, the ancient architecture yields valuable information.

I had visited the Church of Saint Clement fifteen years ago, but judge of my delight when I discovered, in my visit yesterday, that excavations, skillfully conducted for the last ten years, have entirely cleared up the subterranean basilica, which belongs to a much earlier period, and whose oldest constructions may be

referred to the fifth century. Perhaps we there have
the very basilica which Saint Jerome mentioned in
the year 392. The subterranean church is a precise
reproduction of the superior church, which confirms
the ancient type of the latter. It is also divided into
three naves with the *apsis*. The most interesting thing
that I found are the ancient mural paintings, which
take us back quite near the age of the catacombs,
though we discern in them incontestable traces of
the rising Catholicism. They represent scenes taken
from the life of Saint Clement, and, among others, a
solemn celebration of public worship, with all the
officiating functionaries, which presents a faithful idea
of the hierarchy. The date of this fresco must be quite
posterior to that of the church itself; it is of the eighth
or ninth century. One of these frescos deeply moved
me; to my thinking, it is one of the pearls of Christian painting—and I name it because I have nowhere
seen it mentioned. It contains but two figures,
Jesus Christ and Adam. The Redeemer bears a
celestial expression of profound, sympathizing, and
victorious love. He comes to the abode of the dead,
seeking the representative of the fallen race, who has
so long awaited him, and who now sees his protracted
desire satisfied, and the promise of Eden magnificently fulfilled. His glance betrays a serious, astonished joy. This meeting of the first and the second
Adam brings before our eyes the entire drama of
redemption in the most moving manner. Christian
antiquity delighted in this thought. The apocryphal
"Gospel of Nicodemus," which was cited by Justin
Martyr, and consequently goes back to the first half
of the second century, is partly devoted to the visit
of Christ to *Sheol*, a vague region reserved according

to the ideas of the time to the men of the old covenant, until the expected Messiah should open to them the gates of light. Every prophet hails, in his way, the Desire of nations. The first Adam blesses him with emotion as the repairer of his own revolt. Here is truly our fresco. In an apocryphal apocalypse entitled the "Vision of Moses," which Tischendorf has quite recently recovered, the death of Adam is depicted in the loftiest poetry. The earth refuses to receive the body of her lord, of him who should not die. Angels lay it down not far from paradise until the Divine Redeemer shall come to reopen its gates to him. These curious monuments of Christian antiquity explain very well the fresco of Saint Clements; the latter made me breathe the purest perfume of popular poetry in the early ages of the Church.

You will excuse this episode, which moreover falls completely within the scope of this letter. I will come back to my Roman contrasts. A very ingen-ious Genevan author has justly remarked that in Rome itself you find both the city and the village. This at once strikes foreigners. The suburbs are in the very heart of the city; a few paces from a palace built by a Bramante you have a narrow, dirty *vicolo*, with its cracked houses fluttering with rags in the windows. The ox-cart passes by the red carriage of a cardinal, or the gala-coach of a Roman prince. Close to the brilliant coffee-houses of the Corso you have the open air slaughter-house, where you come upon a bloody display of tattered meats which no longer have a name in the language of man. Meats are fried, and exhibited also in open shops, adorned with leafy boughs. In the morning great flocks of white goats invade the city to furnish milk, and give

to certain quarters the air of a sheep-farm of a new sort,
that has palaces for folds ; while the Piazza d'Espagna
and the Piazza del Popolo present the most aristocratic
appearance, other piazzas, far finer in the monuments
that decorate them, like the Piazza di Navone, transport us to rustic scenes.   It is a perfect village fair
with its uncovered shops, its vegetables, and its
fruits heaped up in pyramids, and also its trestles.
The Transteverine quarter contains in its squalor
magnificent Roman medallions ; the women, in their
more than simple costume, have preserved the Roman
type of the Republic, the majestic and haughty
cut of the features with their burning eyes.   The
ancient blood is unmingled ; it has preserved its
vigor, as may easily be perceived by the formidable
uproar that arises on the least squabble.   The Jewish
quarter, the ancient *ghetto*, is hardly more changed,
even though the barriers which formerly closed it at
evening no longer exist.   It is still dirty and hideous, devoted to the sale of old clothes, and the
gratuitous exhibition of vermin.   And yet it was
indisputably there that Christianity won its earliest
adepts in the capital of the empire ; for the passage
of Suetonius, on the agitation raised in the time of
Claudius, by a certain Chrestus—*impulsore Chresto*
—evidently indicates that some Jew from Palestine
had brought a new leaven into the synagogues of
Rome, and that this leaven had quite powerfully stirred up the lower strata of the *ghetto* of that time, so that
the Emperor believed it his duty to meddle with it.
It was in some of these dirty streets that for the first
time the divine words were exchanged that were subsequently to resound over the ruins of the Western
Babylon, and doubtless more than one reader of the

Apocalypse in the first century, from the depth of the opprobrium to which he was banished, hurled at her the prophetic defiance of Saint John. She is fallen, the great harlot who made the nations drunk with the wine of her cup, and stained her robe in the blood of the saints! Alas! she was to fall only to rise up in part as cruel as her pagan predecessor toward the representatives of the pure Gospel.

The contrast in persons at Rome is even more strange than that in the various quarters. In the great cities of the old and the new world a uniform civilization passes its roller over all men; all diversity is blended into one gray tint. On the contrary, a street in Rome is a true diorama, which presents humanity to us under the most diverse aspects. Pass by the foreign colony, which, despite differences in nationality, is molded to the uniform type of high European society: pass by the Roman middle-classes also, who wear the black coat and surtout like everybody else: it is higher and lower that we must seek piquant variety and picturesque originality. To every lord his own honor—and here the lord is the clergy; at every step you encounter a monsigneur in violet, an abbé with his cocked-hat, his delicate air, and intel-lectual glance. Rarely do you cross the street with-out meeting a Jesuit; he feels at home and king at Rome—for his order steers the ship. Capuchins, Dominicans, monks of every garb, and mendicant friars, throng around the churches, or beg from house to house. The carriage of a cardinal, with its three lacqueys in cocked hats, traverses on the gallop the motley crowd, where you notice, particularly on Sunday, frequent groups of peasants, with sun-burnt-faces, and that picturesque costume which

painters are never tired of copying. They come to
the city for their business and devotions. They
throng venerated sanctuaries, come to kiss the worn
foot of Saint Peter at the Vatican, and surround, with
open mouths, the improvisor or itinerant singer who
exhibits a complete little domestic drama, pointing
out with his baton the gross images which illustrate
it. The great source of poetry at Rome is always
the antithesis of ancient art and Christian art. Both
appear in their noblest ideal, and, better than their
juxtaposition, nothing could enable you to measure
the depth of the abyss which separates them. Between these Greek marbles with their unchangeable
serenity and those ecstatic and fervent madonnas there
is the entire drama of Calvary.

Never has classic antiquity appeared so grand to
me as in these days, with that unequaled harmony
of form and expression which is the daughter of
Greece, and the exquisite fruit of her finest spring-
time, which was also the spring-time of humanity.
There was, indeed, but a short season in history for
the production of these masterpieces of serene and
happy grace. It was when the human mind, freed
from the terrible yoke of the divinities of nature
which had, as it were, crushed it, rose up haughty
and free to find itself diviner than all which it had
until then adored. Humanity was its own divinity;
and as it unfolded under a most azure sky, in a splendor of beauty and power that it has not since been
able to regain, with a moral notion of life higher
than all it had until then, possessed it for a moment
imagined that it had no other peaks to climb than
the gilded summits of its own Olympus, where it
worshiped itself. Then it reposed under plane-trees

and olives, and thought it had regained paradise in
the creations of artistic genius. This fleeting moment of enchanted but not effeminate repose, which
results from the equilibrium of its faculties, is it not
fixed in the Apollo Belvidere? This youthful god,
conqueror of the serpent Python, in his joyous and
haughty attitude, and with his divine smile, is he
not humanity itself victorious over the somber religions of the Orient, and finding nothing fairer or
greater than itself to contemplate? To my mind,
this is the idea which breathes in all the Greek statues of which Apollo is king at the Vatican, in those
goddesses, alike smiling and proud, chaste as perfect
beauty, but whose eyes are as limpid as the sky of
their country, though never moistened by a tear. At
the Chiaramonti Museum there is a young faun
which expresses with greater frankness than any
other marble what Winkelmann called the *artaraxie*,
the superb calmness of Greek art. It is an exquisite
work. The marble makes the supple and undulating
forms of early youth palpitate; the expression betrays nothing but the joy of existence. It is a dila-
tion of unreflecting existence, the intoxication of a
flower opening its corolla to the dew of dawn, or of
the lark trilling its earliest morning song. Some
months since a young god, found at Ostia, was deposited at the Lateran Museum. He too brings from
the ruins, where he has slept so many centuries, the
triumphant smile of Greece, but with an inexpressibly disdainful smile, which produces the strangest
effect. But let us not be unjust. Greece is something more than a fine youth admiring himself. She
soon perceived beyond Olympus a vaster and severer
horizon; and a holier divinity than her heroes sculp-

tured by Phidias. Æschylus, Socrates, and Plato,
each in his own way, pursued this high ideal. This
also lives again in the museums of Rome in numerous
and perfect works. The finest of them, as I think,
is the Sophocles of the Museum of St. John de Lateran.
Behold, indeed, the noble poet who celebrated the eternal law of goodness in worthy language, and consecrated it in characters whose purity should make contemporary art blush. In his person you see that second
Greece, no longer simply ingenuous and self-delighted,
but pensive, collected, seeking with Plato the Eternal
One in the multiplicity of things, and attracted with
Aristotle by the changeless beauty of the Prime
Mover of the universe, who is to him as a sacred
lover, yet ever faithful to the worship of art, and
never laying aside its golden lyre. That heroic,
eloquent, and philosophic Greece, here it is again in
this admirable statue of Demosthenes, who seems to
repress within himself the rumbling yet ever-harmo-
nious billows of his mighty oratory. This second
ideal of grandeur, nobility, and force could not be
fixed in a more durable way than the first, because
it was not the divine reparation that the world needed.
In its own manner it opened the way for it by awakening the desire for this reparation, and not satisfying that desire. This rendered it more intense and
more sorrowful, and transformed it into prayer to
the unknown God.

A new art, savoring more or less of decline, expresses this last phase of Hellenism in a religious
point of view, for I am not speaking of that low and
frivolous art which only sought to satisfy the senses.
This new art sprang up under the shadow of those
famous mysteries wherewith men sought to fill the

emptiness of the official religions. In its own manner it very well expresses thirst for renovation through sorrow and death. This stands out clearly from the representation, so frequent at Rome and elsewhere, of the mysteries of Mithra. The warrior plunging the sacred knife into the side of the bull, an image of the natural life, is man awakened from the dreams of infancy and youth which led him to believe in the eternity of happiness on the earth; man comprehending that all terrestrial life must wither and perish, and demanding of death the secret of rejuvenation. You see that a museum is enough to unroll before our eyes the whole religious history of the ancient world.

Yet let us admit that Greece is no longer absolutely herself when she reaches this period of lassitude and melancholy; she has already undergone the influence of the Orient. The mysteries of Mithra are a new molding of Persian mythology. After all, when we think of Greece, that simple name awakens in us a vision of youth, beauty, and harmony—the vision of the Apollo Belvidere, or of the Venus of Milo. Hence the striking contrast between these enchanting works and that Christian painting which at Rome unfolds all its phases. It also had its infancy, like Greece; but what a difference in their inspiration! I never weary of contemplating the ingenuous works of painting in the Middle Ages. They are often stiff enough in their golden setting, but what an impulse toward the *great beyond!* What burning fervor! What frank astonishment, full of adoration, before the divine Child of the manger! What sublime sorrow in the *Mater Dolorosa* at the foot of the cross! Rome is very rich

in works of this period, which go back to Byzantine
art. Let art cast off her heavy swaddling bands, or
the sacerdotal robes, which imprison her in its folds; let
Fra Angelico come, then Francia, then Fra Bartolomeo, you will then recognize what treasures of beauty
the Christian inspiration contained. A complete new
world is won; the world of the inward and the world
from on high, and it is rendered with inexhaustible
wealth. It is not merely the divine that stands out
on these canvasses, but also the true, profoundly human, *the inward man*, who, as St. Paul says, *is also
the spiritual man.* This is what the ancient chisel
or pencil never gave us; that is what Christianity
revealed to us. The painting inspired by it has reproduced this, the variety of her colors has allowed her
to translate this inward feeling in its infinite shades.
When I behold the most ancient and sincere of these
masters of Christian painting I seem to be perusing
again the most moving pages of the "Imitation of
Jesus Christ." Of the demigods of the Renaissance,
Raphael, Michael Angelo, and their rivals, I shall say
almost nothing, because no words are equal to the
impression received before their miracles. They are
to Christian art what Phidias and Sophocles were to
Athens—the eternally radiant summit that attracts
every eye.

Permit me only to remark what a large share they
give to thought. From this they are never distracted
by form, marvelous as it may be. I know no more
striking example of what I assert than the *Dispute
on the Holy Sacrament* by Raphael. He has succeeded in rendering with remarkable plasticity the
difference set forth by St. Paul between faith and
direct vision. Below, on the earth, are the theo-

logians who still seek, though they believe and
only see as in a glass darkly. Above in heaven are
the glorified who behold face to face. This sublime
idea is unfolded in perfect distinctness on the immortal
fresco, without detracting from its artistic beauty, for
that has never been surpassed. This sovereignty
of thought in art cannot be too greatly admired.
Let us not forget that these great masters of the sixteenth century, while painting at the expense of
Leo X., were nevertheless sons of the generation
which produced the Reform.

Next to Greece, and even better than she, does
ancient Rome live again in modern Rome, a nation
of statues whose number is daily enriched. Before
these figures, with strongly-marked features, we constantly hear the fate-spoken word addressed, according to Virgil, to the sons of the she-wolf, *Tu regere
imperio*—to you the command, the dominion of the
world. The Republic and the Empire file past in
their most eminent representatives. I confess that,
before these haughty *Togati*, especially those who lived
before Cæsar, I find the sordid monk, or the plump
abbé, very mean. I beg pardon of the Capuchins;
but seeing them insolently passing before the tombs
of the Scipios, I pitied them. The shade of the heroes
of the Republic was too much for them. I should
certainly have had a very different impression before
the humblest Christian, provided he were really a
man directly mingling in the serious conflicts of life.
I am no blind admirer of the Latin genius; I know
too well how heavily it still weighs upon our race,
and that finally it is the very genius of tyranny; but
at least it was a manly tyranny. For myself, I know
nothing so hateful as the mild despotism of modern

Jesuitism. I cannot tell what I feel in that sanctuary, all covered with gold and precious stones, called the *Gesu*. There it is all perfume of incense, exquisite gentleness—yes, but under this velvet I feel the sharp claw. The other day I witnessed the solemn vespers for the feast of the dedication of St. John de Lateran. All the pomp of Catholic worship was displayed; several Cardinals presided over the ceremony. The chants were splendidly executed, though, as a whole, they had no religious character, nor any real beauty. It was that bastard art, the son of the opera and sacristy, which sings cavatinas to Jesus Christ. While the psalms resounded in roulades, in which equivocal trebles dominated, my heart leaped within me. Through these soft harmonies I thought I heard the cries of the innumerable victims who have been sacrificed to the Roman Moloch; I thought of my Huguenot ancestors proscribed and put to death. I thought of their austere worship, in which they offered themselves as a sacrifice, ready to leave all for Jesus Christ. And then I went back further still into the past—back to that upper chamber in Jerusalem where worship was celebrated for the first time "in spirit and in truth."

This is the pre-eminent contrast which we do not escape a moment in Rome. Under the arches of St. Peter's and her magnificent sister basilicas, you remember the saying, *God is a Spirit*. But in presence of the police, the Swiss and the Zouaves of the Holy Father, you hear the other saying, *My kingdom is not of this world. The weapons of our warfare are not carnal.* Before the oppressive bondage, which enthralls an entire nation, that other word of Christ returns to our memory, " If the Son shall make you free ye shall be free indeed." Hearing this once wherever we turn our steps, no poetry can make us forget this contrast, for it destroys immortal souls, and is one of the worst scourges of the modern world.

But there is another and final contrast which will soon put an end to this whole *regime* of death; it is that which exists between Rome and every thing surrounding her. This is the one black spot on the map of Europe, and this spot grows daily less and less. Every breeze coming from the North and the South brings the breath of freedom; and even the steam of the railways urges on a resistless propaganda which no custom-house can arrest. It would require a Chinese wall that it might endure. The day when the Holy Father permitted a railway to pass through his States, he signed his temporal forfeiture. Those paper ramparts called *Encyclicals* and *Syllabuses* will prove useless here. I am persuaded that we shall not much longer see superannuated Rome as we see it to-day: this encouraged me to describe it before approaching subjects of more immediate interest.   E. de Pressensé.

LETTER III.

Three Pilgrims to Rome: Luther, Lamennais, Hyacinthe—Luther's
Arrival in Rome: his Mysticism; Moral Conflicts; his Ideal Rome;
the Real Rome; his Emancipation and Work—Lamennais: his
Birth; Early Life; Taking Orders; his Early Opinions; Book on
Religious Indifference; Conversion to Democracy; Advocates the
Separation of Church and State; *L'Avenir;* Intrigues of the Jesuits;
Lamennais Appeals to the Pope; *Les Affairs de Rome;* Evasive
Conduct of Rome; Impatience of Lamennais; the Encyclical of
Gregory XVI.; it condemns him; the Shock; his Lapse into Skep-
ticism; Influence on his Disciples; Subsequent Career and Death—
Father Hyacinthe: Birth and Education; Eloquence; Liberality;
First Warning; Visit to Rome; Growing Freedom; Sermons on the
Church; Further Progress; is sent to Rome; the Crisis; returns to
Paris; Speech at the Peace Congress; is Rebuked; Letter to his
Superior; his Future—Interior Discipline of the Dominicans—
Rome desires a Short Council—Assumption of the Virgin—Confi-
dence of the Pope—Anniversary of the Battle of Mentana.

ROME, *November*, 1869.

DEAR SIR,—In the most advanced Catholic circles it is often asserted that Rome is irresistible for
sincere souls, and that she makes every bandage fall
from the most prejudiced eyes. A number of conversions wrought here in the Protestant colony, English or American, are cited in proof. I confess that
I cannot understand the seduction spoken of. I have
witnessed the grandest pomps of holy week. Except
one or two solemn moments, it is a pitiful representation of the most moving of dramas. Without
yielding in the least degree to sectarian spirit, I
think one is particularly struck at Rome with the
bad aspects of Catholicism. This is quite natural, for

it is in its capital that it boldly develops all its principles without tempering or softening them, as it does when it faces a rival Church. A sadly pleasant story is told of two gentleman who had made a solemn appointment to discuss their respective religions. The result of the meeting was that the Protestant went away a Catholic, and the Catholic a Protestant. Each of the disputants had been strong in assault and weak in defense. I can conceive that this affair may, in certain respects, and particularly under certain conditions, be renewed. I admit that in Protestant society, which lacks life, fire, and fidelity to the great history of the Reform, repudiating self-renewal, one may acquire a certain disgust of Protestantism, at least of the type which he has under his eyes; that a weak mind which cannot distinguish between the true and the false consequences of a principle should be for a moment inclined to Catholicism. I avow that I can much easier conceive how at Rome a Catholic might have strong temptations to reject his religion.

I wish to devote this letter to the effect produced by Rome on three great champions of the Catholic cause, who vehemently broke loose from it just after they had witnessed with their own eyes the spectacle which we are told is so edifying. It sufficed them to go up to their holy city to lead them to shake off the dust of their feet against her. These three pilgrims are Luther, Lamennais, and Father Hyacinthe. The first left the Reformation after him, the second raised the standard of philosophic thought, the third that of a Christian liberality which can no longer be realized in the domain of Romanism. These are more than men; they are redoubtable powers, which

the Papacy now finds armed for the war against her.
We should not at all understand the Council if we
did not thoroughly know these three great tendencies
which were not fairly developed until their initiators
had trodden this so-called sacred soil.

I shall say little of Luther, having no intention of
sending you historic dissertations. How often, in
crossing the Piazza del Popolo, have I not imagined
him arriving at Rome by the gate that leads into that
square! He is still a young monk, full of fervor.
He comes from those German convents where the
pure tradition of the Middle Ages is still maintained
in its sincerity. He is a son of that profound mysticism which produced the "Imitation of Christ," and
kindled up the glances of the madonnas and saints of
Christian painting. He has been fed on that hidden
honey. He has learned in the famous book "Theolo-
gia Germanica," which has become a sort of breviary
of tender and introspective souls, to seek the divine
Absolute beyond all intermediaries. This mysticism,
which might have become dangerous by plunging
him into an unconscious Pantheism, is happily tempered by his very serious moral sense; he has felt all
the bitterness of sin, sighed after divine grace, and
saluted its dawn in a book greater than all the masterpieces of mysticism—the book of God. Hitherto
he has lived in his cell as in a hidden world; it has
been for him now the theater of the holiest struggles,
now of the sweetest raptures. It lay open toward
heaven, and not toward earth. He, too, comes to
Rome in his candid ignorance, sure of a terrestrial
realization of religion. He imagines that he shall
find his ideal radiant with glory on the pontifical
throne, and that he shall be able to say, like Jacob

at Bethel, *This is the gate of heaven.* The gate opens,
and he is introduced at once into a world of corruption and servility. He expected the heavenly Jerusalem, and he finds the Rome of Leo X. magnificently
adorned with the spoils of Europe, clothed, like
Dives, in purple and fine linen, and scarcely flinging
the crumbs which fall from her table to the poor
shivering under her marble porches, rearing up to
heaven the vast dome of St. Peter's, but only lifting
up profane songs in place of prayers. The courts of
German princes are pure compared with the court
of the Vicar of Jesus Christ, peopled with harlots
and jugglers, and holding Vanity Fair without shame
beside the pretended tombs of the Apostles. This is
what arrests the young Augustinian monk. He en-
ters the churches, and instead of there beholding, as
in his Fatherland, a people prostrate during the celebration of the holy mysteries, he has before him a
thoughtless assembly, where gay speeches buzz, where
brilliant cavaliers salute with smiles women as completely covered with diamonds as the shrines of the
saints. He approaches the altar. O profanation!
The officiating priest indulges in sacrilegious sport;
he changes words of canonical institution. "*Panis
es,*" he cries, taking up the host, "*et panis manebis:*"
bread thou art, and bread thou shalt remain. If he
would begin a religious conversation people answer
him by talking of some new work of a celebrated
painter or sculptor. He mentions the Holy Scriptures, and they speak of Virgil and Plato. Finally,
with a wounded and indignant spirit, he would try
and do penance for the Church and himself. On his
knees he ascends the holy stairway, to climb which is
worth the greatest indulgences. But he has not

passed over half of it when a mighty voice resounds in him and brings an echo of the apostolic words, "The just shall live by faith." It is a lightning flash in his gloom, but such a flash as laid St. Paul in the dust of the road to Damascus, that he might rise up an apostle of Christ. Luther too rises up. He perceives that there is a nearer way of access to his God and Saviour. A vast joy overflows his heart. Yesterday he was a hesitating, troubled monk; to-day he is a reformer, nay, more, he is the rising Reformation. He goes spreading to the four winds the great word of enfranchisement which has vibrated in his soul, and thousands of poor sinners soon receive it as manna from heaven. The Reformation proceeds from this broken heart, so sacredly consoled, as from a hidden spring—a spring first of all of penitent tears, and then a spring of consolation and joyful assurance. This great stream will never fall dry nor recede; it may cast upon the Roman shore refuse that does not truly belong to itself; but for itself it will pursue its invincible course. A few hundred conversions to Catholicism will produce no effect upon it. There is life, there the main current. The barriers and dykes of the Council will but make it more impetuous and irresistible. Such was the effect of a pilgrimage to Rome in the sixteenth century.

Let us come to the second pilgrim. This is truly a man of the nineteenth century, but at the start he was hailed a new Father of the Church. He is Lamennais. No figure of his time is more original and worthy of interest. To understand the crisis well, which was unraveled even here in his startling rupture with the Church which he had passionately served, we must consider his character, and be well acquainted with the early part of his life. Lamennais was born at Saint Malo, a picturesque cliff in Brittany, incessantly beaten by a stormy sea, and his eyes first opened to those foggy and boundless horizons which are charged with reverie for the Breton race. His childhood was sickly, and his temperament always remained nervous. He grew up under the shadow of that Catholicism, serious even in its superstitions, which has always reigned in Brittany. It is not at all Italian and frivolous. A posthumous correspondence of Lamennais has furnished us the most unexpected information on his entering *orders*. He seems to have had no real vocation. His early letters show him the victim of that more or less sickly melancholy which characterized the beginning of the century, and which was quite natural after the terrible shocks of the French Revolution; it was the only poesy then possible, a species of ruin-flower. Lamennais experienced the grand listlessness, the vagueness, the causeless sadness which Châteaubriand has depicted in his early works. He had embraced the ideas of his family and his province, as opposite as could be imagined to the revolutionary movement. But there was nothing in these which would lead to a vocation to the priesthood. He was forced to this despite himself by his elder brother, and he felt a keen indignation at it, which is expressed without circumlocution in his early letters. But once ordained, he turned with all the impetuosity of his nature to his career. He promptly became the most ardent and most redoubtable defender of Ultramontanism, which he did not distinguish from the most violent political reaction. This was at the commencement of the Restoration. The Empire of Napo-

leon had just been broken up, and the partisans of
the ancient rule fancied that they should soon crush
the remains of the French Revolution ; but they
were gravely mistaken, for it was no longer a question about a man, but about a principle, or rather,
the principle of modern society. They desired to
bring back the good old days of the alliance of the
throne and the altar, and bring to new blossom the
institutions of Louis XIV. in the France of Lafayette
and Mirabeau. It was an insane effort, but one
which, served by sincere fanaticism and high influences, awakened a formidable struggle. Lamennais
threw himself into it with desperation, cleaving particularly to the religious side of the question. The
institutions of Louis XIV. were not enough for him.
He reproached the Great Monarch with his independent spirit toward Rome. For him, as for Joseph de
Maistre, religion was summed up in absolute submission to the Papacy. He then anticipated all the
follies of this hour. In substance, his convictions
were far more social than religious. This explains
the possibility of the complete overset which was
some years later to be effected in him. I would not
deny that he had personal religious impressions, that
his heart beat warmly for Jesus Christ. A comment which he then wrote on the "Imitation" prevents
any absolute judgment in this matter. But we must
always seek the tendencies which rule in a man
through the numerous and varied elements blended
in his moral life. Now it is certain that, in his
Catholic period, Lamennais chiefly saw an ecclesiastical and social system in Christianity. It was the
Church that he worshiped much more than God, and
to him the Church was an external institution, a spe-

cies of colossal cathedral, intended to shelter mankind; it was rather a system than a moral fact. To believe in the Church in this way is believing in a form or an idea; it is depriving ourselves of that direct and living contact with truth, which alone gives well-founded conviction, grounded on experience. Moreover, Lamennais made the authority of the Church, to him inseparable from the pontifical authority, rest on the universality of religious tradition, which he sought through all ages and in all forms of worship. All religion is founded, as he thought, not on a divine manifestation grasped by the individual soul, but on an exterior testimony, which imposes itself on the mind without ever presenting its authority to conscience. The individual must merely bow blindly before the traditional faith of mankind. Thus for this great mind the truth never had that inward and personal character which constitutes living faith, that which says to all human traditions what the people of Samaria said to the woman of Sychar, "Now we believe not because of thy saying, for we have heard Him ourselves." Note, as we pass on, that Lamennais was then a faithful disciple of modern Catholicism. A religion based on authority should not permit free access to the truth; it is lost on the day when men understand that they may come directly to the God of the Gospel. The first of its dogmas is its own authority. "I will believe for thee," it says to its adherent, "believe that I suffice for thee"—this is the law and the prophets. The first work of Lamennais, entitled "Religious Indifference," produced a great sensation. He presented the singular contrast of a doctrine of the past served by the most modern language. Strange, in-

deed! this fiery disciple of the Ultramontane school
had the style of Jean Jacques Rousseau, the most
revolutionary of our writers, a broad and impetuous
style like those mountain torrents which roll and clash
stones together in their transparent waters. Limpidity and fire, these constitute the twofold character of
the language of Lamennais. This apostle spoke like
a tribune, with an impetuosity only equaled by the
harmony of his phrase. He was at once placed in
the front rank of the writers of his generation, and
lauded to the skies by the Catholic party, which
found in him its most eloquent apologist. Soon after
the publication of his first book he approached current polemics, and in these he displayed the same
talent, with a new and truly unheard of degree of
passion, growing more desperate perhaps against the
moderate Gallicans, (who would not make litter of
the ancient independence of the Church of France,)
than against the revolutionists. He demanded, in
fact, the complete overthrow of the French society
that dates from 1789, not hesitating to assault without ceremony the throne of the Bourbons when he
did not find the authorities disposed to trample under
foot all the liberties of the ancient Gallican Church.
He even incurred a lawsuit by the unheard-of violence of his language. He exclaimed, " I will show
them what a priest is ! " alluding to the unconquerable character of his resistance. Lamennais followed
this line of operations and conduct up to the Revolution of July, 1830, which in three days expelled the
ancient dynasty to chastise it for having violated
the charter of public liberties.

This event led to a complete overturn in the political ideas of Lamennais. He who had been the hiero-

phant of the most excessive reaction, was, with no denial of his religious faith, converted in an instant to the cause of freedom. His ardent and passionate nature had received an electric shock from that great victory, worthily obtained without any alloy of sanguinary violence. He perceived that Catholicism was lost if it did not form an alliance with liberty, and he desired such an alliance as passionately as he had formerly combated it. His Ultramontanism had always made him very hostile to the influence of the civil power in religious affairs; he took another step, and enthusiastically accepted the great principle of the separation of Church and State. With an ardent and outgushing soul like that of Lamennais, active propagation immediately followed the formation of these convictions. In 1831 he founded a journal, *l'Avenir*, with the aid of a young priest destined to a great reputation, the Abbé Lacordaire, and that of the illustrious Montalembert. This publication had considerable effect. It was the first time that Catholicism was seen in France associated with liberty, and holding democratic language. The elder clergy were stupefied, the younger ravished. Lamennais did not spare the new government more than he had the old: he and his assistants soon underwent a most exciting lawsuit for opening a primary school without authorization, founding their right on the promised freedom of public instruction. The great lawsuit was not to be at Paris but at Rome. The Jesuit and retrograde party had begun weaving its intrigues against the new party; it was daily denounced to the Holy Father, particularly on account of the warm sympathy it had shown the Polish insurrection. Poland had indeed a claim on

the favor of the Pope, since she was Catholic; but
the crime of her revolt effaced that merit. Lamennais was not the man long to endure these more or
less underhanded and vailed accusations; he declared
that he and his companions appealed to the tribunal
of the Holy Father, and he set off with them for the
Eternal City. He has left us a circumstantial account
of this journey in a book which is, to my thinking,
the most moving of dramas, and is entitled, *Les
Affairs de Rome*. There we see the effect produced
on his ardent soul by contact with the Pontifical
Court.

Do not forget that at this time Lamennais still
believes in the Papacy. To him it is God's representative on earth; from that he expects all light
and deliverance, and he does not suspect that the
sacred oracle will not justify his liberalism, which to
him seems more and more the only means for the
salvation of religious and civil society. He would
gladly kiss the sacred soil he is visiting for the first
time, and he confidently awaits the decisive word.
the enfranchising word, which a divine mouth is
about to speak. First, he must wait long for this
decisive word; his French impatience clashes with
Italian sluggishness, or rather, he neither finds a point
of support nor a point of resistance, but simply a
policy of delay with infinite curves, fleeting, elusive
contours, that supple duplicity of the Monsigneurs
which always shuns clear and precise conclusions.
He sees that they would bow him out, and that they
hope that he too will be overcome by that soothing
atmosphere so well fitted to lay the mind asleep and
lead it to a passive docility. For a time, he champs
the bit; what he witnesses is hardly suited to calm

him. Like Luther, he lifts the vail that covers the
real state of things, the splendid decoration which
hides so much secret corruption ; he perceives above
all that measureless venality which traffics in holy
things, and would obtain all the treasures of Europe
for the pardon of God. The storm rumbles in his
soul, as we may perceive in his private correspondence, where we find terrible words like these : "At
Rome every thing is sold. If they could, they would
sell the Father, they would sell the Son, they would
sell the Holy Ghost." Finally he grows tired ; he
urges the congregation charged with the management of his affairs, he wishes no wiles, he will have
an answer. In vain are they angry at his *furia
Francese*, (French fury,) they have to promise what
he demands with such tenacity, and he leaves Rome
on the strength of this pledge. After some weeks
he receives the desired response, and this response
is the famous Encyclical of Gregory XVI., which
declares his dearest convictions abominable, fulmi-
nates anathema against the most sacred liberties, and
declares that freedom of conscience is a mortal pest.
Thus the oracle had spoken ; but what Lamennais
had taken for the voice of God is the voice of the
Power of darkness, which can only curse the light
and life. Imagine the shock that such a discovery
must produce in a soul like that of Lamennais ! He
strives, indeed, to act in submission. I believe he
sincerely tried this course ; but he was not a man of
Fénélon's sweet and malleable temper, who surrendered without delay at the summons of Rome.
Nor was he capable of that convenient duplicity
which so many Catholics use, who submit in appearance to the authority of the Holy See, let anath-

emas hurled directly at their ideas pass by like
a summer rain, then lift up their heads and think
and act exactly as though nothing had happened.
Lamennais was not made of the same stuff as
those pliant reeds which bend but do not break
—and I honor him for it. For religious diplomacy
is the worst of all. And he soon let loose all
the indignation that was brewing in his heart.
He did it like a volcano vomiting out lava in his
book, *Paroles d'un Croyant,** written in prophetic
style, and directed at all constituted and despotic
authority in State and Church.

This book promptly became a revolutionary Gospel, and was devoured by the people. Unhappily, it
was no calm protest; it overflowed with wrath and
hatred in wonderful eloquence, but an eloquence that
exceeded all due bounds. Yet Lamennais still professed faith in the Gospel. It was gradually effaced
from his heart. He continued ever faithful to spirit-
ualism; he made it the basis of a vast philosophical
system, but he resolutely rejected faith in revelation,
and to him Jesus Christ was nothing but a Saint and
a sublime Friend of the people. He multiplied incendiary pamphlets, and found himself again condemned for offenses of the laws of the press. The
Revolution of February came at the moment of his
greatest popularity; he founded a Republican, but not
Socialist journal, in which he powerfully demanded
the separation of Church and State. Then, on the
establishment of the Empire, he withdrew to a retirement that he was never to leave. With his own
hand he corrected a translation of *Dante's Inferno.*

* Words of a Believer.

Nothing could better suit his implacable genius. One imagines he sees him, like the somber ferryman of Michael Angelo, turning aside from his boat all the rich and the mighty, that he may lead the poor and the oppressed into Paradise. He asked to be interred in the common grave like a pauper, without any religious ceremony. Solitary as were his last years, he nevertheless left a wake of fire behind him. He made a great rent in Catholicism. His old disciples, Lacordaire and Montalembert, never completely escaped his influence, though they separated from him when the great explosion came. Lacordaire always suffered, in his brilliant career, from the suspicions of Rome ; he found himself incessantly menaced with condemnation because he vainly submitted to the letter of the Pontifical Briefs, since he could not accept their spirit, against which his whole soul protested. As to Montalembert, he is now nearer than ever to the opinions of his youth. The step which he has taken in subscribing the demands of the German Catholics is considerable. He has submitted, but, as Alfieri said, like a quivering slave. After all, Lamennais remains a great terror to Rome. He would have been more alarming to her had he not gone over into the camp of pure philosophy, had he continued a Christian. Then he would not only have acted without, but within the Church, and would have served to rally about him all whom the excesses of Ultramontanism excite to resistance. The greatest danger to the Papacy, too, would be to encounter a new and Christian Lamennais. It seems that she is about to find him in the person of the illustrious barefooted Carmelite, who has just declared to the world that it is no longer possible for him to bow, passive and silent, under the yoke of the actual Ultramontanism.

Father Hyacinthe is the third pilgrim to Rome of whom I wish to speak; he leads us back to the center of the religious conflicts of the moment, and to the focus of the complications that precede the great Council. I shall remember all my life the day when I first listened to this great preacher. I had vaguely heard of a new star in the Catholic pulpit. Through chance, I entered one Sunday, in the autumn of 1865, the vast cathedral of Nôtre Dame. I was immediately arrested by the powerful language resounding there before an immense audience; it was indeed great and noble eloquence, proceeding from a heart sacredly moved, and traversing a brilliant imagination, which made both ideas and men live and palpitate, and possessed that electricity which communicates with such extraordinary rapidity to a large assembly. Since Lacordaire, I had never heard any thing like it in a Catholic pulpit. But what was more remarkable than his talents was the substance of the discourse, free from all vain superstition, and permeated with the warmest love for Jesus Christ. I felt at once that this man had a great future before him, and I was not deceived. That very evening, in a general meeting of the Evangelical Alliance, I spoke with emotion of what I had just heard, and of that sentiment of warm and grandly true Catholicity which I had felt at the foot of Father Hyacinthe's pulpit.. Who, then, was the eminent orator that was suddenly rising from obscurity to a place in the front rank? His garb indicated that he had not been content with the priesthood, but that he had desired a place in the Carmelite Or-

der, one of the most rigid in Catholicism.   I speedily
learned that he belonged to a family well known in
the French University; that his father, M. Layson,
had been rector of an academy at Pau ; that one of
his uncles, who died early, had for a moment awakened great hopes as a poet ; that one of his brothers,
formerly a monk, and now in the secular clergy, was
known for his talents and his liberalism.   He was
born, then, in 1827, and grew up in a cultivated and
religious circle.   Early called to ecclesiastical life,
he had studied theology in the best of our seminaries
—that St. Sulpice whence Renan proceeded.   In his
constant aspiration to the ideal he had not hesitated
to embrace the monastic life, which is presented by
Catholicism as the highest degree of piety, because it
most completely lays man in the dust, though unfortunately it gives him a feeling of merit in this act of
abasement.   Father Hyacinthe had been heard in a
few provincial churches, and immediately the effect
of his discourses had been felt.   The Archbishop of
Paris, Monseigneur Darbois, an intelligent and truly
liberal man, had hastened to open the pulpit of Nôtre
Dame to him, and he had there acquired at the outset that royalty by divine right which is exercised by
eloquence, and is surely one of the noblest gifts when
it is wielded in the service of truth.   Such was the
outward history of Father Hyacinthe up to the time
when I first heard him.   Since then his influence
has only grown.   Multitudes thronged the cathedral
two hours before he mounted the steps of the pulpit.
In each new series of discourses a new advance was
remarked.   Those on independent morality had
an extraordinary reverberation.   No subject could
be more opportune in face of the mad attempts

made to separate the moral ideal from the ideal of God.

It was observed that the orator was extremely careful to prove the close connection between Christianity and all generous causes, and that it alone can conduct democracy to her true destinies. In all his words was felt a burning love for Jesus Christ, and of liberty. But what was most significant in his discourses was the freedom with which he honored goodness wherever found, without thinking himself obliged to recognize it only under the particular seal of his own Church. He even dwelt with emphasis on the great aspects of Protestant nations, and especially their respect for the Holy Scriptures, and their scrupulous observance of the Sabbath. He exclaimed, " If Prussia conquered at Sadowa be not astonished, for you will find the Gospels in the knapsack of every soldier. This is what tempers strong nations." The Ultramontane party must naturally have thought such language very improper, yet they dared not openly attack Father Hyacinthe. They merely passed him over in complete silence, while lauding the most insignificant preachers of its school. It is now known that a warning, disguised as friendly advice, had already come from Rome, which betrayed a very natural disquietude. Father Hyacinthe made his first visit to Rome. He preached there during Lent in the Church of St. Louis of the French, much admired, much watched also, and quite ill at ease in this immense gilded cage, whose grates are admirably wrought, but are nevertheless grates. We have likewise an undeniable index of the impression made upon him then by Rome in the marked liberalism of the sermons which he preached at Paris

shortly after his return. Those who heard him in
the autumn of 1868 perceived, with more or less distinctness, that a decisive crisis was approaching for
the great preacher. Never had the arches of the
cathedral resounded with such utterances. These
were not merely flashes of Christian liberalism appearing from time to time ; no, the entire discourse
was permeated and overflowed with it in growing
eloquence. The subject was *the Church*. At the
outset Father Hyacinthe declared that he would not
make it an implacable sect ; that he saw it after the
spirit wherever hearts beat with love for Jesus Christ
and humanity. In support of this generous thesis
he magnificently developed the parable of the good
Samaritan. " Behold," he said, "suffering humanity
laid across the path. He that shall lift him up will
represent the true Church. A priest passes ; he is
very orthodox, this priest, but he passes by the dying
man ; after him a Levite, passes on ; he too is
orthodox, but he also passes on indifferent. Who
pauses ? Who lifts up the poor wounded man,
binds up his wounds, and conducts him to the inn ?
It is a Samaritan. Do you know what the Samaritan was for the synagogue ? The most abominable
being. When the Jewish vocabulary had exhausted
its abusive terms the most cruel of all still remained,
which was to fling in the face of an enemy this out-
rageous name. The Samaritan was the heretic of
the time. Well, he is the Christian in this parable,
for he alone has the compassion of Christ." In another discourse Father Hyacinthe took a further
step : he strongly insisted on the priesthood of parents, and complained of its abandonment through
culpable negligence. " No priest can take the place

of the father and mother beside their child;" and he
made sweet and holy tears flow as he exhibited the
beauty of this household priesthood. He cried out,
" I have just returned from England, where I saw
fathers on their knees amid their children and servants, repeating the prayer that our Lord taught us.
Nothing in the world will keep me from saying that
I there saw true Christians." Finally, these famous
discourses closed with a peal of thunder. The ora·
tor contrasted the Church of Pharisaism with the
Church of the Spirit. He stigmatized in burning
language the religion of form, and of the letter which
can only curse, and he showed that this alone had
torn accents of indignation from the meek and gentle
Master. The synagogue learned to its cost that the
wrath of the Lamb is awful. Though he confined
himself to generalities, all his auditors knew whom
and what he meant. This was too much, not for the
Archbishop of Paris, but for the controlling influences
of the Church. They hastened to send the imprudent Carmelite to Rome. For him this was the decisive journey; it was the final pilgrimage which
makes reformers. There he learned from the mouth
of his superior that the time for gentle dealing with
him could not be prolonged—he could measure with
a glance the depth of the gulf that had been hollowed out between himself and official Catholicism.
An interview with the Pope, whose details have not
transpired, did not lead him to recoil a step. He
now understood how well fitted was that monastic
life, which had appeared to him under such fine
colors in his youthful illusions, to mutilate human
life and abase it under a degrading yoke. He felt
the full weight of the chains of absolute obedience.

In a word, Rome produced the decisive impression on him which she never fails to produce on generous and upright souls who have seen the bands of their early blindness fall. He returned to Paris quite troubled, not yet clear in his aims, but inflexibly decided to obey his conscience toward and against all. You know what followed; you remember that generous speech made before the Peace Congress, for which penance was enjoined upon him by an intimated order.

I have nothing to add to facts known to the whole world, to the simple and sublime letter which announced that the sacrifice was consummated, and that Father Hyacinthe was advancing, confident in God, to meet opprobrium and the unknown, like Abraham leaving the tents of his fathers to attempt a redoubtable mission. Surely he will not be deceived in his faith. We must await the close of the Council to learn whether his acts and words will find an echo in the bosom of Catholicism. But it is certain that when he shall openly engage in his Christian mission among our French population he will collect vast multitudes, and be able to win to Jesus Christ a large number of souls who are not to be reached by the ordinary means of influence. They strive to get rid of this formidable adversary at Rome by the vilest slanders, but none of these poisoned arrows will reach him at the height of public esteem to which he has attained.

A Dominican monk, Father Des Caillot, has lately published a very curious book on the interior discipline of the Order of St. Dominic, from which he has just broken away. He lays bare, in a multitude of details, that frightful spiritual tyranny which makes

man a mere machine or a corpse, according to the
formula of the Jesuits. Father Des Caillot relates
that one day when he was seized with remorse for
very reprehensible deeds enjoined upon him by his
superior, the famous Dono Guisanga, with a view to
generous collections, the latter answered him, "Don't
trouble yourself; I am to answer for the deeds I command you to perform; they do not concern you."
This is truly the *Perinde ac cadaver.* Only here it
is the corpse of conscience. Is it not highest murder
to slay souls! All these revelations are very important on the eve of the Council.

The Fathers who are to have seats in it are beginning to arrive in large numbers, especially those from
the most distant countries. The preparatory committees, called congregations, are hard at work.
They are striving by all possible means to prepare
men for the expected results. A very important
publication has been this week issued from the press
of the *Civiltá Cattolica*, the great organ of Jesuitism.
It is entitled "A Summary History of Œcumenical
Councils." Its aim is very plain; the anonymous
author, who evidently speaks in the name of the
Roman managers, labors to prove that it is not necessary for a Council to be long that it may be good;
on the contrary, the best have been the shortest, and
their merits are complacently enumerated. A few
weeks are enough to effect excellent work. I should
think so, when once it is understood that good Councils are those which show themselves docile toward
the Holy Father and surrender their powers into his
hands! Why prolong vain deliberations which are
after all a simulacrum? The ideal Council would be
one that opened and closed the same day, in one in-

stant, by a great acclamation to the Infallible Pope and the Immaculate Virgin.

It is evident from this work that the favorite plan of Rome is to have a council of a few weeks' duration that may solemnly and forever pronounce the abdication of the Church, or rather the Episcopacy, in favor of the Holy See. Henceforth it would be truly useless to convoke new Councils; they would not even play the part of the old parliaments of the France of Louis XIV., which merely registered the royal edicts. When once it is understood that all pontifical briefs fall directly from heaven, it will suffice for the Holy Father to publish them, that Catholic Christianity may receive them on its knees. This morning announcements of new publications on the Assumption of the Virgin are posted up on the walls of Rome. This also is one of the dogmas which they would have proclaimed by the high assembly. It would do well to reveal to the world the historic documents which its supernatural inspiration has enabled it to discover, since the fact in question must have had witnesses. Where are they except in the pictures of Raphael, Titian, and Correggio. This is what people of little faith would be glad to learn.

The Pope is very confident of the issue of the Council, just as a sovereign is sure of a legislature which he has nominated by his agents or by his state council. He has given a truly astonishing proof of his confidence. On the confines of the Transteverine district rises a hill whence we have certainly one of the finest views in the world. On this hill is built San Pietro in Montana, a doubly sacred place, where tradition locates the martyrdom of the Apostle. You trace in its least windings the course of the

Tiber, which loses itself in the rank vegetation; to
the right is the great city with its innumerable domes.
Before you rise the Sabine Mountains, with their har-
monious lines.   The spectacle has a majestic grandeur that is quite unparalleled.   There, before the
Church of St. Peter in the Mount, the Holy Father is
rearing at this very moment a column in honor of the
Council, and as a sign of its success.   Surely his nature is hardly that of Thomas, who must see to believe; his faith is a strong " evidence of things not
seen."   This confidence would be much more touching and admirable were it not founded on past success, on the docility of the Episcopacy in accepting the
dogma of the Immaculate Conception, and on means
well known here for acting on recalcitrant minds.
This column of expectation is nevertheless a curious
index of the imperturbable assurance of the Papacy
on the eve of the Council.

Last week the anniversary of the battle of Mentana
was celebrated with great pomp.   There was a mass
and a banquet, and the officers of the Pontifical
Zouaves swore to spill their blood for the Holy See.
Just now they only spill the liquors they drink from
shop to shop, in the most idle garrison life conceiv-
able.   The regular French troops are encamped in
the provinces; here we only see the famous Zouaves
and a few Swiss, whose party-colored uniform suggests the rainbow.   All this military array devoted
to the defense of the Holy Father deserves to be
dwelt on a moment, for it brings before us one of the
gravest questions of contemporary politics.   This
will be the theme of my next letter.

E. DE PRESSENSÉ.

LETTER IV.

THE ROMAN QUESTION.

Peculiar Position of Rome: The Pope guarded by Foreign Troops;
The Practical Phase of the Matter — The Origin of the Temporal
Power — Its Security under the Old *Régime* — The Shock of the
Revolution of 1793 — An Election Trick — Napoleon I. and the
Papacy — Count d'Haussonville and Father Thenier — The Pact of
1815 — The Revolution of 1830 — Its Consequences — Foreigners
first guard the Pope — 1847 and its Changes — Election of Pius IX.
— His Position and Measures — The Pope in Exile — Intervention
of the French — Craft of the Prince President — Return of the
Pope — His Rule — The Italian Movement: Its Results — With-
drawal of the French — Garibaldi Advances on Rome — Return of
the French — Arguments of the Catholics — The Near Close of the
French Occupation.

ROME, *November*, 1869.

I TOLD you, at the close of my last letter, that Rome
is placed in the peculiar situation of being under the
direct guardianship of foreigners, for the national
forces there are insignificant, while the troops
furnished by other countries are considerable in pro-
portion to the number of inhabitants in the Pontifical States. A powerful nation, in particular, shel-
ters under its flag the power of the Holy Father,
which would long ago have been overturned but for
its protection. Thus the temporal power of the
Papacy exists and lasts only through succor from
abroad; that is, it no longer exists of itself. Abandoned to its own strength it is certain that it would
fall in twenty-four hours before the antipathy of the
populace. If there be an abnormal situation in the
world surely it is this; the crises which threaten it

are also renewed at regular intervals; the Roman
Question is the order of the day in European politics,
in such a way that it will not lose that status until
it shall be finally settled. It may be adjourned, but
not set aside. In reality no question is more important; it presents, in a most inextricable knot, the
great problem of the union of the temporal and the
spiritual powers; it brings it to light from the theoretic stand-point through the discussions it awakens,
and it certainly has contributed much for the last ten
years to enlighten the public on this point, and to
rally the liberal party on the separation of Church
and State, for their union at Rome enables us to lay
our finger on their gravest mischiefs. But the
Roman Question has also a purely practical importance; the mutual relations of civil and religious
power are regulated in most European lands by concordats which were drawn up on the basis of the political
sovereignty of the Holy Father; should that sovereignty disappear, these concordats would be immediately abolished by that fact; the relations of the two
powers would have to be constituted on a new basis,
and, with the wind that is up, that basis would, perhaps, be that which your grand Republic so gloriously
laid down when it first proclaimed and applied the
great principle of the absolute separation of Church
and State. It is very important, then, for us to know
what supports prop up that rampart, which, of
itself, would grow weak, and be laid in the dust at
the first whiff of internal freedom. By showing
how fragile in themselves and unjust these supports
are, we shall the better comprehend the singular
condition of this country and all that we are entitled
to expect, for the latter part of the century, in the

way of political renovations.   It is likewise certain that the Papacy will seek to strengthen its temporal power by some action in the Council, and that anxiety for it will weigh on that high assembly.   I shall begin with a rapid history of the question, then we shall see what stand-point the Catholics who defend the temporal power of the Pope assume.

I shall not dwell on its first establishment.   Its most intrepid champions dare not make it a primitive institution, for they know too well that, in the matter of domains, the early conductors of the Church of Rome had only the space needful for their burial. The catacombs are there under their very feet to show that the early condition of the Church, like that of its Master, was one of persecution.   The temporal power of the Pope was formed, like any other sovereignty in the Middle Ages, by a series of incidents, each less edifying than its predecessor; apart from a few donations like that of the great Countess Matilda, spoliation has played an important part in the extension of the pontifical domains.   Cæsar Borgia rendered it important services, and that name tells all.   The pretended donations of Constantine and his successors are impostures demonstrated to all the world except Rome.   The false decretals are the most distinguished, and also the most fruitful, of historic lies.   The Papacy is in the position of a proprietor who possesses his domains under a forged title-deed.   That he should profit by long possession, that he should silently, and without quarreling, cultivate his estate, may be conceived from the standpoint of a none-too-scrupulous delicacy; but that he should lift up his voice in the country and cover the frauds and spoliations of his ancestors with the name of God, would be scandal and confusion. This is, in fact, the conduct of the Papacy. It would gladly win credit for a second dogma of immaculate conception, and cause the foundation of its political sovereignty to pass for a divine work, pure from all human alloy. It will succeed in this design less than ever in a century, where the past is inundated with a vivid and implacable light through the progress of historical science.

The Holy Father might peacefully enjoy his temporal power through the entire period of the ancient rule, when the idea of popular sovereignty appeared only as an impossible dream. The shock of the Reform did not modify the political condition of Italy. Vainly was Rome taken and sacked by the Constable de Bourbon in the fortunes of war, the Pontifical domination was never brought into question in an age when the Church was every-where incorporated with the State, and the Throne was backed by the Altar. Every thing was destined to change with the new era introduced by the French Revolution, which shook all thrones, and almost every-where awakened democratic sentiments. The Papacy, guided by the sure instinct of despotism, perceived at once that there was her true enemy; she was not content with protesting, as she might rightfully do, against the encroachments of the revolution on purely religious territory, and condemning that famous civil constitution of the clergy which was an essay at revolutionary theocracy, since the new power aimed of itself to regulate simple religious affairs. The Papacy would have been entirely right in putting forth the most vigorous appeals in favor of those unfortunate French priests who were odiously persecuted

for refusing an oath offensive to their consciences,
even though it might have been answered that they
did but apply her own principles to herself. But
she assumed a very different part; she fulminated
anathema on anathema against the principles of the
New France; she took part openly for the ancient
order of things; in a word, she put herself into open
war with the Republic. It was very natural that she
should undergo the consequences of such conduct,
and that, as she had put herself on the level of ordinary political powers, she should share their common
fortune. She did also share the terrible blows in-
flicted by France on Italy. The Roman State was
dismantled, the Pope went to die in exile—and the
Pontifical States only regained a little quiet by
allowing themselves to be dismembered at the treaty
of Tolentino, signed by the young General who
had just astonished the world by his overwhelming
victories.

Here belongs a most curious episode, which has
been fully revealed in the Memoirs of Cardinal Consalvi, a capital document in contemporary history.
The author has narrated, with astonishing frankness,
the circumstances of the election of the substitute for
Pius VI. in the year 1800. We may judge from the
manner in which he describes the intrigues of a Conclave what the inspiration of a Council is worth, since
the results of both assemblies are placed by Catholic
orthodoxy under the direct influence of the Holy
Spirit. The Conclave assembled at Venice was in
the greatest embarrassment on account of the opposite intrigues of the powers which had their agents
among the cardinals. Strange thing. Austria and
Naples, which were then at the head of the Catholic

States, had only one project in mind, namely, to get
a Pope of the right stamp named, who would permit
them to retain the fragments of the pontifical domain,
of which these States had taken possession under pretext of exercising a salutary protection over them.
The cardinals who were not sold to these two powers would not listen to such a nomination. They
did not know how to get out of these inextricable
difficulties; they had, indeed, an excellent candidate,
full of piety and gentleness, who also had the great
recommendation of being personally agreeable to the
puissant Dictator, who had just taken possession of
power in France. This was Cardinal Chiaramonte.
Another Cardinal moved heaven and earth in the
conclave, and exerted a preponderating influence.
The task was to gain him over to the proposed combination; but as he was a proud and independent
man, they knew that he would only support measures resolved on by himself, or which he thought he
had taken up of his own motion, and there was nothing else to do but to get his private secretary, an insignificant Abbé, to suggest to him the plan they
wished to have succeed. He fell completely into
the snare, and came gravely to declare to those who
had secretly whispered his lesson to him, that after
much reflection he had come to think that the election of Chiaramonte was the sole means of salvation
for the Conclave. His inspirers loudly praised his
superior wisdom, and thus Pius VII. was nominated,
according to the recital of a Cardinal of the Holy
Church, who was subsequently his Secretary of State,
and whose testimony certainly is not open to suspicion. Do we not seem to witness a low-grade comedy? Does not the superb Cardinal, who gives the

idea of others as his own opinion, remind you of
that personage so dear to the Italian people, who
does whatever you please, thanks to the skillfully-
handled string behind the curtains? To call him
by his proper name, is he not a merry-andrew?
This anecdote, whose authenticity is unquestionable,
does not fail to illuminate in its own way the great
pending question of the personal infallibility of the
Holy Father. Behold, then, in what way and by
what measures he whom they would now make the
very organ of the Holy Spirit may be called to the
Pontificate. An intrigue, for which one should blush
in a political election, would be enough to give the
new Council its celestial inspiration. For the grand
exhibition of infallibility that they are getting ready
it would be better to close up the green rooms, and
not allow profane eyes to see the background of the
theater.

The pontificate of Pius VII. was quite agitated.
As for himself, he was worth more than the system
which he personified. He was a priest full of gentleness, uprightness, and always desirous of obeying his
own conscience; but it was a terrible thing for him
that he had to deal with the most violent and cunning despot of the modern world. The Count
d'Haussonville has just published a most remarkable
book on the relations of Napoleon I. and Pius VII.,
remarkable, not only for its talent, but for its thorough investigation, and abundance of unpublished
documents, which cast the most vivid light on that
important period in the religious or ecclesiastical history of the nineteenth century. Here we learn especially how false is the pretense of those apologists for
the temporal power who see in it the safeguard of the

independence of the Holy Father. It is certain that
all the faults committed by Pius VII. are attributa-
ble to his anxiety to regain intact the domain of the
Holy See. If in the famous Concordat of 1802 he
makes concessions on the constitution of the Church,
if he comes to Paris to crown Bonaparte, still stained
with the blood of D'Enghien, it is because the General, then omnipotent, has perfidiously hinted to him
promises of territorial aggrandizement which he is
fully determined not to keep. His unlucky power,
which gives him no real means of self-defense, is like
the ever-vulnerable heel of Achilles ; there precisely
is his spiritual power attainted. His imperious protector makes him forsake the neutrality which alone
befits his pontifical character, and wishes to impose
on him measures hostile to any given power with
which he is at war. The Pope resists gently, but
with perseverance. Napoleon, intoxicated with the
triumphs of Austerlitz and Jena, cannot allow any
sort of resistance ; he will have every thing bend to
his yoke. He who had boasted of being the restorer
of altars, a new Constantine, did not hesitate, after
unheard-of violence in language, to have the Pope
carried off from the Vatican by his police, and flung
into a State prison, where he subjected him to odious
treatment. You must read in the fine account of M.
d'Haussonville all the episodes of this infamous persecution of an aged man, shut up in secret, and separated from all his counselors.

The perfidy matches the brutality of the means.
M. d'Haussonville has found proof that the physician
of the Holy Father was bought up, and that he was
paid to act in his way on the nerves of the unhappy
victim, who had hours of hallucination. At the same

time, all the members of the French and Italian
clergy who did not admire these high exploits were
hurried into prison or exile; students for the priesthood were sent to the army, to the posts most dangerous for their health, where they nearly all died.
Rome had been annexed to the French Empire, and
Napoleon caused his scribes to prepare very fine dem-
onstrations of the incompatibility of the temporal and
spiritual power; of the gentle law of the Gospel, which
would have the priest remain in his own domain,
and is summed up in the great precept of obedience
to the prince—a precept which the imperial controversialist caused to be inserted in the first line of the
catechism published by his order, with the menace of
eternal damnation to him who would not love and
serve Napoleon I. with all his heart, with all his
soul, and with all his strength, while naturally hating
his English or Austrian neighbor as the Emperor himself hated him.   Thus Napoleon wished to abolish the
union of the two powers at Rome only to unite them
the better on his own head.   He wished to be the Czar
of the West, and to put ukases in the place of briefs.
Surely the remedy was worse than the disease, and we
do not hesitate to justify in this quarrel the unhappy
Pontiff, who was weak only one day—when he signed
the mocking Concordat of Fontainebleau—a weakness quickly redeemed by the most honorable recanta-
tion.   It would seem as though, if the book of M.
d'Haussonville ought to meet a good reception any
where, it would be at Rome, since it greatly exalts
the memory of Pius VII.   The praise would be the
more valuable because it comes from a perfectly independent man, who does not belong to the Catholic
party.   But not at all.   His book is ill received.   So

much so, that they have caused a refutation to be
fabricated by Father Thenier, with a great display
of diplomatic documents. This refutation has been
made with the evident co-operation of the French
government, which has largely opened its most secret
archives to the reverend Father, while they had been
hermetically closed against Count d'Haussonville; a
fact which did not hinder his having, thanks to his
extensive connections, the most curious and authentic
documents. The interest of the French government
in this affair is clear; it would, as far as possible,
justify the chief of its dynasty and wash itself of the
just opprobrium merited by its violence toward an
aged man from whom it had obtained all the concessions compatible with his pontifical charge. But
what is inconceivable in this justification of Napoleon
I. is its having the Holy See for an ally, whose interest ought to be of an opposite kind. In fact, whatever exalts the Emperor abases the Pope. One arm
of the scales cannot ascend unless the other descend.
On reflection we find two quite profound reasons,
fully worthy of the Jesuits, for the publication of the
huge book of Father Thenier. The first is, that the
cause is more important than the man; now the book
of M. d'Haussonville, while awakening a very just
sympathy for the unlucky old man who was both the
victim and plaything of imperial despotism, paints
with great frankness his tergiversations, anguish, and
the sudden changes in his decisions. Now it is dangerous to give the world such a spectacle at the very
moment when you would make the Pope a god. It
is much better not to make the hearts of men so tender toward him, and conceal that embarrassing past
in the accumulated waste paper of documents bor.

rowed from the heirs of the persecutors of Pius VII. The second reason is, that those old persecutors are now the necessary protectors of the Holy See. They are really detested, because it is hard to lean on a power so slightly Catholic and so versatile, but it is important to treat it well, especially at the moment of striking the great blow in the General Council. That is the only possible explanation of this strange publication, which I ought to call attention to as a very characteristic symptom of the present situation of the Pontifical Power.

Let us pass rapidly over the period of the Restoration. In 1815 the Papacy recovered its domain almost intact. It is related that at the Congress of Vienna, where Europe was pieced out according to the will of the conquerors of the moment, Cardinal Consalvi, Secretary of State to the Holy Father and his representative, said with a smile to Prince Metternich, "We will give you whatever you like on high, but give us another city or district." The Pontifical Government, like the Bourbons and the French Emigrants, had neither learned nor forgotten any thing during the period of its exile. It came back with all its old errors, and the long peace which it enjoyed was turned to advantage by it in completely re-establishing the old despotism. It fancied that its subordinates were perfectly satisfied because no complaint reached it; thanks to the *régime* of repression which prevented any manifestation of public opinion. It is the bloody saying of Tacitus again: *Silentum faciunt et pacem appellant*—They make silence and call that peace. As all Italy was subjected to the same rule and was bowed under the saber of Austria, the liberal contagion was easily arrested on the frontiers, and the Pontifical troops, despite their meager valor, which was somewhat elevated by Swiss mercenaries, sufficed to maintain calmness from a political stand-point, if they did not always suffice to subdue brigandism, the scourge of Southern Italy. The Revolution of July, 1830, disturbed this convenient lethargy of the Italian nations, who, in the preceding period, had only had a few sudden fits of conspiracy, promptly stifled in the blood of their authors. It was fickle France again, that can never be reckoned on, which uttered the cry of liberty after having in three days overturned the throne of her perjured King. The shock was formidable throughout Europe, and we cannot say what it might have produced had not the first aim of Louis Philippe been to shun all foreign wars, and introduce his dynasty into the European Council. Yet the appeasement could not be so prompt as he desired. While Poland shook her chains and entered on an heroic struggle—while Belgium got clear of Dutch domination—all Italy strove to rise up; but she could not succeed. The Pontifical yoke rested in its full weight on Romagna, without the compensation of the splendors of Rome, which procure great profit for the inhabitants of the Eternal City, and satisfy them so long as they are content with being church beadles and keepers of museums. That rich province also lifted up the standard of insurrection in 1831; it had the encouragement of seeing two princes of the Bonaparte family take arms in its cause; these were both the sons of Queen Hortense; one died in consequence of the expedition, the other is now the Emperor of the French; and some pretend that he has not in reality changed, and that he does not love the government of the priests more than in his youth. The revolt of Romagna was too isolated to succeed, and it was promptly stifled. Nevertheless the Holy Father perceived that he could no longer trust entirely to his own troops; he obtained an Austrian garrison to occupy Bologna. France, unwilling to surrender all Italy to the influence of Vienna, and particularly the Pontifical States, with which she was to have constant connections, sent a garrison to Ancona. The defense of the temporal power of the Holy Father by foreign troops dates back to that period.

The French bayonets nevertheless disturbed him, because he knew that they were too intelligent to approve all that they protected; he was well pleased to see them resuming the road to France in 1838. From that hour the Papacy was able to exercise its heavy and senile despotism in full security, carefully measuring out the respirable air to the intelligence of its subjects; killing, as far as it could, the spirit of independence and progress; stifling it in secret dungeons whenever it exploded; exiling all who disquieted itself; and merely offering its people the monotonous pomp of an almost idolatrous worship to relieve their weariness in a narrow and wretched existence, whence all the great interests of modern life were carefully banished. That was the fine time, the good old time, of which the Roman prelacy only thinks with bitter regret.

However, about 1847, every thing was changed; again the breath of freedom breathed over Europe. France showed herself discontented with the neither grand nor frank policy of the old King Louis Philippe, whose fault it was to see only the impertinent rancor

of a conquered opposition in a very general and quite
profound movement. From north to south, Italy
prepared to revolt against Austria and those princes
who were her docile lieutenants. The King of Piedmont, Charles Albert, took the direction of the national movement, and began by giving a Constitution
to his people. Far stranger thing! Gregory XVI.
was replaced on the Pontifical throne by a liberal
priest. Pius IX. proclaimed a general amnesty and
sketched out a Constitution for his people, which left
a large part to laymen and to their control. His
name was adored in the whole peninsula, and for a
moment he became the standard-bearer of the nation.
But there are edifices so worm-eaten that they cannot
even be repaired without tottering from base to crest.
The Holy Father perceived this only too soon. The
tocsin of the Revolution of 1848 every-where precipi-
tated affairs; all Italy was up with the cry on her
lips, *Fuori i stranieri!*—Away with foreigners!
Charles Albert put himself at the head of the liber-
ating army. The King of Naples for a moment pretended to follow him, but it was only till he could
recall the troops needed to check his subjects; he shot
or sent to the galleys all the Liberals that he could
lay hands on, after having abominably deceived them
with a lying constitution. It was the hour to judge
of the inextricable impropriety of the temporal sovereignty of the Pope. He was at once the common
Father of the faithful and the sovereign of an Italian
Principality. If he made war on Austria, he would
lose the former title; if he did not, he would incur
the execration of his subjects, who passionately desired
the enfranchisement of their Italian Fatherland. For
a moment, the Pope was carried away by the desires

of his people; he sent a brigade, commanded by
General Durando, to support the operations of Victor
Emmanuel, but he saw speedily that he was thus sac-
rificing his part as the chief of the Church, and followed the example of the King of Naples. This was
the first discord between him and his people, who no
longer desired such subjection, and had, more or less,
imposed on him a constitution which the illustrious
economist, Rossi, was charged to apply. But it was
an impossible task; an infallible priest cannot be a
constitutional sovereign; all the more so because religious or ecclesiastical affairs are constantly blended
at Rome with political affairs. Moreover, the effort
was bruskly interrupted by the abominable murder
of M. di Rossi, on the very steps of the Legislature,
which he was about to open in the Pope's name.
The latter succeeded in taking to flight, and betook
himself to the protection of the King of Naples at
Gaeta while the Republic was proclaimed at Rome,
under the influence and preponderating direction of
Mazzini.

It is to this period that the present French occupation goes back, and it is very important distinctly to
note its origin. It must be said that its origin was
a distinguished trick, of which the French National
Assembly and the Republican authorities at Rome
were the victims. The business is not to defend the
Republic of Mazzini; that is not the question. No
matter if that administration should seem hardly suited
to the character and situation of the Roman people.
It ought to fall only before the manifest wishes of
the people, and not before a foreign invasion. If the
latter were legitimate, all others are equally so; and
in the last century the Prussians were entirely right

in passing the French frontier to destroy the hot-bed
of revolution at Paris. But particularly, it was in-
admissible to lie to France and to Italy to disguise
the true aim of such an expedition. Now this was
done in the most indisputable manner. In the spring
of the year 1849 France had not yet replaced the
Republican Assembly of 1848 by the Legislative Assembly, of which a majority was committed to reaction. Prince Napoleon, President elect, after the
second of December of the previous year, was following with docility the advice of the reactionist
party, to which likewise he chiefly owed his election.
He was fully decided to interfere at Rome to give
satisfaction to the Catholic party, of which he stood
in great need for his ulterior designs; but he, as well
as his advisers, knew that there was no way to obtain
authority to intervene from an Assembly which was
very firm, very honest and moderate, but inflexibly
attached to republican principles. He used subter-
fuge. Some months earlier, General Cavaignac had
prepared a maritime expedition solely to protect the
Holy Father. The Prince President augmented the
number of vessels and troops which were to take part
in the expedition, and demanded of the National Assembly authority for their departure, still to watch
over the security of the Holy Father, and to counter-
balance the influence of Austria, which, after the
great victories of Radetzky over the unfortunate
Charles Albert, was becoming preponderant. The
latter reason was well suited to touch a French assembly. It granted the subsidies demanded on a
report from M. Jules Favre. A few days passed,
and people learned with stupefaction that, scarcely
disembarked at Cività, Vecchia, General Oudinot,

Commander-in-chief of the expedition, held very different language from what was to be expected of him ; that he took more or less the attitude of a restorer of the pontifical power. But the public indignation kept no further bounds when it was known that he had demanded of the Republican Assembly at Rome permission to land and select a salubrious position near the gates of the city, solemnly promising to respect the independence of the Roman people ; that when he had obtained what he had demanded he revealed the true object of his expedition, and unmasked his batteries, which did not save him from a repulse in the first assault that he made, and from being forced to undertake a regular siege. The National Assembly declared that it had been deceived, and, in spite of the embarrassed explanations of the ministers, voted an order of the day, which implied a severe censure of what had been done. Unhappily it had but a few moments more to live, and the Legislative Assembly was won over in advance to the Catholic policy. Accordingly, after stormy debates, which brought on the marked insurrection of the 13th of June, an entire approbation was accorded to the policy of the Prince President. Thanks to the reinforcements sent him, General Oudinot took possession of Rome despite the heroic defense of Garibaldi, and the Holy Father soon returned, supported and defended by a full corps of the French army.

The Prince President hoped that the sacerdotal rule would not be restored, with all its abuses, and that the Pope would make some concession to the French flag, which henceforth sheltered him, and which, although faithless to the principles of '89 from the moment that it floated at Rome, had been

too often filled with the breath of freedom to find
pleasure in protecting a tyrannical theocracy. For
this purpose he sent his aide-de-camp, M. Edgar Ney,
to the Holy Father with a very imperious letter, demanding serious reforms in civil affairs, as a gift on
his second accession. But at Rome they were deafer
than ever in that ear; they were glad indeed to receive French soldiers, but not French advice, and
they knew very well that the Catholic party disap-
proved the President's letter. The Pope came back
from Gaeta a most desperate champion of absolutism,
like all backslidden Liberals. He restored the old
Roman machinery on its former footing; his States
were again surrounded with the thick net of minute
precautions, that there might be no contraband commerce in liberal ideas. The priestly yoke rested
with its full weight on the population, the lay element was more and more excluded from public affairs. Meantime the *coup d'état* of the second of December, 1851, had come on in France. Every mouth
was gagged that might have spoken in favor of the
freedom of the Romans. The Catholic party, which
hoped to derive advantage from it, with a few honorable exceptions, greeted this event with enthusiasm.
L'Univers, the most violent and influential organ of
Ultramontanism, lauded the new power, born of perjury and massacre, to the skies, and at Rome the
astute old men who wished to keep an entire people
in squalor chanted the most sincere *Te Deum* they
had ever intoned. These are the unhappy divorces
between religion and morality which do the former
more harm than all other attacks. Ours is a century
when things move so fast, and possess such a power
of transformation, that we should never deem any

situation long compromised. The Roman authorities fancied that they had only a slumbering people to deal with, and thought they could resume the nice mummified life of past centuries, when a new thunderclap came to procure them a most disagreeable awakening. It was almost the whole peninsula rising up for its independence. Count Cavour had succeeded in stirring up the old Italian leaven in the heart of the Emperor of the French by presenting political prospects, of which the baths of Plombières, where they met, guard the secret. The rapid and victorious campaign of 1859 freed all Northern Italy, and its first whiff swept away the garrison of Bologna. To Italy the treaty of Villa-Franca was a cruel deception ; it arrested her at the famous Quadrilateral, suspending over her the perpetual menace of a return of the Austrian army, which, established in its fortresses like a bird of prey in its inaccessible eyrie, could select at will the propitious moment for an invasion. Besides, the combination favored by the Emperor of the French was a division which might become a confederation of States, wherein Austria, through Venice and Florence, would have a considerable influence, and over which the Holy Father should preside ; he, the greatest enemy of national independence. This detestable treaty, though never applied for a day, was a stimulus to the genius of Cavour, who, moreover, felt himself in harmony with the aspirations of his nation.

What followed is well-known. Florence and Parma intimated to their Archdukes an order to remain in the Austrian camp, where they had thought good to take service. Never was the overthrow of any dynasty more legitimate. Garibaldi, at the head of his volun-

teers, took possession of Sicily, and triumphed at
Naples, quite as much by the astute policy of Cavour,
whose means we are far from approving, as by the heroism of his red-shirts. At last the whole Pontifical State
was agitated and shivering under its degrading yoke.
The people of Romagna succeeded in their prompt
revolt. During this period of contemporary history
the French government pursued an equivocal policy.
Though mounting guard at the Vatican, it secretly
favored annexations to the new kingdom of Italy.
When Cavour decided to strike a great blow after
the organization of an army of Pontifical volunteers
under the command of Géneral Lamoricière, it is
related that General Cialdini, who was to command
the Italian army, came to pay his respects to the
Emperor, then in Savoy, and that Napoleon simply
said to him, *Fate presto*—Act at once. Cialdini did
not fail to follow this advice, and it was easy for him
at Castelfidardo to crush the army of the Pope, quite
inferior to his own in numbers and organization,
though its chief was one of the most intrepid generals and one of the most generous men of France.
The domain of the Pope was reduced to its present
boundaries; outside of Rome it had lost its most
precious jewels—and it retained the Eternal City
only by the aid of a French corps of occupation.
How long would she still retain that? This was a
very dubious question after all that had taken place
within two years. Did not the Emperor cause a
pamphlet to be written by one of his confidants, which
hinted that the Holy Father might well be content
with the Vatican and its dependencies? Events had,
moreover, raised the question of the temporal power
of the Papacy in all the European press, public

opinion was agitated and impassioned in various
directions, and the new kingdom of Italy, which had
been recognized by France immediately after the
death of the illustrious Cavour, did not fail on every
convocation of its Parliament to declare that Rome
ought to be its capital. Surely the position of the
temporal sovereignty of the Holy Father was quite
grave, despite the very irregular subsidy of Peter's
pence and the enlistment of many volunteers. It
became much more so when a convention was ratified
between France and Italy in September, 1865,
according to which the Emperor withdrew his troops
on condition that the King, Victor Emmanuel, should
prevent incursions on the Pontifical States. The
French troops were in fact withdrawn; but two
years had not elapsed before Garibaldi again attacked
the Roman State with his bands. This was a solemn
moment for France; the question was whether the
Emperor would resume the old error of occupation.
His hesitation was great; but, yielding to high and
dear influences, the Chief of the State, who then
possessed his personal power in its fullness, ordered
the fleet to sail from Toulon to Cività Vecchia. The
Chassepot guns did wonders, according to the happy
expression of General de Failly, who commanded the
French troops. The Garibaldians were crushed, the
Pontifical power consolidated, and M. Rouher declared at the French tribune, in the memorable debates
which took place on that occasion, that never would
France abandon the cause of the Pontifical sovereignty. For the present, the army of occupation is in barracks at Cività Vecchia, and at Viterbo;
they are not numerous, but a corporal's guard with
the French flag would be enough for the occupation

to have its full effect. People know that France is
near. What am I saying? She is there, with her
power and prestige, in the least of her soldiers. Further, the Imperial Government has authorized the
enlistment of a French legion, called at first the
Legion of Antibes, whose members retain their
rank and their rights on retirement whenever they
return to France. The Pope also has in his service
a Swiss legion and six battalions of Pontifical
Zouaves, volunteers enlisted among all nations, and
most ardent Catholics in their opinions. It is a fine
blossom of legitimist aristocracy. They are as the
apple of the Holy Father's eye ; he sees in them his
defenders from conviction, and is never weary of
showering benedictions on them ; they are encountered in large numbers kneeling before holy relics
in the churches ; on certain days they all commune
together, and they are spoken of as confessors of the
faith. This does not keep them from leading garrison life at other times, except a few who are perfect
enthusiasts. The Holy Father has several times
reviewed them, blessed their cannon, a very singular
office for the Vicar of the Prince of Peace ; he is
nearer his true office when he blesses the lambs on
Saint Agnes's day. Such is the military position of
the Roman States—whose most characteristic feature
still is the French occupation. The Swiss and the
Zouaves cannot pass for national troops. It is,
then, incontestable that the Holy Father needs foreign bayonets to guard him against his own subjects.
We shall see in the next letter that this comes from
the intolerable tyranny of his government. But is it
not itself a grave thing to see the representative of
the Catholic religion reduced to employ means before

which the worst lay despots would recoil? He is
the only present representative of those petty Italian
tyrants of the Middle Ages who could reign only by
turning the point of a foreign sword against the
breast of the nation on which they imposed themselves. I know that it will be said that the Pope
has to deal not merely with his own subjects, but
also with the intrigues and conspirators of Italy. But
after all, the Romans too are Italians, and for them
you will never be able to identify their great common
country with a foreign power. Between the Florentine and the Swiss, though arrayed as a halberdier,
he knows well which is his true compatriot. It is
likewise certain that all the gallant, energetic, and
youthful portion of the population is in exile; it is
these who wish to re-enter their homes occupied by
men who do not speak their language nor love the
grandeur of their country. Does not all Italy know
that Rome is a focus of conspiracy against her, that
there she is profoundly hated, and that the Holy
Father desires nothing so much as her abasement
and division? Yet justice compels us to blame her
policy so far as it has been tortuous and violent;
let her renounce these means, which are chiefly peril-
ous to those who use them, and just leave the breath
of freedom to blow over the nations! Let her also
have full confidence in the infallible imprudence of
her adversary! One Encyclical like that of 1865 is
worth ten Garibaldian expeditions to her.

The great argument of the Ultramontane Catholics
to justify foreign occupation at Rome is, that the
Eternal City belongs not to herself but is the sanctuary of true Christendom. If walls, temples, and a
city of stone were meant, such an argument might

be understood; but this city is inhabited; it is a city, and not merely a sacred hostelry. Now by what right, under pretext of serving your faith, do you trample under foot the liberty of human beings with the same moral destiny as yourselves? What! your religion need idiots and slaves! What! you need a eunuch people to guard your great sanctuary, as if it were a Mohammedan seraglio! What! human victims needed for your Papal idol! Then you do not know that the whole world is not worth one man, and for the good of religion you inflexibly load your brethren with chains which you would not wear a single day! But what then is your religion? Ah! if you think to serve it by such an administration, come then into the popular assemblies now held at Paris, in the capital of the Empire which you would make soldier to the Pope. Listen to those terrible outbursts of hatred against God. They come from the fact, that a people which has always been assured that Catholicism and Christianity are one and the same thing sees God only athwart your Pope-King and athwart the blood of Mentana. You are venturing the spiritual power of religion on the miserable stake of the temporal power.

Whether it please the Ultramontane party or not, their excesses have poured the most vivid light upon the question of the relations of these two powers. The French occupation of Rome has done more to advance the cause of the independence of the Church than the most eloquent books. To-day the whole liberal party is won over to it. And the liberal party is the France of to-morrow. When they come to power the Roman soil will not retain one of our soldiers, for the occupation of the Pontifical States does not merely wound the rights of the subjects of the Pope, but also the rights of Frenchmen. According to her Constitution, France is not a Catholic State; all religions are to be alike protected by law. By defending the Holy Father, the government ceases to be lay; it devotes itself to the service of a special Church, and forces us, who do not belong to her, to sustain her. This is a defiance of justice that cannot be continued. Its approaching limit is also foreseen. This is perceived, too, at Rome. Therefore their haste to hold the Council. France will be its halberdier—but patience! That will fill up the measure and the cup will overflow! A notable fraction of Catholicism begins to long as ardently as we for the fall of the temporal power. They are indeed right, for the Catholics ought to be the most impatient to see the end of a state of things which is truly the dishonor of their religion.

E. DE PRESSENSÉ.

LETTER V.

Cause of the Uneasiness of the Romans — Modern Liberty and Theocracy — The Prince and the Pope — Pope elected by Ecclesiastics — The Sacred College — The Conclave — The Congregations — The Courts of Law — The Signature — *Consulta Sacra* and the Robe — Trials not Public — Special Rights of the Clergy — The Police — Impunity of Crime — Conspirators — The Prelacy — Clerical Establishments of Rome — Foundations, Masses, and Begging — The Press and the Censorship — Enforced Hypocrisy of the Romans — No Reform possible — Ignorance of the Masses — Higher Education — The Jesuits as Educators — Their Triumphs over History — A Roman Apologue — Singular Consequences of Theocracy — Approval of Theaters and Lotteries — A Suggestive Incident.

Rome, *November*, 1869.

Dear Sir,—Should it be asked, Whence comes the immense dissatisfaction of the Roman population with its government? the reply is only too easy. We need only remember the nature of that government. Surely there is none more detestable in the world. It combines every thing that can exasperate a nation which has drawn a few breaths of modern liberty. To tell all in a word, it is Absolute Theocracy pushed to its final consequences. Let us try to present a rapid picture of it, to show what Catholicism, left to herself and without any counterpoise, does with humanity when she can dominate it at will. This question is important in relation to the religious controversy; indeed, as I have already said, liberal Catholics, who are singularly annoyed by the Pontifical Encyclicals, strive to lessen their sweep by a strained exegesis. But all their commentaries are annulled by that which we have under our eyes at Rome; the Pontifical rule is the Syllabus turned government, and incarnated after a sort in an administration which is daily applied. All the fine phrases that can be made on the harmony of freedom with Catholicism, dash and break on a reality which cannot be denied. Be fore leaving his diocese to come and sit in the Council, Monseigneur Dupanloup pronounced a very eloquent discourse on taking leave of his priests. He indignantly protested against the impious wretches who fear that the Council may pronounce a divorce between modern society and the Church. On this head he repeated his famous explanatory pamphlet on the Syllabus, and affirmed that the Church could not hate and condemn that society of which she is the mother. These grand words mean nothing—it is not enough to talk vaguely about the conciliation of the Papacy and modern society; they must be brought face to face. We are about to tell, or rather, remind, Monseigneur the Bishop of Orleans what he will find at Rome. He knows the principles on which modern society reposes: he shall see whether there is one of them that is not resolutely trodden under foot in the Eternal City, and systematically denied. I imagine what the bishops from your free America would feel on this despotic soil should they for a moment lift the vail of unreflecting respect which will cover their eyes—should they forsake the wholly perfumed and obscured atmosphere of incense which will envelope them, coolly to consider things. I imagine that they would be in haste to return to their great and noble country, and that they would say to themselves that the most detestable wish which the deadliest foe of the United States could utter,

would be, that they might exchange their government
for that which prevails in the Holy City.

If there is an elementary principle in modern society it is that of popular sovereignty ; that the government, whose form may vary, should represent the
will and interests of the country, and not represent
itself, nor serve its own grandeur. That is, indeed,
royalty in the modern sense, nay, I will say in the
Christian sense, for this great idea comes directly
from the Gospel. What becomes of this principle
before a power which affirms that it is descended directly from heaven, not by some mysterious species
of divine right, which loses itself in the night of time,
but by the direct designation of the Holy Spirit, so
that it represents not its own people, but God himself, and may claim an obedience as implicit as the
Jehovah of the Old Covenant demanded of the
twelve tribes of Israel! This power can neither be
shared nor limited. It is vain to reserve infallibility
to questions of doctrine. It is not possible that he
who thinks himself the mouth of God to interpret
religion should not deem himself illuminated with
celestial light to guide public affairs, all the more
because these are constantly blended with religion—
because civil and ecclesiastical affairs form an inextricable network. The Pope needs to be an absolute
king to preserve his independence, unless he would
be no king at all, and move exclusively in the spiritual sphere. But if he has any temporal sovereignty
it ought certainly to be wielded free from control.
We cannot imagine a Pope obliged to yield to the
vote of a deliberative assembly when a treaty with
any given power should be in question, for all the
treaties which he contracts have a religious side, and

are concordats; consequently they affect ecclesiastical interests. The Priest could not be constrained by the Prince, therefore the Prince should never know bonds. Please note that what the Papacy does at Rome it would wish to do every-where; that it has' not abandoned the pretensions of Gregory VII. and Innocent III.; that it is still ready to affirm that the temporal power in all places is in respect to the spiritual power as the earth in respect to the sun; that in any case the Church should be mistress. There is something more than a fact in the Pontifical absolutism, there is a principle, a dogma; the unhappy nations who undergo it have not even the hope of any improvement for consolation. They will move eternally in the circle of their present institutions, a circle which cannot become more supple, but must either be broken or drawn ever tighter. The palliatives that have repeatedly been devised could never be applied; the Council of State had not even the right to regulate expenses. It could only attest them and submit. It is a hundred times better, too, that this shadow of parliamentarianism should disappear, and that no oil should be poured on the wheels of absolutism; it is desirable that the horrible gearing should play in all its harshness. There have been, furthermore, intelligent despotisms, at least in the measure in which they are possible. These offered the people a bargain, and in exchange for their freedom favored their material prosperity and their national grandeur. Under Frederick II. Prussia was doubtless subjected to an iron yoke, but she found consolation in the feeling that she was being conducted to glorious destinies. Understand me well. I do not say this to excuse despotism; it is always immoral and mischievous. I simply remark that, though it can never be excused, it sometimes offers compensations. But nothing of the kind is possible in the Roman Theocracy. The Holy Father has no right to lay to heart the interests of the country. He governs his principality only with reference to the Church universal. To him Rome is merely a vast episcopal throne. He is not an Italian sovereign, but the chief of Christendom. The Roman people is likewise assured that never will their Prince assume the stand-point of their interests in forming alliances. He offers them as a sacrifice to the cause he personifies. The sacrifice would be touching did he offer *himself*, but the expense of the burnt-offering is borne by his people. As for him, he hovers in the empyrean, and sniffs the incense of Christendom. The troops he pays will never serve except as a guard to his personal authority; they will not weigh an ounce in the political balance, and the Roman people will have the pleasure of thinking that they are treated like old men and women in general politics, and that the haughty speech which might reveal manhood is never expected of them. Thus they are kept in constant humiliation.

Should it be claimed that the elective character of the Papacy is an amelioration, that would be a great mistake.

First, the Holy Father is elected solely by an ecclesiastical body, without any communication with the people. Then the fleeting nature of his government prevents his having extensive aims. A family which becomes a dynasty is more associated with the country and its interests than an old bachelor, who, when he has loaded his nephews with favors, (which

the present Pope has never done,) has nothing more
to wish for himself. His name stirs no memory ; he
has nothing in the past to care for, nothing to pro-
vide for in the future, in which he has no concern.
His government also is the most barren imaginable
in public affairs. The Cardinals constitute the Council of the Papacy, a Council which it names, and
which can never influence its decisions. They are
divided into three orders : the order of Bishops, the
order of Priests, and the order of Deacons. Together
they make up the Sacred College, which is transformed into a Conclave when a new Holy Father is
to be chosen. They guide all civil and ecclesiastical affairs, and are divided into Congregations. The
chief are those of the Inquisition, the Propaganda,
Rites, the Council, and the Index. The Apostolical
Chancery is the depository of the Papal bulls ; the
Datary is charged with the dispatch of benefices,
indulgences, and dispensations. The Penitentiary
sends off absolutions. The influence of the Cardinals
and the clergy is not less in civil than in religious
affairs. Do not forget further that you must never
separate the former from the latter in a theocratic
constitution. The religious life of the inhabitant of
Rome belongs, as much as his civil life, to the power
on which he depends. He is responsible, then, in a
multitude of cases, to the Congregations that I have
just enumerated, to which he must account for any
failure in the duties of piety. The Congregation of
the Inquisition is doubtless rather a phantom of the
past than a very redoubtable power ; the history of
blood and tears written on the walls of its dungeons
has had no new chapters in late years, because it is ad-
venturous to be old Papal Rome. The pressure of the

circumambient air is nevertheless felt, and the courage fails to turn wish into deed. Yet be not too confident. I am well assured that should any movement of evangelical propagandism be taken in the act of distributing the Scriptures the Inquisition would be found again, not indeed to slay, (her teeth are broken,) but to imprison. She is still called to busy herself with a multitude of cases of conscience.

This leads us to the organization of Justice at Rome. It is in this domain that especially all the principles of modern society are set at naught. First of all, the preponderance here belongs still to the clergy. How could it be otherwise? Is it not a moral institution, the father of the people? To intrust to laymen the care of discerning evil, characterizing and punishing it, would not that be the pitch of abominations, the overthrow of all rules? Hence care has been taken to exclude them as much as possible. The principal courts at Rome are in reality only ecclesiastical tribunals. They are the tribunal of Signature, a species of superior court charged to interpret the laws; the Consulta Sacra, which has an appellate jurisdiction in criminal causes; the Tribunal of the Robe, which is the Supreme Court of the Roman State. Judicial trials are not public; they are conducted in the shade; no appeal to the public is possible. The law may be strangled between two doors by the dumb officers of the Roman authorities. It is easy to conceive what arbitrary measures such an administration must produce. Proceedings by documents are substituted for the voice of defense, which, moreover, would be lost in the void without arousing an echo. The clergy finds its advantage in such institutions. All its misdoings are buried; it has immunities which are infinitely precious to its members in exemption from the common law ; the jurisdictions under which it is are very careful to keep its peccadilloes concealed. Thus ecclesiastical charity covers a multitude of sins. The regular clergy is exposed, not to more scandal but to greater perils. Every convent has its own jurisdiction, its *in pace* secret prisons. God knows how many tears they have drank up, how many unfortunates have there been punished, perchance for good impulses !

Besides, in a despotic State justice has but very slight action compared with that of the police. The latter spreads its protecting wings every-where, keeping its Argus-eye ever open, even in the most secret confessional. Yet it does not use brutal means. It walks with measured steps, disguising its movements. It is a gentle and discreet person, who has been at the seminary of Gesu, who has learned his best tricks of the good fathers. It has borrowed of them the paternal smile, the honeyed voice, the patience that can watch for hours, and then, when the hour for action comes, can unite rapidity with mystery, and the blow has fallen before the hand has even been seen which inflicts it. No guarantee can arrest it ; personal liberty is a concession and not a right ; justice is not bound to act after limited delays ; it may easily leave the prisoner to rot in an unknown dungeon. Relatives make some outcries, but they are bound in so many ways that silence is quickly imposed on them. An order of exile is expedited without any notification, and no demurrer can get it revoked. The other day the " Rome Journal," speaking of the indignation caused in the Eternal City by the brief appearance of an Italian Representative,

well known for his liberal opinions, rejoiced that the
Pontifical police would know to prevent the recur-
rence of such scandals, and that in its underground
ways it would succeed in removing from the Holy
City every element of mischievous propagandism.
The Roman police naturally has so much to do in
watching over the Liberals that it is often very lenient
to ordinary offenses, especially when the criminal has
potent friends.   One day an unlucky brigand had
been caught plunging his dagger into the breast of a
Frenchman in a fit of jealousy. He thought to get
out of the affair because he had great friends who
could well cover up his peccadillo. But for once he
had reckoned without his host, who was this time
the French police, because his offense must be answered before the military authorities of France.
He complained bitterly of his misfortune to him who
told me the story. "Our Roman police," said he,
"they understand, they understand;" meaning, that
with good recommendations you can always escape
them.   M. Ampére, the celebrated writer, who knew
Rome better than any body else, used to tell the following story.   One day he encountered a good old
man, with the placid and honest air of a patriarch.
He asked him what his calling was, not doubting
that he had filled the most honorable offices. "I,
sir," returned the good man, "I was formerly a brig-
and." "What! a brigand with your excellent figure?" "O, sir, you talk like my father! At the
moment of my decision he said, 'Why turn brigand?
Become a prelate rather. You will steal in the office.' But I loved glory." Thus may retired brigands peacefully consume their savings at Rome, while
the most honest man, if suspected of liberal meas-

ures, is flung into prison or exile, without judgment or debate, on a mere suspicion.

And yet this skillful police cannot find the true nest of the Roman conspiracies. There exists a National Committee at Rome which urges on by all possible means deliverance from the Papal yoke. It is known that it sits permanently; that its communications with the Garibaldians are numerous; and that it waits patiently to attain its ends. Well now, they never have succeeded in getting hold of the principal members. They are perhaps in some branch of the administration, or in the antechambers of some Cardinal, bowing, as need is—perhaps they swing the censer. On great occasions their presence and activity is disclosed. Some fine morning the walls of Rome are suddenly all covered with proclamations, which give the general watchword. The entire prelacy is furious, but their wrath must exhale in vain imprecations; the offenders are invisible. They may be close by, all steeped in devotion; but their punishment is impossible.

The Italians excel in these underground maneuvers. They are the best conspirators in the world; prudent, discreet, skillful in misleading, and in putting the bloodhounds of the police on the wrong track. As I have spoken of the Prelacy, I must explain this singular institution. It constitutes a species of aristocracy with no very well-defined functions, but from which are drawn all the dignitaries of the Church, and part of those of the State, which is never separated from the former. This body furnishes the Pope his high domestics, and occupies the most important functions in the ministry. It may be known by its violet stockings. The number of the prelates is considerable. The clergy, moreover, in the proportions to which it has multiplied, is a perpetual cloud of grasshoppers, busy in consuming this country. Rome numbers three hundred and eighty-nine churches, several of them important basilicas; each has a numerous train of servitors to maintain; some have canons magnificently paid. Add to these the College of Cardinals, each of whom receives yearly six thousand dollars, a multitude of Bishops *in partibus*—immense seminaries and convents of all orders, which would of themselves constitute a great city. You cannot take a step in the street without crossing files of monks of every name, Franciscans, Dominicans, and Carmelites, with all their divisions and subdivisions. No doubt the money that supports this numberless clerical body comes from ancient endowments, but it is none the less drawn from the country which it exhausts. Mirabeau said justly, when the difficult question of the estates of the clergy was in discussion at the tribunal of the Constituent Assembly in 1789, that the State must always have a right of resumption upon these estates of corporations on condition of generously indemnifying the actual generation still in possession. He said, "The dead, if their right were absolute, might occupy the entire soil of any country with their tombs, so that not an inch of land would remain for the living to cultivate and subsist upon." Well now, this argument, which at first seems a paradox corresponding to no reality, has its full value on this Roman soil overloaded with those pompous endowments, by which so many of the rich, anxious about their eternal future, have sought to purchase the pardon of Heaven by paying for it in cash to

those in whose hands they saw the celestial keys.
Rome, as has been well said, is the great *mortmain*
proprietor of the Occident.   But if the endowments
are insufficient, the mass-market works in the most
fruitful manner.   It has been greatly perfected in
the last few years; it is a true branch of trade.
There is now a free exchange of masses with the
various Catholic countries; they are exported with
benefices.   Thus a given Church has considerable
orders for masses, which it cannot meet all alone; it
arranges the task with some less favored Church,
which performs them at a cheaper rate, and the former Church gains the difference.   This custom is not
peculiar to the Roman States; it is very general, and
has given occasion to some passably scandalous law-
suits.   I believe that, through the telegraph, the
mass-market will yet be found beside the stock-
market.

Mendicant monks like the Franciscans are another
sad sore for this unlucky population.   Their rule
obliges them to live on alms; at Rome these alms
are a regular tribute levied on the poorest houses.
The Capuchin friar knows all the arts of his trade;
he approaches his patient with a benign air, offers
him a pinch of snuff, speaks his dialect with great
facility, for he is from the common people, like his
victim, and then he reaches out his bag or wallet,
and the wretch must acquit himself, unless his
poverty be past doubt; otherwise he would be ill-
liked, and the Church has long arms.   The blood-
sucker returns to his convent quite gorged.   Beggary
has its third estate at Rome, which is largely represented; it is recognized and patented; every mendicant wears a medal from the government and goes

with a nasal whine to church doors, as though he fulfilled some State function. Naturally he has to make a great display of devotion to succeed in his business. I am persuaded that more than one capitalist lifts with one hand the tapestried door of a large church, often while his other hand is often extended to you.

The Pontifical Government can be under no illusion on the discontent that is brewing in the hearts of its subjects. It knows that a single spark would fire the powder. It also takes the most jealous care to remove every thing which might awaken the least liberal aspiration. What the press is, under such rule, may be imagined. It is purely and simply the organ of the government. That alone speaks and writes. Never can the slightest abuse be named, never the least objection be uttered. Foreign news is dressed up in Roman style before it circulates; the telegraph, that free child of the air, is under the most minute watch. But one strain is heard in all the Roman journals, a perpetual halleluiah to the wonderful and heavenly rule which they enjoy, and a constant anathema against revolution and its abominations, especially against the new kingdom of Italy. Dull sarcasms rain upon that like hail. Geography itself must lie for the benefit of the Holy See. None of the new titular styles is accepted. The King of Italy is still the King of Piedmont; the province of Naples is never mentioned except as the Kingdom of the two Sicilies. On the government of the press let us listen to the *Rome Correspondent* — a very well-meaning journal. I find the following passage in its issue of November sixth: "No, the Papacy is not an extinguisher. It favors social activity while restraining it within those limits which befit the welfare of the people, morality and justice. As to literary activity, Rome numbers thirty-four newspapers, in which, thanks to the watchfulness of the authorities, none can offend either morality or reason, or the authority which represents them." What could be more ingenuous? Reason and morality are incarnated in the government; whatever is opposed to that is immoral and irrational. There is nothing to do but to receive and repeat its teachings. These thirty journals are merely its speaking-trumpets. Do you not admire the number thirty-four? Is it not an answer to all objections? What! our press not sufficient? and we have thirty-four journals; count well, not one is lacking. Well! had you two hundred they would none the less be one and the same journal—yours. Be there two hundred or ten parrots in a cage, it is ever the same babble. The censorship, which is always preventive, does not bear merely on the newspapers, but on all publications. Every book is subject to it, whatever topics it may treat. It is certain that no scientific discovery would be allowed to pass which should bear hard at any point on Romish orthodoxy. Its famous blunder with Galileo has taught it nothing; it has found means to reconcile his discoveries with its dogmas, and it permits Father Sacchi, the illustrious astronomer, to have a magnificent observatory in the College at Rome, and even to borrow some of his discoveries from foreign profane science; but it would not grant an *exeat* to a compromising discovery, however well-founded it might be on irrefragable documents. It is well known how carefully the door of the Vatican Library is closed; it possesses treasures on the history of the later Middle Ages and on the struggles of the

Reformation. But so long as the present rule endures, history will never get its eyes upon them. Night must be created in the past as well as in the present, that the Pontifical Star may blaze alone in all its splendor. The sun is its great enemy; the Reformation showed this well by inscribing on its standard the device, *Post tenebras lux.*

The censorship pursues irreligion or heterodoxy in the humblest publications, and even in the opera *libretti.* Every literary work must bend to the proportions of its Procrustean bed or undergo the outrage of its scissors. The word liberty is everywhere excluded as incendiary. It is not allowable to put into an opera any term that nearly or remotely appertains to the ecclesiastical tongue. Thus, to cite a recent example of the scruples of the censorship, in a certain piece there was mention of the *angelic beauty* of some heroine. The censor found nothing more urgent to do than to put in the room of those words the *admirable beauty.* But the Pope thought this was too much, and he hinted his feeling with witty neatness when, passing in a carriage along the street of the Holy Angels, he inquired its name, as if he had forgotten it, and chided his informant by saying, " You are mistaken, it is not the street of the *Angeli;* it is the street of the *Mirabili.*" But above all there is one book which is carefully banished from Rome, and whose circulation is guarded against as though it were poison—the Bible. You may ship a cargo of romances, French or English, to Rome, except those of political tendencies; but apart from your pocket Bible, you cannot openly introduce a copy of the sacred volume. The great Bible Societies, which are the honor of Protestantism, occupy the chief place in the anathemas of the late Encyclicals; they are denounced as Satanic enterprises.* Indeed, we might say to the Papacy, " If you are God, the Bible comes from the devil, since whatever you do, and, further, all that you mean to do, is blamed and branded by that book. I seem to see the God of the Gospel entering your proud basilica with the scourge of small cords, which drove the buyers from the temple, and the fearful anathemas which turned the Pharisees of Jerusalem pale. You do well, from your point of view, to banish the word of God to your frontiers. You are right in fearing it—it will slay you!" I have not yet said a word about the holiest liberty—liberty of conscience—because it would be ridiculous to speak of it at Rome, where every thing is organized against it; it is the great stumbling-stone. I have already cited the terms in which the Encyclical of Gregory XVI. and Pius IX. characterize it.

In all the Concordats signed by the present Pope it is expressly interdicted; we need only remember the famous Concordat of Vienna, in which, after Sadowa, Austria rightly recognized the cause of her defeat; that rule was after the heart of Rome, since it subordinated the education, literature, thought, and will of the country to the good pleasure of its clergy. The Concordats, proposed to the republics of South America, are conceived from the same standpoint. It is there that we must seek the true Romish idea, and not in liberal countries where, in order to obtain something, she is obliged to make important

---

* I believe a copy of the Gospels, with Catholic comments, may be had at bookstores. But this has nothing to do with the free circulation of the Holy Books.

concessions, but without ever touching her great principle, that the only freedom pleasing to God is that of the Church, a freedom that consists in her oppressing souls at will. But it is at home, in Rome, that this fine system must be seen at work; there the word of God cannot resound except in little chapels of embassadors, which are yet covered by some foreign flag. The least attempt at private religious propagandism would surely lead to imprisonment or exile. They celebrate with great pomp the abjuration of blind Protestants, who are caught in the snare of a wholly exterior worship; yet the abjuration of a Catholic would be not only forbidden, but severely chastised; thus what the Sultan allows is here forbidden, and Romish fanaticism exceeds Mussulman fanaticism. What could you have more abominable than the carrying off of little Mortara on the pretext that his nurse had him baptized on the sly? That enormous scandal is forgotten, and yet it continues, for Mortara is now a priest, forever separated from the family from which he was stolen.

Whenever we enter the Sistine Chapel to admire the frescoes of Michael Angelo, do we not see, on the walls of the passage which the Holy Father traverses to reach his private chapel, the frescoes of Vasari, which represent the triumph of the Church on St. Bartholomew's eve? The memory of that execrable massacre is thus religiously preserved, not on account of the merit of the work, which in itself is only mediocre, but for its own sake, and to attest forever in what sense the saying is true, that the Church shrinks from blood.* What a cry of indignation would arise in France should she consecrate at Versailles a great

* Abhorret a sanguine.

picture in admiration of the massacres of September! What is the difference?

I have not yet mentioned the most frightful consequence of the rule I am describing; the hypocrisy to which it, perforce, condemns a good share of the population. Every Roman is obliged by law to fulfill his religious duties, and after the great festivals to produce a ticket of confession, else he can exercise no trade, or he is subject to various penalties. His moral dispositions are of little account; he must at any rate commune. In such a state of things the confessor must necessarily be very tolerant—there are well-known means of procuring these confessional billets on easy terms. If there be a sacrilege committed under heaven, it is surely that which is renewed at Rome on all the great festivals—a sacrilege ordained by him who proclaims himself the Head of the Church. You remember those terrible anathemas with which the book of the Prophet Isaiah opens against the formalist worship of degenerate Judaism, bowing down like a reed in solemn festival days, while the heart retained its indomitable pride; against that theatrical worship which covered up injustice and violence. "I cannot endure your solemn feasts," cried Jehovah; "they are an abomination unto me. Who hath required you to present yourselves before my face?" Well, the Romans might justly answer, "He who has not only required, but exacted this of us, is the Pontiff who claims to be your Vicar and Representative. It is he who has appointed these solemn feasts, whither we are constrained to come by the urgency of his soldiers; and if we bow our heads over the pavement of the basilicas with souls full of pride and selfishness, it is because the halberd of the guards of the Holy Father constrains us. Therefore we come, as we think, to eat and drink the flesh of your Christ without one of the feelings required by that august sacrament. Our solemn feasts are to many among us public falsehoods decreed by the law of the State." Can we imagine what demoralization such a government must produce, and what becomes of conscience in such a school! It either produces the most resolute impiety, most contemptuous toward a religion so travestied, or, indeed, it impresses an incurable duplicity on the soul. Where the essential relation of life is thus falsified, the entire being receives a bent to falsehood that can no longer be remedied. And yet people will be astonished, and perhaps indignant, that nations molded by Papal Catholicism should have some difficulty in getting clear of it, and should retain its traces even after their chains have fallen off. The greatest curse of this sacerdotal absolutism is, that even when revolution has overturned it for a time, it renders freedom almost impossible. There are evils so inveterate that they even infect the means intended to heal them.

There is no hope of seeing the Roman people elevated so long as it shall be dependent on the Holy Father. No reform, small or great, is possible. Cardinal Consalvi, in those curious memoirs of which I have spoken, relates that while he occupied in his youth an important position under the government he sought to banish certain abuses, but that he stirred up so much wrath on the part of those who lived on them that he was obliged to yield. This old tale is ever new in the Roman States. What hinders any serious improvement in their moral condition is the fact that the great agent of progress, public education, is in a deplorable state. In reality, the Papacy dreads to educate the people; it has every thing to lose from putting them in a position to understand history and the real state of things. It would not be content to say with the Apostle, that Satan can sometimes transform himself into an angel of light; it would openly declare that the light is a demon. It imagines that what ruined humanity in Eden was not its rebellion, but knowledge; and it takes good care that the accursed tree shall not extend its boughs over the population which it governs. That tree would, indeed, find a soil hardly propitious for its growth and nourishment in these unwholesome lands of the Roman Campagna, which are of themselves the proof and the result of gross ignorance. The rustics of the environs are half savage; only on the confines of your great forests, among the fragments of the Indian tribes, would you find a race so devoid of culture, despite something unspeakably sad and proud that appears through their tatters. There is a certain number of infant schools at Rome, but the children are taken to them in their cradles; they are rather cribs and asylums than educational establishments, and what is almost solely learned there is to spell out the Catechism.

A large part of the urban population cannot yet read. Good heed is taken not to shake off its ignorance. Here a book is a foe; and they do not forget what asylums printing-houses afforded the Reformation in the sixteenth century. All that concerns education appertains to the clergy; with the Papacy this is an absolute principle, which it from time to time recalls in a doleful voice to the memory of emancipated nations. To her mind, the Church is

the intellectual mother and nurse of the rising generations; she must harden them into her image and
fashion their minds in a sacred mold. The Bishop
of Orleans, Monseigneur Dupanloup, in a quite pitiful warfare which he conducted in France against
the freedom of lay education, said that at least the
women ought always to be reared on the knees of the
Church. Here all the youth receive from her whatever light they have. There is indeed a University
for the sciences and for law, but under control of the
clerical extinguisher. Secondary education is given in
convents to young ladies; to young men in the great
ecclesiastical establishments in which Rome glories.
Apart from the Propaganda College, where young
men from all nations are admitted, and where nearly
all languages are spoken, and a few special Colleges,
like the Irish, the most considerable educational institution is the Roman College. It has a magnificent
edifice, perfectly adapted to its purpose, where it may
conduct its instructions from the rudiments of Latin
up to transcendental theology. It is wholly in the
hands of the Jesuits. They have ever been very
skillful, insinuating, and gracious masters, with a
certain easy and agreeable bloom of literature, yet
without ever developing a love for true beauty; they
dote on trifles of form; the art which they like, as
we may be convinced from their churches, is a pretty
art; they every-where prefer the pretty to the beautiful, because sovereign beauty is a summit where
we breathe free air. Any generous admiration gives
the soul an upward impulse which is not without its
dangers. But the Jesuits obtain their greatest triumphs in historical studies, or rather *over* history,
for they have infinite art in getting clear of testimony

that would embarrass their cause. To-day they no longer dare to push their audacious falsifications so far as they did in the period of political and religious reaction that followed the fall of Napoleon. It was then that the Manual of the illustrious Father Loriquet appeared, which quite tranquilly suppressed the French Revolution, and dated the reign of Louis XVIII. from the death of Louis XVII.; making the Victor of Marengo and Austerlitz a Lieutenant General in the service of the Most Christian King. The courageous Jesuit thought it just and proper to give Providence a lesson since it had failed in all its duties by allowing the eldest Son of the Church to be kept in exile by an adventurer. I almost prefer these cynical falsifications, so promptly desired for youth, to the artful falsification of history now made by the reverend Jesuits; the lying is not less, but it is more skillful, more difficult to perceive and refute; it is ever a perversion of history, which only glorifies the past and curses the future. The procedures of the Jesuits remind me of certain Gnostic sects of the second century, who hardily took sides with the Prince of darkness. Their adherents were called *Ophites*, or the Serpent's men, because they took pleasure in glorifying Satan; their saints were precisely all the enemies of the true light, from Cain to Judas Iscariot; they carried it through to the very end. Well! the Jesuits, though they stop short of this, do something like it. In history they are always and every-where for darkness against light; they are for the oppressors against their victims; their great men are Philip II., the demon of the South; Louis XIV., he who revoked the Edict of Nantes, and not he who resisted the Pope; Sixtus Quintus; Saint Pius V.; the Inquisi-

tion; while all who have labored for the emancipation of mankind are criminals. The theology of the
Roman College is famous; it is taught by the most
distinguished masters; at their feet the purest and
most absolute Romish orthodoxy is learned. I con-
versed one day with one of my countrymen, an intelligent young priest, trained in this school. He
unrolled to me in the easiest fashion frightful theories
of religious tyranny founded on the principle that it
is the right and the duty of the Infallible Church to
save souls despite themselves. He also told me
that the great target of the polemics of the Reverend
Fathers was not unbelief, but Liberal Catholicism.
Here is the dangerous adversary which must at any
cost be crushed. After hearing him for some time I
could not help saying, " I hear you, Abbé, with the
same feeling of painful astonishment which I should
feel before some fearful physical deformity. They subject your minds to a sort of dislocation which places
you and your like in the category of intellectual mon-
strosities." Indeed, I can compare the method of
the Roman College, in deforming the understanding,
only with the art by which certain gymnasts succeed
in unjointing themselves in order to become clowns
of the highest grade. Nor do I allow myself to be
caught by the air of gentleness and good-nature that
reigns in this superb establishment, nor the kiss which
every pupil leaves at the close of the lecture on the
hand of his master. I know too well what these fine
appearances conceal. As to moral education, it
should be remembered that informing and espionage
are its fundamental principles.

The Romans deeply feel the mischief done them
by the Society of Jesus. A cutting speech is attrib-

uted to them on this topic. The Piazza di Gesu, which is before the church and convent of the Reverend Fathers, is famous at Rome for always being very windy. The people have turned the matter into an apologue. One day, say they, the wind met the devil before the Gesu—wait for me here on the square, said the devil to his companion; I am going into the church for a second, and will be out in a moment. He went in, says the apologue, but he has never been seen to come out. For this reason the wind continues ever blowing in that accursed place. The Romans are gentle, keen, and amiable. The champions of the temporal power proclaim them perfectly happy, and draw an argument from their patience. They forget two things: first, that the energetic party is in exile, and that there remain here hardly more than those who let furnished apartments and the shopkeepers. The second is, that when slavery has become agreeable to him who undergoes it the crime is truly consummated, for it has reached the moral nature by destroying its power of resistance. If you say that the Romans are happy under such rule, you furnish your adversaries the most terrible argument against you. That is the proof that you have killed them by asphyxia. The most redoubtable of chains are those whose weight is no longer felt. But it is not true that the Roman people is content, and the foreign occupation is the proof. How should it be happy with no prospects before it, when all outlets are closed against its most legitimate ambition, and upon all the paths of public life it encounters a forestalling clergy which monopolizes the chief offices. I beg a thousand pardons, I had forgotten the most illustrious Roman Senator,

the heir of a great name for a very little thing, for in
vain does he lodge at the Capitol; he is only President of the Roman municipality, which is merely
charged with a few vulgar highway cares. One
would say that in this august appellation, which recalls an entire glorious history, there is a final irony
addressed to the Roman people, the better to make
them feel their nothingness.   Senate, tribuneship,
and *comitia* have all disappeared and come to melt
into the absolutism of a Pontiff, from whom every
thing comes, to whom every thing returns.   This
absorption of power in sacerdotal hands often has
very droll consequences.   Thus the theaters depend
directly on the Holy Father, who has them conducted
by a prelate; no buffoonery is played, not a ballet is
given without the express authorization of ecclesiastical authority.   It is the Holy Father who by his subordinates keeps the Roman lottery—a very immoral
institution, a perpetual bait to evil lusts, an ever
open gulf for the savings of the people.   Thanks to
this sadly won money, some of the pomps of worship
are maintained; and the Papacy seems to say, with
Vespasian, that money never has a bad scent; for the
lottery is never closed, even when all the coffee-houses
are shut in the solemn festivals, and when the so-
called Apostolical Benediction is given to the city
and the world—*urbi et orbi*.   Finally, it is the representative of Jesus Christ, who upon occasion confirms
death sentences, and sends a soul, perchance impenitent, into eternity.   This last touch finishes the
picture.

An unhappy Roman, condemned to the highest
punishment for political offenses, saw a priest approaching him in the cell which he was about to

leave, bringing him the final consolations of religion. He repelled him with indignation as the representative of a rule that he abhorred, and which was putting him to death; then he flung his face to the earth before a large crucifix to show that he was no impious wretch, and that he could distinguish between the Papacy and Christ. Liberal Catholics! come to Rome and open your eyes! May you then show as much intelligence as that wretched man, for unless you make the distinction which he made before dying your religion will die, and you will be responsible for its death.

E. DE PRESSENSE.

9

LETTER VI.

Religious Worship in Rome: its Magnificence Contrasted with the
Primitive Type—Culmination of Roman Art at the Reformation—
Its Previous Condition — Gothic Architecture and the Roman
Churches—The Cathedral at Cologne and Saint Peter's—Transfor-
mation of Pagan Temples into Christian Churches—The same con-
trast in Painting—Fra Bartolomeo—The Last Judgment of Michael
Angelo and that of Fra Angelico—Raphael, Julius Romanus, and
the Decline—Similar Phases in Church Music—Ancient and Modern
Church Song—Church Music and the Reformation—Testimony of
M. de Laprode—Defects of Protestant Worship—That of the Post-
Apostolic Period—Ceremonies of Holy Week and Easter—Taking
the Vail—Grotesque Appeals to the Populace—Mercenary Spirit of
Catholic Worship—Its False Supernaturalism—Its Absolute Idola-
try—A Touching Ceremony.

ROME, *Nov.* 22, 1869.

DEAR SIR,—Before coming to the direct preparations
for the Council I wish to inquire what are the
characteristics of worship at Rome. It is here that
we learn to grasp the dominant trait of Catholic
piety in its peculiarities, but without forgetting the
multitude of souls who attain their God in the impulse of adoration, and in order to worship Jesus Christ,
raise the heavy and splendid hangings which separate
them from him. To judge any religion well we
should not take it in those who, by dint of intellectual elevation, transform and idealize it. There are
many Catholics, alike distinguished and sincere, who
object when gross errors in their worship and doctrine are pointed out. They always reply; " You
understand nothing of the matter. You take the
exceptions for the principle, and what offends you

has a very plausible and Christian interpretation.
They transport their Church with themselves to Tabor, where they gladly rear their own tabernacles, and
see, under a sort of celestial atmosphere, all that
seemed most contrary to the Gospel. Thus they deceive themselves in perfect good faith, and prolong
illusions dangerous to all. We must descend from
that mountain which soars into the pure ether of a
transcendental mysticism and regain the plain; there
we find the popular, practical religion, that which
acts on the masses; there we see it in its regular
play. I freely compare actual Catholicism with one
of those old·manuscripts, so well deciphered by Cardinal Mai, which are called palimpsests. They contain two layers of texts, one pagan, which is primitive, then a Christian text, which has been traced by
the hand of some monk, so as to cover the previous
characters. Put a sponge across it, and you recover
the paganism. Well, now, it is this touch of the
sponge that I would send across the evangelical text
laid over the primitive text by noble minds who
create a Catholicism in their own image, and for
their exclusive use; it is truly idolatry that I shall
find.

Now since the spiritual and Christian upper text
does not exist at Rome, it is very easy to discover the
true state of things. What strikes us at the outset is
the pompous and theatrical character of the worship.
Its magnificence expels depth and inwardness. This
feature also appears in the architecture, paintings, music, at least in all that belongs to positively Roman
and Catholic influences. Pass over the most ancient
period of Christianity which preceded the great development of the temporal power. I have already

described the ancient basilica, and shown that it remained faithful to the great notion of a spiritual Church distinguished from the general life of the world, and brought that distinction to mind as well in the arrangement of its edifices as in its institutions. All the basilicas of this type, which are numerous at Rome, present the same character. The paintings of the pulpits are perfectly simple without excluding pathos. It is ever the Good Shepherd, surrounded by his sheep, for whom he gives his life; the mystic vine, whence the Christian soul must draw its vigor; or, indeed, the Master surrounded by the martyrs who have given their name to the Church, as *Saint Comus and Damien*, or *Saint Pudentiana*, near great Saint Mary's, whose frescoes go back positively to the close of the fourth century, for Sig. Rossi found the exact date inscribed on the holy volume in the hands of the Christ. Doubtless we are no longer in the times of primitive simplicity and freedom; but the Christian character is nevertheless strongly impressed on these antique edifices. As to the sacred music, it must have had a moving grandeur, to judge by what Saint Augustine says of the impression it produced on him at the decisive epoch of his conversion. He says in his Confessions, "With what rapture did I hear, O God, the holy songs of thy Church! They brought tears to my eyes, and I was glad to weep." *Et currebant lacrymæ, et bene mihi cum eis.* Remember that at this time he was passing through the doleful crisis which made him a new man; that he was tired to death of the false pomp of worldly life. Hence it is not the artist, but the Christian who speaks. But then, despite the growing and continuous progress of the hierarchical idea, we are yet far from the time when it will fashion a world to its own image.

To my mind, the truly Roman Catholic art dates from the Renaissance and the Reformation; it then reached its culminating point, and revealed itself in full sincerity. Until the Reformation the Church contained in its bosom all the elements which subsequently separated and even fell into open war. All these tendencies existed within her in a sort of embryonic state, and all drawn up under the Papal crook, but preserving their special direction, and not coming into clear rupture. Who could deny that long before the Reformation German Catholicism was distinguished from Southern Catholicism? The mystic fervors that the convents of the North shelter already reveal the need of direct and immediate communication with Deity. Even in Italian Catholicism there are many divergences which sometimes burst out, as in the grand figure of Savonarola; but I prefer to compare these explosions of a freer Christian feeling to the sudden jet of a current of water which has long flowed under ground. It exists before darting up to the free air in a sparkling and echoing sheaf. Well, the Catholic art of the twelfth and thirteenth centuries profited by this yet undiminished wealth of the Church, when it still possessed all its treasures in their fruitful variety. I exaggerate nothing. I do not pretend that the Catholicism of that age was a species of anticipated Protestantism; nay, it was truly the Church of unity and hierarchy, the new theocracy; but it was, nevertheless, a Catholicism entirely different from that which was established after the great separation effected by the Reform, a Catholicism not yet bent to the Romish type, full of

vigor and originality despite its errors, mystical and
learned, austere and puissant.   To that Catholicism
we owe Gothic art, which has never been able to
take root in Rome, and which failed from the very
moment that she exercised a decidedly predom-
inant influence in all the domains of that Church.
What is Gothic art but precisely the grandest manifestation of that Germanic Catholicism whence the
Reform was to proceed ?   Men may discuss its origin
as much as they like; they may credit the Romans
for the arch, the Arabs for the broken lines of the
ogive; it nevertheless remains true that Gothic art
was creative, and that it set its seal upon all the elements that came to it from elsewhere ; it created as
human genius does create, which is no God to draw
its works out of nothingness ; but it is enough for it
to have impressed on them a truly new meaning, an idea and a feeling that are its own, that men
should be unable to dispute its originality.   Now
what is the meaning, the idea of the Gothic?   Enter
the Cathedral of Cologne, and you will grasp it in a
moment.   In that vast edifice, and in its fellows,
Gothic art desired to express the world and society
as it conceived them.   It is indeed a theocracy, but it
brings it back to a truly Christian type ; it impresses
on it the sign of redemption, then especially it flings
it into the region of the infinite and the eternal with
the bold spire which it directs to heaven.   Stand in
the Choir of the Cathedral, there you see all the lines
come thronging together in a species of irresistible
impulse.   The *ogive* reproduces the same characteristic on a smaller scale.   By the arrangement of its
lines it also cries *Excelsior! sursum corda!*—Up, ever
higher !   It should be observed that nothing like this

had been seen before in the history of art. The pagan temple, especially under the enchanting form it took on in Greece, is an edifice of restricted proportions. It is solely intended as a habitation for the Deity. It sufficed that the cella was well adorned, that a statue of perfect beauty was deposited there, and that space was reserved for the altar of sacrifice. In its beautiful, sunny marbles it had preserved the smile of its religion. The Roman basilica, which is the most remarkable architectural creation of the kingly nation, is fully conformed to its genius; it only admits the horizontal line; it is all length and breadth. Nothing carries the glance beyond this world, which is the sole empire that Rome has ever coveted. The Gothic cathedral, on the contrary, is like a great *memento* of the eternal life which Christ has won and given to us. Thus, as a poet has said, it is as though, having knelt down in its robe of stone, it prayed. I prefer, to be sure, the upper chamber at Jerusalem with its tongues of fire; but it cannot be denied that the Catholicism of the Middle Ages, through all its obscurity, had its tongues of fire to celebrate the God of the Gospel. I appeal to those sublime chants of the twelfth and thirteenth centuries, which, with the hymns of Luther, are the finest, most pathetic things produced by Christian song.

Now compare the religious architecture of Rome with these monuments of the North! The contrast is absolute. Is it not especially remarkable that it should have completely shunned the Gothic, even in its great epoch? A single church, that of *Santa Maria della Minerva*, shows traces of it. Still they have hastened to spoil that by covering it with gilding, and overloading it with ornaments in bad taste. Except this,

all the Roman churches are patterned on the ancient
basilica; I know that they are arranged in the form
of a Greek or Roman cross, but what decidedly prevails is the idea of external grandeur; it is *extension*, and not *elevation*, which characterizes them.
There we hear the incessant echo of the old Roman
device, Thine the empire! Think above all, of rule,
dominion!

Most of these churches are very mediocre, except
in the interior, where works of art are piled up, but
where decoration is lavished till the eye wearies of it.
The architects have spent their pride in the arrangement of façades, but have never abandoned their
routine in the general arrangement.

If one would have a complete idea of Roman religious architecture, he should consider Saint Peter's.
I know of no more complete contrast than that which
exists between the splendid basilica of the Vatican
and the Cathedral of Cologne. I do not restrain my
admiration of the former. I admit that you rarely
obtain a grander view than that of the mass of monuments of which it is the center. The semi-circular
porticoes which surround the square, in the midst of
which an obelisk rises, form the finest introduction
to the basilica itself. The latter is so harmoniously
arranged that its grandeur is not at all overwhelming,
because no part is salient or inharmonious. The cupola,
which rises to a dizzy height, seems a natural development of the building. The five naves of the interior
are connected with the apsis, like the branches of a
gigantic trunk; and yet all this grandeur does not
soar. It extends and unfolds in space, but does not
truly tower. The Sainte Chapelle of Paris, an ideal
creation of the reign of Saint Louis, would disappear

in one of the chapels of Saint Peter's, and yet it lifts
you far higher; it has an impulse, a something inexpressibly winged, in its Gothic lines, which bears
the soul aloft.   Elevation is not a matter of dimensions, but of direction and inspiration.   Saint
Peter's, with all its magnificence, does but produce
the effect of that high mountain whence is seen, not
heaven, but all the kingdoms of the world.   Has not
the bargain of earthly domination been proposed to
the Roman hierarchy, and accepted by them in exchange for spiritual dominion?   In this respect has
it not imitated the degenerate Judaism of the synagogue, and clung to that mastery more than to the
Divine Master, who said, "My kingdom is not of
this world?"   Saint Peter's, and the other great
basilicas of Rome, seem to me to express this devia-
tion from primitive Christianity by the most striking
symbol.   Every thing recalls Christ the Ruler, and
nothing leads us back to the Crucified, his opprobrium and his inward glories.   Saint Peter's is the
capitol of the Papacy.   At least, it reveals the high
art and bears the impress of the haughty genius of
Michael Angelo.   But what shall we say of the architecture of the Jesuit churches?   This introduces us
to the second period of the Roman domination; the
Reform has shaken its torch over the world; the
empire of Europe is disputed with the Papacy.   The
times of its haughty royalty are gone; absolutism
must grow supple, but bend like steel without ever
breaking.   This medley of ruse and unconquerable
force is the whole of Jesuitism, that great and skillful
prop of Pontifical authority in these difficult days
when an adroit and artful policy must be united with
obstinacy.   But in this game men lose their grandeur,

and the architecture of the Jesuits is all delicate and
complicated. Seeing the overwrought ornamentation of their churches, one thinks of the processes
used in glossing up a pretentious old woman. They
have laid down velvet carpets on the road to paradise,
and striven to enlarge its entrance. Their history, and
also their genius, may be read on the stones of their
edifices. This is likewise a decisive test for Roman
architecture. It has always been able to appropriate
without effort the ancient temples or pagan edifices,
like the temple of Faustina, and that of Venus and
Bona, and the baths of Domitian, transformed by
Michael Angelo into the fine Church of Saint Mary
of the Angels. Never could any Gothic edifice have
had such an origin.

If I pass from architecture to painting I might
make similar remarks. It is indisputable that the
great mystical and religious school of painting also
preceded the time when Roman Catholicism established itself in opposition to the Reform, and that its
highest inspirations belong to the same movement
which produced Gothic art and reared the cathedrals.
I have already spoken of the profound impression
produced on me by that ingenuous and mystical style
of painting which preceded the Renaissance, and still
profited by its first jet without denying what forms
its religious grandeur. It was in Flanders and Germany that it was born and perfected its methods.
The purest Christian ideal sparkled in the profound
glance of the Virgins of Van Eyk, Albert Durer,
and Holbein. Italy followed the movement, and
tempered its austerity with that inimitable grace whose
secret is hers. It was, indeed, between the fifteenth
and sixteenth centuries that this great Christian art

attained its height. What exquisite tenderness, what
celestial candor, what burning ecstacies in those
pictures and frescoes of the Fra Angelicos and the
Francias! There is a chapel at the Vatican, painted
by the former of these masters, which people often
neglect to visit because it is not in the usual programme. It is the chapel of Saint Laurence and
Saint Stephen. Here is great Christian painting; a
little too sacerdotal, but the soul itself breaks out in
those living colors, and repeats to us its love for
Christ, its immortal hope, and its sympathy for all suffering. I also remember the famous fresco of the Convent of Saint Mark at Florence, which groups the
principal saints and doctors around the cross in one
impulse of devotion. How well I there recognized
the painter who shed abundant tears when he took
his brush to portray the features of Christ or of the
Madonna!

As I think, the last and the greatest of these truly
Christian masters was Fra Bartolomeo, the Dominican
disciple of Savonarola. Roman Catholicism cannot
claim the faithful friend of the Florentine Reformer
who was burned as a heretic. His picture of the burial
of Christ by Mary, Saint John, and Mary Magdalene,
which is in the Pitti Museum at Florence, is an act
of adoration; here the brush has lost nothing; it has
all its suavity, all its splendor, all its firmness; but it
is impossible long to contemplate that work without
feeling that blended tenderness and profound respect
for Christ which is expressed with a sort of impetuosity in the prostration of Mary Magdalene, with
angelic sweetness in the glance of Saint John, and an
immeasurable sadness in that of the Madonna. Well,
this profoundly Christian art is not the child of

Rome. Doubtless its works are · numerous there, because the Papacy has contrived to form the most magnificent of museums in the Eternal City; but the inspiration of these mystical paintings came from elsewhere. Raphael, who understood and expressed every thing, may be adduced against us, but his genius unfolded under the soft sky of Umbria. I know well that it was at Rome that he painted the Dispute on the Holy Sacrament; but among the seeking and doubting theologians have I not seen the noble countenance of Savonarola? Can we deny that the breath of the Reform has passed that way? At any rate, it was at Rome that he painted the Fornarina, the Galatea and Psyche, exquisite but not at all Christian works. As to Michael Angelo, none is ignorant how far the leaven of the Reform had fermented in him, as shown by his letters to Vittoria Colonna. When he gave himself up without reserve to the inspiration of the place, he painted at the Sistine Chapel his fresco of the Last Judgment. That, I grant, is quite Roman. I admire its power and fire, especially when I contemplate it under the purple light of evening. But I cannot think it a religious painting. That Christ who resembles an antique Hercules, and who curses the reprobate with such a terrible gesture, is truly the Christ of the Vatican, of the Inquisitors, whose arm is only lifted to crush. All the pagan details that surround the pincipal figure remind us of the court of Julius II. and Leo X. Compare this formidable fresco with the picture of Fra Angelico on the same subject, that is to be seen at the Corsini Palace. Here the drama is purely moral ; the inconsolable sorrow which appears in the features of the impenitent is not the simple reflection of the flash of avenging lightnings; it springs up from within. This is the Gospel. Touching the soil of Rome, Christian painting speedily loses its truly religious character, though it sheds a dazzling splendor with Raphael, whose genius was too great not to escape local influences more than any other artist, though he also underwent them toward the close of his short and brilliant career. Do not forget that one of his pupils was Julius Romanus, whose brush, when no longer restrained and guided by his master's sketches, promptly became voluptuous and sensual. With the Pontificate of Gregory XIII. (1572) the decline begins; mannerists encumber churches, convents, and palaces with their conventional art. The Cavalier d'Arpino, (1569,) whose works swarm at Rome, is the representative of that school, without grandeur or lofty inspiration. The religious character is more and more effaced. Bernino in architecture, and d'Arpino in painting, are truly Roman artists, and such as Catholicism under the yoke of Jesuitism must love.

Church music passes through the same phases as painting and architecture. The plain chant is the echo of that of the Middle Ages; it is grave and sad. Then you have a few truly great masters, who, like Allegri, write in a grand and almost monumental style. The *Miserere* of this composer, which we hear on Holy Thursday and Friday at the Sistine Chapel, without organ accompaniment, produces an imposing effect. But if the Pope's Chapel on its great days be excepted, the music heard here is deplorable in composition. In churches of the second class it is bad at every point; they have not confined themselves to pillaging celebrated operas which are sung with all

the vivacity of theatrical choirs. At Saint John de
Lateran and Saint Peter's the execution is careful. I
have already spoken of the chapel of the former
basilica. As to the second, which is famous at Rome,
and rivals the Sistine, I heard it on a great and
solemn occasion, the 18th of November, the anniversary of the dedication of Saint Peter's. Two choirs
responded to each other with organ accompaniments.
The execution was perfect; the magnificent bass
voices, the sopranos, ever strange and questionable;
though it is claimed that they are no longer permitted
to purchase their voices on the terms at which they
were procured in the last century. But hearing
those *roulades* and *cavatinas* which formed a true
artificial fire of dazzling notes, who would ever have
imagined that they were singing the Penitential
Psalms, and that the sighings and sacred impulses of
our prophets gave occasion to this effeminate vocal-
ization? Theatrical music, when it is truly fine and
passionate, is far superior in seriousness to these bastard
compositions, a vestry *pot-pourri* style of airs brought
together from all the musical works which have had
any popularity. No doubt that where Catholicism has a different inspiration; it has treasures of
Christian music. Mozart's Requiem, the masses of
Beethoven, Weber, and Rossini, reveal a very different inspiration, but this does not please at Rome.
They prefer soft harmonies, which lull the soul and
deliver it, fast asleep, to ecclesiastical authority. It
is not here, but in Germany, that true religious music
is to be heard. Listen to the Passion of Sebastian
Bach and his sublime hymns, and you will no longer
allow yourself to say that the Reformation ignored
high art. Here it is by turns majestic and profound,

rising far above those profane masses which are sung
to strains too light to satisfy human passion. For
myself, I would give all the music of Rome for the
choral of Luther, chanted in a German church by
thousands of manly and vibrant voices. To show,
moreover, that my judgment is not dictated by par-
tiality, allow me to support it by the testimony of an
illustrious Catholic, Victor de Laprade, who has just
published the following lines in the *Correspondant :*
" It seems to me that the license now allowed in
church music exceeds all that the religious sentiment
can tolerate. When I hear military flourishes howl-
ing, grating, and barking beside the altar, I do not
feel sure that I am in this world. Finally, when I
see bands of actors, to give them their true name,
introduced into the choir, mingling with the priests
during the sacrifice, in vain do I hear musical masterpieces ; it is impossible for me to feel more pious
or devotional than at the opera. A Catholic from
conviction, I content myself with sighing before such
symptoms, and remembering that there are fleeting
abuses in the Church ; but were I a freethinker, I
should say to myself, There is the music of a vanishing
religion. For myself, it seems to me that in the Catholic ceremonies of our days, music has broken the
discipline which the Church had wisely imposed. I
can allow none of the bad reasons, useless to enumer-
ate, and not very religious, which have led ecclesiastical zeal into this evil path. It is not by a profusion
of hymns and candles that souls are drawn to the
truth and retained in the faith."

Having spoken of the accessories of worship, let us
now speak of worship itself—the truly Romish worship. I do not assume a sectarian stand-point, as

though the ideal of worship were attained in the bosom
of Protestantism.   I think that, with few exceptions,
that worship has followed its inclination too far; and
that, from the legitimate desire of never lacking spirituality, it has fallen into barrenness, especially in our
Calvinistic Churches.   That severe devotion is the noblest of all when fed by fervent piety—it transports
the mind to a naked and austere summit—and, if the
soul then spreads her wings to rise toward invisible realities, it certainly comes nearer God than in any other
religious form.   Yet adoration does not here occupy
sufficient space; too much is granted to pious speech:
the unutterable sighings of a heart burning with holy
love are too far stifled by logical formulas.   I think
that almost perfect worship once existed in the Church,
after the apostolic epoch which in all points is incomparable: this was at Alexandria in the time of
Clement and Origen.   The liturgic fragments which
have been preserved are admirable; their spirituality is
complete, but adoration pours out its vase of perfumes
at the feet of Jesus like Mary the sister of Lazarus.
The center of the worship is not the altar, which does
not exist, (*aras non habemus*, says Minutius Felix,)
but the eucharistic table, which reminds the Church of
the greatest of the gifts of God, though without forgetting the others.   I hope to set this characteristic of
the worship of the second century in clear light in
the last volume of my history of the Church; I will
not now dwell further upon it.   I am persuaded that
we have much to learn from that great period, and
that, by satisfying legitimate wants which appear on
every hand, and of which Puseyism is a false and exaggerated expression, we shall avoid many dangers,
and shall labor efficiently for the development of

the Church according to the necessities of the times. Catholicism has preserved a few traces, a few recollections of the primitive adoration, and we shall do well in seeking to glean them up from those troubled waters and clear them of their alloy. But we must admit that the alloy is so gross, especially at Rome, that the pearl is completely buried. Let us try to characterize in a few touches that abased worship which is a perpetual contradiction of the Evangelical type.

The first characteristic of it that strikes me is what I shall call its absolute ritualism. I do not blame rites in themselves; I know that they are indispensable, that public adoration should have certain forms regulated beforehand, so that every thing may proceed with order and propriety, and that piety may not be troubled with constant surprises. But Christian rites should be simple, and should not stifle spontaneity; they should be so conceived as to appeal to the living sentiments of the soul, to awaken them, and speak to the heart and the intellect. At Rome rites are so conceived as to take the place of every thing; the prescribed form is not the stimulant or the expression of piety, it is a species of ready mounted machine which performs its functions like the prayer-mills of the Orientals, but not without crushing the moral life in their complicated wheels. The individual completely disappears before the Church; it is she that prays by his lips, that kneels with him at the prescribed moment, who rises up at command; at every moment is heard in the basilica of Saint Peter's, as in a ship, the whistle of the machinist. The sacred language is dead; it is the voice of the past, most commonly unintelligible to

10

him who makes himself its passive and momentary
echo. The Gospel or Epistle is not read, but chanted
in a nasal tone, which does not allow a thought to
reach the mind. The sacred book is cut and slashed
up day by day without the believer's being ever able
to bring his thirsty lip to the leaping fountain. The
spirit is thus always and every-where sacrificed to
the letter; rites understood and practiced as they are
at Rome are truly the petrifaction of worship.

Its second characteristic is, that it is an exhibition
of the Christian mysteries, or, rather, a daily effort to
renew them. In this point it approximates the ancient mysteries of paganism. In those mysteries the
pagans in reality adored nature and her hidden
forces; their effort was to represent to themselves in
a complete manner her constant revolution, and especially that great law which draws life from death, and
in which they sought to find a promise or a hope for
themselves. That was all their consolation. Thus,
in the most celebrated of those mysteries, the Eleu-
sinian, they represented in the carrying off of Pro-
serpine to hell, and her return to the light, that marvelous law of nature which carries a grain of wheat
down into the earth in order to bring forth from it a
brilliant sheaf; it was tracing out to the eyes, and, as
it were, renewing, the permanent history of the natural
divinity which they adored. The God of the Gospel
belongs to a very different domain. He is the God
of the spirit and of liberty. He consummated the
salvation of the world by a free sacrifice offered once
for all, which is not repeated like the periodical
crises of nature. It was necessary for the pagan to
reproduce them before his eyes in all their successive
evolutions, for it was in these very evolutions, or in

the profound acquaintance which he might obtain
with them, that he placed all his hope of salvation,
at least in the mysteries. It is enough for the Christian to grasp with his heart and mind the divine act
to which he owes the redemption of his soul; his worship should be its memorial at the same time that it
should express his profound gratitude. The Eucharist combines these characteristics. It does not play
the drama of the passion; it brings it to mind and
confirms it; it is likewise the spiritual sacrifice which
unites the disciple with his Master. The Romish
worship has very different pretensions. It aims on
the one hand, like the pagan mysteries, to represent
in very truth the history of its God; on the other
hand it plays the passion; not believing that the
sacrifice of the cross was sufficient to cover all sin, it
pretends to continue it by the hand of its priests.
The mass is very decidedly an attempt to represent
the immolation of Calvary. It is at Rome that this
character of Catholic worship appears complete and
unvailed, especially in the ceremonies of Holy Week.
Day by day they unfold the scenes of the passion before the eyes of the faithful. Thus on Holy
Wednesday, while the *Miserere* is chanted, twelve
lighted candles represent the twelve Apostles; these
are extinguished one after another, to show their base
desertion of the Master.. On Holy Thursday the
pretended Vicar of Christ prostrates himself before
twelve poor priests and washes their feet; then he
makes them sit down at a table prepared for them
and serves them. Holy Wednesday is the day of the
burial of the host; it is deposited in Saint Paul's
Chapel as in a sepulcher; all the candles are extinguished, not a bell resounds. It is a complete con-

trast with Palm Sunday, when the Pope, still representing Christ, makes his triumphal entry into the
basilica of Saint Peter's while the sacred branches
shade him and bend before him. The morning of the
third day they go in great pomp to seek the host;
it is brought out of the tabernacle which served as its
sepulcher, and presented to the people as the Divine
Arisen, and the Pope celebrates with the confession
of Saint Peter the grand mass of Easter Day. When
he elevates the holy elements before the assembly
they all bow down. A very beautiful hymn rises
from the depths of the *Confession*, or from the pretended tomb of the Apostles. The people think
themselves before their newly-risen God; then the
Holy Father ascends a balcony of the basilica and
gives the benediction to the city and the world, (*urbi
et orbi.*) Is not Rome, then, truly the Eleusis of Catholicism—the place of the great mysteries where the
history of God is solemnly played? At Jerusalem,
where the pomp is naturally much less imposing,
they have in one point improved the spectacle.

In the Church of the Holy Sepulcher I saw a doll,
the image of Christ nailed to a wooden cross. It
was detached with all reverence from the gibbet, and
they went to bury it till Easter morn. It is well
known that at Christmas mangers are arranged in
most of the churches, and that the mystery of the
nativity is represented as in spring they represent.
the mystery of the crucifixion. You can very well
understand after this that the theater sprang from
the Church in the Middle Ages; we may say that at
Rome it has decidedly remained in it. Nothing is
more striking in this regard than the taking of the
vail. I witnessed this ceremony at Naples when it

was under the rule of the Bourbons, a worthy chapel of ease to Rome. A number of young girls, among them one particularly fair and sad, were conducted by their parents to the altar to pronounce the vows which were forever to separate them from the world. The drama was divided into two acts. In the first gay and brilliant music recalled those worldly pleasures which the young girls were about to renounce. Then a priest pronounced a truly frantic discourse as he pointed them in the Host to the Spouse to whom they should give themselves. He spoke with a specious and passionate realism, which produced the strangest and most painful effect. The final ceremony at length came on, to the sound of mournful music, their locks falling under the shears. Then the vows.

The Church likewise delights in giving extraordinary exhibitions to awaken and pique curiosity. The other day I saw near a little chapel a few steps from Saint John de Lateran, grossly made, but very expressive, figures in wax, which displayed a frightful execution of Catholic missionaries in the Orient. People thronged before the horrible spectacle, and offerings for the work fell thick into the wooden bowls of the collectors. This fair-day measure is not disdained, and is very productive. Strangely enough, in this southern land, where people feel an extraordinary horror for all that hints at death, it has been surrounded with the most dismal circumstances in order the better to act on the imagination. Nothing is more funereal than the long train of a confraternity, with its cowls dropped down, as it accompanies a coffin to the cemetery. The Capuchin friars here present a permanent funeral display. They have be-

thought themselves to arrange in the vaults of their
principal church a whole army of skeletons, recruited
from the dead of their order, who have the privilege
of obtaining an immortality of terror. What strikes
me further in the Romish worship is its mercenary
character. I speak not merely of the money it demands to sustain its sumptuousness, and the Peter
pence exacted in all lands with so much urgency
and skill : I particularly mean to designate that sad
error consisting in purchasing heaven by our works
and merits. Here it displays itself without modesty
or check. As a counterpoise, or rather, as a comple-
ment, it has the indulgence market. Its treasury is
freely opened in the Pontifical City. Every Church
disputes for a share, and assures the benefit of them
to all who submit to given practices : these fallacious
promises are read on its front. Nowhere do men
more ingenuously imagine to expiate relished worldly
pleasures by the weariness of reciting litanies, and
wearing out their knees on the pavements of churches.
The division of the year into profane and festival
days rests on no other principle. The distinction
between Lent and Carnival is most marked at Rome.
There the latter shakes in full security the bells of
gross folly. It, too, is an ecclesiastical institution.
Balls, theaters, joyous and unrestrained feasts, can be
multiplied at pleasure. The antique bacchanal is
mistress of the streets of Rome during this period of
liberty or license on condition of stifling its laughter
at the fixed hour, changing its comic mask for a
mask of mourning, and covering its head with ashes.
The Church, like a kind mother, receives into her
courts the vinous turbulence of yesterday, diets it,
and makes it listen to masses on masses. The mis-

chief is, that the sin was foreseen and accepted as well as the penitence; it is a calendar affair.

A fourth characteristic of Catholic worship, as presented to us here at Rome, is the marvelous or false miracle every-where supplanting true miracles, and banishing them to the shade. Ridiculous legends spring up like weeds in a badly cultivated field; they almost entirely conceal the great evangelical realities. The great Christian supernaturalism is thus compromised by the fantastic supernatural, which seems to be one with it. You know how popular Madonnas that moved their eyes have been. Several notable conversions have been attributed to them. There is no sanctuary which has not its marvelous history, beginning with Nôtre Dame de Lorette, which was transported through the air from Palestine to Italy. At Naples the frightful jugglery of the miraculous liquefaction of the blood of Saint Jannarius goes on every year without any interference from the Pontifical authority, which accepts and patronizes it, even though the process by which the coagulated blood of the saint is made to flow is well known. The Salette Springs, and those of the Grotto de Lourdes, which are said to effect miraculous cures, are patented at Rome, who, not content with her own prodigies, every-where encourages this species of gross magic, which recalls the most shameful times of the decline of Rome, but which is very fruitful. It is easy to comprehend the way in which belief in false miracles springs up. We have only to take the commemorative chapel reared near the Church of Saint Agnes, in memory of the great peril which the Pope escaped some years since in that very spot, where the lower floor of the edifice suddenly sank under him without his experiencing any mischief. Surely nothing is more natural than to feel a lively emotion of gratitude to God in such circumstances, and publicly to express it ; but he was pleased to see in the providential protection which saved his life a miracle of the highest order, a special intervention of the Madonna. He caused a large picture of the whole scene to be painted in vivid colors. In the foreground the Pope is seen, calm and smiling amid the peril ; while those present, and among them certain French generals, display the basest dismay. The epaulettes of our braves are not spared by the artist, who did not fear to depict them trembling in presence of the august serenity of the Holy Father. Saint Agnes appears above him in the air shielding him with a protective hand ; then in the background of the picture the Madonna, surrounded by angels, commands the whole scene. This complaisant interpretation of a very simple fact by the painter, or rather by those who ordered the picture, passes for a fact in the eyes of most spectators. It is understood that Saint Agnes and the Madonna appeared to the Holy Father. This is Gospel truth, and future ages will recount the great prodigy. Thus we witness the formation of the legend.

Let us indicate finally the last characteristic of the Roman worship, which is an unbridled idolatry. It need not be pretended here that the images are not adored, and that the homage paid them is meant for God. They are as positively worshiped as fetiches. This cannot be doubted when we have seen with what ardor the foot of the pretended statue of Saint Peter is kissed in the basilica of the Vatican, which is quite worn by the lips of its thousands of worshipers. The image of the Bambino, (babe,) exhibited by the Capuchins in Christmas festivals, receives veritable worship. Madonnas, covered with sumptuous ornaments, are elevated to the rank of miraculous virgins, and treated as the most celebrated statues of Venus and Juno were in antiquity. As to the relics of the saints, they shoot up in an abundance which cannot but be very disquieting, since more than one villain is the object of profound veneration under the name of some martyr. There is no end to the fables told about these pretendedly sacred remains. If they do not show us, as in the Armenian Convent at Jerusalem, the stones that " would have cried out," or, as at Florence, the relics of the Holy Trinity, which are a new mystery, and the most astonishing of all, added to those of the faith, they furnish you with a bit of all the saints known and unknown ; the gold or diamond setting makes the pretended bone pass. Nothing excites the devout part of the multitude more than this type of piety. But there is another more subtile idolatry, which is daily growing, and which consists in exalting the creature at the expense of the Creator and the Redeemer. I have already dwelt on that frightful apotheosis of the Madonna, which must transform the Trinity into a quaternity. Since the proclamation of the Immaculate Conception it has been assuming an unheard-of development, unlike any thing known in the past. Catholicism has but two ever-present and adored divinities—Mary in heaven, and the Pope on earth. Thus in every solemn ceremony incense is burned before the Pope, his Cardinals, and Canons— before whoever personifies the hierarchy. In presence of the Pope the Romish worship cries out by all its organs, " The voice of a god, and not of a man."

Thus there is growing up from day to day a gross materialism in worship ever in quest of new idols. Saint Joseph is now in great favor ; his medals heal body and soul. To-morrow it will be some other favorite of this gross piety—gross even in its liveliest ardors—which, with its false miracles, its effeminate ditties, and its unlimited credulity, is a continual defiance hurled at the human mind at a moment when the true supernatural has enough to do in defending itself against the assaults of unbelief. We should rather shed bitter tears over such deplorable things than rejoice at them with sectarian satisfaction. Let us not forget that it is athwart this abased form of Christianity that a large part of Europe sees not merely the Christian ideal, but the divine ideal ; and are we astonished after this that she plunges headlong into Atheism ?

Before closing this letter suffer me to speak of a fine and touching ceremony which I have just witnessed. To-day, November 22, was the Feast of Saint Cecilia. In her honor they had likewise illuminated the famous catacombs of Saint Callistus, of which I will send full details in one of my approaching letters, for it is one of the most remarkable discoveries of Christian archeology. Those somber passages, bordered with the tombs of the early Christians, were enlightened with a trembling light, as in ancient days when they assembled on the anniversary of their martyrs to fortify themselves by recalling their holy memory. A considerable multitude inundated the crypt, where a pious commemorative service was celebrated. It was a scene from past ages standing out against the sad and obscure background of present circumstances.   It sufficed also to ascend from that subterranean place to the open air to sadly perceive what invincible paganism is displayed on this old Latin soil, which has, however, drank up the blood of so many glorious martyrs of the religion of the Gospel.

E. DE PRESSENSÉ.

LETTER VII.

Preparations for the Council — Arrangements of the Council Hall —
—Sessions Secret—Name of the Council—Its Memorial Column—The
Entertainment of the Members—Ceremonial of the Assembly—Pre-
cedence of the Members—Labors of the Preparatory Committees—
Publication of the Proceedings—The Proceedings to be in Latin—
Confusion in its Pronunciation—Other Differences—French Bishops
mainly Ultramontanists—Chorus of Priests—The French Liberals:
Bishop Dupanloup, Prince de Broglie, Abbé Noirlieu, and Professor
Tassy—The American Prelates—Devotion of the Irish Bishops to
Rome—Subserviency of the English Bishops—The Belgians—The
Austrian Martyrs—The German Liberals—The Demonstration at
Fulda—The Letters of Janus—Reforms demanded—Döllinger on
Papal Infallibility—Probable Conclusion on this Question.

ROME, *November*, 1869.

It is now time to speak of the preparations for the
Council, since I shall soon have to talk about its opening. Yet the preparatory phase has its own importance ; it also bears a special character belonging
solely to itself. Many opinions which subsequently,
after the conclusion, will think themselves obliged to
blend in the final grand *Te Deum*, and rally to the
decisions of the Council, appear to-day in singular
vivacity, and yield the true measure of that famous
unity which is a mere myth. For I expect likewise
to be shown how convictions may change between
to-day and to-morrow otherwise than through per-
suasion. And the proof that they do not change is,
that when once the grand parade ends, they will rise
up again, and put themselves in quest of elastic inter-
pretations, which they will surely find ; for what
does not the human mind find when its position is

already taken? However, when once the Council shall have spoken, more prudence and circumlocution must be used. This is also the favorable hour to hear the sound of the diverse bells of Catholic Christendom before the great thorough bass of Saint Peter's shall have drowned every thing with its echoing clamor, and filled the air with volleys of formulas and anathemas. I shall strive not to quit the solid ground of attested facts, not to get upon the quicksand of hypotheses, for all wagers are open and all suppositions possible, as to what is soon to take place in the metropolis of Catholicism, and the influences which will finally predominate. I shall begin by speaking of the external preparations, to which great importance is attached in this land of spectacles, where religious masters-of-ceremonies play so great a part. You may confide in the information that I send you; I draw it from a very sure and well-informed source, and in no respect do I change its substance. Only do not forget that this source is Catholic, and consequently that things are presented in their most favorable light.

The material labors on the inclosure of the Council, in the basilica of Saint Peter's, are nearly finished. Admission to this inclosure has just been forbidden to the public. The partition which separates it from the rest of the church only extends to the arch of the transept; it does not exceed two thirds of the height of the pillars. It is very solid, and, moreover, is covered with thick linen. A large door, whose leaves, it is said, will be unclosed during the public sessions, has been opened in its midst. In the background of the inclosure the seats of the Cardinals are seen, arranged in a semicircle, and elevated seven steps above the floor of the Chapel of Saint Processus and Saint Martinien. The throne of the Holy Father forms its center, and is exalted four steps higher. Behind the Pontifical throne is a passage through which the Holy Father will come to the sessions without needing to traverse the inclosure; this issue ends in an invisible corridor, and a secret staircase leading to the Vatican. At the height of thirteen feet above the seats of the Sacred College two desks rise, one on the right and the other on the left, capable of containing a dozen persons each. I am assured that they are intended for stenographers. Above these desks runs a woodwork, which will be decorated with twenty-four medallions, representing the popes who have convoked Councils. These portraits are none other than the cartoons, in mosaic, which adorn the circumference of the Church of Saint Paul without the walls. The Holy Father has likewise ordered two pictures, representing Saint Peter and Saint Paul, which will be suspended in the inclosure. From the seats of the cardinals proceed, in straight files, the seats of the bishops along both sides of the semicircle. They are arranged in six rows. The first is on the level of the ground; the others succeed, ascending in due order like the benches of an amphitheater. You perceive four intervals, cutting perpendicularly the files of the seats and serving to admit the members of the Council to their respective places. These places are overlooked on each side by two superposed desks, intended for the Theologians, which fill up the breadth of the two arcades of the right lateral nave. It is thought that the tribune for orators will rise at a short distance from the Pontifical throne, near the seats of the

Sacred College; the Patriarchs will be placed immediately below the Sacred College.

As to the tribunes of the Christian Princes and
their representatives, or their orators, as they were
called in former Councils, they will be constructed at a
short distance from the Papal throne. The Holy
Father recently said that if the sovereigns or their representatives desired to attend the Council they could,
but that in no case could they set up claims and
insist on rights which do not comport with the times.
Further, no invitation has been addressed by the
Pope to princes or governments.

There is some talk of covering the entire inclosure of
the Council with a glass arch, to keep the voice of the
orators from being lost in the depth of the edifices
whose extreme sonorousness would drown their words
in a multitude of echoes and a prolonged reverberation of sound. They would seek by this means to
render the inclosure of the Council fit for the most
important debates. Until now it had been proposed
to reserve it exclusively for the solemn public sessions,
those where it is not indispensable that the discourses
of the orators should be heard by all the fathers.
The most important debates were to take place in the
hall which surmounts the fore-court of the basilica, and
which serves on Holy Thursday for the ceremony of
the Supper. It seems that this project has been
modified, and that they would, as far as possible, introduce unity of place into the sessions.

Firemen watch constantly over the safety of the
inclosure of the Council, to prevent any misdeed by
the party of action, to whom, rightly or wrongly, is
attributed the criminal intention of burning the
estrades and the seats of the fathers.

In all probability, the public will not be admitted to the circle of the Council; but exceptions will be made for some distinguished persons who will be authorized to be present at its solemn sessions. Yet it is said that, during these, the two leaves of the large door will remain open, and that from the threshold of the inclosure people may enjoy a glimpse of the venerable Areopagus.

The magnificent carpet which will completely cover the floor of the Chapel of Saints Processus and Martinien, itself vaster than many a cathedral, is said to be a gift of the King of Prussia. This monarch, having learned that the Holy Father desired to pay little by little the great sum which the carpet costs, believed it a duty, though a Protestant, to come to his aid in this pinch.

It has been decided that the approaching Council shall bear the name of the "First Œcumenical Council of the Vatican." On the 14th of October the cornerstone of a monument (of which I have already spoken) intended to perpetuate its memory was laid. This monument will rise on Mount Janiculum, at the center of the platform that extends before the Church of Saint Peter in Montorio, built on the spot where the Prince of the Apostles was crucified. Its base will be hexagonal, and on five of its faces will present bas-reliefs, representing the five sections of the earth, indicated by allegorical figures holding standards, on which the labarum floats. The sixth face, adorned with the arms of Pius IX., will bear the dates of the opening and the close of the Council. Such is the pedestal on which will be erected the magnificent column of African marble, discovered in the excavations of the Emporium Romanum. A contemporary inscription indicates that this column was intended for Nero. The ceremony of laying the corner-stone was performed by Cardinal Joseph Berardi, Minister of Public Works and Commerce.

A special committee, composed of prelates who speak foreign languages, is charged with the reception and lodging of the bishops quietly, and as fast as they arrive at Rome. A special arrangement has been made for the reception of the bishops. The authorities of Cività Vecchia, Orta and Ceprano, have orders to telegraph to Monsignore Serafini as soon as one of them presents himself on the frontiers. On the arrival of the train at Rome a committee takes care to have as many carriages at the railway station as there are bishops designated by the telegraph.

More than one hundred and forty bishops have already asked entertainment at the expense of the Pope. New demands of this nature are daily made. Every bishop, provided he expresses the wish, is entitled to the hospitality of the Holy Father for himself, his secretary, and a servant.

The lodgings which have been prepared by order of the Pope for the fathers of the Council are quite numerous, and it would be impossible to give their address in detail. It will suffice to indicate those which are found in the convents of the Dominicans on the Piazza di Minerva; of the Lazarists on the Piazza di Monte-Citoris; of the Oblates of Tor di Specchi at the foot of the Capitolinus; of the Franciscans at Saint Peter's in Montorio; in the Cortoni Palace at the foot of the Aventine; in the Senni Palace at San Celso; in the Chapter-houses of Saint Peter and Saint Mary the Greater. In the large house belonging to the canons of Saint Peter, near Saint Martha's, more than forty bishops will be lodged together. They will have very convenient, and even comfortable, apartments, and a vast hall where they will take their meals in common. They have transported large quantities of chairs, carpets, mattresses, hangings, etc., from Marseilles to furnish all these lodgings.

Prince Alexander Torlonia has put at the disposal of the Pope for the bishops the great and splendid palace built by Raphael opposite the Church of Scossacavalli, which enjoys the advantage of being only a few steps from Saint Peter's. Prince Borghese and Prince Massimo delle Colonne have followed the example of the celebrated banker by opening their palaces to the venerable guests of Rome. A French gentleman living at Rome has assumed the maintenance of a bishop till the Council closes.

The Pope desires that the bishops, as supreme judges in questions of faith, representatives of nations, and interpreters of the Holy Ghost, should be received with the highest honors.

As to the ceremonial of the Council, it is the object of the constant study of a special committee, which holds its sessions now at the house of Cardinal Patrizi, its president, now with Monsignore Ferrari, inspector of apostolical ceremonies. As there is necessarily a lack of traditions about ceremonies that have not been repeated for three hundred years, the committee has had much labor in searching and ransacking old parchments and dusty folios in order to obtain practical rules.

They have striven to define the question of precedence as exactly as possible. It will be generally

regulated, not according to the degree occupied by
the different dioceses of Catholicism in the hierarchy
of the Church universal, but according to the senior-
ity of the precognition of each of the members of the
episcopate in the category to which he belongs. These
categories are five in number—Patriarchs, Primates,
Archbishops, diocesan or effective Bishops, Archbishops, and Bishops *in partibus infidelium.*

Further, and with a view to simplify the question
of etiquette, the Holy Father has decided that all
bishops taking part in the Council shall be named
assistants of the Pontifical throne.

The cardinals, in their quality of counselors of the
sovereign Pontiff, candidates for the chair of Saint
Peter, and members of the supreme senate of the
Church, form the immediate surrounding of the Pope,
and consequently have precedence of all other ecclesiastical dignitaries.

The question of the admission of Abbés, called
Nullius, and of the Generals of Orders, has been settled in the affirmative, agreeably to the traditions of
the Council of Trent.

The Holy Father is about to nominate four Cardinal Legates to represent himself in the sessions of the
venerable Assembly whenever he shall not preside in
person. Two of these Apostolic Legates will be
Cardinal Reisach and Cardinal Bilio, who is supposed
to have been the principal author of the Syllabus.

Monseigneur Fessler, Bishop of Saint Plöten, Secretary General of the Council, is exceedingly active.
He is studying all the innumerable questions that
the preparatory committees, forming separate bodies,
each following its own specialty, have separately
elaborated. Besides the General Secretary, other

secretaries, chosen from the members of the committees of the Council, are soon to be nominated.

Cardinal Reisach, director of the special committee charged to elaborate the matter of the politico-religious questions which are to be debated in the universal Assembly, has fallen sick, and been obliged, according to the prescriptions of his physicians, to travel for his health. He is temporarily replaced by Cardinal Capalti, an old secretary of the Propaganda.

The greatest secrecy rests on these preparatory labors, and, apart from a few questions, we obtain only imperfect information, incomplete news, and vague rumors.

When the preparatory committees are dissolved, there will only remain a certain number of Italian and foreign prelates at the disposal of the Holy Father for the studies which he may see fit to require of them. The preliminary labors are completely finished, and it is said that they are drawing up this very moment the formulas of the decisions and decrees which will be presented to the Council.

It is claimed that the most complete freedom will reign in the debates of the assembly, and that the Pope himself quite recently said to a great personage that he desired the Bishops to have full opportunity to display all their ideas and sentiments, and that the questions which should not be determined on with unanimity, or which should not have at least a striking majority in their favor, should be dismissed *ad acta.* The multitude of questions of every kind requiring solution is so great, that Monsignore Gionnelli, Secretary of the Permanent Congregation of the Council, as well as of the Committee of Cardinals, designated for the revision of all their labors, lately said that it was not even possible for so many subjects to be exhausted in a short time.

It is not yet known what mode of publicity will be adopted by the Council to keep Catholicism informed of what passes in its bosom. Some would have the official "Journal of Rome" publish daily reports of the sessions and the decrees of the assembly, as is done in secular parliaments; others propose that the *Civiltà Cattolica*, becoming the official organ of the Council, should appear more frequently, and give, with a periodical account of the debates, the decisions proclaimed; finally, others think that the secrecy which has presided over the preparatory labors ought also to surround the Council, and that only at its close should an official report of it be published.

A practical question, which does not fail to prove very embarrassing, is that of the reproduction of the debates by stenography. But one language indeed will there be spoken, the sacred tongue, ecclesiastical Latin; but the Tower of Babel will nevertheless assert its rights through the different manner in which the Latin is pronounced. The distance is great from the English to the Italian pronunciation; it needs well-trained ears to recognize the same word on the more or less closed lips of the Anglo-Saxon and in the sonorous articulation of a man from the South. They intend, likewise, to have stenographers of the diverse nations, but these will not enable the honorable orators to understand each other. There will be, then, rather successive monologues than a contradictory debate. This will not greatly displease the Roman managers, who would gladly have the Council content itself with their Latin, laying the accent on certain well-known words, the infallibility of the Pope and the divinity of the Virgin.

Let us now take account of much more important differences than those of Latin pronunciation, and which, awaiting the issue of the Council, freely show themselves. Let us consider, in turn, the various nationalities which will be represented, and inquire what are the dispositions which animate each of them. We shall thus see that there is cause to complete the famous comparison of the seamless coat, which they have tried to make an image of Catholic unity, and add that it is as variegated as Joseph's coat.

Let us begin with our French Bishops, who for some days have been flowing into the Eternal City; for the moment, I will deal only with ideas and not with individuals, to whom I shall subsequently come. It is certain that a majority of these Bishops come with the most ardent Ultramontane dispositions; many of them have expressed these opinions in furious pastoral letters on occasion of the book of Monseigneur Maret against the infallibility of the Holy Father. For some days the journals have been inundated with their prose, that heavy episcopal prose, which contrives to be at once without nerve and without moderation—soft and violent as the impotent anger of old age. Some of them made a very pompous scene before leaving their dioceses; they assembled their clergy to address them in pathetic farewells, as though they were setting off on the most dangerous missions, while these courageous confessors only set out to cast down in their own persons the ancient rights of the episcopate before the Roman idol. The priests who are absolutely dependent on them—for the priesthood is as much abased before the episcopacy as the episcopacy before the Holy See—these priests, who are merely their creatures, pretended to charge them with a solemn mission, by urging them on in their own Ultramontane direction. Further, many of these priests have followed them to Rome; permission has been very freely granted them to remain.

A considerable number of French curates and monks are here, mostly fanatics in Ultramontanism, and impatient to kiss the dust under the feet of the Great Pontiff. They will not sit in the high Assembly, but they will encircle its debates; they will contribute to form an atmosphere of ardent enthusiasm to weigh upon and envelope the Council.

I understand very well then why the bishops leave so many parishes deprived, for the moment, of their regular pastors; in the great spectacle which is preparing, they are to play the part of the chorus in the antique tragedies, which, in the minds of the authors, gave their true signification. A few bishops only are exceptions; the Archbishop of Paris at the head, and the Bishop of Orleans, who has just published a new circular wherein he pronounces with some energy against the timeliness of the new dogma of the Immaculate Conception. The manifesto of the *Correspondant*, the organ of Liberal Catholicism, has been published as a pamphlet since I mentioned it to you; you know that it is from the incisive pen of Prince Albert de Broglie, and that, through much circumlocution and laudation of the Holy Father, its conclusion is that of the Bishop of Orleans. The *Correspondant* has acted like Pius IX., it too has set

up its column commemorative of the Council, and
engraved on it the idea which it hopes to see triumph
in the high Assembly. It can already anticipate
that it will have singularly to abate its triumph, for
its manifesto has been the object of the most violent
attacks; it has been abused by the *Univers* as an
academician, a philosopher—which, for that devout
journal, is the highest abuse—and denounced as a
violent transporter into the religious domain of· that
abominable parliamentary rule which it incessantly
cries up in the political sphere. The *Correspondant*
will be at the Council in the person of Monseigneur
Dupanloup, the Bishop of Orleans, and he will there
reveal the measure of his influence and his courage.
The Church of Paris numbers many enlightened and
learned priests, at once pious and liberal. I will cite
in the first rank the Abbé Martin Noirlieu, curate
of the Church of Saint Louis d'Antin—a venerable
old man, who is an heir of the noble spirit of Port
Royal—who beholds Ultramontane follies with a
grief which he openly expresses, and who ardently
desires the triumph of the Gallican tendency over
Romish novelties. I have often met young priests
full of talent and piety at his residence, who spoke
with indignation of the paths into which Jesuitism
was plunging the Church. Among laymen, I will
mention M. Garcin de Tassy, a member of the Insti-
tute, and Professor of Oriental Languages, who has
never ceased to protest against Ultramontanism with
an energy which age does not enfeeble. These representatives of a profoundly liberal and Christian Gal-
licism will not be in Rome, but their worth is known
there; they are dreaded, and the thought of them
may well prove a weight in the balance, at the de-

cisive hour, in preventing the triumph of the papal party.

From France let us pass to the fathers of the Council who will come hither to represent the great Anglo-Saxon race. Of your American Bishops I can tell you nothing which you do not know better than I. It is claimed that Ultramontanism counts many a convert among them within a few years, but there is one point on which they are more rebellious to Romish influence, namely, the question of the union of the temporal with the spiritual power; because they know by experience the value of the opposite policy to the Church—what dignity, what power she finds in it. Perhaps it will seem hard to them to say, *Truth on that side of the Atlantic, but error on this.*

The Canadian Bishop, who was one of the first to arrive in Rome, is, on the other hand, noted for his enthusiasm for the Pontifical army. He has addressed the Zouaves furnished by his diocese in a discourse quite to the taste of the Roman leaders. The Irish episcopate naturally has at heart all the passions which long oppression produces. It will beware of dwelling on the great act of liberation which England has just accomplished in behalf of Ireland, because that act is, after all, a step toward the separation of Church and State; and because, if they like its favorable consequences for Catholicism at Rome, they blame its principle. They even openly expressed that blame on occasion of the memorable debates in the House of Commons, whence the law of separation proceeded, which will, more than any other measure, immortalize the name of Gladstone. The Irish clergy belongs body and soul to the Papacy; they are counted on as a picked corps which is to be wielded decisively in critical moments. They count no less on the clergy of Great Britain and Archbishop Manning. He has all the zeal and fire of neophytes, precisely because he is a recruit from the Protestant camp. The proselyting activity which Catholicism has exercised in England for the last thirty years has been great, though it has been exaggerated. It has revealed all the inconsistencies of the Episcopal Church, which, by the way in which it exalts the traditional and sacerdotal·element, lays a well-constructed bridge between Westminster and the Church of Rome. Puseyism and Ritualism, which are its most authentic form, are already half Catholic; they will not miss the crown of the edifice, which is the Papacy, and most of the adepts of Pusey do not consent, like their master, to leave the work unfinished. The doctrinal shock, also, which was produced in the Anglican Church by *The Essays and Reviews*, and of which the publications of Bishop Colenso are the gravest symptom, has disgusted many minds with her institutions; especially when it has been so evident that the institutions of Anglicanism would not permit the removal of that peril, and that doctrinal suits brought before the Court of the Queen's Bench would come to no issue, for the reason that questions of religious conviction can never be put on the same footing with questions of procedure stifled under papers and parchments. Hence, while the Low Church, which is scarcely Episcopal, has grown considerably, Catholicism has also made important conquests among timid minds that feel the need of a tangible authority. It is also more or less becoming an affair of fashion and custom, since some of the first families in the aristocracy have allowed themselves to be won by it. But it is a long way from this fact to the belief that England therefore runs the risk of abandoning the Reformation. She will neither deny her genius nor her grandeur; the heart of her people is invincibly Protestant. The episcopal form will probably perish, but only to assure the triumph of a more consistent Protestantism, better founded on its immortal principles and clear of any bond with the State. But let us return to the English Catholic episcopacy. Archbishop Manning has also published his pastoral letter, which is a fervent glorification of the Papacy and the author's pledge to sustain it in all its usurpations, which, in his eyes, are assertions of the most legitimate rights. The English priests who are in Rome will sustain him with all their energy; they will blow up the Ultramontane flame, should it chance to languish. One of the most distinguished members of the clergy of Great Britain, Dr. Newman, will have no voice in the Council. He does not belong to the same tendency. He is a man of great learning, of a distinguished and liberal mind, which does not incline to exaggerations; unhappily he does not openly combat them; he is timid and silent when he should speak. He will not check his brethren who will be able to give themselves up to all the heat of their fanaticism.

Belgium will not make herself heard in discordant words. She is a nursery of Pontifical zouaves, and docile priests, who are spiritual zouaves; habituated to struggle against the Belgian Liberals, they have learned in this conflict to use the weapons of discussion, though their journalists do not forget those poisoned arrows of calumny with which the arsenal of the Jesuits is ever well stored. Their chief is Mon-

signore Deschamps, the Archbishop of Malines, who
was one of the first to proclaim the necessity of for-
mulating the dogma of the infallibility of the Holy
Father—this act secured him a brief of approval.
This prelate has good eyes to discover in history what
science has never been able to detect there, to wit,
the regular play of the Pontifical absolutism from
apostolical times. He will certainly be one of the
chiefs of the right wing of the Council, and one of its
champions should there be any serious discussion.

If we come to Germany, the spectacle is quite different, at least as we approach the North. The Austrian episcopate signed the Concordat which was so
dearly paid for at Sadowa, and which conducted the
country quite gently to an incurable senility. The
prelates who put their hands to that odious treaty,
through which they hoped to tyrannize quite at ease
over the public mind, and who sustained with imprudent zeal the indignant protestations of the Romish
Court against civil marriage and lay education, also
form a part of the picked battalion of the Gesu.
Several of these are looked on as martyrs, because
they have incurred some slight penalties for having
resisted the most righteous laws of their country.
But they are merely the martyrs of their folly, and it
will be hard for them, despite the desires they may
have, to produce in the Council of the Vatican the
effect which those old confessors produced who, at
Nice, bore the scars of the Diocletian persecution.
In Bavaria, Prussia, and the other countries of Germany, Catholicism bears a very different character.
It has not breathed with impunity the air of scientific
freedom which breathes over the German Univer-
sities; it has become learned in its turn, and has

enriched science with remarkable works. The illustrious Möhler, author of the best Catholic work on Symbolics, had visibly undergone the influence of Schleiermacher. Daily contact with German science cannot fail to place transrhenish Catholicism in quite a special situation, so long as it does not deny its nationality and remains faithful to the genius of its race. No doubt Ultramontanism also has adherents in Germany; they have even held a very spirited meeting in which priests and laymen echoed the theories of the Encyclical; but the most eminent members of the German clergy were absent from that rather noisy than intelligent gathering whose importance finally was small. The manifestations of Liberal Catholicism have been far more notable. I pass rapidly over those already known to every body. I name, for the sake of memory and completeness in this important matter, the manifesto of the German Catholics of Rhenish Prussia, published in the month of July, in which they very distinctly protested against Romish tendencies, against the union of the two powers, and quite particularly against that Congregation of the *Index*, which pretends to regulate the reading of all the faithful, and consequently to trace out the limits of contemporary science. This manifesto has been completed by a very solid book which demonstrates historically how much the actual pretensions of the Papacy lack foundation, and how questionable are the proofs it invokes. *The Letters of Janus* are more than a party programme; they are a complete treatise of compact and irresistible argumentation which it will be easier to condemn than to refute. A far bolder work has just appeared in Germany; this emanates from the most advanced wing of the same party. It is not a simple protest, but a very precise demand of the reforms desirable in the Church, and which the Council ought to proclaim in order to serve her true interests. The bare title of this work reveals its scope; it runs thus: *Reform of the Romish Church in its Head and in its Members—The Task of the Approaching Council.* The first reform required is the decentralization of the Churches by the weakening of the bond which binds them to the Papacy, so that each may have, as in the past, its own physiognomy. Secondly, they should abolish the exaggerated matrimonial impediments which introduce the Pontifical power to so many family firesides. Those perpetual vows which are rash engagements should be abolished. Let the national tongue of every people replace a dead language in the celebration of worship. Give laymen a share in the administration of the Church. Let clerical education be completely renewed; and finally, let the Church abandon forever all the theocratic elements contained in her present rule. Such are the desires expressed in this work, which speaks with all skillful precautions and all the reserve of ecclesiastical language. This certainly is a sign of the times.

Another equal sign is a pamphlet against the Infallibility of the Pope, which has just appeared at Ratisbon. It bears the name of no author, but all its readers name an illustrious theologian of Munich, the learned Döllinger, who really was the inspirer of the German Catholic manifesto of Bonn and of the *Letters of Janus.* Contemporary Catholicism has no more distinguished master. His history of the preparation for Christianity in the bosom of Paganism is a vast monument of solid learning, entirely faithful to the rigorous methods of contemporary criticism. His book on the temporal Papacy is a masterpiece of impartiality; he proves in the most peremptory way that it is not of divine origin, that it is the product of a purely human history, and that nothing is more senseless than to make the destinies of Christianity depend on that. He has also written a book to refute the famous work of Bunsen on Callistus and Saint Hippolytus, a book which maintains him in Catholic tradition, and prevents his being ranked with schismatics when he interferes with the inward debates of the Church, as he is now doing with so much learning, with an influence so legitimately acquired, and with a manly and precise style which avoids the endless windings of German periods. This time he desired to write in a language more generally known than his own, and he has chosen the French. I must give you a rapid analysis of this remarkable work, which will be a capital document in the important cause to be pleaded in Rome, a cause which would surely be carried in the interest of Döllinger were not the judges prejudiced, and did they weigh votes instead of counting them. You will remark that all the arguments presented against Infallibility bear with equal force against the Immaculate Conception.

The pamphlet begins thus: "In past ages the Church has always rejected novelties by dwelling particularly on the antiquity and immutability of her dogmas. When we can prove of any dogma that it was unknown for some centuries, that it did not arise till some definite epoch, or that it was not professed by the entire Church, and that it is not contained potentially, as logicians say, as a logical, inevitable,

necessary consequence in other dogmas, then that doctrine is adjudged from the Catholic stand-point; it
bears the brand of illegitimacy on its brow; it should
not and cannot be elevated to the dignity of an article of faith. Now all these features are combined in
the notion of the Papal Infallibility." Such is the
theme to be argued. The learned author asks them to
produce some text from one of the Fathers that concludes in favor of that Infallibility; he easily shows
that those which the Jesuit theologians oppose to him
are audacious falsifications of citations detached from
their context, and that partisan spirit has done them
violence. He says that "the history of the Catholic
Church during its first thousand years must of necessity be an insoluble enigma for all the partisans of
Papal Infallibility. They are not the least in the
world able to explain the long duration, the profound
and internal complication, and, in a word, the entire
series of the great contests on revealed dogmas." In
fact, how can we conceive of so many debates, so
many folios, and such care to understand each other
well on doctrine, if they already possessed an infallible oracle who had only to open his mouth that all
difficulties might vanish? Heavenly light illuminate
all the problems of Christian metaphysics and practice! Whence comes it, then, that in all great dog-
matic contests they have hastened to convoke a
Council and appeal to the Church in its totality?
Why did Pope Leo trample under foot his own rights
by declaring it necessary to convoke an Œcumenical
Council, and how strange the scruple which seized
on Pope Siricus that he should excuse himself for not
being able without such a Council to give a decision
on a disputed doctrinal question? Cardinal Orsi

was truly right, from the stand-point of the partisans of infallibility, in complaining of " the useless *fracas* made by the convocation of Councils," and casting the blame of it on the emperors.

Approaching the question of principle, the learned author then shows that it is to the Church as a whole, and to her alone, as well in her usual condition as in her representation by a Council, that infallibility, that is, divine protection and light, is promised. In proof, he invokes the first Council, that of Jerusalem, where nothing was decided by an authoritive decision of Saint Peter, but where the discussion was entirely free, and James the Lord's brother exercised a preponderating influence. The vote took place *in the name of all.* The first great Councils dispensed entirely with Papal confirmations, witness that of Nice and the second Œcumenical Council of Constantinople, whose decisions had the force of law without any mention being made of the Holy Father. The texts of the Gospels on which the partisans of infallibility rest are here interpreted with a very loyal exegesis. It is well known that they cite mainly the prayer of Christ for Peter, (Luke xii, 32,) *that his faith fail not,* joined with the exhortation which the Lord adds to it, that, *after his own conversion,* he should strengthen his brethren. But this interpretation will not bear serious examination. Particularly is it in flagrant contradiction with the constant tradition of the Church for the first seven centuries, since none of the Fathers of the Church understood the passage in that sense. All who expounded it, like Cyprian, Hilary, John Chrysostom, recognized that the only question was of the individual virtue of his faith, and not of an inability to err in doctrinal decisions. It was Pope Agatho who first essayed in the year 680 to deduce from this passage the proof of a prerogative granted to the Roman See, but he excused himself by declaring *that great ignorance in theological matters then reigned at Rome.* Have the Bishops who maintain the opinion of Agatho forgotten the oath which they take in their ordination, agreeably to the so-called Confession of Pius IV. and an explicit canon of the Council of Trent, (Session IV,) by which the Catholic Christian is referred to the consent of the Fathers of the Church, and therefore of the first six centuries, in the interpretation of the Holy Scriptures? Hence they commit a species of perjury by seeking to introduce a comment which is in flagrant contradiction with all primitive Christianity. Finally, historical facts cast decisive light on this question. If it were true that the privilege of doctrinal infallibility had been granted by Jesus Christ to the Papacy in the person of Saint Peter, it would be necessary to show that for eighteen hundred years never had a Pope erred in doctrine. The contrary is far too palpable. This assertion would not be true even in regard to Saint Peter, since at Antioch, far from strengthening his brethren, he rather led their faith astray by his hypocrisy, as Saint Paul was obliged to tell him. If Zosimus approved a profession of faith which denied original sin, if Liberius subscribed an Arian formula, if Honorius, by giving his approbation to an erroneous formula, aided the spread of the heresy of the Monothelites, as an Œcumenical Council judged—and how many similar facts might not be added—nobody will be able to recognize in these diverse errors the fulfilling of the command to "strengthen the brethren in the faith." Here, indeed, is a club-stroke, from which the doctrine of infallibility will find it hard to recover. The author justly calls our attention to the fact, that if they would found it on the application of the words of Jesus Christ to the person of Saint Peter and his successors, there is no good reason for limiting it to the *public* declarations of the Holy Father; he is himself the pure and leaping spring of doctrinal truth, and that spring flows whenever he opens his mouth. Returning to the testimony of the Fathers, the author shows in peremptory style that when Saint Cyprian, with the whole African Church, refused to submit to the decisions of the Bishop of Rome on the question of baptism administered by heretics, he thereby showed what he thought of the infallibility of the Papacy. Saint Augustine, though differing from him on the value of baptism conferred by heretics, fully justified his ecclesiastical stand-point, for he declared that he was not bound to adopt the view of Pope Stephen. If it be pretended that the Popes can be judged by nobody, what shall we do with the Œcumenical Councils of Basle and Constance, which very clearly proclaimed the contrary doctrine, and affirmed the superiority of the General Council to any Pope. Further, Pope Martin declared in an express bull that they who reject the decisions of the Council of Constance are guilty of heresy.

The author next approaches a series of considerations whose importance in the present circumstances of society will escape none. If the Papacy has always been infallible, then we must accept as true, and seek to exalt as salutary, all its political and social declarations. There is no principle which the popes have more loudly proclaimed than the duty of the prince to use his sword in the violent suppression of heresy. Once proclaim the dogma of Papal infallibility and it will follow that this doctrine must pass for a divine truth, according to which Catholic states will be bound in conscience not to allow the profession of any other religion than Catholicism. More than fifty popes have called the Inquisition the Holy Office, and popes have lauded it on occasion of the canonization of certain Inquisitors. For centuries they have also sanctioned the rule that all who obstinately depart from a single article of the faith should be punished with capital punishment. If they proclaim the infallibility of the Papacy, it will be forbidden any Catholic to say or think that the institution of the Inquisition was a grave error. It would be necessary to pronounce an absolute divorce from modern society and plead against the verdict of conscience. The doctrine of Gregory VII. on the right of the Papacy to depose sovereigns at will, must be made an article of faith.

The gravity of the silence observed by the Council of Trent in this matter cannot be overlooked. It is certain that the question was there discussed and contested. By not pronouncing, they showed clearly that it was considered indifferent to the faith. The opinion of infallibility has been able to gain ground only through constraint and violence. In Italy, Spain, and Portugal, the Inquisition stifled all other instruction. Similar violence occurred in the great corporations of the Church, in the Religious Orders. In this regard, the Jesuits have wielded the most despotic pressure, and have caused all works to be put in the Index which submitted that opinion to a scientific examination. Now where freedom to instruct has been refused there can be no talk of the agreement of the Church, (*Concensus Ecclesiæ;*) the word consent excluding in advance all ideas of constraint. Compare the theologians who have combated Papal infallibility with its furious advocates. On the one hand we have Bossuet, the learned Benedictines of Saint Maur, all the German Catholic theologians of any worth; on the other may be arranged Torquemada, Cajetan, Baronius, Bellarmine, Orsi, all the Cardinals; then the Generals of Orders resident in Rome, and above all, *the entire Gesu.* The theologians of the Roman court have not feared to make use of controverted documents and forgeries to stay up their position. They have incessantly invoked the Decretals of Isidore, a scandalous historical fraud, and forged texts of the Greek Fathers. They do not trouble themselves with the historical discoveries which brought those audacious falsifications fully to light; they use them like the words of the Gospel. In the last works published by this school we find all this apocryphal rubbish—witness the books of Neutra Roskowani; of the Jesuit Weninger, who has written especially for the Catholic clergy of the United States, who has the face to feign a history of the Council of Nice to produce the belief that the authority of the Pope was regarded as superior to that of the Council. The same reproach may be addressed to the treatise of Bouix on the Pope and to the little work of Archbishop Deschamps of Malines.

Let us cite the conclusion of this pamphlet, whose importance is plain to all.

" In the supposed case [namely, of the adoption of the infallibility dogma] an unequaled grip upon us would be given, and a vast advantage to separatist

Churches, as well the Greco-Russian and Oriental as the Protestant. There is every appearance that the whole controversy, as hitherto conducted against the Catholic Church and doctrine, will be concentrated more and more on this sole doctrine, which would then have become in fact the test of a standing or falling Church, in which contest her adversaries would find the most efficacious arms, the most conclusive arguments in the very bosom of the Catholic Church herself, in the writings of her greatest and most celebrated theologians, and in the controversialists by whom they were formerly overwhelmed. What reply will the defenders of the Church have to make when told that, for more than eighteen hundred years, this doctrine was first unknown, and then rejected and refuted by a considerable part of the Church, and that precisely the most learned part; that the most respectable scientific corporations of the Church, like the University of Paris, have taught the contrary doctrine through four entire centuries? What will they have to answer, finally, when their adversaries shall refer them to the writings of Bossuet, Fleury, Noel Alexandre, and so many others of equal or nearly equal weight? It would be needful in that case to gradually give quite another form to the doctrine concerning the Church, and particularly to change entirely our instruction in regard to *the conditions and distinctive characters of a Church dogma or article of faith.*

The enterprise of proclaiming the hypothesis of the Papal infallibility as a dogma of the Church would, among other consequences, have that of enfeebling the authority of the Church in an incalculable degree. For nothing can be more harmful to the authority of the Church in the eyes of the faithful, as well as in those of strangers, than the sight of a doctrine forming henceforth a part of the teaching of the Church, and proved by means, or at least by the aid of, designedly-invented, long-continued, and sustained fictions. Now it is clear and indisputable that such is the case with the doctrine of Papal infallibility. The fictions by whose aid the way has been prepared for this opinion, recommended and introduced at last into scholastic theology and into the canon law, begin in the sixth and were continued down to the thirteenth century; and Thomas Aquinas himself, whose authority has had so decisive an influence in propagating and strengthening the opinion of the infallibility of the teachings and the decrees which emanate from the See of Rome, was deceived by testimonies invented willfully, and attributed to the Greek Church."

I have aimed to make you acquainted with this courageous plea of a truly self-consistent liberal Catholicism, which closes without that promise of cringing and absolute submission which is the binding conclusion of the most independent episcopal circulars. At Rome, doubtless, they will disdainfully pass over these worthy pages and peremptory arguments; according to the stinging saying of Pascal, they will bring on monks in place of reasons, in order to finish up every thing by a majority vote. Instead of monks, they have all those fine bishops of the East whose long white beards are as venerable as their minds are ignorant; they have a good number of *bishops in partibus* who will be in the Council what chamberlains are in our assemblies; they will have the entire Italian clergy, who, with rare exceptions, are furious at the sale of their estates; they will have, besides, all the throng of the Roman Monsignori.   Yet it is possible that they may not dare to formulate the dogma of the infallibility of the Pope, and that they may avoid extremes by an equivocation sufficiently neutralized by the recent proclamation of the doctrine of the immaculate conception.   But in my next letter I will resume the chapter of hypotheses in speaking of the future heroes of the Council—those who will be its orchestral leaders.

E. DE PRESSENSÉ.

LETTER VIII.

Leading Actors in the Council — The Absentees — The Pope — Antonelli — Bishop Tosti — Archbishop Manning — Bishop Hoefele — Bishop Hanneberger — Cardinals Donnet and Bonnechose — Bishop Plantier — The Bishop of La Rochelle — Bishop Dupanloup — Archbishop Darboy — Louis Veuillot, the Lay Delegate — Anticipations in Liberal Circles.

Rome, *November,* 1869.

AFTER conversing with you on the diverse tendencies which will encounter each other in the Council and surely clash if there be serious debate, I must now draw your attention to the persons who will figure there in the front rank. We know the subject of the action or drama; let us now try to obtain an idea of the actors who will play its principal parts.

There are several of these whom the eye will seek in vain, and who will shine there by their absence: these are the chiefs of countries formerly submissive entirely to Catholicism, and who by their embassadors held a place of honor. People remember that at the Council of Trent the Legates of Rome constantly turned an uneasy eye toward the seat whence the Spanish embassador often set up claims full of pride, and toward that where the French embassador expressed with much grace, but firmly, the opposition and the reserves of his court. The importance of the intervention of the Catholic Princes in the High Assembly depended on the ancient order of things, which closely associated politics and religion. The Popes claimed that decrees of the Council

approved by them should obtain the force of law in
all countries, and that the civil authorities should sustain them with all their resources. That class, then,
could not be uninterested in the resolutions taken in
the name of the Church, and they had to see that
these in no way compromised them. This necessity
of an understanding with the great powers was a
check on ecclesiastical eccentricities; yet it was not
always sufficient, since the Kings of France saw in
the disciplinary measures fixed on by the Council of
Trent a dangerous encroachment on the rights of the
crown, and forbade their publication in the kingdom.
All this is changed to-day; the separation of the
Church and civil society is every-where begun; there
is no State in Europe which follows in the wake of
the Papacy for its interior organization, and which
appears disposed to give the force of law to its decisions. Consequently none is directly interested in
them; the Council will have all the more freedom because it has less power. Further, some of these powers
have to look so carefully to their moral credit with
the people that they dread accepting the least share
in the exaggerations of the Papacy. The presence
of their embassadors would, from this stand-point,
present grave inconveniences for them, since, unable
to prevent any thing, they would seem to approve
every thing. Let us not talk of princes called schis-
matic; the Emperor of Russia, justly rated at Rome
for his persecutions of the Polish Catholics—in which,
note as we pass on, he has merely applied the principles of Rome to Rome—can only look with disdain
on a Council where the Pope will try to gain a religious absolutism which belongs solely to himself as
the Czar of Holy Russia and the personification of

the Orthodox religion. He knows how recalcitrant bishops are made to walk, and how the human conscience bows under the heel of his boot. The King of Prussia and the Queen of England can see nothing more in the Council than the Emperor of Russia; they are both quite decided to respect the liberty of their Catholic subjects; that is the proper way to avenge the abuse addressed to the religion which they profess.

The Emperor of Austria, since his rupture with the Concordat which delivered his equally vast and diverse States to the Papal yoke, has had only to strengthen his independence toward the Church. He knows very well that his embassadors at Rome would only receive sharp remonstrances on all reforms which have turned on the emancipation of lay society. Like his English sister, he depends on a Parliament that obeys no countersign, particularly none that comes from beyond the mountains. The parliamentary governments would indeed be forced to submit any resolutions in which they might take the least share to the deliberations of the representatives of the nation. Not for a moment could that be allowed. As to the King of Italy, he is plumply excommunicated for having taken possession of the estates of the Church. In his late illness, this excommunication did not keep him from finding, like Cavour, a priest to give him the sacraments when he thought himself at the point of death. It is asserted at Rome that this priest was charged by his bishop to first require a promise to restore to the Papacy all fraudulently acquired estates—that the King gave incontestable signs of penitence—that, consequently, much is to be hoped from this provi-

dential illness. They also affect to rejoice greatly on
his recovery, as though he were going to repair many
iniquities. Those who write these idle tales and
seem to believe them, forget an Italian proverb that
says, *Passato il dangiere, gabbato il santo*—Danger
over, the saint is set aside. In the day of peril he
is invoked with the most fervent devotion ; he is
promised all kinds of offerings : but on the morrow
they are eager to forget these fine resolutions, and
the poor saint may drop asleep again in the dust of
abandonment. Suppose Victor Emmanuel had promised all imaginable reparations to the Papacy, we
may be assured that as soon as he could whistle a
hunting air he would no longer remember the night-
mares of his fever. But he promised nothing, because
he could not promise any thing; for he well knows
that he has to deal with a parliament that will not
jest on these subjects. He now has difficulty enough
in calming its impatient ardor to take possession of all
that remains of the Papal States ; he will not risk his
crown in going backward and undoing the kingdom
of Italy. He would be perfectly sure, should he
make the attempt, to join at the Eternal City
the alienated majesties, and meditate quite at his
ease on his past plunderings. I do not think him
of that humor. The *monsignori* will be cheated
in their felicitations in respect to his recovery,
which will not lead to the restoration of an inch
of territory.

Italian royalty has even taken its precautions with
regard to the Council; it declares beforehand in a
ministerial circular that, while granting full leave to
the bishops under its jurisdiction to go there, it
protests in advance against decisions of the High

Assembly which may be in conflict with the constitution and laws of the kingdom.

It is well known that the Emperor of the French is still the Eldest Son of the Church, yet he will beware of sitting in the Council. He will no more occupy a place there than at Saint John de Lateran, where he is an Honorary Canon. Yet this question was debated seriously in the cabinet. They even talked at one time of sending as Extraordinary Embassador to the Council, M. Baroche, the old Minister of Public Worship. But this was renounced for the reasons indicated; it is known that at Rome French influence would not weigh a straw on the resolutions of the Assembly; that they would distrust whatever came from that quarter; and that the Extraordinary Embassador would have the pleasure of receiving constant checks. It is in itself disagreeable enough to be obliged to mount guard around the Council, and be charged to protect, with French bayonets, deliberations whose clearest result may well be the condemnation of all the fundamental principles of our social system. France will remain then, arms in hand, at the door of a Council whose threshold she will not cross; she will be the sentinel of the Holy Father, with his Swiss in their yellow array. Admirable role, of which she would do wrong to complain! Is there any better suited to mortify pride and lead to the practice of humility? To be sentry and beadle of the Vatican in this great solemnity—that must content her ambition. Let her smite her breast for all her past imprudence, and chiefly for that disorderly love of liberty which formerly made her to-day, like proud Clovis, burn what she adores.

I vainly inquire what other sovereigns might well

figure in the great spectacle soon to be given. The
poor Queen of Spain could only bring hither the
Golden Rose which the Holy Father granted her the
last year of her sad reign, as a homage, if not to her
virtues, at least to the energy of her Catholic faith,
which made her send Bible readers to prison. The
Spanish Provisional Government is quite devoted to
the search for that rare bird called a good king, who
can be made whatever they please. They know, besides, that the revolution in which they took the lead
is abhorred and cursed at Rome; they have such
great fears of compromising themselves with the
Papacy that they did not even wish to lend the
palace of the embassy to the Archbishop of Valla-
dolid for his reception as a Cardinal, and that
ceremony was pitiful; before ten o'clock the argand
lamps were extinguished. There is, indeed, a royalty
of the old order present at Rome; unhappily it is a
royalty without a realm. The poor little King of
Naples, Francis II., will not leave his Farnese Palace,
where he is expecting an heir, alas! without an in-
heritance, even though he should cause him to have
all the provinces of the former kingdom of Naples for
his godfather. He can only offer the Holy Father
the purity of his absolutist and Catholic orthodoxy;
but that does not suffice to establish the ancient rule;
he is only the shade of a dead and buried past, save
in Rome, where he exists in a mummified state.

As to your Great Republic, nobody thinks of
her on this occasion, and nothing does her more
honor than the universally recognized incompatibility between her and any blending of religion and
politics.

Having spoken of those who will not be in the

Council, let us speak of those who will be present. *A Jove principium*. Let us begin with the god of the Catholic Olympus, the venerable and dangerous Pius IX.; one of those men destined sincerely to lead the convoy of ancient institutions, and whom we may call the Louis XVI. of the Papacy, except the tragic end which, thanks to God! is not to be dreaded. Like the august and unfortunate victim of the French Revolution, he bears the crushing weight of an entire past of which he is innocent, but whose responsibility he finally accepts with blind enthusiasm. He also began with projects of reform and smiles on liberty, to end with the most unbridled reaction. As to the purity of his life and the sincerity of his faith, calumny herself has never raised a suspicion against them. Let us seek, as far as the profane may, to penetrate this complex nature, which, through its medley of good qualities and defects, will have exercised a great influence on the fortunes of religion in the nineteenth century.

Pius IX. is two years older than people commonly think. He himself told our embassador in these charming terms: "They are always taking something from the poor Pope. They have even taken two years from me in consequence of the confusion into which the events of the close of the last century had thrown registers of birth in the Pontifical States." This rectification makes the Pope nearly eighty years old. He belongs, moreover, to a family in which longevity is traditional. His father died at the age of eighty-eight years, not through senile weakness, but in consequence of an accident. This very year the Pope celebrated the jubilee of his ordination. Now, before being a priest he was a

soldier. Very young, he entered the noble guards.
Thus with the sword he served that temporal power
of the Papacy which he was afterward to defend in
his Pontifical quality with so much energy and obstinacy. Few details are known about the obscure
years of his priesthood. He owed to his nobility—
for he belongs to the great family of the Mastai—as
much as to his ecclesiastical qualities, which however were real, his elevation to episcopal dignity,
and then to the Cardinalship. He became noted for
his piety and gentleness. His diocese was as well
administered as is possible in this country ; that sufficed to give him a great reputation as a popular
bishop. His election on the death of Gregory XVI.
in 1846, was effected with astonishing rapidity, and
without the usual intrigues. One of the first acts of
his reign was the proclamation of an amnesty, which
filled not only Rome, but all Italy with enthusiasm.
To comprehend the almost delirious character which
that enthusiasm assumed, we must go back to the
political and moral circumstances of Italy. The moment had come when the movement for emancipation had gained a development which nothing could
arrest. Proud and shivering, all Italy was rising up
against those who had insolently told her that she
had no right to exist as a nation, and that she was
only a convenient geographical circumscription. On
the other hand, some of her most illustrious patriots
dreamed of a close alliance between the Papacy and
national independence, forgetting the part of the
Holy See in the past, and the maledictions of Dante,
who truly was the inspired voice of Italian patriotism,
irritated at being always wrecked on the œcumenical
sovereignty, which could not espouse that cause with-

out diminishing itself. These generous theorists of the future mentally recast the Pontificate in their own image, and intrusted to her the care of representing and defending, by a purely moral authority, enfranchised and regenerate Italy. Abbé Geoberti, in his famous book on the "Primate," had developed these ideas with great eloquence. In that work people found a medley of elevated philosophy and liberal demands which secured it considerable credit. Under this impulse all eyes turned toward Rome on the death of the old Pope, from whom they could only expect new editions of his Encyclical against liberty of conscience. It is easy to comprehend what raptures seized this ardent and changeful people, which feels things as much with its imagination as with its heart, when it saw proceeding from the urns of the Conclave a sympathetic name compromised by no reactionary measure. These favorable dispositions became a true intoxication on the proclamation of an amnesty, which was, however, less general and liberal than might be supposed. People applauded in it all that it seemed to promise; they hailed the future in the present, and the name of Pius IX. flew from lip to lip as the symbol of a risen country, as the pledge of all progress and deliverance. Popular enthusiasm no longer saw things as they were, but as it desired them. Though wide awake, Italy dreamed of the accomplishment, of her aspirations, and she thanked the new Pope for her dream as if it were already realized. Instead of contenting herself with a recognition of the very modest reforms already granted, she drew from them all that she could desire with an ingenuous faith which was to be cruelly deceived. This enthusiasm itself reacted on

13

the ardent soul of Pius IX. He tasted all the sweets of popularity, and gave new pledges in the organization of a State Council, wherein all the cities of his States were to be represented by laymen, and in the organization of a national guard. Yet those who were thoroughly acquainted with the Holy Father knew how precarious were these reforms, since they did not repose on firmly fixed principles of conduct, but on essentially changing impressions. He suffered himself to be guided by the inspirations of his heart without subjecting them to reflection, and he was quite disposed to take these inspirations for direct communications from the Holy Spirit.

I was told at Rome that before deciding on some simple police measure, the Pope kept his eyes long fixed on a crucifix, then he determined it suddenly as though he had received advice from Heaven, though it was a minute administrative detail. " Thus," said the eminent and sprightly man from whom I have this anecdote, " does Pius IX. bring the heights of heaven into the dens of politics." I surely understand that the disciple of Jesus Christ may do all in his name, according to the apostolical precept ; but he ought to consult his Master with his conscience and reason, and strive to grasp the spirit of his precepts or example. Nothing is more dangerous than wishing in all things to proceed by inspiration, for men then excuse themselves from reflection, and give way to every caprice of the imagination, and to all the fluctuations of the sensibilities. To-day the wind blows from the north, to-morrow it will come from the south, and men allow themselves to be turned about at its will.

The north wind soon replaced the south wind with

the Holy Father. In treating the Roman question I have already related the grave incidents which induced this sudden change, without at all palliating the faults and crimes of a violent demagogy which did not recoil before the murder of the Pope's chief magistrate, the illustrious Rossi. Yet it would be unjust to impute this crime to the entire party, since it was the deed of an isolated fanaticism. But even before the revolutionary movement had displaced progress in regular ways, when all Italy was echoing from end to end with the cry, *Viva Pio Nono*, the Holy Father was beginning to turn from his liberal policy. On this very curious phase of his reign we have a document of prime importance, which permits us to follow from day to day the crisis of his mind, if I may so speak. This is the correspondence of Massimo d'Azeglio, who played a considerable part in the Italian renovation, and whose honesty is universally recognized. It was he who nobly said as he assumed the direction of the Piedmontese ministry in an hour of great danger, " I am not in power, but in duty." He has left the purest and most respectable reputation. He was, moreover, a Catholic in conviction, of liberal and sincere piety. The King, Charles Albert, had sent him in 1848 as Extraordinary Embassador to the Holy Father, in order to induce him to give the cause of national independence the support of his popularity and moral authority. In another letter I have explained why the common Father of the faithful had not thought it possible to take part in this conflict, though really, by withdrawing his troops from the Italian army, he espoused the Austrian cause ; this he openly did shortly after. What is especially interesting in the letters of Massimo

d'Azeglio—charming letters, written in French, in
simple, living, and picturesque language—is a species
of psychological study of Pius IX. made as events
progressed. These letters always speak of him with
the greatest respect, without any slanderous spirit, but
they lay bare all the secret springs which act in the
Pontifical Court on the will of the chief of Catholicism ; they make us follow in all their windings the
hardly edifying channels through which the so-called
celestial inspirations pass before being transformed
into *motu proprio.* Nowhere have I seen presented
with more truth that terrible Roman machinery
which works only in a miserable sacristy interest.
It was of this that Massimo d'Azeglio said with energy, " At Rome they fabricate an artificial conscience, which they substitute for the human conscience." A profound saying, which perfectly explains the overthrow of morality in behalf of religious
despotism. Good is whatever profits the hierarchy ;
evil is whatever compromises it. Deeds are arranged
in these two categories, and tried by this test. Massimo d'Azeglio disengages with Italian neatness, and
judges with his probity as an honest man and a convinced patriot, the Jesuit intrigue, whose nets gradually entangle the soul of Pius IX., and lead him back
to the true traditions of the Papacy. One day he
believes he has shaken him, and led him back to the
Italian cause. He is charmed with his goodness,
gentleness, his mind so free from pride. A few
hours later he returns ; every thing is changed.
Some Jesuit has been able to trouble the soul of the
Pope, to awaken its scruples, and the sacred weather-
cock has turned anew. I recommend the perusal of
this correspondence to all who wish to acquire a pro-

found knowledge of the Roman Court and of the character of Pius IX. We see that the author sought as long as possible to lull himself in illusions. His piety made it his duty to abandon hope only at the last extremity. We see his inward struggles in these various phases, until at length, all vails being rent, and the true condition of things appearing in full light, he breaks out in words of indignation, and he too shakes the dust off his feet in turn, not against Catholic institutions, in which he did not cease to believe, but against the Roman Court and its detestable policy. Let the blind admirers of Rome, and especially Protestants, who feel themselves attracted by its splendors, hear and weigh the indisputable testimony of this pious and chivalrous Catholic, who speaks only of what he saw with his own eyes in the Eternal City!

Gaeta, whither the Pope fled, was his rock of Patmos; at least, this is what is pretended by those sad councilors who, at the epoch of his hegira, took possession of that feeble mind; there he perceived that liberty is of the devil, that whatever resembles or leads to it should be accursed. Did it not proceed from the hell of a republic to enter the paradise of an absolute monarchy, a paradise which, it is true, needed to be guarded by foreign troops against the dull irritation of its inhabitants; but what! did not the garden of Eden itself have its cherubim and flaming sword? Only the business was not to keep those under who had first dwelt there, but to prevent their return, which shows a slight difference in the two situations. It was ever the government of the Bourbons of Naples, which had combined treason with violence, and cast into prison citizens whom it

had attracted into its councils as into a snare, that
seemed in all points admirable to him, and was the
ideal model which he sought to propose for the imitation of Christendom. This absolutist tack of the
liberal Pope of 1846, shows his mobility and mental
weakness. It was at Gaeta that, a new Moses, he
received the tables of the political and religious law
which thenceforth he was never to grow weary of
presenting to the world; his two Encyclicals and the
Syllabus are its summary. Unhappily for his people,
he could pass at will from theory to practice, and
try on the shoulders of the Romans a yoke which he
imagined had been forged on a celestial anvil by the
holy angels.

I am not narrating the reign of Pius IX.; I limit
myself to trying to make him known. Since his return to Rome he has always remained what his exile
to Gaeta had made him. The doctrine of Jesuitism
is incarnate in him; I do not mean its morality, for
nobody accuses the Pope of duplicity. It is his very
sincerity which is his strength, and an invaluable advantage to his inspirers. He transforms their calculations into fervor and enthusiasm, and appears to
purify them by contact with his soul. It seems like
a muddy spring, so long as it is subterranean, which
regains its limpidity the moment it leaps up into the
open air. The resolutions of Pius IX. indeed come
from the subterranean springs of the Gesù, and proceed from that tortuous policy which defrauds at
ease *in maximam Dei gloriam;* but he shows so
much good faith in them that he takes away their
odious morality, while preserving their native brand
of civil and religious absolutism. His personal piety
is indisputable, while in the past his purity of life

has never been touched by suspicion. He bears up
his eighty years magnificently, without an infirmity.
His figure is full of keenness and gentleness, but it is
the gentleness of invincible obstinacy : he has not a
doubt, not a hesitation, on the course he has taken.
He is proud of his ideas, sure of himself. He feels
himself a prophet, and acts as if he were. Moreover,
the prophet unbends; his domestic life does not
cease to be very simple, it is the life of a monk; yet
he delights in amiable speeches, in conversational
familiarity. In the audiences which he grants to all
that ask them, he suddenly drops the tone and bearing of the Pontiff to speak like a simple mortal of
the health of his visitors and of the incidents of their
journey. This is what especially charms English
neophytes. Is there any thing more amiable than a
smiling and jesting God? The Romans are harder
to please; have they not imagined that the Pope has
an evil eye, and that his benediction brings misfor-
tunes? They shun it, too, as far as possible.

If bondage to his system is perfect in Pius IX., his
heart is full of kindness. In an Encyclical, he will
not hesitate to devote all heretics to eternal flames,
but he will tolerate no anger at individuals. One
day he said to a young French priest who was going
back to his own country : "My child, you cannot
hate error enough; but love him who has fallen into
it, I do not say like a brother, but like a mother."
It should not be forgotten that this maternal love
exacts the doing every thing for the salvation of
the soul which is its object, and that to tear it from
doctrines which ruin it they will refuse it air and
light, and send the body to rot in some dungeon of
the Inquisition. We must not be deceived by

this clerical gentlenest, sincere as it may appear in the Pope.

Such seems to us the President, the Chief, the Inspirer of the future Council; an upright and ardent soul, fixed forever, despite his early mobility, in the doctrines of Jesuitism; uniting fanaticism with goodness; following his own impulses as inspirations; believing in himself as in a dogma; without pride, because he thinks himself at an inaccessible height, and believes that so indisputable a superiority need not be asserted; indulgent and inflexible; incapable of political management, following ever his path, his idea; as ignorant of the times as the lowest monk; able to be a sincere Christian in his humility, and a Pontiff usurping the rights of God and of his Christ. Behold the man! Never did Saint Peter's bark, so called, have such a dangerous pilot in a more tempestuous voyage. The Holy Father, as the Vicar of Christ, will vainly say, "It is I; be not afraid;" it is he that directs the tacking of the ship. For that very reason should the crew tremble!

Among the Italian Cardinals, the only one who is now of real importance is the famous Antonelli. He will not figure in the front rank among the doctors of the Council, for he has, perhaps, never opened a theological work. He is Cardinal Deacon, and has never received priestly orders. But if he dogmatizes little, he acts much; and he will certainly be as influential behind the scenes of the Council as he will be silent in its deliberations. Cardinal Antonelli differs in every point from the Pope. He does not ask his political inspirations from heaven. Secretary of State to the Holy Father, he really governs; he does it with that short-sighted skill which only considers the embarrassment of the moment, and which gets out of them as Figaro got out of the imbroglios into which he plunged. Cardinal Antonelli, who is not thought to have serious convictions, who has always been a frivolous and worldly prelate, has put himself entirely at the service of the Jesuitical reaction; he has there sought his point of support. He has, then, no excuse; for nothing can be more abominable than to play the fanatic through policy, and to use a crafty prudence in violence. He indeed revealed the measure of his disinterestedness in the jealousy which he showed toward men most devoted to the Papacy when he had reason to fear lest they should eclipse himself with the Holy Father. Thus, when the generous Lamoricière came to offer his sword to the Holy Father in the redoubtable and decisive struggle which ended with the battle of Castel-Fidardo and in the loss of all Romagna and Umbria, he constantly clashed with the ill-will of the Cardinal Secretary of State, who looked with evil eye on those who were serving his cause without his aid, and crossed, irritated, and weakened the General as much as he could. Monsiegneur de Mérode, brother-in-law of M. de Montalembert, a brilliant and convinced man, who seriously sought to form a Pontifical army which could be counted on, was forced to undergo a daily struggle with Cardinal Antonelli, who had no rest till he had deprived this useful servant of the Papacy of his high position. He also delights on occasion, and with more reserve, to show his ill-will toward the chiefs of the French army of occupation, and his proceedings have sometimes led to an outburst. Cardinal Antonelli, who feels his full worth, desires to preserve himself as long as possible for the Papacy.

His fear of death is proverbial. It is said that when
the cholera broke out in Rome some years ago,
Antonelli, under pretense of watching over the
Holy Father and preserving him from the malady,
shut himself up in the Vatican and forbade all communication from without. One of his enemies who
had something to avenge, and who, prelate as he
was, counted on indulging in this satisfaction, came
to the Vatican declaring that he must speak on serious affairs with the Cardinal Secretary of State.
The latter could not decline the interview. "Whence
do you come?" he asked the importunate prelate. " I
come," replied he, " from the hospital, where I have
been chafing cholera patients." To paint the wrath
and terror of the Secretary of State is impossible.
That vengeance was perfect. Moreover, we have
only to consider him closely to judge him. At sight
of that sly, weasel-face you comprehend his past and
his career. What is most astonishing is, that honest
Pius IX. should so long have kept this unloyal and
unspiritual adviser beside him as the director of his
policy. No doubt the Pontiff regards this as a
necessity of his sovereignty, and we have thus a new
proof of the full moral independence which it secures
him.

Of the other Cardinals I shall say nothing, because
their work is insignificant beside that of Cardinal Antonelli, whose compeers they hardly are, since he alone
holds the clew of all the business and the intrigues.
The whole Sacred College at Rome belongs to the
extreme tendency. The Neapolitan Cardinal Andrea
alone had shown some feeble good-will to the national
cause, but he was drenched with disgusts, severely
reprimanded, and returned to die sadly at Rome some

months since, to teach all his colleagues and his successors that they cannot accept the purple without taking with it all the countersigns of the Roman Court. I know but one Italian entitled to sit in the Council who is a friend of freedom: this is Father Tosti, the superior of the celebrated Convent of Monte Cassini, a distinguished scholar, nourished in retirement on the finest studies. Drawing in his convent on one of the richest ecclesiastical libraries in the world, he has distinguished himself by a very erudite history of the order of Saint Benedict, on which he is still laboring. He has also interfered in contemporary struggles with writings in which breathes a true Christian liberality; he has combated the Ultramontane and Jesuitical tendency with rare frankness in eloquent pages which have widely echoed. He is much disliked at Rome, whither he has just come to sit in the Council. It is certain that he will there support the Gallican party with all his power. Unhappily, he occupies only a secondary position in the episcopate, and he will be made to feel it.

If I come to the eminent prelates of other nations, I encounter first Monseigneur Manning, the Archbishop of Westminster, an old graduate of Oxford. He is a convert to Catholicism; he has all the fervor and all the narrowness, though not the eminent talents, of Cardinal Wiseman, his predecessor. His pastoral letters are prolix, and very weak in argument. He will do well to vote as others do in the Council rather than defend his party in speech, for he has only a limping logic and a hardly profound science to devote to that service. His importance comes much more from his position than from his powers, and also from the promises which he makes of the near return of England to Catholicism.

Among the German Bishops who made a protest at Fulda against the proclamation of the new doctrine of the Papal infallibility, in language full of respect, but whose bearing escaped none, I will mention Bishop Hœfele. He represents very honorably that German Catholicism which has gained much from the contiguity of the Reform, and which has taken up habits of serious study on that classic soil of science. Hœfele was long a professor of theology at Tübingen; he has published a well-reputed edition of the Apostolic Fathers, and a History of the Councils, which must furnish him useful information for the debates soon to open. I will mention further Bishop Hanneberger of Bavaria, a friend and disciple of Döllinger, animated by a truly evangelical spirit. I remember hearing from him, in the Church of the Holy Sepulcher at Jerusalem, a very simple and very fine discourse, animated by a truly evangelical spirit, without the least trace of superstition. He, too, is a man of learning. May these German prelates not undergo the soothing and lulling influence of Rome, but quit themselves as men in the grand debate! It is greatly hoped here that, when once they have touched Italian soil, they will leave their protestations in their baggage, and suffer themselves to be carried away by the general enthusiasm. People already see them at the feet of Pius IX. I hope truly that Rome reckons without her host.

I come to the French bishops, and shall try to make you acquainted not with their opinions, on which I have sufficiently dilated, but with themselves. Let us begin with the Coryphei of Ultramontanism. You have first our Cardinals. I will say nothing of Monseigneur Donnet, Archbishop of Bordeaux, because you may be assured of his nullity in the Council. He is a prelate of very noble bearing; the most notable event of his life was being buried alive when he was merely a young Abbé whose existence did not seem so precious as since he has occupied one of the chief Sees of France. The mistake was seasonably discovered, and he has furnished a very brilliant ecclesiastical career—at least from the stand-point of preferment. He will represent to advantage in the Council that Bordeaux vineyard of which he has such a varied and profound knowledge. In the French Senate, to which he belongs, he has only made weak and insignificant speeches; the bench of Cardinals, however, was never resplendent there, and in religious questions, whenever there is an unskillful thing to do or say, the prelates are never found wanting. Nothing is heavier or more trailing than this ecclesiastical verbiage. However, an exception must be made from the oratorical stand-point in favor of Monseigneur Bonnechose, Archbishop of Rouen, and Cardinal. He can speak with elegance and distinction. I perfectly remember his first efforts at Paris thirty years ago. He was then a young Abbé, sweet and sympathetic in his eloquence. There was even a gleam of Liberalism upon him. He was the most faithful disciple of the celebrated Abbé Bautain, who had been censured at Strasburg by his bishop. It is true that his resistance resembled that Russian aristocratic opposition which reproaches the tyrant for not being despotic enough. The Abbé Bautain asserted the insufficiency of human reason in a way which seemed exaggerated even at Rome. But they did

not then give much attention to the basis of his doctrine; they saw him struggling with his bishop; that
was enough to make him a Liberal Catholic and bring
his disciples into favor. In the front rank of these
shone the Abbé Bonnechose. He was very popular
at Paris, about 1840, in the little chapel of Foreign
Missions, where he preached, if I mistake not, during
Lent. People liked his unction and agreeableness.
However, he remained in the temperate regions, and
was not destined to enter the phalanx of the Ravig-
nans and the Lacordaires. He early became Bishop
of Perpignan, and showed great administrative gifts.
Scarcely nominated to the Archiepiscopal See of
Rouen, he received a Cardinal's hat. The courtier-
like tone of the discourse which he addressed on this
occasion to the Emperor Napoleon was observed. He
gave the ultramontane party pledges, but always with
a certain prudence, as to political applications of the
system which might annoy him as French Senator.
It was he who said in open Senate that he considered
his clergy as a regiment of which he was colonel, and
that he meant to exact military obedience. In the
Council he will neither compromise himself with the
Holy See nor with the French government.

Most of the provincial bishops reach Rome in a
state of true Ultramontane fervor. Monseigneur de
Montauban is distinguished for his fanaticism; this is
his sole title to notoriety, for his circulars are masterpieces of bad style and absurdity.

Monseigneur Plantier, Bishop of Nimes, follows the
same flag, only he gives it so much the more glaring
and visible colors because he began by hoisting the
opposite standard   He is a converted Gallican, but
he is truly converted. Bishop of a diocese where

Protestantism is largely represented, he thinks it his
duty constantly to provoke it, which is a culpable imprudence in a country so often deluged with blood in
religious struggles, and which in 1815 was the theater of true massacres accomplished by brigands who
pretended to be champions of the Catholic faith.
The ultramontane pastoral letters of Monseigneur
Plantier exasperate the nerves of France, when she
reads them, by their bilious tone and their bitter rubbish.   But let us admit that he is outdone in this holy
war by Monseigneur Pie, Bishop of Poictiers, who
should be called the Zouave Prelate, after his famous
adventure in a funeral oration over a living thief, who
was reported to have died in the service of the Holy
Father.   I believe I have already mentioned this
affair.   Monseigneur Pie is himself a zouave of the
infallible Papacy, ever ready to charge Gallicanism,
his episcopal rapier in the air, shooting out his circulars right and left like grape-shot ever at his disposal,
patronizing the grossest superstitions, founding religious festivals for relics that can only be named in
Latin ; finally one of those useful adversaries who render a hundredfold more service to the causes they
combat than to those they defend.   It is with a certain pleasure that I see him at Rome ; he reserves a
few weak chances of success for the Gallican Prelates
of whom I must now speak.

I count three of these, Monseigneur de la Rochelle,
a learned and eloquent prelate, known for his liberality ; then Monseigneur Dupanloup, and the Archbishop of Paris.   You know all the noise made by
the former in his recent manifesto against the infallibility of the Pope.   I confess that after his attitude
of late years I did not expect such clear and decided

language from him. Monseigneur Dupanloup is a
man of vehement impulses, incapable of arresting
his pen. Whatever crosses his heart or his mind
must at once explode. His ruddy face reveals a
sanguineous temperament; he can only work with
all the windows open, and he tires his secretaries out,
as some cavaliers harry several horses in their day's
ride. He has written enormously. His best claim
to literary distinction is a large book on education,
which opened the doors of the French Academy to
him; but his circulars and pamphlets have produced
a far greater sensation, for he has the pen of a true
journalist, and shuns the jeremiads of his compeers.
He has a lively turn, the *granum salis*, irony and
passion. He dilutes far too much these ingredients
of a good style. It is largely to him that we owe
the detestable law on public education which still
rules us, and which gives the lion's share to the
clergy in the direction of the University. Last year
Monseigneur Dupanloup waged a deplorable campaign against lay instruction, upon which he invoked
the severities of the civil authority, while seeming to
demand the complete freedom of education; a sure
means of strengthening the evil tendencies which he
denounced. But he has flung fire and flames at new
Italy, and defended the temporal power of the Papacy with more passion than any of his colleagues.
Yet he is not disposed to follow the Papacy quite to
the proclamation of its infallibility; the services
which he has rendered will prevent their treating his
opposition too contemptuously should it continue.
Despite all his ardor as a Catholic controversialist,
Monseigneur Dupanloup is nevertheless a hundred
leagues from the doctrines of the Encyclical, which

he has striven to color with a liberal hue in a complaisant commentary. Despite his enforced confidence in the result of the Council, he must go there in fear and trembling.

The Prelate who will quite certainly feel least at ease in Rome is the Archbishop of Paris, Monseigneur Darboy. Observe that fine and distinguished physiognomy, somewhat sad in its nobleness; you recognize in him a modern man so far as it is possible to remain one under an archiepiscopal miter. Monseigneur Darboy belongs to the most decided tendency of liberal Catholicism, as is proved by the sympathetic protection he so long accorded to Father Hyacinthe. He stoutly resisted the encroachments of religious corporations on his authority, and openly broke with all the popelings who sought to impose themselves on him. He is also greatly attached to the grandeur of France, which he confounds a little too much with the fortunes of the empire, and the Syllabus has no more decided foe. Judge if the air of Rome can suit his mind, and how he is there considered. I am very curious to know what his attitude will be in the debate, and how far he will be able to express all his thoughts.

Laymen will not enter the Council, but the influence of some of them will there be very puissant. One layman like Louis Veuillot is worth twenty bishops. The Editor of the *Univers* will be in the High Assembly, like Agrippina in the councils of Nero, "invisible and present," according to the expression of Racine in his beautiful tragedy. Louis Veuillot has elevated abuse and invective to the height of an institution. This harsh guardian of Ultramontane orthodoxy has been very well called the

14

King of Abuse.   He is well esteemed at Rome ; there
his journal brings rain and fair weather.   We may
be sure that he will play a great part during the
Council.   He will represent the lay element and
the universal priesthood by the broadsides of
scarcely canonical abuse, which he will let fly at
all who will not fall in with the pace of Ultramontanism.

To give you an idea of what is expected in the
Liberal camp at Rome of the High Assembly, I will
introduce you into one of the most distinguished
Italian houses, which I cannot otherwise designate.
There I found a freetalker, as bold as any in the
most independent drawing-rooms of Paris.   Here is
about what I heard from very well-informed and
very sprightly lips.

" The Pope vainly says, as he did the other day,
pointing to the sun, ' *My infallibility is no less evident.*'   As well go to a cardinal's reception this
evening in a Merry-Andrew's costume as assume infallibility before Christendom ; since this does not
seem less mottled with divers colors when we reflect
on all the opinions which in turn it has sanctioned in
the past.   Here at Rome we see the reverse side of
religion ; it is the counterpart of every thing that it
was at its origin.   It is no longer a religion, it is a
court.   The great politicians who retain the Papacy,
when they have rejected Jesus Christ, are unworthy ;
which does not hinder me (said the speaker, with an
inimitable smile) from being a good Catholic."

" The Council," said one to him, " will probably
be a vain effort."

" Say rather, a stinging blow," replied the
Italian.

These are the thoughts of a large part of the galleries, where the spectators are most intelligent. It is well to glean them up, and I send them to you in their sincerity and freedom. The phrase *a stinging blow* will remain ; it may well prove prophetic.   E. DE PRESSENSÉ.

LETTER IX.

At Naples—A Festival—The Bourbon Rule in Naples—Francis II.—
Stains on the Cause of Liberty—Garibaldi's Capture of Naples—
Measures of Cavour—Justice of History—Present Irritation—Popu-
lar Liberty—Education—Philosophy—Religion—The Buffoon on the
Stage and in the Pulpit—Brigandage—The Camorra—Perplexities
of the new Government—Italians in Politics—Evangelical Labors at
Naples—Political and Religious Outlook of Latin Races—Pagan
Naples—The Decline of Paganism—Revelations at Pompeii—Im-
pure Gods, Gladiators, Slaves—Discoveries in Art—Manuscripts—
The Victory of Christianity.

NAPLES, *December* 1, 1869.

I MUST transport you from the City of Ruins and from
the Council to Naples, which may be called the great
enchantress of Italy, and which has, as it were, intoxicated with her filters the numerous generations who
have in turn fallen asleep on her coasts. I arrived
here just as they were celebrating the great festivals
in honor of a new-born prince, grandson to Victor
Emmanuel. The occasion is excellent for judging of
the condition of the new kingdom, at least in the
southern provinces, and also to appreciate a new aspect of classical antiquity. Thus the most actual
present and the past are constantly meeting in my
letters, as in this Italian country, where we cannot
take a step without meeting some great ruin.

Fifteen years ago I visited this same Naples. It
was then bowed under the yoke of its Bourbon, who
prided himself on imitating under this fine sky the
harsh and austere despotism of Nicholas, and displayed all the graces of a corporal without ever

having seen fire, unless in the fuses of cannon which he had caused to be fired at his people. He resolutely applied to them a system of brutalization, and conscientiously began with his own house, for he kept his eldest son, heir to the throne, in dense ignorance, and denied him a share in public life. He had so well succeeded in this work that when he desired to marry him at Munich he dared not send him to a foreign court, and it was necessary that the bride should be brought to Naples that the imbecility of her husband might not appear to every eye. It was while conducting his son to the frontiers of the kingdom to receive the Princess that the King took the disease which carried him off at fifty years, his conscience burdened with abominable treasons, for which his Jesuitical confessors enthusiastically amnestied him, since they bore hard on the infamous Liberals. His son, Francis II., found himself on the throne before he had the slightest idea of politics, and he was content to continue the system of which he had been the first victim. The machine was set up; it went alone until one fine morning, when it broke down in the shock with triumphant Italian liberty.

This triumph, let us frankly confess, was obtained by means that were not entirely laudable. Garibaldi's Sicilian expedition remains a truly epic episode, although it is now proved that he was positively aided in secret by Cavour; yet it abides true that he incurred the greatest dangers, and that the struggle was heroic. Garibaldi has committed great political faults. He has often compromised the national cause by his speeches and his deeds; he nevertheless remains a figure full of grandeur, which has no need of the halo of a demagogic prophet, with which he

allows himself to be enveloped. His courage and
disinterestedness have never been belied. He is likewise the idol of this ardent and imaginative people,
which finds in him the expression of its passions.
Garibaldi is the explosion of the popular volcano,
which has long left its wrath to rumble in its bosom
against religious and political tyrannies. The tor-
rent of fire sweeps on many pebbles with its lava.
Generous feelings are blended with utopian dreams,
with imprudence, and abusive imprecations.

The capture of Naples itself was much less admirable than the conquest of Sicily. People have greatly
celebrated the entry of Garibaldi into the capital of
the kingdom of the Two Sicilies without an army or
escort, in a simple open coach. But every body
knows to-day that Piedmontese gold had purchased
many defections in the army and navy of Francis II.;
that the confidence of the unhappy young King had
been laid asleep by the assurances of Cavour to his
embassador while they were playing him false; and,
finally, that Gaeta was not taken by the Red Shirts,
but by the regular troops of Victor Emmanuel. This
explains why the work of assimilation is much slower
in Naples than in the other parts of Italy. History,
after all, executes the justice of God; every fault is
severely punished and expiated by the very difficulties which it inevitably causes to arise. If I blame
the measures of the Piedmontese policy, it is not, I
confess, because I feel any great tenderness for its
victims, for they were truly the scourge of one of the
finest countries of the world; and they have left it in
a demoralized condition which will not be, for a long
time, transformed. Despite contrary assertions I am
convinced, by exact inquiries made on the spot, that the

ancient kingdom of the Two Sicilies is much more attached to the Italian monarchy than is commonly thought; or at least, that it experiences no temptation to put itself again under the yoke of its former masters. The taxes excite great irritation, because they are really exorbitant; but they do not prevent the circulation of life and activity in the country, while it was stifled and died under the iron hand of the Bourbons. For the last two days I have witnessed great national festivals on occasion of the birth of an heir of the House of Savoy. I can affirm that the city is not adorned only by official hands, and that the illuminations are not merely by order. The inhabitants of the provinces troop to Naples, and encamp in the streets, so as to miss none of these festivals. Were they so opposed to the present dynasty as people say, they would not be so eager to celebrate the birth of a Piedmontese Prince; they would follow the example of Northern Italy toward the Austrians. It would be entirely absurd and unjust to compare, as the Catholic press does, the feelings of the Neapolitans toward Victor Emmanuel with those of Milan and Venice before their enfranchisement toward the Emperor of Austria. I do not deny a certain discontent, but declared hostility does not exist. Brigandage itself, that last prop of Francis II., who has expended the greater part of his fortune in paying it, is beating a retreat at every point. No restoration is, then, to be feared, unless from a general overturn in Europe.

The new government has granted to Naples, as to the entire Italian kingdom, the principal liberties of constitutional government; but the moral condition of the people of these provinces, to which I shall

presently return, renders this present for the moment
nearly useless, because ignorance and idleness do not
know exactly what to do with it.   What is infinitely
more important, is the development of public education from the high to the humble.   Popular schools
have multiplied, though they are still insufficient, and
not persistent enough; but salvation lies in the formation of a new generation that can read and write.
The Italian government will doubtless walk resolutely in this path.   Superior instruction is set up on
a grand scale in the University of Naples.   Unhappily, the youth, habituated to the sweet idleness of
this delicious climate, improve it only very imperfectly.   They were recently obliged to quell a mob
of students, who rebelled because they thought the
theme required for the baccalaureate too difficult;
they indeed desire the diploma, but not the study
which it ought to represent, that it may not be a
vain simulacrum.   Superior instruction, through an
anticatholic reaction, which is only too easy to understand, belongs almost entirely to the most advanced tendencies of pantheistic philosophy.   One
of the most popular professors lately opened his
course with these words: "Gentlemen, we shall begin
by showing how baseless and insane is the idea of a
God.   We shall then proceed to serious studies."
Such a philosophy will not elevate the people.   Were
it to decidedly triumph in the higher classes, while
blind devotion continued to rule in the ignorant
classes, the decline would be incurable.   The most
excellent institutions in the world would not restore
their moral and mental health.

It is here that we must see, next to Rome, what
papal Catholicism makes of a people when it can

mold them as it will. We have a school in France that teaches independent morality; that is, entirely separate from religion, and self-sufficient: in Italian Catholicism we have religion independent of morality; devotion considered as a means of escaping the obligations of the eternal law, or of conveniently expiating transgressions. Nothing more surely and more deeply perverts the human soul than religion thus understood, for it becomes a sort of plenary indulgence granted to evil. It produces security in vice, and almost in crime. A thousand times better is the absence of religion than such devotion, which is only a base terror of hell, and a material and derisive means of self-insurance. It is also to Catholicism, fashioned in the image of the Jesuits and ruled by them, that this nation owes the gravest of its defects, which prevents the possibility of building up any thing solid upon them; I mean its facility in falsehood, its inveterate disposition to cheat. Not only is there no respect for truth, but it is mocked, and people would think themselves duped did they not deceive their neighbors. Hence none can trust any body; distrust is universal. The bond of true human fellowship is sincerity, according to the profound saying of Saint Paul, "Speak every man truth with his neighbor, for we are members one of another." Speech is, indeed, the sole mode of intellectual exchange among men. To lie is to substitute bad money for good coin. A land over which falsehood rules is like a country where the true gold can no longer be distinguished from counterfeit pieces: exchange has become impossible, the social bond is relaxed, and disorder is universal. This is the great sore of these southern populations—a sore which will be mortal if it be not promptly healed. A man who knows and loves this land well said to me energetically, "There, conscience is dead, it is rotten." Consequently the corner-stone, the rock on which we might build, evades us; we find only a mobile and fugitive surface. Intelligence surely is not lacking; it is quick, thoughtless, piercing, free—but it has no compass, no fixed star in the moral heavens. Its brilliancy resembles the phosphorescence of these southern seas—which does not really shine—all the more because education is nothing, and the taste for learning is still quite undeveloped. The *lazzaroni* spirit is only too generally diffused in the circumambient air; it is an influenza found under the embroidered coat of the courtier. The Neapolitan is at once sober and sensual; he only needs a bit of bread, an orange, and a cup of coffee for his morning repast; he quite easily earns what he strictly needs; he then delights to roll himself up a ring in the sun, like the white of an egg, or at evening under the chandeliers of his theaters. His abode is neither comfortable nor very neat; but his gloves are faultless, and his wife is adorned like a shrine. Every thing is for the world, for the gratification of vanity. His true fireside is the public square, the street, the theater. He loves sallies, and executes them with sprightliness. The buffoon remains the most original and truthful type of his literature. It has been said that ancient Russia was an absolute monarchy tempered by assassination. The old Neapolitan rule was despotism tempered by the jests of the Merry-Andrew. The boards which he trod were a sort of escape-valve and solace for the repressed public spirit. A gesture, a word on the tip of the lips, escaping in the flash of a rapid and

malicious smile, suffice for allusion.   Yet one should
not be unjust even with a buffoon.   At Naples he is
a real artist, full of spirit, caustic, a perfect mimic of
the ridiculous wherever he encounters it, skillful in
speaking the various popular dialects, and besides a
very good fellow, and in his way, religious.   The
actor who spends his time in making the Neapolitan
populace laugh twice a day is an excellent father,
and cares with devoted tenderness for his sick wife.
The Molière of his times, he constantly renews his
repertory, and plays what he has composed.   Alta-
ville has displayed true talent in this coarsely flavored
literature; in the city he is the most excellent man
that you will see, and he is surrounded by affection-
ate esteem.   Do not forget that we are in the land of
contrasts.

Under the former rule, the most successful buffoon
was not at the theater of San Carlino, but in the
pulpit of the Capuchins.   There should we look to
see the popular orator exert himself with many gri-
maces and puppet gestures.   What he chiefly sought
was to excite the nerves of his auditory, mainly composed of women, to make them faint, and lead them
trembling to the threshold of the confessional.   They
told me here of the effect produced by a certain
Capuchin, who painted hell with such fearful realism
that he tore cries of terror from the women who heard
him.   He closed a frightful description of the flames
of hell with the picturesque expression, *Quella frit-
tura!*—What a frying!   And the good women cried
out, Jesus, Mary!   What shall we do?   How escape?
The Church opened its arms, and they flew to it;
stretched out its hand, and they brought their offerings.   But another preacher employed an image of

the same class in an address to the King. The latter, who had heard of his reputation as a popular preacher, asked him to let the King hear him. "Look out," replied the Capuchin, "I cannot disguise the truth; you do not know my genius, otherwise you would not ask me." The King insisted, but, as a precautionary measure, he had him preach with closed doors. The Capuchin opened with the words, "I have always observed that when a fish rots, the head is first tainted." The King did not ask for the rest, and he did not insist on hearing him in public. This preacher at least united courage with originality, and his bold language made his audacious metaphor pass.

The manner in which the last revolution was effected is an index of the moral condition of the people; never were seen more accumulated treasons, more brokerage or stock-jobbing of consciences. On the other hand the means employed by the royalists to regain power are still more blamable. We have already spoken of its paying brigands. If we reflect on it, can we find any thing more monstrous than to pretend to restore true order in any country, civil and religious order, by taking into pay, or at least encouraging or sustaining by subsidies, wretches who would have the green cap of prisoners-for-life in all the prisons of Europe, who carry fire and massacre through the villages, and who extort ransom from prisoners under penalty of death or slit ears? What has so long rendered the efficacious suppression of brigandage impossible is its always finding a sure asylum in the Papal States, whose frontier was an inviolable barrier against the Italian police. This, however, has been seen and done before all Europe in the name of the pre-eminently conservative party, and with the notorious support of the Pontifical Government! For some time brigandage has sensibly diminished; this comes chiefly from the depletion of the treasury of Francis II., and from the redoubtable energy of the measures of repression.

The ancient rule has left behind it another scourge which there will be much trouble in extirpating; this is the *Camorra*, a species of secret, but not political organization, which has spread its network over the entire country. It is quite difficult to know its origin, which is lost in the night of time. Perhaps it was at the outset an attempt to supplement the deficiencies of justice, and to replace it when its action paused too soon. The *Camorra* then, in those remote days, would resemble the Free Judges of the Middle Ages, who followed up those whom they had condemned until they had reached them and made them undergo the penalty which, in a solemn session held perhaps underground, had been pronounced against them. But if the *Camorra* had such an origin it has truly been transformed; it has become a species of Free Masonry in oppression, which has no other aim than to plunder the people. We cannot comprehend how it has been able to get an authority accepted which is more burdensome than the best organized governmental tyranny. Doubtless it is through terror on the one hand, and on the other by making its victims hope one day to share its profits—for the *Camorra* is of good composition, like the House of Lords; it is not limited by rights of birth, and it opens its ranks to new adepts who seem worthy to sustain its cause. Initiation must be difficult; proofs of courage are demanded of the candidate, a very

easy courage moreover, since it consists in giving a
dirk-stab on the order of the chiefs, and dirk-stabs
from behind are willingly given.   The adept belongs
soul and body to the association, as in secret societies,
only he serves no political ends; he is merely the instrument, and also the beneficiary, of a money making
association, which gives dividends to its stockholders
by means of the poniard.   It is certain that the secret
power of the Camorrists was recognized by a considerable portion of the population—that they raised
their imposts quite at their ease.   The peasant who
carried provisions to the city remitted a tenth to some
mysterious personage whom he found near the gate,
and he dared not defraud these popular customs.
The petty coachman remitted a portion of the money
which he had received to a passer-by, who gave him
a sign only too easy for him to recognize.   The Camorrist made himself obeyed from the depth of the
prisons, whither his exploits frequently led him.
Sometimes blood flowed, when the task was to subdue unexpected resistance, but that blood only ce-
mented the pact between the Camorrist and the
Neapolitan people.   It has no doubt diminished since
the fall of the ancient rule; but it is far from being
abolished, for it withdraws into the shade, and its
secret is almost never betrayed.   It is divided into
squads of ten men; each has its chief.   When he
wishes to confirm his power he flings a piece of money
some steps before him, and asks whoever wishes to
replace him to pick it up.   If a hand is stretched out
it must be immediately armed with the knife—for
the old chief only yields if he is overcome in the combat which candidature induces.   Ever the knife!   It
is the sign of this religion of pillage and murder!

I would not be unjust in the picture I am drawing of the Neapolitan nation. Much should be forgiven it in consideration of the education it has received, without forgetting the numerous and honorable exceptions which show what it might become under better influences—those courageous citizens who, like Poerio, have languished in the prisons of Ischia as the price of their patriotism, and who have never desired a pardon which seemed to them a true insult; those upright, honest, and truly pious hearts which are encountered here, as every-where. And then we must turn with confidence to the future, and expect the regeneration of this intelligent people.

The new government encounters very great difficulties in the moral condition of the Neapolitans, as well as in that of Southern Italy in general. Thus one of the most insuperable obstacles to a good establishment of the finances is precisely that facility in falsehood which is so common in this country. Vainly are the imposts so arranged as to meet the enormous deficit which weighs on the kingdom; they come in very imperfectly; the channels may be well hollowed out, they too often find supplemental ditches to drain them, and a good share stops on the way. Either the tax-payers find means of escaping them through ruse, or the subaltern officers ply their wits to appropriate them to their own use. This is the shameful sore of this country, through which some of its best resources flow away. A good observer said that what it had mainly lacked for some time was honest functionaries. The North possesses some of these, but they are rarer than tenors in the South. Add to this grave inconvenience an excessive mobility in the financial regulations, which leads to disorder

and endless delay—all causes of impoverishment for
the public treasury. The lack of persistency and
stability in political life always hinders its regular
movement. The unbridled babbling of the Neapolitan is also a cause of weakness in the discharge of
civic duties. I was told that when a simple municipal election was held at Naples, the result was not
known till six weeks after the ballot. The reason is
very simple; every old municipal councilor wished to
make a speech, and he gave way to his oratorical vein
as though he alone were to speak. Italy invented
discourses of two or three days' duration which set
and rise with the sun. The moral life is in danger
of running away in this unbridled prattle. However,
to be just, we should recognize a political instinct in
the Italian which always brings him up on his feet,
and which in very critical hours enables him to find
the practical issue with a skill which would rebuke
many old diplomatists. It is still the race of Ma-
chiavelli. They are also like the Athenians in the
insatiable curiosity which consumes them. The cof-
fee-house is to them what the *ayora* was for the brilliant loafers of Greece. They are not content with
the public news, they would know every thing of the
private life of those whom they encounter. It is not
rare to hear a Southern Italian ask his neighbor in a
box at the theater the amount of his income, or a
lady whom he does not know how many children she
has, and whether she has hopes of more. The language easily lacks modesty; it has the intrepidity of
the old Latin in calling things by their names. When
we reflect on the condition of this people at the moment when it came from the hands of the Bourbons,
we comprehend the characteristic words that slipped

from the illustrious Cavour in his mortal agony:
"No siege; *le lavi, le lavi!*"—wash, purify them!
He was right; it is indeed a regenerating bath that
the Italians of the South need. The bath has begun
with the diffusion of public education, which has
carried its budget for the old kingdom of Naples up
from about $10,000 to about $180,000, and which
has every-where organized courses of evening lectures.
The disappearance of a large number of convents in
consequence of the sale of the ecclesiastical estates is
likewise a benefit; for those idle monks, who shot up
in all the country as in ancient Spain, served only to
maintain ignorance and false devotion. But the
great instrument of regeneration would be the propagation of the pure Gospel, which alone can reach the
evil at its root by renewing conscience. Let us
glance at what has been done in this particular.

It would seem that, when the barriers reared by
Catholic absolutism had fallen, and freedom of conscience had become the law of the land, the preaching of the pure Gospel would have the most rapid
success. It has not been so, because precisely the
first effect of the former administration was profoundly to shake that moral basis on which alone
Christianity can build. It is a great error to imagine
that outward circumstances have a preponderating
influence on religious development. The Christian
Church won its finest conquests under the yoke of
the Roman tyranny, because it encountered a well
prepared soil; because if the evil was great, it was
truly felt, and the aspirations of men's hearts anticipated the Gospel. It was the same in the sixteenth
century, which surely was not an age of free conscience. The Reform grew and conquered under

the most tyrannical rule that can be imagined. It also found a predisposition in the hearts of men. It came at its hour, and a spark sufficed to kindle up an immense flame. This moral predisposition for evangelization did not exist in Southern Italy. No doubt it was in many hearts, for in a more or less latent manner it is in the soul of every man ; but no breath of evangelical inspirations had passed over this soft and frivolous people. Individuals might be won by Christian preaching, but the masses were not then capable of being stirred. Men have been forced to abate their early hopes. Naples has long had a Swiss chapel, which has ever been a focus of religious life. M. Valette, one of its first pastors, had acquired a great and legitimate influence, but it could only be exercised in a limited circle. He had not even leave to visit the hospital of Swiss Protestant soldiers, who would have desired the succor of his ministry. After the annexation every thing was changed. There was a moment when people might hope for a reformatory movement. Father Gavazzi, an old Dominican, preached in the streets to large multitudes, who displayed the liveliest enthusiasm. He was an orator after the heart of this ardent and mobile people. He spoke with that expressive pantomime which pleases them, in imaginative, picturesque language, sprinkled with daring metaphors, and biting and violent remarks. He blended politics with religion, and thundered vehement invectives at the Bourbons and the monks. The danger of such preaching is, that it draws the attention of the audience wholly to controversy, and runs great risk of seeing them withdraw whenever it shall turn to great Christian themes, and no longer be seasoned with those high spices which

please southern palates. Thus it fared with Father
Gavazzi. He did not long keep up his fire at Naples.
The Marquis of Cresi, a Neapolitan, who was won
over to the Gospel before the Revolution, conducted
a more serious work. He established regular worship
in Naples itself, and with certain foreign aid organized
a system of colportage which was entirely suited to
this period of commencement. The Marquis of
Cresi had the advantage of belonging to the nation
which was to be gained to the Gospel, of understanding it well, and speaking its tongue. For some time
he had real success. A committee on Italian evangelization was founded to encourage these efforts.
Public discourses on religious themes were held in
its name, and collected quite numerous audiences.
A Wesleyan work was likewise begun. The Vaudois
Church of Piedmont had hastened to plant its standard at Naples. Evangelical schools were opened for
the people. Things then wore their best aspect; they
were full of hope. The middle classes themselves
seemed disposed to follow the movement; they thronged to the evening discourses, the schools were filled.
Unhappily sad divisions broke out among the directors
of these different efforts. Christians of Italian origin
could not bend to the rules of the Vaudois Church.
Thence arose struggles which became envenomed,
which degenerated into quarrels, and which unhappily became public in the sequel of the foundation of
a journal representing the Italian element, with great
violence of language. The Marquis of Cresi soon left
Naples quite discouraged. The discourses for men
ended. There only remained the Vaudois Church
and the Wesleyans; the former scarcely collected fifty
auditors. The schools, happily, are full of prosperity.

They gather up more than five hundred children,
and the efforts of the Directing Committee of the
Work of Evangelization are concentrated on them.
This is the result of the first missionary campaign at
Naples. It is far from brilliant. Elsewhere Italian
evangelization has had better success, as I shall have
occasion to inform you when I shall have collected exact information. The Committee on Evangelization
does not mean to discontinue its labors; on the contrary, it intends to renew them with fresh zeal. The
prosperity of the schools is very encouraging. Bib-
lical colportage grows more important as a taste
for reading spreads. The discourses will no doubt
be resumed; but we must not be deceived, the great
shock will not come thence for Italy. I have a like
conviction respecting France. These efforts, which
should be pursued with courage and perseverance,
because they contribute to save souls, are not enough
to produce one of those great currents which gives
the Christian mission the impulsive force of the early
days. The plowshare of God must pass over these
Latin lands—light and brilliant lands, where the seed
of eternal life only slightly penetrates the soil. The
furrow must be plowed deep, and it will be, do not
doubt that, by the great crises which will not be
lacking at the close of this stormy century. Modern
society must learn what it costs to reject the Divine
Idea, and abandon itself to Pantheistic Naturalism.
It will know the worth of a democracy without God,
and the disasters to which it leads. On the other
hand, Catholicism is charged to wage the most incisive
controversy against herself by her own excesses. But
these evolutions will not be accomplished without
laceration and sorrow. Now our Europe needs pre-

cisely these sorrows to awaken her Christian aspirations and rear her altar, if not to the unknown God, at least to the forgotten God. Then the evangelical mission, finding a well-prepared soil, watered with tears, and perhaps, alas! with blood, will be able to extend its labors and its conquests as it has not yet done, and the reformatory movement will resume its course, as in the sixteenth century, for the salvation of modern humanity. I know no other salvation for it.

I should be grieved were the preceding reflections to discourage existing evangelical labors. It is a great thing to be even an obscure link in that chain of pure faith which is never to be interrupted. At certain periods, Christianity finds itself like a railway train before a mountain; it must tunnel the mountain. The position of those employed in the work lacks apparent grandeur and splendor; but let them be consoled, the obscure tunnel leads to richer plains; it was a defile necessary to pass. This is our history for the moment on the European continent. Let us be resigned to our mission; the important thing is to fulfill it in the name of God.

II. Permit me now to use the freedom of correspondence and pass to an entirely different subject. It is no longer of the Naples of the present time that I would converse, but of antique Naples—of that voluptuous paganism the decline of which we learn to know on these charming coasts better than elsewhere, and whose prestige and dangerous beauty make us the better appreciate the grandeur and the difficulty of the conquests of Christianity. And first, how can we refuse to recall in a few words the framework, still the same, of a picture which has changed less at bottom than people would think, for in many regards it has preserved its pagan coloring. There is no contrast more marked than that between the scenery of Naples and the scenery of Rome. It is not that grand sadness, that majesty of immense mourning, which wraps you in melancholy; on the contrary it is the most ravishing unfolding of an eternal spring which nothing can destroy, and whose smile cheers even the ruins of a crumbled world. Contemplate the gracious curves of its shores, that seem fondly sketched; those softly rounded gulfs kissed by the azure wave; those islands scattered, each a paradise, on the sea whose infinite perspectives they soften and limit; that gay, luxuriant vegetation, where the striking fruits of the South ripen among olive-trees and rounded pines! See those cupolas of verdure, those orange-trees and lemon-trees that perfume the breeze! You will then comprehend the full seduction of nature here. There is not under heaven a more dangerous Armida, or one that presents man a more intoxicating cup. Asia Minor doubtless has some Edens comparable with this, but the waves which bathe her are often terrible—they are transports that speak of death. Greece has outlines of equal grace, but their contours are firmer; we might say that they were drawn with the great art of Phidias; at Naples we are rather reminded of the chisel of Praxiteles. They who would enjoy the complete vision of that incomparable scenery should follow the route from Castellamare to Sorrento, between the picturesque hills and the coast, with its infinite sinuosities, which projects its magnificent olives and its gardens of orange-trees above the blue waters, and is incessantly cut into capes and scooped out into gulfs. From the heights which overlook Sorrento the horizon extends from Cape Misenus to Vesuvius, and includes all the grace and magnificence of the country. The pole has often been called the throne of winter. I shall place that of summer on the summit of the Camaldulas. It is not yet the terrible sovereign that scorches Africa; it has all the splendors of that sovereign without his flames. It has poured out its largess over these dazzling plains which we see at our feet; its mantle of gilded and purple harvests surrounds the mountain, and its joy breaks forth on the purple sea. It was truly in these places that the religion of nature found its chosen sanctuary and shed its final splendor; it was there that, in the eve of the ancient world, it desired to taste its final inebriation and crown itself with roses in a feast that combined all pleasures. People may reply by pointing me to Vesuvius, whose smoke rises in the blue heavens like an eternal menace of destruction—as if to suggest every moment that the least thrill of its burning entrails would suffice to ravage and destroy all these wonders. Does it not rise from the mass of ruins accumulated at its foot, like a glutted lion among the bones of its victims? But who does not know that the ancients loved to combine images of death with those of voluptuousness, and that they sometimes made a skeleton preside over their orgies—not that they might grow wiser, but hasten to enjoy, and, as the poet of Epicureanism said, Pluck the rapid moment as we pluck the quickly withering flower whose full fragrance we would inhale!

There existed, then, a pre-established harmony between this enchanting land and the declining paganism which was developed here in all its splendor

and in a morbid bloom.   Nowhere can we study it
better than in this Neapolitan country.   In Greece,
we have eyes only for the ruins of art in its great
period ; at Rome, what rules is the ideal of power,
unconquerable energy, the ineffaceable mark of the
talon of the eagle, which embraced and consumed
the world.   We have seen at Naples that effeminate
paganism which no longer believes in itself, which
has but one God, pleasure, and which seeks in these
brilliant waves a less somber and bitter Lethe than
that of the realm of shades ; it is Epicurean paganism, the last word of antiquity at the moment when
the Cross was planting its austere symbol in the face
of all these refinements of a corrupt civilization
which exhausted the treasures of the world in grati-
fying its lusts.   The Museum at Naples, and especially Pompeii, evokes under our eyes this paganism
of the second period, if I may call it so ; it presents
itself to us with all its distinctive features.   The excavations of Pompeii have been prosecuted with·
redoubled energy since the annexation.   Every day
new houses arise from the ground with their frescos
and mosaics.   These artistic treasures produce very
different effects under their natal sun and in the hall
of a museum.   Temples, forums, private houses,
shops, villas, theaters, circus, every thing lives again
as fresh as it was eighteen centuries since ; this is
not pagan life arranged and embellished as in pagan
literature, which always selects from the diverse elements of reality ; no, here is the complete reality of
pagan life, reappearing in its nakedness, undisguised,
unvailed, with a frequently fearful sincerity and
cynicism.   On the walls we still read gross inscriptions which reveal defiled imaginations.   Death en-

tered the city, like the thief in the Gospel, in the
hours of night; it had no time to make its funeral
arrangements. It is there before us as it was in its
every-day life, with its elegance and its vice; it enables us to grasp an entire epoch in itself, whose confession it brings to us from the moment that it shook
off its ashes. Completing what we see at Pompeii
with the masterpieces heaped up in the Museum of
Naples, we have a perfect image of Greco-Roman
paganism at the advent of Jesus Christ, *minus* the
more elevated side of its sadness and its aspirations,
which was kept in the shade by the ease and charms
of existence in sweet and fertile Campania.

What impresses me in this Neapolitan or Pompeiian paganism is, that the position of honor is there
accorded to divinities of the second order, especially
to those that favor pleasure, Venus and Bacchus. It
has made an Olympus to its own taste, where pleasure
reigns sovereign. There we do not find the Jupiter
of Homer, who, changeful and passionate as he is,
has gleams of justice and moral grandeur, like a
Greek of the heroic age. Still less do we find there
the Jupiter whose noble and proud image had been
sculptured by Phidias,

"The great Immortal whom the blessed praise,"

according to the sublime verse of Pindar. The fa-
vorites of this abased religion are the goddess of
beauty and the god of wine. The Neapolitan Venus
is not that proud divinity who expels or sets aside
evil passions with her ideal beauty; the Venus of
Milo, compared with the Callyjuga, is like a Madonna
of ancient art. She who was adored in Campania is
a ravishing woman, but a dangerous beauty. The

marble palpitates; Pygmalion has animated his
statue with the culpable fire which consumes him.
The Pompeiian Bacchus recalls in nothing the mysteries celebrated under the name of that god, which
had a deep meaning. He is purely and simply the
the god of the bacchanals, crowned with vine-leaves;
the pupil of old Silenus, who is also reproduced with
favor. The great mythological legend is constantly
sacrificed to piquant or sentimental anecdote : Venus
lamenting Adonis; Diana ravished before Endym-
ion, or indeed chastising Acteon ; Leda and her swan,
the carrying away of Europa, the abandonment of
Ariadne. These are the favorite subjects in the Pompeiian frescos, often treated with much grace and
feeling, but sometimes with libertinage. *Genre*
work every-where replaces high art; it is not the
ideal of which they strive to afford a glimpse, it is
reality that they like to evoke for the gratification of
the eyes. The Pompeiian paintings show a great
predilection for the combats of gladiators; in this
they are fully in harmony with the morals of the
times. For declining paganism, the gladiator was
what the hero was for ancient Greece. The bloody
games of the circus had replaced the sublime dramas
of Æschylus and Sophocles. It has always been remarked that voluptuousness loves blood; the soul
relaxed by guilty pleasures is animated only by the
spectacle of suffering, and cruelty alone can make its
unstrung fibers vibrate. In the Museum at Naples
we see a great many gladiatorial suits of armor, which,
in their beauty and ornaments, resemble the armor
of knights in the Middle Ages. I have also encountered in the Pompeiian frescos the images of several
slaves loaded with burdens. I found likewise at

Naples a striking type of ancient slavery in a very fine bit of sculpture, which represents the giant Atlas bearing the world on his robust shoulders. The figure is noble and hopeless; it breathes weariness and vast sorrow. It is truly the type of those millions of men who were regarded as outside and below society, toward whom any thing was permitted, as Seneca said, who bore up by their obstinate labor that world of elegance and pleasure which lived by their sweat. Impure gods, gladiators, and slaves! did not the Greco-Roman world rest on these three pillars when it grew feeble and was decaying in its own corruption? The little temple of Isis at Pompeii suggests that invasion of foreign and Oriental religions to which paganism in its desperation had recourse. But in reality this was not a foreign religion, for Isis, as the goddess of Ephesus, of whom the Museum at Naples possesses a very fine statue, was ever the great goddess, Nature, who replaced all other gods in a debasing pantheism.

What Pompeii especially reveals is the inside of the pagan home, domestic life. Nothing less resembles a family hearth than these charming abodes, with their porticoes, peristyles, gardens surrounded with columns, their triclinium surcharged with ornaments. Every thing is for show, elegant idleness, sumptuous repasts, and pompous, though never numerous, receptions. The dwelling-rooms are little, voluptuously decorated boudoirs, arranged in two rows, and forming two parallel passages around the atrium and the garden; they are solely intended for sleep, and are only looked upon as accessories. Domestic life did not exist. The frescos that adorn the walls acquaint us with the life led there. We witness the

toilet of the great Roman lady surrounded by her
slaves; we can count the vases of perfumery which
she used.   We behold family repasts in their scarcely
chaste freedom.   The dancing women who figure in
ceremonial feasts are represented to us in their light
and provoking grace.   Still further, we are introduced behind the scenes of a theater, where they are
getting up the spectacle ; and into the house of the
tragic poet, at the moment when he is about to recite
his new productions.   Excellent art, though at Pompeii it seems to have been a good copyist, adorned
these pleasure-houses of a middle class whose fortunes
must have been moderate.   For them were wrought
those fauns, dancing, sleeping, or plunged in intoxication, whose attitude is rendered with such astonishing
suppleness in that little Narcissus with his delicate
grace of self-intoxication, and especially that tired
Mercury, who has all the somewhat painful carelessness of lassitude ; for these abodes were painted the
ravishing frescos of Ulysses disclosing himself to Pe-
nelope, the sacrifice of Iphigenia, whose pathos is so
affecting, and those three Graces, whose serene beauty
not the pencil of Raphael has surpassed.   It is at
Pompeii, too, that we read a frightful commentary
on the picture which Saint Paul has traced of the
infamies of the Roman decline, of that fondled and
insatiable voluptuousness which, seeking the infinite
in sensual life, found only the monstrous.

Art extended its domain on all sides.   It could
give an elegant form to the utensils of ordinary life.
Lamps, pottery, and jewels received its seal.   The
pagan of that period would have all his senses flat-
tered at once.   It is but too easy to find the explanation of this wholly brilliant and infamous life in the

papyri discovered in the ashes of the destroyed city, and which are unrolled to be deciphered by the most ingenious processes. They are all treatises of Epicurean philosophy. This philosophy, more surely than the flames and ashes of Vesuvius, was to destroy the society that had surrendered itself to it, crying, " Let us eat, drink, and be merry, for to-morrow we die !"

It is after such spectacles that we admire the moral power which made the cross triumph not only over the Cæsar of Rome, but the Venus of Naples; which purified the pagan abode, and created the Christian home; which finally made the lily of purity grow up amid such slime. To conquer brutal force was much, but it was more difficult still to subdue the syren of this gulf, and the enchantments of a refined voluptuousness, which was the conclusion and the prestige of Greco-Roman paganism.

E. DE PRESSENSÉ.

LETTER X.

RECENT EXCAVATIONS AT ROME — THE PALACE OF THE CÆSARS AND THE CATACOMBS.

Napoleon III. and Archæology—Signor di Rossi—The Late and the Present Aspect of the Palace of the Cæsars—Temple of Jupiter Stator—Cicero's House—Two Frescos—Christian Relics in the Palace—Importance of Christian Archæology—Nature of its Disclosures —Rossi's Roma Sotteranea—Bosio's Explorations—Arringhi and Marchi—Rossi's Method—The Catacombs used for Burial, not Worship—Three Periods in their History—Dates of Monuments—Christian and Pagan Burial—Symbols of the Christian Tombs—The Catacomb of Saint Callistus—Callistus Himself—Visit to the Catacomb —The Consecration of Labor—Testimony of the Catacombs on Catholicism and Protestantism, the Primacy of Peter, the Adoration of Mary, the Sacraments, the State of the Dead, the Invocation of Saints, the Canonical Books, and Image Worship.

ROME, *December*, 1869.

WHEN the Council shall open it will be hard for me to speak of any thing else than what may be learned of its deliberations, or of the spirit of its members. I take advantage, then, of the few days that remain before the solemn inauguration of the High Assembly to converse with you on a subject which well deserves to occupy the attention of the friends of science, and of all who take an interest in Christian antiquity : I mean the truly magnificent discoveries made of late years in the domain of profane and sacred archæology. Let us first speak of the former.

Follow me to the hill which overlooks the Forum on the right.   It is the famous Mont Palatine, the cradle of antique Rome, which was to her like the pompous tomb where an oriental king desired to die surrounded with all his luxury and voluptuousness; for there arose the palace of the Cæsars; there was that colossal orgy of the imperial decline organized, in which was spent all the force and energy of the conquerors of the world. Some years ago this illustrious spot was marked only by a few shapeless ruins. There people admired one of the finest views in Rome, the Forum, the Colosseum, the mountains of Latium and Albania, then the immense plain ending in the countless domes of modern Rome. But it was only in imagination that people could represent to themselves the magnificence which had been displayed on these places, and for which the treasures of the world had been exhausted. Within ten years all this has changed; the wand of an enchanter has evoked the past before us. This wand is nothing but the intelligent will of the French Emperor, served by a skillful Roman archæologist, Signor de Rossi, who has pursued these excavations with equal talent and energy. He has needed both, for the Roman Court has more than once seized on the precious opportunity to be disagreeable to its mighty and inconvenient protector. But the Emperor Napoleon III. clung to his project. It is well known that he feels a very lively interest in Roman antiquity, to which he has devoted a considerable book, "The Life of Cesar." He is not merely guided in this taste by love for science, but by a sort of moral affinity, which likewise he openly avows, with the General who crossed the Rubicon and founded the Empire. He sees in him the type of those providential men, as he calls them, who save society as he thinks by placing themselves above the laws. His history of Cæsar, and his liking for that period, remind me of a quite piquant anecdote which is found in the History of Pius VII. by Chevalier Artaud. He relates that Cocault, Minister Plenipotentiary of France at Rome under the Consulate and Empire, conversing one day with Napoleon I. on the Cæsars of Rome, his mighty companion grew angry with Tacitus, and accused him of having calumniated Nero, Caligula, and Domitian; "Kindred minds, kindred minds," replied Cocault; a bold speech, which attributed his defense of the Roman Empire to a moral likeness. Napoleon understood, smiled, and showed no ill will to his sprightly embassador. We may apply this remark to the taste of the Emperor Napoleon III. for all that relates to the family of the Cæsars, without forgetting that if he has drawn from them his liking for personal government, he has left to them its useless rigor; and that, apart from critical moments when nothing arrests him, he is the mildest of men. Whatever may be his motives, he has nevertheless rendered an immense service to science in causing the active prosecution of the excavations of Mont Palatine, which daily lead to new discoveries.

At first glance it seems as if nothing had been changed. You have before you only the ordinary entrance to a Roman villa. But hardly have you mounted the staircase when the scene changes. You are at the heart of Roman history. Descend again on the right, toward the Colosseum; you are on the spot where a rabble of brigands constituted themselves a nation, invoked the gods, believed in its fortune, and began by petty conquests of the surrounding tribes that invading movement which was only to pause at the limits of the known world. We are confounded at the contrast between the humble origin of Rome and the unheard-of extent of its dominion. It was merely a stronghold at first; the eye at once measures its area. They have found the shapeless ruins of the temple of Jupiter Stator, which was reared in gratitude for the first victory of Romulus. From the start, the religion of the Romans bore a wholly material and local character. It honored the gods only for services rendered ; these were to labor for their advantage as well as in their pay. They also honored only agricultural and warlike divinities. They needed wheat and victory. Such is the basis of their worship, addressed in reality to themselves, for they had made their religion a sort of historic memento of their success. Mankind never knew greater utilitarians. If you descend the hill on the left of the Capitoline side you will have before you the rich habitations of the Roman aristocracy at the close of the Republic, and at the beginning of the Empire. Here are the remains of the house of Cicero, who could almost perceive from his abode the tribune which was his throne. Every thing here has larger dimensions than at Pompeii. The houses were spacious, and might suffice for the luxury of that corrupt period. The bridge has been found which Caligula caused to be thrown from the Palatine to the Forum, so that they could pass directly from the Palace of the Cæsars to the Curia, and note the promptness with which the Senate obeyed directions. In this place we see the ruins of a city, and not merely of a private edifice. If we now place ourselves on the summit of the Palatine we are positively before the Palace of the Cæsars. It has sprung

16

out of the ground with all its principal dispositions
which disclose themselves to the eyes in an incontestable manner. Two magnificent columns of white
marble mark the position of the grand portico which
preceded the Palace. This portico opened first upon
the basilica of Jupiter, where justice was administered, and which in these places produces the effect
of a frightful irony. It is of itself a considerable edifice. Beside the basilica, and parallel with it, is the
Palace itself, properly so called. The atrium leads
into a vast reception-hall. Then comes the peristyle,
which ends in the triclinium, the shameful theater
of imperial gluttony. On the right is the *nympheum*,
intended as a bath. It is an elegant hall, where
every thing is calculated to please the senses. The
triclinium is followed by the library and academy,
devoted to rhetorical declamations. In the garden
are found the sites of several temples.

Close beside the Palace of the Cæsars a patrician
house has been discovered, which still bears the impress of the noble simplicity of the Republic. The
ornamentation is in exquisite taste and soberly elegant. This discovery has brought to light one of the
finest frescos of ancient painting: it represents Io
between Argus and Mercury; the young maiden is
touching and chaste in her beauty, the glance of
Argus has the fixedness of an implacable guardian.
Mercury is a winged creature whose foot hardly
grazes the earth; the color has retained its vivacity.
Pompeii has no painting superior to this masterpiece.
I do not even know whether it possesses one which
can be put in the same rank. Another fresco, found
beside the former, has a peculiar interest; it gives us
the aspect of a street in Rome at the close of the

Republic. We see a woman coming out of her house in ceremonial costume, probably for some sacrifice. She is followed by the solicitous glances of the members of her family, who are placed on the balcony of an upper story, while two slaves consider her through a window of the lower story. This is a perfect revelation concerning the arrangement of Roman houses. Unless I am mistaken, the balcony is a true discovery. We can now perfectly conceive a street in Rome as it was eighteen centuries ago. As the excavations are actively pushed forward, they daily discover some new site, some statue, some shaft of a column, or some jewels. Yet few objects are found intact. We can very well understand that rapacity would fling itself on the Palace, where it was well known that all the riches of the world were heaped up. Thanks to the statues and the innumerable busts of the Vatican and the Capitol, it is very easy to re-people it. Every Emperor appears with his own physiognomy, and Tacitus restores life to this dead past; his terrible graver traces under our eyes those scenes of horror wherein insatiable voluptuousness is combined with a not less eager cruelty; where the madness of omnipotence had its furious fits; where humanity might learn what monsters she is capable of producing. Here should we read afresh that history of blood, and it is with this great avenger of the human conscience that we should traverse these accursed places.

Strange fact! among the ruins of the imperial palace certain Christian memorials have been discovered belonging to the early ages of the Church; among the rest, one of those little funeral lamps, adorned with evangelical symbols, which were carried among

the Catacombs. This need not astonish us. Saint Paul
tells us that his bonds had become known in the
pretorium, and even in Cæsar's Palace. Thus, while
the persecuting Emperor fancied that he had annihi-
lated an odious sect by his cruelty, it was growing up
in his own Palace, and with it that moral power
which was to overturn the world which he so faithfully represents.

I do not speak of other discoveries which have been
made in late years, particularly at Ostia, where admirable statues have been found. I shall have occasion
to speak, when describing the Catacombs, of the
excavations on the site where the temple of the
Arvolles brethren arose. I have aimed to draw your
attention to the most capital of the archæological
labors of these late years. This fruitful excavation
of the Palace of the Cæsars is a considerable event
for science, and it will doubtless provoke numerous
and important publications.

II. I come now to Christian archæology, which
has especially occupied my time at Rome. I had
important information to require from it for the last
part of my History of the First Three Centuries of
the Church, which will turn on the development of
Christianity at the family fireside and in the primitive worship. The Fathers of that age, no doubt,
cast vivid light on this theme. But the Christian
necropolis restores it to life; it gives what books never
give, an intuition of the past; it in some sort makes
us their contemporaries. How often under the somber arches of the Catacombs, before some mutilated
fresco, have I seemed to leap over ages, and mingle
with the affected multitude that had just deposited
the ashes of some confessor in these places! What

forms the great interest of the Catacombs is, that we there find not merely the expression of the piety of the chiefs of the Church—her bishops or theologians—an expression which has always taken on a more or less literary form : here you glean up the ingenuous testimony of popular faith. A father has lost a son and repeats his affection and his hope ; a wife laments her husband, a brother his brother, a friend his friend, and all together the courageous confessor who perished under the tooth of the lion or the sword of the executioner. The Christian heart reveals its true nature on these somber walls in some thrilling fresco, some rapid touch, or in some brief word, and does it in that funeral hour, great among all hours, when, broken by sorrow, it exhales its deepest sighs as a crushed flower yields its sweetest perfumes. The Catacomb, thus interpreted, gives us that every-day history—that history of the lowly and humble—which in general is forgotten for pompous parade, and which is the very tissue of human condition in all times.

I had already come to Rome, fifteen years ago, to undertake this fruitful study ; but since then the discoveries in this domain have been so considerable that Christian archæology has been entirely renewed. I have been able to fully acquaint myself with the present state of this science, to which sufficient importance has not yet been attached, thanks to the *Roma Sotteranea* of Signor Rossi—a large work of which two volumes in folio have appeared—and thanks chiefly to visits made in his own company to the Catacombs. Permit me first to render homage to this illustrious scholar and the invaluable services which he has rendered the history of the Church. We can-

not attribute the precious results of his researches to
the happy success of suddenly lucky excavations; for
the new excavations have only been successful through
the admirable method with which they have been
begun and pursued.   Doubtless Signor di Rossi had
predecessors.   Bosio, in the seventeenth century,
first directed his attention to these Christian burial-
places, which had been forgotten for centuries.   He
had collected in the Acts of the Saints all their information relating to them, and had traced out an
inventory of future researches—a plan of discoveries
to be made.   His book is still exceedingly valuable.
He had gone to work, not by directing excavations
properly so called, but by striving to penetrate the
Catacombs through all accessible openings, and carefully describing all that he had seen with his own
eyes.   He more than once risked his life in these
dangerous researches ; he repeatedly lost his way, and
passed three days without light or food in some of
those infinitely meandering subterranean passages.   I
have read with emotion this courageous inquirer's
name, traced by himself in the Catacomb of Domitella.   On more than one point his indications have
proved erroneous, but he opened the breach.   In the
eighteenth century the Catacombs were excavated
anew by Arringhi, who wished to continue the studies
of Bosio; but he worked hap-hazard and without
method, and, unhappily, he pillaged and destroyed in
his imprudent researches more than one catacomb
whose primitive state we can now no longer conceive.
In our times Father Marchi, of the Roman College,
has certainly laid open the way for di Rossi; his
works on the Christian architecture of the Catacombs
are valuable ; his descriptions of the structure of the

Catacomb of Saint Agnes deserve to be read. He showed in an irrefutable style, as I think, that we must not confound the Christian cemeteries with the quarries or sand-pits of the pagans—that the former were arranged the reverse of what the quarrying of stone or any other industrial labor would have required—that their narrow passages were arranged solely for burial. Unhappily, Father Marchi lacked a truly critical method, and he fixed at hazard the dates of monuments. Thus the honor of having completely founded the science of the Catacombs recurs fully to Signor di Rossi.

I shall give you a rapid glance at his way of proceeding; then I shall relate the general results of his investigations, and finally, I shall associate you with my visits to subterranean Rome, a sure means of not transforming my letter into an archæological treatise. Signor di Rossi had recourse to all the still existing means of information for determining the location of the Catacombs. Unhappily, the capital document has perished. Saint Augustine informs us that on occasion of the quarrel with the Donatists, an exact catalogue was prepared of all places of worship or burial which had belonged to the orthodox Christians of the preceding period, and which had been destroyed in the persecution of Diocletian, together with the Sacred Books and chronicles of every Church. Had this document been regained, the topography of the Christian section of Rome would be fixed. Signor di Rossi consults, with the greatest care, the ancient calendars which connect the churches with the names of martyrs, the martyrologies, the lives and acts of the Pontiffs, and the ancient topographies of Rome; but he does it with rare sagacity, applying the great methods of modern criticism to these documents, often surcharged with legends. He rightly thinks that it is as needful to know how to discern truth blended with error as to reject error blended with truth. As especial guides, he has taken the itineraries of the old pilgrims who had come to Rome when the Catacombs were still open to devotion, and which marked with great exactness the sites of the holy places they had visited. Thus he found, in the sequel of a book by Alcuin, quite a detailed itinerary of two pilgrims from Saltzburg, who had come to Rome to visit the Catacombs, and especially that of Saint Callistus. Their indications were very precise. They told by what gate they went out, how far they were from the tomb of the celebrated Metellus. With this itinerary in hand, Signor di Rossi went to these places, and he only saw a vineyard and a garden. The first impression might well make him despair. Yet he was not discouraged; he caused excavations to be made in the vineyard designated. Judge of his delight when, after a few days' labor, he saw appearing one of the vastest Catacombs of Rome, that of Callistus, where Saint Cecilia was buried. I shall hereafter speak of the archæological treasures which this underground cemetery contains, when I come to narrate the visits I made to it with the illustrious archæologist. I will first sum up the explanations which he gave me concerning the places themselves, and which bring before us the general results of his discoveries, consigned to his great book, "*Roma Sotteranea.*" We should distinguish three periods in the history of the Catacombs: the first is that of persecution, when they served for the burial of the martyrs, and for the interment of simple Christians who loved to repose near those glorious confessors of Christ. Worship was then but rarely celebrated there, and only in moments of violent persecution. The second period begins with the peace of the Church. For nearly a century the subterranean burials continued, though in restricted numbers. The Catacombs became essentially a place of pilgrimage. Saint Jerome has eloquently described the impression which he experienced on descending into that sacred night, and contemplating the burial-places of confessors. Unhappily, every thing was sacrificed to this new destination; the bishops of Rome caused vast staircases to be constructed to lead to the most celebrated crypts; they enlarged the passages around them, and even added inscriptions to the primitive inscriptions. Thus they considerably changed the aspect of the subterranean cemetery; and to grasp it in its primitive condition, it is needful to go back beyond the embellishments of the period of peace. It is here that a sagacious criticism has a chance for development. Signor di Rossi believes that he has discovered sure signs for determining the dates of the symbols. He has been able to collect a large number of dated inscriptions, and to group them according to their dates; he has formed classes and families; thus a type shows itself which permits the classification of other inscriptions. For example, the monogram of Constantine, barred crosses, is found only since his time. The ancient inscriptions are of excellent calligraphy—very fine and perfectly simple. The Christian inscription becomes surcharged from the time of the peace of the Church; it grows more detailed, more human, dwells more on the part played by the defunct in

his earthly life.   The Greek characters are also an
index of high antiquity.   As to the symbols painted
on the tombs, they are not numerous in the primitive
times ; they mostly have a hidden, mystical sense,
which is natural in times of persecution.   The
anchor, the dove, and the fish, occupy the principal
place.   The ornamentation of the early period is
much finer and more classical than that of the times
of peace.   The same difference is remarked between
these two types as between the Arch of Titus and
that of Constantine.   Signor di Rossi has not failed
to consult even the bricks, for they bear their trade-
mark and their date.   When he finds them in large
numbers of the same date, this is to him a certain indication of the epoch to which the structure belongs.
It is by these diverse means that he strives to distinguish between the monuments of primitive Christianity and those of the following age.

The third period of the history of the Catacombs
is that of the invasion of the barbarians, who were in
a rage with the Christian crypts as well as with the
pagan temples.   The popes completed what the
barbarians had begun, though with a very different
purpose.   As far as possible, they had the sacred
remains and the funeral ornaments carried away ;
then they closed the Catacombs.   Visiting them was
forbidden.   During the night of the Middle Ages
their memory gradually perished, save the small
portion on which basilicas, like Saint Sebastian, were
built.   Without suspecting it, the Church of Rome
for centuries had her finest monuments under her
feet ; neither for science nor for piety did they exist.
As I have already said, Bosio was the first who sought
to regain this great past.   I have explained how his

successors rather harmed the progress of Christian
archæology. To Signor di Rossi belongs the honor
of having found his way in this vast and obscure
labyrinth, amid the confusion of dates and of having
borne thither the torch of a sure criticism.

Let us in few words recall the origin of the Catacomb. It is, properly speaking, a Christian institution. The pagans knew nothing of this nature.
First, with the exception of the Etruscans, who
buried their dead and laid them in sarcophagi, the
Romans and the Greeks burned corpses and gathered
up their ashes into funereal urns. Most commonly
the great families built them magnificent sepulchers,
belonging solely to themselves. The *columbaria* were
private property, and they only received the ashes
of the freedmen of some illustrious house, but they
had no relation to the Christian *cœmeterium ;* the
slumbering together of the members of a spiritual
family. The sole non-private burial that was known
in antiquity was the species of common tomb near
the Esquiline, where were flung the ashes of slaves
and of men from the dregs of the people. Two Jewish Catacombs have indeed been discovered at Rome,
one near the Via Portisa, which was also a common
grave, and on the Appian Way another, much more
ornate. But the latter seems to belong to a period
posterior to the Christian Catacombs. It was truly
the Gospel which inaugurated fraternity in death
after having consecrated it in life. It loved to repeat,
over the perishable dust of its followers, that in Christ
there is neither Greek nor Jew, male nor female, slave
nor noble. The tomb of the martyrs is the center of
the Catacomb ; near them all Christians loved indis-
criminately to repose. The form of burial was bor-

rowed from Judaism; the disciple of Jesus desires
to be like him in death as in life, hence he strives
to repeat in his own burial what he knows of the
burial of the Master. He was interred in a grotto;
the Christian also desires to repose in the bowels of
the earth. In the Catacomb of Saint Agnes is found
a closed grotto, which was certainly the earliest form
of Christian burial. But it was soon needful to
modify it in order to satisfy the necessities created
by the great numbers of the proselytes. The Catacomb was formed of several stories of narrow passages, in whose walls quadrangular openings were
pierced where corpses were deposited. They were
closed up with slabs covered with stucco, on which a
pious hand engraved the name of the defunct, an image
of hope, a word of tenderness. When the burial of
some martyr or eminent Christian took place, they
gave an arched form to the sepulcher, and it was
called an *arcosolium*. This arrangement allowed the
multiplication of symbolical frescos. Sometimes they
formed true chambers, or funeral chapels, with four
arcosolia.

The Christian Catacombs extended over an immense
space, which corresponds perfectly with what the authors of that time tell us about the prodigious progress
of the new religion. Did not Tertullian say to the
pagans, " We are every-where. We fill your camps
and your armies; we are found even in the Palace of
your Emperors ? " Persecution increased the Church
instead of diminishing it. " It has a real charm,"
said Tertullian ; " the blood of the martyrs is the
seed of the Church "—*Sanguis martyrorum semen ecclesiæ*. Yet the persecution was a great hinderance
to the outward display of the proscribed worship.

People ask how it was possible for the Christians to excavate this subterranean city, with its vast proportions, under the sword of their executioners. Signor di Rossi has resolved this problem in the happiest manner. He has demonstrated, texts in hand, that the Emperors, always greatly opposed to associations among the citizens which might menace their despotism, had made a solitary exception in favor of funereal associations, which might monthly collect means to procure the interment of their members. The superstitious ideas of the pagans concerning death, which led them to closely connect the destinies of the soul with those of the body, had evidently weighed in this unique point on the harsh and intractable imperial legislation. The Christians confined themselves to conformity with a custom, and made use of an existing right. Signor di Rossi has found inscriptions which prove that they used forms of language analogous to those used by the pagans to designate their funereal associations. The latter called themselves *cultores* of the citizen who had made them a generous gift of land, or had granted them a large estate. The Christians were designated as *cultores Verbi*—those who cultivate acquaintance with the Word. Funereal associations were styled fraternities. It was easy and pleasant for the members of the Church to assume a title which corresponded so well with their feelings. Signor di Rossi cites decisive texts, which show that these concessions had sometimes been withdrawn from the Christians by their persecutors to be ultimately restored to them, which establishes in an irrefragable way the fact of the primitive concession. Thus a problem finds its solution which had long appeared insoluble. Signor di Rossi found a material proof of his assertion in the excavations made in 1865, in the cemetery of Domitella, or of Achilles and Nerea. They found a splendid entrance to the Catacomb. On both sides of the door, stone benches are arranged with all that is required for the *agape*, a deep well, and a fountain. Now we know that the funereal associations were wont to celebrate a sort of solemn feast in memory of the dead. The Christians turned this repast into an agape, and thus conformed to custom, while modifying it according to the spirit of their religion, in order to preserve the right so dear to them of freely burying their dead. We may say that on this important point Signor di Rossi has brought his proofs to a demonstration.

Christian burial is profoundly distinguished from pagan burial in the fact that the latter turns toward the past. It calls that past to mind in every way, and even strives to perpetuate the terrestrial life. Viands are placed near the dead, his arms are at hand; his honors and dignities are produced in a pompous inscription. The pagan only turns his eyes with alarm to the somber region that opens before him beyond the tomb, and he seeks to project over that darkness, which is enlightened by no well-founded hope, the warm tints and colors of the sun of this world. He would have death like one of those fine sunsets which continue their brilliant farewells long after the star of day has disappeared. The Christian tomb, on the contrary, turns toward eternity and heaven; what is behind is very pale and very wretched compared with what is ahead, and especially above. The soul's fatherland is beyond this abode of darkness and sin; the true life is not exhaled with the last breath; it has just begun, and this true life proceeds not from

man, but from God; it is the gift of Christ, the
bloody and glorious prize of his sufferings. Such
are the blessed certainties expressed by the funereal
symbols of the Catacombs. The dove represents the
happy soul which has flown away to God; the palm
recounts its triumph; and the anchor, which often
assumes the form of a cross, expresses its invincible
hope, and its point of support. The *Alpha and
Omega* suggest that all these favors come from Christ,
who is the beginning and the end of salvation. Those
simple words *in pace* suffice for the consolation of
survivors. And especially in the early days all accessory circumstances were neglected, all that con-
cerned the earthly lives of their beloved friends.
Were they rich or poor, illustrious warriors or slaves,
—dignitaries in the Church? No matter. The inscription tells nothing of this; they were Christians,
and that was enough. There was no harsh and
haughty stoicism in this; no, for the heart speaks
loudly over these tombs. Expressions of tenderness
are very frequent. We light incessantly on the word
dulcissimus applied to the dead. Human and divine
love and glorious hope, that is all, but it is enough;
for this is all that is immortal in the present life, all
that death cannot destroy. The contrast between the
Christian and pagan tomb stands out with singular
force in the inscriptions borne by both: *Vixit*—he
hath lived—is the pagan formula; *vivit*—he liveth—
is the Christian formula.

Now that we know the general character of the
Catacombs we can undertake a visit with profit. The
excavations are far from having laid open the greater
part of subterranean Rome. For the present, people
can only visit the Catacombs of Saint Agnes, of

Achilles and Nerea, of Saint Priscilla, and of Saint
Callistus. I would particularly speak of the last, for
we shall here find the most precious discoveries
made in late years. I must first say a few words
about this Callistus, under whose name the vast
cemetery has been placed, because the guard of it
had been confided to him by Bishop Zephyrinus,
whose deacon he was before becoming his successor.
Here I shall no longer have Signor di Rossi with
me; but whatever his knowledge may be, I think I
am in the right on this point against him. Callistus,
of whom the Roman Church has made a saint, was a
cunning trickster. It is possible that he died well,
and that martyrdom covered his questionable past.
Cardinal Richelieu said one day that his red robe
covered all his doings. It was the same, and for
better reason, with the blood-stained robes of confessors; these also covered whatever defects there might
be in their lives, and only their heroism was remembered. I can understand that their heroism should
have been the sole memory of them which was
guarded; but it is not permitted history silently to
pass over evil deeds which have not had merely an
individual bearing, but have acted in the most fatal
way on the destinies of the Church. Now an old
manuscript, discovered some years ago in the dust of
Mount Athos, has come, bringing an overwhelming
testimony against Callistus.

This is the famous book of "Philosophoumena,"
discovered by Minos des Minos in a scientific mission
undertaken in the name of France. The learned
world immediately recognized the value of this book,
which contains the most complete and fresh information on the heresies of the early ages of the Church,

with original citations from the chiefs of the Gnostic
school. Nobody emits a doubt on its date; it goes
back quite positively toward the middle of the third
century. The latter part of the book was devoted to
an inside chronicle of the Church of Rome in that
period, and traced out the frightful usurpations of its
bishop, Callistus. Who was this indignant witness
of the intrigues which contributed most in preparing
the way for pontifical despotism? Origen had been
named, and that pleased the Catholic party, which
could dismiss as heresy whatever annoyed them in
the document. But as the author of the work called
himself a bishop, and as Origen was only an elder
or presbyter, this hypothesis could not be sustained.
I hold it certain to-day that the author of the " Philosophoumena" is Saint Hippolytus, who was Bishop
of Ostia about the middle of the third century, and
died a martyr, one of the most illustrious doctors of
the time, a disciple of Irenæus and Alexander. Whoever has attentively read the undisputed works of his
pen which remain to us can easily conceive that he
alone could have written the "Philosophoumena."
It was, moreover, known that he had devoted a book
to the heresies. But without engaging in this great
debate, I will confine myself to pointing to the decisive
proof which Rome furnishes us. At the Museum of
the Lateran people admire a very fine statue of Saint
Hippolytus, on the pedestal of which is drawn up a
list of his works, among which figures a writing which
is positively cited in the " Philosophoumena" as being
from the author of that book. We have before us,
then, one of the most worthy representatives of Christendom in the third century. What does he say of
Callistus? First, he depicts to us the earlier periods

17

of his life. That he was formerly a slave, and was afterward elevated to the highest ecclesiastical dignities, would only be a fact honorable to himself and to the Church. That proves how high she placed herself above all social distinctions. Unfortunately, Callistus rose by dishonorable means. He began with simple villainy. After having gone through a fraudulent bankruptcy at the expense of the Jews of the Transteverine quarter, he sought to conceal his crime by going to play in their synagogue a comedy of Christian heroism, transforming a vile affair about money into a doctrinal quarrel. Sent to the mines of Sicily for this daring act, he took advantage of the momentary good will of Commodus toward Christians and returned to Rome, where he became the eager servant of the old Bishop Zephyrinus, hardly an intelligent man, and fond of money. He employed his position to gain friends by flattering all the dogmatical opinions which were then in conflict at Rome, by giving pledges and fair words to each, without shunning, despite all his prudence, a lapse into heresy, through the ambiguity of his language, which bordered on Pantheism. Through these measures he became the successor of Zephyrinus, and he turned against his allies of a day. Once seated in the episcopal throne he thought only of the methods of increasing his power. He employed the surest means of success by relaxing all the bonds of the ancient discipline, flinging wide open the doors of the Church to all who desired to enter without renouncing a sinful life. This calculation was profound; a holy Church is a free Church, for Christian people only abandon their rights when they have renounced the fulfillment of their duties. The sacerdotal priesthood grew up on the ruins of the universal priesthood. Callistus was particularly easy toward the improprieties of great ladies whom their whims brought into the Church. He compared the latter to Noah's ark, which carried in its bosom unclean animals as well as clean. This confusion required a firm hand in the pilot, and the Bishop of Rome was charged with the business. Saint Hippolytus openly resisted him ; he chiefly combated the most fearful of his usurpations, which consisted in directly remitting sins in his own name, without any regard for ecclesiastical discipline. This is what made the valiant defender of ancient Christian liberty shiver with indignation! But he was resisting a current stronger than he—stronger than the resistance of the Origens and Tertullians, the current of worldliness and formalism whose billows the union of the Church with the Empire, was soon to precipitate in an irresistible manner. The book of Hippolytus nevertheless remains an overwhelming witness against the early attempts of the Roman Episcopacy to found a divine power. Surely it is a favorable hour to hear the voice of this champion of liberty and holiness, on the eve of the day when one of the successors of Callistus will strive to ascend the last step of the altar where he would be adored by Catholic Christendom. Let not the name of Callistus prejudice us against his Catacomb. He was merely charged to arrange it ; he could not dishonor the holy confessors who repose there ; besides, his remains are not here. The sanctuary has not been profaned. I have already related how Signor di Rossi succeeded in discovering this Christian cemetery, one of the most vast and important. It really includes two cemeteries, that of Callistus and that of

Lucina, which have been combined by subterranean galleries. The latter was by far the more ancient; by bringing together fragments of inscriptions scattered in the ashes, Signor di Rossi succeeded in reading the epitaph of Cornelius; and by prosecuting his excavations he discovered his portrait painted in fresco on the arcosolium which served for his tomb. Now Saint Cornelius was one of the most eminent bishops of the third century. In the Catacomb of Callistus he got together by the same process the fragments of a great inscription of Pope Damascus, which in the most precise manner indicated the location of the episcopal tomb in the third century. The epitaphs of four bishops of that epoch have also been regained in the same crypt, which is situated near the crypt of Saint Cecilia. Thus Signor di Rossi has very truly discovered the most important Catacomb of the second period of the Church of Rome. In gleaning up all the inscriptions which were buried there, he perceived that the land belonged to the illustrious family of the *Cecilii*, which explains its proximity to the pompous tomb of Cecilia Metella, the wife of Crassus. Some of the greatest names of ancient Rome and of imperial Rome are encountered in the funereal inscriptions of the Catacomb. The Christianity of that epoch then did not merely attract to itself the poor, the slaves, the ignorant, but also an important section of the Roman aristocracy, women akin to the imperial family, men destined to the highest offices in the State. Nothing can better show how universally souls were then wrought upon by religious aspirations, and how they sighed for a worship which might give them peace. The higher classes of the nation had particularly flung themselves into Oriental superstitions, but the superstitions of Mithra and Isis had quickly revealed to them their nothingness, and, impelled by the same needs of heart and mind, they now came knocking at the doors of the Church.

After all these explanations, it is time for us to penetrate the Catacomb of Callistus. We go thither by that incomparable Appian Way, which to my mind is the finest thing in Rome. Coming out by Saint Sebastian Gate we encounter the Quo Vadis Church, whose touching legend I have already related; then, not far from the tomb of Cecilia Metella, you reach the gate of a vineyard—a turfy mound overlooks the entire landscape. When the golden rays of the setting sun impurple the immense plain, girdle the Albanian and Sabine Mountains with a halo, and come breaking on the aqueducts, you say to yourself, This is truly perfect beauty, and you are not mistaken. You descend into the Catacomb by a very steep staircase; you light a candle and advance, full of tender respect, along these somber walls, which contain the remains of several Christian generations and the ashes of confessors. You imagine the scenes that have taken place under these arches in the days of persecution. You see a multitude in tears accompanying the corpse of one of its pastors who has just been sacrificed; prayer and sacred hymns rise amid sobbings, and the words of eternal life resound as a mighty consolation and a sure promise. A pious hand traces the memory of this holy hour in a fresco rapidly engraved on the unslaked lime. It is Elijah borne away in his chariot of fire—a sublime image of the glory of the martyr. There, it is the youth in the furnace, repeating to the Church that the Son of God traverses it with her. Next, it is Daniel in the lions' den, or Noah in the ark—a lively image of the protection of God over the loosened waves of persecution. The Christians of those dolorous times delighted in the symbols of triumph ; rarely do they depict those' of suffering. Why should they? Were they not plunged in it? What they need is, to greet in advance the happy shore whither their hopes tend. Yet I found at Saint Callistus a very beautiful fresco, which represents the appearance of the Christians before the tribunal of the Emperor. We see the haughty judge on his seat; the pagan priest who has denounced the Christian is fleeing basely, and full of wrath ; he perfectly represents the persecuting Church which says that she abhors blood, *abhorret a sanguine*, because she does herself slay those whom she has delivered to the secular arm. Nothing is so fine as the glance of the confessor; it has that inflexible sweetness which nothing can overcome : and he too, in his indomitable resistance, repeats after the Master, I am a king, for I bear witness to the truth. Symbols which speak of the resurrection are also very numerous. Jonah is its most frequent type ; he is represented as he is swallowed by the whale, and then as he proceeds from his jaws, which represent the jaws of the sepulcher. The resurrection of Lazarus is likewise constantly represented. A very significant painting in the Catacombs, which indicates one of the greatest revolutions wrought by Christianity, is that which shows us a laborer with his instruments of toil, a blacksmith with his tools, a ditcher with his pick. Till Jesus Christ came, manual labor was despised and given up to the slave ; it is now honored as being required by God. In the Christian cemeteries we are constantly reading the great text of Saint Paul : *Do*

all things in the name of God. We feel that the
entire life is animated by a new breath, that is sancti-
tified in all its legitimate elements, and that the
barrier is not yet reared between the sacred and the
profane ; as if all that we are, all that we have, and
all that we do, did not belong to God. A mother
has desired to have the plaything of a child prematurely snatched from her tenderness, represented on
his little resting place. Christian symbols have been
found on utensils, on fragments of furniture, which
were incrusted on the tomb as signs for recognition.
I was particularly struck by one inscription gleaned
up by Signor di Rossi at Saint Callistus, and which
runs thus in Greek : *Dyonissas presbytes iatros—*
Dyonisias priest and physician. The Church of the
third century, then, saw no incompatibility between
the exercise of the ecclesiastical office and a purely
lay calling.

You would, no doubt, ask me whether the frescos
and inscriptions of the Catacombs bring any confirmation to Catholicism or Protestantism ? I should
reply concerning both in the negative. What is
found there is very different from either; the Christianity of the second and third century, with its freedom and fervor, with all the complex elements that
were blended in it. There is not a single inscription,
nor a solitary fresco, that implies the primacy of Peter,
for the inscriptions which put his name over a Moses
Smiting the Rock are of later date. The Virgin
Mary appears only as the humble mother of Jesus, to
whom alone adoration is visibly addressed. As to
the sacraments, they have sought to make much of
the frescos of Saint Callistus, which represent Baptism by the miraculous draft of fish, and the Supper

by a mystical repast around a table laden with loaves
and fishes. I can see nothing in these frescos which
implies any thing more than the celebration of
these two sacraments, connected with the evangelical stories which have always served as their
symbols. At any rate, there is no trace of any
other sacraments but Baptism and the Lord's Supper.
Most of the inscriptions imply the immediate blessed-
ness of the dead. Some contain a vow in his behalf, and others entreat his prayers. This is nothing
astonishing ; the Church of the second and third century believed in the continuation of redemptive action
beyond the tomb.

It is remarkable to note that all the symbols
used in the Catacombs are drawn from our canonical books. It is only at Naples that you find
something drawn from the *Shepherd of Hermas*—
two maidens building the mystical tower. We can
infer nothing from the Catacombs concerning the
worship of images, since it is admitted that they did
not serve for places of worship. The vials wherein
it was claimed that the blood of martyrs was deposited bear inscriptions which imply that they were
used in the Eucharist. In this, then, there is no
certain indication to discern the tombs of martyrs,
apart from topographical designations. I do not
speak of the other Catacombs which I have visited,
and which I have already named, because I have
grouped about Saint Callistus whatever has seemed
to me most worthy of interest in my studies of
Christian archæology.

I take leave to express the wish that the Fathers of
the present Council may often descend into the
Catacombs, in order that they may measure the dis-

tance which separates the Roman Church of to-day from the Roman Church of the early times ; and that they may explain how the actual Pontificate proceeds from the primitive Episcopacy; and above all, how it continues its tradition in the bosom of the wealth of material power and by the exertion of an oppressive policy.

E. DE PRESSENSÉ.

LETTER XI.

The Council Chamber—Preliminary Session—An Unpleasant Incident
and a Conversation—Bishop Dupanloup and M. Veuillot—The Op-
position—The Pope's Allocution in the Preliminary Session—Its
Spirit—The Manifesto of the Civilta Cattolica—On the Eve of the
Council—The Letters of Janus put in the Index—Wrath of the
Liberals—Opening Ceremonies of the Council, with Comments—
The Committees on Faith, Discipline, and the Religious Orders—
Their Duties—Parleying Protestants—The True Issue—Unmeaning
Distinctions—The False Supernatural.

ROME, *December*, 1869.

I SHALL write the last two letters in the form of a
journal, in order to follow more closely the incidents
of these important days. Here we are decidedly on
the eve of the Council. The preparations are advancing from day to day. I went this morning to
Saint Peter's. The chapel where the deliberations
will take place is quite ready. The benches are covered with velvet, the Pontifical Chair rises in its
majesty and solitude, a symbol of the dogma which
they are eager to proclaim at Rome. In the basilica
itself, in the rear of the confessional of Saint Peter,
benches of the same kind are prepared for the great
religious ceremonies which will precede and accompany the Council. This morning, Tuesday, December 2d, a preparatory session was held in the Sistine
Chapel, and I saw filing past bishops of all nations,
tongues, and costumes. The session no doubt dealt
with the ceremonial question. Priests are arriving
at Rome in ever-growing numbers. Their minds
appear quite heated. Returning from Naples this

morning, I had a very significant conversation with two Jesuits. The occasion of it was original enough, though hardly agreeable to me. It happened that yesterday evening, on leaving the station at Naples, a thief had nimbly and skillfully abstracted quite a sum of gold from me. The company was all clerical. They shared my vexation, but it did not fail to inspire a certain contentment in my cassocked companions, because they thought it a new proof of the moral lapse of a nation that is shaking off the yoke of Catholic absolutism. In vain did I suggest that my thief did not belong to the new generation, by observing that justice required us to blame his early teachers rather than the new government. It would not do, and they came near accusing Victor Immanuel of having had his hand in my pocket. Once on this ground the conversation did not pause. My friends of the Gesu expressed a profound indignation at the late manifestations of Monseigneur Dupanloup, as if he were dishonoring the close of his career. They lauded Veuillot and his journal to the skies. For them he is the Archangel Michael, sword in hand. They turned a deaf ear when I told them that this archangel more frequently took mud from the highway to besmear his adversaries than the sword of speech. When I invoked freedom of conscience, ever trampled under foot by this desperado, they replied that the truth alone had rights—that it was like the sun—that people ought to submit to it or be punished—that the Pope was as God. When I declared to them that I felt horror at an Inquisitor-Christ, they did me the honor to say, *You are a Protestant.* Thereupon they fell to abusing our missions and our great Reformers. "Study, sir, study

the history of the Church," said a monk quite ludi-
crously to me, " and you will see whether there is any
likeness between Saint Peter and your Luther." I
might have asked him, with a smile, to show me the
likeness between the boatman of Lake Tiberias and
the Sovereign Pontiff. He talked of pride, rebellion,
and always came back to that frightful theory of the
right of persecution. This is the staple of the Roman
idea. In the eyes of the two Jesuits you should have
seen the gleaming of the stern and somber fire of
fanaticism. Be not deceived—it is this inflamed atmosphere which will surround and weigh upon the
Council. It will have, like the Convention of 1793,
its mountain and its tribunes, which will exercise a
moral violence on its deliberations. Decidedly the
presence of all these monks is not useless.

December 3.—To comprehend the irritation of the
Ultramontanes against the least of the Gallicans, one
should read the letter of the Bishop of Orleans to
M. Veuillot. I send you a reproduction of it, for it
is a capital document on the question of infallibility.

" SIR: In the letter which you published, November 18th, in regard to my observations on the
controversy raised in relation to the definition of
infallibility, you excuse yourself for having been one
to awaken this controversy. You pretend that, if I
have determined at last to speak on this question,
you had nothing to do with it; that it was not your
fault.

" Here I am obliged to contradict you.

" Yes, sir, it is your fault, and I cannot accept your
excuse.

" You ask, ' Why has Monseigneur the Bishop of

Orleans brought this question before the public?' I will explain to you.

" You deny the seasonableness and justice of my act: I will make you comprehend them.

" You say that it would not be becoming to provoke from me a new condemnation. I come not to condemn, but to warn you.

"I might neglect your provocations, were they personal to me. But what you have been doing for ten months is another matter.

" You assume, sir, a bearing in the Church which is no longer tolerable.

" You, a mere layman, of whom one of our holy bishops said yesterday, in your own columns, that they have no authority and are nothing in the Church. You usurp strangely—you agitate and trouble men's minds in the Church; you are raising a sort of pious mob at the doors of the Council; you prescribe its course; you raise questions that the Holy Father has not raised; you talk of inevitable, as you deem them, definitions; you tell their upshot and form; you decide questions of doctrine and discipline; you make yourself a judge between bishops, to dishonor some and rule others; you take sides for or against them, on the gravest, most delicate, and complex theological questions; you abuse, denounce, and put under the ban of Catholicism all Catholics who do not think and speak like yourself; you do not even allow them to abstain, through a sense of incompetency and through reverence, from discussions against bishops; in your eyes, not to meddle with controversies raised by you as you do, is a desertion!

" This is too much, sir. It was time to answer you. Therefore I spoke. You say that 'I have just given a head to an armed revolt.' No, sir; what I have done is no revolt, but a defense.

"For the moment has come to defend ourselves against you.

"In my turn, then, I raise my voice, and hasten to oppose enterprises against which I utter a solemn warning.

"I accuse you of usurpations over the Episcopacy, and of perpetual intrusion into the gravest and most delicate affairs. I denounce especially your doctrinal excesses, your deplorable taste for irritating questions, and for violent and dangerous conclusions. I accuse you of accusing, abusing, and slandering your brethren in the faith. Better than you, none ever deserved that severe phrase of Holy Writ : *The accuser of the brethren.*

"Above all, I reproach you with making the Church a partner in your violence, by presenting as her doctrine, with rare audacity, your most personal ideas."

M. Veuillot has replied with his accustomed daring. He has hurled at the Bishop of Orleans the phrase which is his climax in abuse. When he has exhausted his vocabulary which however does not lack wealth, he has a crowning epithet, Academician. In his eyes that represents all baseness and all hypocrisy. And he did not fail to let that arrow fly at Monseigneur Dupanloup, who indeed is one of the Forty of the French Academy. M. Louis Veuillot, by what I was told last night, has reached Rome. He is no doubt to represent one of the tongues of fire in the new Pentecost, and breathe upon the assembly that rage against all liberty which consumes himself. I have received new information concerning the divisions of opinion in the Council. It seems that the Hungarian and Portuguese bishops form the extreme party against the Pontifical infallibility ; they come here full of animation, and will sustain the Germans and the few bishops who have resisted the general current. The Pope has had a table prepared which gives him a view of the probable votes of the diverse bishops. How singularly that savors of worldly policy ! What matters all this information, if it is true that all the bishops, when once assembled, will be lifted to the heights of inspiration ? What they think to-day is of no importance, since to-morrow they will become oracles of the Divine Spirit. But the Holy Father himself acts as if he had to deal with an ordinary deliberative body, as the Queen of England would do on the eve of the opening of her Parliament. This is because the Pope, in his desire to see the triumph of the dogma of his infallibility, slightly forgets that the Council is to be inspired, and relapses unconsciously into the reality of facts. The thing will be much more patent when the deliberations shall have begun and shall appear doubtful. There will be great anguish at the Vatican ; they will ask if the good party may not receive a check, and will talk, on occasion, as though the Holy Spirit lacked wisdom. Sarpi, the enlightened historian of the Council of Trent, relates that the inspiration came to the sacred Council in the valise of Rome, which brought benefices and presents. To-day the presents flow to Rome and do not proceed from her. There is, then, no such abominable simony to fear. Unless they succeed at the outset in creating a blind enthusiasm, discussion will be needed and the result doubtful. It will, moreover, be difficult for

the deliberations to produce any great effect at the
time. The speeches will scarcely be heard, and little
understood, by auditors not belonging to the same
nation as the orator. Stenography will gather them
up, and the prelates will read them at home, sipping
their chocolate. Thus will they form their opinions.
We ask ourselves how the sacred spark will be
loosened in an assembly so split up.

December 4.—The discourse pronounced by the
Pope in the preparatory session, the other day, when
he had the oath administered to the officers of the
Council, has just been published in the *Rome Journal.*
The Holy Father limits himself to the expression of his
joy on finding himself surrounded by the bishops, and
compares himself with Jesus Christ surrounded by
the disciples when he formulated the loftiest doctrines.
People perceive the sense and aim of this comparison.
The Allocution closes with pious words, which for a
wonder are unmingled with anathemas. As if to contrast with this pacific language, the *Civiltà Cattolica,*
which appeared yesterday, published a true manifesto
under the title, *The Council of the Vatican.* The
organ of the Jesuits inquires, What are the diverse
dispositions of mind which appear on the eve of the
8th of December? It finds three principal ones, joyful expectation, declared ill-will, and the disquietude
of men of little faith. The last are the Liberal Catholics. Against these is directed its heavy artillery.
They would reconcile Catholicism and modern liberty.
But this liberty is precisely the great heresy which
the Council should condemn. Under the name of
liberty they try to withdraw the family, the State, and
the school from the Church, from the saving power
of the word—since the first principle of that liberty

is the secularization of civil and political life. This must be at any cost hindered and condemned. The word is life, light, and salvation. The duty of the Church is to subdue the State as well as the family and the school, and to make an end of freedom of conscience, which denies her this sacred right.

The Council will not fail to condemn the miserable indifferentism that tolerates all religions and all opinions. The Ultramontane party will not be reproached with carrying its flag in its pocket on the eve of the Council. It hopes for the restoration of the law of the Middle Ages. One faith, one law, one king! People observe the guarded silence of the famous review on the late productions of the Bishop of Orleans, while it extols the most mediocre circular of the most unknown South American bishop. It behaves like the ostrich, which thrusts its head into the sand in order not to see the approaching peril, and assumes the air of despising what at bottom it dreads.

December 7.—Here we are on the eve of the great day. This is truly the moment to speak of a French pamphlet advertised on all the walls of Rome, and entitled, " On the Eve of the Council." A masterpiece of bigotry and stupidity, it is sure to be greatly relished in orthodox circles. The author feels compassion for those whom he calls *good-natured* Catholics—by whom he means the simple and credulous who fill the churches, at least in the lay ranks—who allow themselves to be snared by antichurch accusations. The author makes me feel that he merits an honorable position among the *good-natured* of whom he so disdainfully speaks. He seeks to prove that all the anxiety which has been circulated on the issue of the Council has no foundation. He does not comprehend how the doctrine of infallibility can disturb people, and I confess that on this point his reasoning seems to me well founded. He says, "After the publication of a not yet defined dogma like the Immaculate Conception, done by the Pope alone without a Council, who could seriously, and without offense to his own conscience, to-day maintain the so-called Gallican ideas on the infallibility of the Pope and the Council? These ideas then received a mortal blow from the hands of the entire Episcopacy. Was not that infallibility more than proclaimed in 1854, since it was publicly and unanimously obeyed? Shall it be inscribed in the Council in the great book of the defined rights of the Holy See? It seems to us that after having read it in the consciences of the whole Episcopate, that this is nothing to stir up serious men." This time the "Good-natured" does not lack skill. He gives us to understand that, proclaimed or not, infallibility nevertheless exists. Then he pours out his bile, vile vestry bile, on the recalcitrant bishops, and he can only abuse Father Hyacinthe by rejoicing in his fall, as he styles it, because it has rent the vail in which the Catholic Liberals were wrapped. He seeks to reassure the bishops, who are a little vexed that simple priests should know more than they about the programme of the Council, having been admitted into the preparatory committees. He elegantly inquires, "Have they not understood that the cook is not better fed than his master because he sees the dinner which he prepares before the master, who does not see it till he has the chance to eat it?" It is well understood, then, that the Council will be completely *cooked* before its opening; that the bishops will only have to shut their eyes and open their mouths to proclaim what has been decided on for them. The author trounces those governments soundly who have some anxiety concerning the wisdom of the resolutions that may be reached on the relations of the civil order and the religious order. These decisions will be conformed to eternal truth ; and besides, the princes have denied the Christian faith since the State has become secularized. They will not have, then, to employ their swords in the service of the decrees of the Council, which, however, is a great pity. Let the Church and the world be reassured as they behold Pius IX., who, since he proclaimed the Immaculate Conception of Mary, combines in recompense the penetrating charms of woman with manly energy. Let them fall upon their knees, and into silence. Such is the substance of this pamphlet, which at Rome doubtless seems a marvelous work. At the very moment it appeared, they were placarding on the walls the last decisions of the Congregation of the Index. It condemns in the front rank the "Letters of Janus," a grave and learned book, which very clearly expresses the views of the most distinguished section of German Catholicism. It is the Catholicism of Döllinger that is here condemned in advance, and stifled by the mutes of the Roman seraglio at the moment when they are about to open the so-called deliberative Assembly of Catholicism. This shows the measure of freedom which recalcitrant opinions will there enjoy. I regard this condemnation on the eve of the Council as a scandal. The Papacy would see its opponents only with their hands bound and their lips gagged ; but then it might have spared us this comedy of a senate of bishops which can only decide with what sauce to serve the fish, that is, with what sincere or equivocal formulas they will wrap the dogmas already decreed at the Vatican. How well I understand the wrath that rumbles in the hearts of intelligent and liberal men at such a spectacle. Here is what I heard the other evening in a Roman abode of the highest distinction : " The temporal power is every thing here. It has mounted the spiritual power, and uses it as its steed. Islamism is perhaps not so far from primitive Christianity as Papistry. Celestial Empire, Sublime Porte, and Holy See—these are a triangle, of which each angle is equally distant from the Gospel. What a distance between Calvary and the Vatican, between the Holy Sepulcher and the Holy See ! The Papacy once abolished the Society of Jesus. The latter returns the favor to-day by dragging it to its ruin. Christianity will be reborn in these lands only from the ashes of the present structure." Such are the motions of many consciences. As I write, all the bells of Rome proclaim the great festival of to-morrow. On me they have the effect of a battle clarion. They excite in me the ardent desire to fight more energetically than ever the great fight of Christian freedom.

December 9.—Well, it is over, the famous day so long expected in Catholicism, which is to inaugurate, if we may believe its sincere defenders, an era of glory and power with which nothing in previous ages can be compared ! Let us try to give a faithful picture of this great spectacle, which under the arches of Saint Peter's had incomparable scenic advantages, and which had some very fine moments. The skies were not favorable ; the weather, which had seemed to promise sunshine, was detestable. The dull gray light, leaving the immense basilica in demi-obscurity, was a great pity, for a rich golden light would have added much to the magnificence of the ceremony. From five in the morning the multitude began to flow to the porticoes of Saint Peter's. Near half past six, the doors were opened. The church was speedily more than full. Never, even at Easter, did I see it so greatly thronged. It was a moving ocean of human heads, where all the ecclesiastical costumes were blended in an often picturesque variety with brilliant uniforms, the toilets of the great ladies, and the simple garments of the Roman peasant. The ladies all wore black vails. Fortunately no breath of terror passed over that human sea, for one dare not think what would have happened had such a multitude been of a sudden wrought upon by one of those inexplicable frights which too often arise in great assemblies—it would immediately become a blind element, and irresistible in its wrath, which would destroy itself. Nowhere in my life have I seen so many men assembled. Fortunately the Italian crowds do not resemble our French throngs in their promptness to lift up and dash together their waves; and there was no accident to regret at Saint Peter's. The basilica is happily not susceptible, on account of its size, of being overloaded with ornaments; otherwise they would not have failed to spoil its magnificent arrangements, as is done in all the other churches on great festivals. Its immensity triumphs over the false elegance of its tinsel. Overflowing thus, it produced a truly grand effect; there is certainly no other edifice on earth capable, on such a day, of presenting a similar vision of mankind. However, I noticed one change accomplished in favor of the opening ceremony of the Council; the famous statue of Saint Peter, whose

great toe is worn away by the kisses of the faithful,
was splendidly adorned for the ceremony; instead of
the usual image, which is that of an apostle from the
ranks of the people, they had made it the representation of the royal pontificate; they had flung over his
naked shoulders the mantle of a chief of the hierarchy,
and circled his brow with the tiara. This act is
symbolical, it very well expresses what Roman Catholicism has done with Christian antiquity in sur-
charging it at a later date with the deceitful signs of
its usurpations. It could not more frankly confess
that it found an apostle, born and abiding in poverty, as well when he became a fisher of men as when
he flung his nets into the Sea of Tiberias, and that
despite himself, it made him a prince of this world, a
civil and religious despot. This avowal is at the
same time a hint to the Fathers of the Council to
bow before the successor of Peter, and not to cherish
foolish ideas of independence. The hall of the Council, which has been opened in one of the arms of the
transverse cross of the basilica, is as I have already
described. They have depicted on its walls some of
the greatest Councils, beginning with that of Jerusalem. The painter has received new information
on that great event, which he surely did not draw
from the narrative of Saint Luke. He shows us the
assembly with the Virgin Mary presiding, seated between Saint Peter and Saint Paul. To her all eyes
are turned, as it is in her name that prayers are to go
up to ask of Heaven the illumination of the bishops.
To us nothing appears more logical than this honorable position of the Virgin in a Council opened on
the anniversary of the proclamation of the Immaculate Conception, and convoked with the special

design of justifying forever this grand, authoritative stroke of the Papacy.

About eight o'clock, the troops which were to keep the way open for the cortege took their place in the basilica; the Swiss are arrayed as halberdiers of the Middle Ages, with coats of mail and red plumed helmets. The cannons of Saint Angelo announce that the ceremony is about to begin. The Fathers of the Council are assembled in the galleries of the Vatican; they descend the princely staircase. They pass the threshold of the basilica, and the singers of the Sistine Chapel, who precede them, intone the *Veni Creator* in simple and noble style. The aspect of Saint Peter's at this moment is imposing; never yet had such a procession swept through it. The bishops are estimated at eight hundred. Each of them is accompanied by his theologian. At the head of the procession are the dignitaries of all sorts who abound in Rome, then representatives of all the congregations. Then follows the long file of the bishops, who advance two by two. It is truly an assembly from every tongue and nation. Beside the Italian bishop, with his delicate and long profile, advances the German bishop, with somewhat gross but manly features. Here is a French bishop near a Spanish, English, or American bishop. The Oriental bishops are remarkable for their long beards, and the majestic calmness of their expression. The most distant missions are represented; the Bishop of Siam is beside the Bishop of Geneva. The entire hierarchy unrolls the links of its chain. While the ancient hymn vibrates powerfully under the arches, the patriarchs and cardinals, covered with their purple, precede the Holy Father, whom his noble guards, all bedizened with gilding,

announce. He is followed by the apostolical prothon-
otaries and the generals of the great religious
orders. He lays his golden miter on the threshold
of the basilica. He pauses before the Confessional of
Saint Peter, prostrates himself, and intones with his
sonorous voice the prayers for the day; then he proceeds to the throne which has been prepared for him
in the further end of the Hall of the Council. Then
begins the great opening mass, performed by Monseigneur Patrizzi, the Cardinal Vicar, which is chanted
by the choir of the Sistine Chapel.

This choir is the musical glory of Rome. It always chants without accompaniment, and it entirely
shuns the theatrical effects of the Chapels of the
Canons of Saint Peter's and of Saint John de Lateran; it does not like interminable roulades and
brilliant cavatinas. The music which it prefers is in
general very ancient; melody is rare, but the whole
effect is marvelously powerful. Nowhere have I
found such consummate art in passing by gradation
from the softest *piano* to the most reverberating
forte. You would think it a single voice running
over the entire scale of the diapason, with shades of
infinite delicacy, to end in a superb and triumphant
outburst. The Sistine Chapel is the faithful guardian
of a musical tradition which goes back to the finest
days of Catholic art, and it is this that preserves it
from the invasion of the refined and effeminate melo-
dies which Church music now affects. Will it long
keep that tradition? I doubt it. It will finally share
in that indescribable softness which the Catholic
worship has taken on, since the adoration of Mary
has occupied the central place. For the moment,
this musical revolution is not yet effected at the Sis-

tine. Let us profit by this to admire their somewhat
strange chants, which appear in their sharp tenuity
to attain the extreme limits of the human voice, then
to melt into majestic harmonies; sublime echo of
tradition. Yesterday the "Veni Creator," as well as
the opening mass, were chanted with unequaled per-
fection, in a way that filled the soul with religious
emotion in which there was nothing artificial. Let
us grasp in their flight these good moments of the
Catholic worship, for they do not last long, and they
are soon replaced by great parade. I ought, however, to concede that the forms of the opening services
of the Council appeared to me in general fine and
well conceived, and, at any rate, much superior to
the habitual ceremonies of modern Catholicism. I
can very easily explain this superiority. The Romish Church has held no Œcumenical Council for three
centuries. In the determination of the ceremonial
then she is obliged to recur to a tradition quite an-
terior to her innovations. Mariolatry and the un-
measured exaltation of the papal power were not
developed three centuries ago as they are at the
present time. They were on the morrow of the
Reform; the Society of Jesus had not attained the
degree of influence which it has since acquired. The
business was to defend themselves against a powerful
adversary, whom they might indeed burn and exter-
minate, but could not despise. The breath of the Reform, though weakened and cooled, had reached some
of the Fathers of the Council of Trent, especially the
French prelates. It is, then, very easy to comprehend that the necessity of conforming in the opening
of the present Council to a tradition which belongs
to a period when Catholicism was very different from

what it is to-day, should have impressed on the ceremony of the 8th of December a character evidently
superior to the present level of Romish piety.

Immediately after the mass, Monseigneur Peucher
Passavolli, charged with sermon, proceeds to ask the
benediction of the Pope and leave to begin his preaching.   It is a formal sermon, without any precise meaning.   The Cardinal Vicar then read the first words of
the Gospel of John : *In principio erat verbum.*   After
that Monseigneur Fessler, the Secretary of the Council, went to deposit a copy of the Holy Scriptures on a
reading desk in the form of a throne which had been
set up over the altar.   This was surely an admirable
ceremony, which calls to mind a profound saying of
my illustrious master, Vinet.   He said that certain
Catholic ceremonies affected him like those buoys
which are fixed at certain spots in the sea near the coast
to mark the place where some precious object was lost.
Does not that Holy Bible laid on the altar suggest
with great eloquence the treasure, lost to present Catholicism, of that veritable authority before which every
Christian should bow?   In the early General Councils, which, however, were not free from human
influence, especially from that of the pretendedly
Christian Cæsars, the sacred texts truly had the force
of law.   Herr Professor Piper, well known for his
fine works on Christian archæology, and for his evangelical "Year-books," has discovered at the Imperial
Library of Paris, in an old manuscript, the representation of an ancient Council.   The Bible is not
only laid on the altar, it is put wide open in the chair
of the president—on that is conferred the presidency
of the Council.   That is the true doctrinal infallibility; it is there and not elsewhere.   Were not the

act of depositing the Bible on the altar a vain form
for the Council of the Vatican, it would not be so
anxious on the question of knowing how far infallibility should be divided between the Pope and the
bishops. Both would lay their hands on the sacred
book and every thing would be said. I well know
that if they submitted to its teachings, consulted directly and not athwart tradition, there would soon be
neither bishops nor popes, and that, according to
the command of Saint Peter, nobody would longer
dream of lording it over God's heritage. At any
rate, it should not be forgotten that the Christian
soul is the true altar of Christ, and hence that the
Holy Book should not Le kept from it, as though they
would profane it, nor impious powers be encouraged
and blessed in their criminal devotion who have flung
into galleys and prisons persons guilty of having read
together the volume pompously laid on the altar of
the Vatican !

The ceremony quickly came back to its true spirit.
Beside the Bible is likewise laid on the altar the
pallium, or sacerdotal mantle of the Holy Father ;
then he is adorned with it in great pomp, that he may
receive the fealty of the bishops, after having intoned
the psalms of the day. The bishops then proceed
one by one to kiss the hand of the Holy Father and
do him homage, thus showing that they are not
ministers of the Holy Gospel, servants of the divine
word, but the ministers or subjects of the Pope.
They pass before the Bible, and leave it on its golden
throne, to bend the knee before a man. Is not this
reducing the Bible, and Him who speaks to us in it, to
the illusory royalty of the Merovingian princes, under
whose name the mayors of the palace governed, while

waiting to shear their locks and send them to die in some monastery? Here the mayor of the palace is the mighty lord of the Vatican.

After receiving the fealty of the bishops, the Holy Father pronounced a truly beautiful prayer, in which, for himself and the bishops, he begged Jesus Christ that they might be kept from sin and error, that they might not turn aside, but follow the right path without undergoing any pressure. Here is another of these confounding anomalies. What! you are infallible as you pretend! You are so by your very office as successor of Saint Peter, as the common Father of the faithful, and as the organ of eternal truth—and still you entreat God that you may be kept from error and fall. Either your prayer, O Holy Father, is a mockery—which I do not admit, knowing your personal piety, and all that renders your old age respectable—or it implies that you may err, that you do not possess infallibility by divine right, that you are exposed to our uncertainties and weaknesses. Then by what right, and with what face ask the Council to proclaim what you confess you do not possess? You demand that they shall no longer examine any of your opinions in doctrine or morals, and that they shall no longer weigh in the scales of the sanctuary any of your judgments, and yet in your prayer you confess that in those scales you may well be found wanting, did not the grace of God, which you ask as we ask it, keep you from lapse. It is absolutely impossible for me to comprehend how a Catholic theologian escapes this difficulty. I would also ask him how the infallible Pope should need daily to prostrate his infallibility at the feet of a confessor. I shall be answered that infallibility is not impecca-

bility ; but is not this to forget all the laws of exper-
imental psychology, and to neglect the close relations
that subsist between moral and intellectual life ?

Let us recur to the opening session. The most
solemn moment was when the litanies of the saints
of the day, intoned by the Pope, were chanted by the
entire Council and the vast assembly. At that
instant the aspect of the Council was very imposing.
The hall is arranged as an amphitheater ; in the
center is the altar, at the rear the Papal throne.
Two vast tribunes stand one above the other ; one is
divided into two parts, for the diplomatic corps and
the sovereigns, among whom shine the old Duke of
Florence and King Francis II.—fallen royalties which
are still recognized at Rome. The second tribune is
for the Sistine choir. Seated in their places, all the
bishops wear the miter. The Papal Chapel chants
a verse of the litany, which is majestic and simple ;
then the Council, with the assembly, repeats it. It is
an immense chorus, whose mighty concord fills the
naves and ascends to the cupola. It is impossible to
avoid a very lively emotion as we hear all the
oriental and occidental bishops uniting their voices
in that antique hymn. It is a splendid representation
of Catholic unity, which would ravish us did we not
remember that it is founded on mental slavery, and
that, after all, it is a pure chimera. Ah ! could all the
dissensions covered up by appearances break out at
this moment, how many sharp notes would mar this
fine harmony, and how many discords would come
smiting our ears. Reflection comes then to calm
enthusiasm, yet it must be confessed that the first
impression is powerful, and the effect of this chant
considerable.

After the chanting of the litanies, the Holy Father
addresses an allocution to the Council. We cannot too
greatly admire the beauty of his tones. This old
man of eighty years has a full and melodious voice,
whose sonorous and modulated vibrations are heard
at a great distance. He employs great emphasis in
his delivery; you feel that he is moved and happy
to have seen the dawn of this great day. His allocution is very significant; it expresses very clearly in
what spirit he hopes the Council will be held. Here
is a summary of it:

The Holy Father began by expressing his joy on
seeing the great assembly of bishops about him, "on
this day, favorable above all others, of the Immaculate
Conception of the Virgin Mother of God!" "Venerable Brethren, let us all bear witness to the word of
God in order to show the path of truth to all men,
and to judge, under the guidance of the Holy Spirit,
the oppositions of science falsely so-called." Then
follows the usual picture of the deviations of contemporary humanity, the cry of distress from a power
which feels that the world is escaping it. The Holy
Father says, "You see the impious conspiracy of
which Satan is the head; it spreads afar, it has on
its side wealth and institutions, and vails itself under
freedom that it may wage war on the Holy Church
of Christ." This language, in the mouth of the author of the Encyclical of 1867, is clear. "But," he re-
sumes, "nothing is mightier than the Church. 'Heav-
en and earth shall pass away,' said Jesus Christ, 'but
my words shall not pass away.' Hear them: 'Thou
art Peter, and on this rock I will build my Church,
and the gates of hell shall not prevail against it.'"
Such is the important thing in the allocution, and

we may add the watchword of the Council in the mind of the Holy Father. The Holy Father then explains that it is to remove these evils that he has convoked the Council, which at this very moment presents the image of the Church Universal—which in the person of its Bishops shows its piety and its obedience to the See of Saint Peter. The Holy Father feels a burning desire to labor with this great Council for the salvation of souls perishing without the pale of the Catholic faith. His eyes move with comfort over this great and noble city of Rome, which God has not abandoned to Gentile pillagers, and to the Roman people, who encircle him with their love. What particularly sustains his courage is the union of the Episcopacy with the Apostolical See; in these difficult times nothing could be more useful to the Church. These bonds should be drawn still closer, for in the war waged on the Church, union with its Chief Pastor is more than ever necessary. In this spirit let us labor to give peace to kingdoms, the law to barbarous nations, repose to the religious orders, order to the Church, discipline to the clergy, and thus reconstitute a people well-pleasing to God. The discourse closes with an invocation to the Holy Spirit, to the Virgin, Queen of the Church, to the Angels, and to the Martyrs whose relics are at Rome.

After his allocution the Holy Father arose, holding in his hand the pastoral crook, which is the sign of his universal dominion, and gave the Council the triple benediction. Then the Cardinal, who fills the functions of first deacon, said to the Fathers, *Orate*, (pray.) They knelt, and prayed in silence for five minutes. Then the same Cardinal said to them,

Erigite vos, (rise up,) and they arose. I hardly like
this intervention of the master of ceremonies in
prayer, nor the supplication begun on the minute and
closed at command. Still less was I pleased that
Cardinal Antonelli should be the leader in prayer, he
who has hitherto shone in other spheres than those of
inward piety, and is better acquainted with the
mountain whence we see all the kingdoms of the
world than with Tabor!

After the prayer and the gospel of the day, the
ceremony underwent a modification which does not
seem unimportant. According to the original programme, the moment had come when the master of
ceremonies should pronounce these words: *Exeunt
omnes qui locum non habent in Concilio*—Let all
who have no right to sit in the Council, depart. The
embassadors, sovereigns, and Sistine choir should
have left at this moment, and the doors of the Assembly been closed, that the Fathers of the Council
might hold their first deliberation in the prescribed
forms, depositing their ballots in the election urns.
It is only when the deliberation has taken place in
this way that the doors should open again, and that
it should be proclaimed before the entire Assembly
that the Fathers themselves had decreed the opening
of the Council. Instead of conforming to this rule,
the Holy Father caused the Fathers to vote in public
by simple acclamation. I well know that the subject of the deliberation was of no importance, that
the business in hand was a mere resolution agreed on
in advance by all, namely, the opening of the Council. But derogations from the forms of deliberating
assemblies are always grave matters; on occasion of
an incontestable decision, a precedent is thus created

which will subsequently be used in relation to much more important questions. For my part, I should not be astonished if there was in the acclamation of yesterday an attempt to hasten matters, and demand from enthusiasm what reflection would refuse. Perhaps I am mistaken, but it notwithstanding remains true that the forms were modified yesterday in the direction of summary proceedings. In the second place, the Council decided that its first public session should be held January 6, Epiphany day. Again they chanted the *Veni Creator*, and then the ceremony closed with the *Te Deum* in the Gregorian style, chanted by the Council and the assembly. Worthy coronation of this ceremony! whose memory will long be preserved, and which none of our contemporaries will probably see renewed. I besought God from the depths of my heart, while they were invoking the Holy Spirit, that he would send upon mankind his Spirit of freedom and holiness, that His breath might pass over Catholicism to startle and renew it, and that this audacious attempt at a Council might turn to the confusion of Jesuitic Ultramontanism, through some check, or through one of those insolent triumphs which bury evil causes. I took care not to forget that I have more than one brother in Jesus Christ among the Fathers of the Council, and that it is testifying my love to such to desire that their bonds may be broken. I forgot to say that the Knights of Malta, representatives of an order that no longer exists, have asked to serve as guards of the Holy Council. It is a phantom which may well end by guarding a ghost, for I fear, from fresh information, that the Council may be led to decisions so little in harmony with the present state of the world and

the Church that they will, as it were, be null and
non-existent.

I learned yesterday from a very reliable source
that the Council will begin by naming a Committee
on its Ceremonial, which will likewise serve as arbiter
should any differences arise between the bishops.
This is a species of quæstorship, at least what we
designate by that name, in our parliamentary assemblies. Then will come, also this week, the nomination of the three most important committees: that on
Faith, that on Discipline, and that on Religious Orders.
They will nominate another Committee on Missions
and the Christian Orient. The Committee on Faith
will be charged to draw up all decisions on the relations of philosophy and religion—on all doctrinal questions. There will come the famous question of Papal
Infallibility, and probably, too, that of the Assumption of the Virgin. The way in which the first Committee shall be made up will show how the majority of
the Council inclines. The Spanish, American, English, and Italian bishops will vote for the papalist idea
—I employ this expression, which would be thought
very inharmonious here, for brevity, and because it
very well depicts the situation. But a portion of the
French and German bishops will examine more nar-
rowly. Yet they are very hopeful in the Ultramontane camp. It is pretended that Bishop Dupanloup
is universally blamed for having put out his pamphlet at the very moment of coming to sit in the
Council. They would even be disposed to tax this
haste with impropriety, while they admire the putting of the Letters of Janus into the Index. It
would be becoming, no doubt, to vote silently what
has been prepared beforehand by the Roman man-

agers. They have ravishing explanations of the dogma of infallibility. It is said, and I am now reporting what I have heard, that at bottom this is a Liberal dogma ; that the Episcopacy, since it no longer presents independent and princely positions, is entirely subject to the civil powers, and that henceforth the Holy Father alone represents the independence of religion ; that consequently the Liberal party is the Ultramontane party, and that it has proved it by more than once allying itself with the most advanced democracy. I need not remind you of the high exploits of the Jesuits in this line ; they have not even recoiled before regicide. We well know that they are ready for any thing to serve their party, and that they would sing the Marseillaise if it would lead to their goal. Only we must not forget this goal. The paths that lead to it are diverse and tortuous, but their firm purpose is to end in the concentration of all advantages in the hands of the Papacy. The Ultramontanists mock us when they affirm that by fortifying the authority of the Holy See they fortify the spiritual power, since, according to their own theory, they never separate the temporal power from the spiritual power, and since they openly aim at theocracy. Surely I am the sworn foe of Cæsarian Papacy. I never have ceased, and never will cease, to combat it even in its mildest forms, in the guise of Concordats ; but I none the less detest Papal Cæsarism as it appears in the Roman theocracy. Let them call things by their names, and let them not color with the name of liberty the criminal efforts of civil and religious absolutism.

This leads me to speak of the task of the second Committee, that on Discipline. This will have chiefly to consider the relations of the Church and State. It will begin, to judge from what I am told, by laying down the principle which is at the basis of the Ultramontane system, the necessary subordination of the civil to the religious power, the duty of the State to be the prop, the defender of the Church, to deliver to her the rising generation, to watch over the periodical and literary press from her stand-point, and to punish heresy as an offense or a crime, according to its gravity. On this point I do not think they will capitulate; the Holy Father would deem that a condemnation of his Encyclical which he could not accept. It is probable, then, that in more or less covert words they will condemn modern law, which is identical with the secularization of the State.

"But," I said to the eminent man who imparted these ideas to me, "nothing is more opposed to Christianity than the use of constraint in defending or propagating the truth." "Constraint!" he replied; "but we do not desire it. Nothing is more opposed to our ideas." "But," I returned, "how will you deal with those who are not convinced by your teachings, for men are not born Christians." "We will persuade them by addressing their hearts and minds." "Very good, if they listen, but if they are obstinate?" My companion kept silence, for people know too well what the Ultramontanist system implies for opponents and schismatics.

They gave me to understand that, in view of the unhappy times, they might abate somewhat from the rigor of their principles wherever it was necessary, that is, wherever they are not the stronger; for it is well understood that when the Church finds a government after its own heart she concludes Concordats

such as Austria and South America know.   She
strives as nearly as possible to approach her ideal,
which is at Rome.   Prudent men, who understand
the requirements of politics, would wish them to
regulate in a uniform manner the *mode of living*
with what they call, by a delicious euphuism, *hypothetical* governments.   This is the customary expression for States which have not submitted themselves
to the sway of the absolute law, or the Papal law.
With them every thing is but hypothetical—freedom
of conscience, freedom of education, that of the press,
vacillating hypotheses—all, like the philosophy
whence they spring, destined doubtless to pass away;
but as these hypotheses for the moment are quite vital
—as considerable powers side with them—it would not
be amiss to make terms with them while waiting for
the return of the reign of God.   This is the opinion of
prudent bishops, but the zealots do not hear with
that ear, and they triumph; they will issue new editions of the Syllabus and the Encyclical.   Surely the
Committee on Discipline will have wherewith to occupy their leisure, and all the more so, because they
will have to treat the thorny question of ecclesiastical
estates.

As to the Committee on Religious Orders, it will
have to look closely to their present constitution, and
to study the modifications that should be introduced.
The Committee on Missions will have a very delicate
question for its order of the day, that of the relations
to be formed with Oriental sects which more or less
approximate the Catholic type.   One would be terrified at the labors which would be incumbent on
the Committees of the Council had not the Roman
managers provided against their fatigue, and greatly

abridged their labors, through a well-adjusted com-
miseration in arranging all questions. I have been
given to understand that they hope to profit largely
by the light of the preparatory congregations. They
will also have to consider the means of approximation with the Greek religion.

The Sultan gives his full approbation to these
efforts, because he is very glad of any thing that can
enfeeble the power of Russia. They are busying
themselves, too, with Protestants who may be tempted to use the occasion to treat of their reunion with
the Church. The Holy Father has named a certain
number of theologians with whom they can confer.
Already certain English pastors seem disposed to
hold a parley. They speak also of ten Rhenish Prus-
sian pastors who declare their readiness to return to
the pale of the Church, if they will concede to them
priestly marriage and communion in both kinds.
We shall soon know what will result from these
efforts at approximation. In my eyes they are of no
importance, because they come from men who in reality are already Catholics. The reserves which they
still make are insignificant when compared with what
they have conceded. For myself I should without
sorrow see the Catholic elements retained in the
Reformed Churches following their affinity to the
end. Positions should be clear and marked in the
great religious struggle that is preparing. The ritualism that is striving to stifle spiritual religion, and
the Neo-Lutheranism awakened by sacramental materialism and sacerdotalism, are out of place in Protestant Churches ; they are enemies in the place.
Let them move out with flying colors and draw up
under the standard of Rome, unless they will purge

out the Romish leaven which is in the depths of their hearts and minds. I cannot grant that any son of the Reform, truly consistent with its principles, can have for a moment the notion of coming to treat with the Council of the Vatican. Whatever concessions he may obtain, he sacrifices every thing by recognizing the authority of such an assembly to decide sovereignly, and in the name of God, ecclesiastical doctrine and discipline. He thus abjures the essential principle of evangelical Protestantism, which puts no authority above Holy Scripture, or rather, Jesus Christ speaking in the Scriptures.

Besides, how can we forget the profound modifications which the ancient constitution of the Church has undergone? I admit the indisputable authority of no Council, not even of the Œcumenical Councils of the fourth and fifth centuries. But at least they might claim to be true representatives of the Christian Church. The bishops were not named by one of themselves, trenching on the monarch; they were elected by the members of the Church, and laymen were not reduced to the condition of helotism to which the Catholic hierarchy condemns them. They received no watchword from the Bishop of Rome, whose presence or absence did not greatly disturb them. The decisions of the Council of Nice did not need his sanction that they might be universally received. But if I would find a true Christian Council, I have only to turn back to that which was held in the upper chamber at Jerusalem, and whose deceitful image is presented us in the painting that adorns the hall of the Council of the Vatican. No president by right directs its debates; each speaks with entire independence. In place of bishops I see elders of the

Church named by it, exercising over it a purely
moral influence; simple believers witness and share
in the deliberations.   So little do the Apostles claim
the right to impose their opinions that the idea which
prevails comes from James, the Lord's brother, who
is not an Apostle, and the decree of the Council is
sent in the name of the entire assembly.   " The
Apostles, elders, and brethren to our brethren among
the Gentiles who are at Antioch, in Syria, and in
Cilicia, greeting.   It seemed good unto us, being assembled of one accord, to send unto you chosen men.
It hath seemed good to the Holy Ghost and to us to
lay no other burden upon you than these necessary
things."   This simple introduction to the resolutions
of the Council of Jerusalem scatters all the pretensions of the Councils of the hierarchy, and truly I do
not know how they can get clear from the precision
of these simple terms, which show what a true representation of the Christian Church is.

As to the infallibility of the Council, the same
eminent personage observed to me yesterday that it
should not be confounded with inspiration.   The
Scripture is a divine word, but the word of the Council is a human word divinely preserved from error.
Here is another of those distinctions whose meaning
entirely eludes me; how can a human word divinely
preserved from error be other than an inspired word?
But every thing in these pretensions to infallibility
amazes me; the Council sees no tongues of fire resting
on the heads of its members; every thing goes on as
in a deliberative body; they discuss, they vote: formerly they put more than one vile spring in play, as
is evident in the case of the Council of Trent.   Up
to a given point we are fully in the order of nature,

then all of a sudden the supernatural begins; it triturates, if I dare say it, to the bottom of the urns wherein the Fathers deposit their votes; it comes forth from it glorious and immaculate. And yet it does not attach to all the votes! The majority alone is the object of the miracle; the minority has nothing to do with it—remain in the low regions of the fallible reason. Here are miracles of a very peculiar type—half prodigy, half natural. We can know the precise means employed to bring about the result. These means are very simple, but the result itself is divine. Thanks to God, the true supernatural bears no analogy with this which I have just characterized, and of which Rome is about to give us probably the last representation, for I have a presentiment that what we see to-day will never be repeated.

E. DE PRESSENSÉ.

LETTER XII.

Another Contrast — The Oratorio of the Pontiff of the Immaculate Conception — Review of the Papal Army — Its Composition and Condition — The Committee on Conciliation — Regulations of the Council — Social Life at Rome — The Expenses of the Council — Fruits of Mariolatry — Vexation of the Liberals — Their Policy — A Morning Ramble — The Bull of Excommunication — Comments — The Committees on Faith and Discipline — The Anti-Council — Its Follies and End — The True Anti-Council — Probable Success of the Ultramontanists — The Italian Government and its Difficulties — Protestant Missions — Savonarola — Needs and Hopes.

Rome, *December*, 1869.

Dear Sir,—For the sake of greater freedom I still employ the form of a journal. Permit me to lay before your eyes yet another of those contrasts with which Rome abounds, and which I strove to depict to you in my second letter.

I went last Sunday to Saint Peter's to witness one of the solemn Advent masses over which the Holy Father presides. It was a representation, with a full orchestra, of the Catholic worship in all its magnificence. The sun shed vivid light on the basilica; the bishops were present in a body at the ceremony. The choir of the Sistine Chapel chanted the office. Going to his throne, the Pope passed through long lines of halberdiers and noble guards, then he put on his miter and received the fealty of the prelates. Mass was performed by a cardinal. You see that nothing was lacking in the pomp of this service, rendered more brilliant and solemn by the presence of seven hundred bishops. This was truly the monarchical Catholicism of the present time, the religion which speaks to the senses and fascinates them in order the more easily to subdue the understanding and the will. Thence I went, without any gradual transition, into two Catacombs generally closed to visitors, and for which I had obtained special permission, the Catacombs of Saint Priscilla and of Saints Peter and Marcellinus. Nothing is finer than the road which conducts to the second. We go out by the major gate, which is an antique gate; we pace alongside the aqueducts which impart such a poetic sadness to the Roman Campagna; at every step we encounter some abandoned ruin. On the left is Mount Soracte and the Sabine mountains; while the Albanian hills, with their graceful undulations, bound the horizon. The melancholy inspired by the imposing ruins with which the way is sown is involuntarily softened before a landscape whose sweet harmony is not to be surpassed. Reaching a remote farm, we find the entrance of the Catacomb hard by an ancient pagan temple, and descend into the Christian necropolis. What a change of scene when, under these somber arches, we think of the mass of Saint Peter's! What an eloquent refutation of the pretensions of the Pope King! I indeed found two crowns in the Catacomb, but they were like that of Jesus Christ, and girdled the bleeding brow of a confessor. Among the numerous symbols with which these Catacombs abound, I have not encountered one to justify the Catholic system. Instead of a ruling and tyrannical religious power, I only saw the merciful love of the Good Shepherd seeking his lost sheep; instead of a Christianity triumphing proudly over its foes, I only saw a militant Christianity, engaged in

the most redoubtable struggle, and unweariedly repeating her immortal confidence—now with the three
youth in the furnace; now with Jonah, who was
swallowed for three days only to be born again to a
better life; now with Noah, saving his ark amid the
waves of the deluge; now again with Daniel in the
lion's den: all these symbols, speaking of a humble
and courageous faith which clung to things invisible
and cast its anchor within the vail, are multiplied in
these two Catacombs. They are likewise filled with
prayer. The Christian men or women whose remains have been deposited in these vaults are presented to us with hands lifted toward heaven. The
incense of the saints has burned under these arches
as nowhere else. Contemplating them, we breathe
its sacred perfume. Finally, there is no trace of
legends in any of these frescos. The most interesting, and now the most celebrated, is in the Catacomb
of Saint Priscilla; it is a representation of the nativity of Jesus Christ. Mary holds the infant Jesus
pressed to her bosom. The star of Bethlehem has
paused above her. A prophet designates the child
and seems to say, Lo, the Desire of all nations! You
think you recognize Isaiah in him. This fresco seems
to belong to the highest antiquity, perhaps to the
first half of the second century. Very ancient inscriptions have been discovered in its neighborhood.
The ornamentation of the vault is in simple and exquisite taste, which suggests the classic style, and
cannot be later than the second century. They try
to draw great advantage from this picture in favor of
the worship of Mary. I do not see the least indication which can be interpreted in that way. The
Virgin has no halo, she is not the object of adoration;

it is the child that is designated by the prophet. I should even say that what constitutes the beauty of this first of the Madonnas is, that it is not set over the altar, that she has not the priestly stiffness of sacred art; she is living, her beauty is simple and expressive, she is truly a daughter of men, a flower of Galilee that has retained its grace. That inexpressible Raphael-like touch which forms its charm depends precisely on this absence of idolatry. The more idolatry grows, the more art is abased; nothing then equals a miraculous image. They would give all the masterpieces of the Renaissance for a Madonna which, according to some gross tradition, has moved its eyes. I attribute to the development of Mariolatry, in part, the abasement of the artistic inspiration in the religious domain. They wish to make idols, and they will no longer create types wholly human and divine, that let the inward fire breathe athwart expressive loveliness.

But in the matter of abased, hypocritical art, blending the sacred and profane, nothing can equal the burlesque representation given last Sunday in the Church of the Holy Apostles in honor of the Council, before a large number of cardinals, bishops, and priests. The theater is interdicted on the Sundays preceding Advent, which did not prevent the organizers of the great spiritual Council of the twelfth of December from drawing largely upon it. But why should not the most worldly airs be sanctified when once they have been sung by the Pontifical Academy of the Immaculate Conception? This association, we read in its printed programme, is wont to celebrate every year a great concert in honor of the Virgin. It could find no more solemn occasion of being faithful to this custom than the opening of the Œcumenical Council. This year it will assign a high place to the praise of the Pontiff to whom we owe this convocation. A cardinal will open the solemnity with a *prose*, which will place the Council under the protection of the Virgin. Then we shall execute hymns in divers tongues. The Academy will make these hymns alternate with three parts of an Oratorio entitled " The Pontiff of the Immaculate Conception," in which the glory of the Holy Father is associated with that of Mary. The Virgin will deign to bless our poor homage. She who is the mother of eternal wisdom, the holy protector of our faith, can only bless the labors of an Academy which thinks solely of developing true knowledge.

Let us now see in what manner it develops this knowledge. The first part of the Oratorio is set to the air which opens Bellini's opera of " The Puritans." It represents the faithful people praying God, during the Conclave, to give his Church a chief after his own heart. Then comes a joyful chant from the Roman people after the election of Pius IX. The chorus celebrates the benefits of the amnesty to an air from Meyerbeer's " Robert le Diable," blended with an air from the Sappho of Saccini. The hymn devoted to the hegira of Gaeta is sung to an air from Verdi's Macbeth. The patriotic master, whose attachment to the Italian cause is well known, also contributes the cavatinas necessary to celebrate the happy return of the Holy Father, "accomplished through unhoped-for succor," says the libretto ingeniously, which seems to suggest an army of angels descending from heaven. Alas! it is well known that these angels wore the red pantaloon of our troops of the line. The libretto adds, " O thou Holy Virgin, who alone hast crushed the serpent's head, thou alone canst scatter the infernal throng which has invaded the See of the Holy Father." For once the miracle was not complete, being complicated with artillery. The triumphal hymn of the Immaculate Conception is borrowed from the " Nebuchadnezzar" of the same Verdi. After the canticle of the Immaculate Conception we have that of the Syllabus, still to an air from Nebuchadnezzar, an opera whose theme suggests the dangers men risk in taking themselves for God. The protection of the Virgin seems to have extended a very weak shield over him whom it sheltered, for it did not prevent his losing the finest jewels of his crown. But this is the stand-point of proud reason. Faith perceives her intervention in the proclamation of the Syllabus, which is better than all provinces. I think the kingdom of Italy would very gladly join in that hosanna. I only detach from the canticle of the centenary these words addressed to Mary, " O Mary, who dost protect the Church, we have confidence in thee alone ! " The music of Meyerbeer's " Robert le Diable " accompanies a chant in adulation of Pius IX. on occasion of the jubilee on the fiftieth anniversary of his ordination. Its flattery is so gross that nowhere else is there a theater so low in grade that it would not be hissed there if addressed to the sovereign of the land. Rossini and Donizetti are also put into requisition. The " Eleanore " of the latter master furnishes the romance of the Virgin's memorial with a strong reinforcement of amorous roulades. This fine masterpiece is continued in the triumphant hymn of the Council, in which an air from Sappho alternates with those of Rossini's La

Charité. The Holy Spirit is totally eclipsed by Mary, who is to animate the bishops with divine fire. The oratorio closes with an obedient homage paid to the Holy Father in the name of Christendom. Rossini has the honor of furnishing the music with his two operas, William Tell and the Siege of Corinth. The Council is only named for form's sake. The chorus chants, "We swear, O our Lord, to render thee the homage of our thoughts, for thou only canst dispel this night of error; thou art the fountain of truth. We promise to follow thy faith were it at the price of the most cruel martyrdom."

It is odd that this oath of enslavement should be set to the air of the famous oath of Helvetian freedom in "William Tell." It is a strange way of preparing for martyrdom to sing a medley of worldly music. Nothing could better depict the abasement of Catholic art of Rome, and also the religious jugglery which forbids the opera at the theater in order to transport it to the foot of the altar, with an accompaniment of frenzied applause. It is true, that the hands which made the uproar were hands wonted to consecrate the host. No female voice was heard, and principles were all safe; yet the sopranos went up very high, and suggested the Orient in its most hideous customs. I forgot to say that in guise of a ballet between the various parts of the Oratorio, we had the diversion of hymns to the Virgin and the Pope sung in different languages by the pupils of the Propaganda. High privilege to hear the same idolatrous platitudes in Arabic, English, Latin, and many other tongues! This buffoonish and religious solemnity bears the complete stamp of the Gesu. I thought I ought to make it known to you somewhat in detail, for it seems to me one of the most characteristic of present circumstances. The Council will also be celebrated by a great review of the Pontifical troops at the Villa Borghese. Let us doubt no longer, this one will far surpass the Council of Jerusalem, which lacked the accompaniment of tender roulades and cannon salutes.

December 16.—The review took place at the Villa Borghese in splendid weather, under the magnificent shade which forms the beauty of that promenade. There all the Pontifical troops were assembled: Zouaves, the so-called Antibes Legion, whose framework is French, carbineers, artillery, chasseurs, dragoons, and police. People noticed especially a corps of mountaineers of agile aspect in picturesque costume. They are meant for the repression of brigandage, at least of that which forgets time and place, for, long permitted and encouraged on the Neapolitan frontier, it turns culpable in the Sabine mountains. It is pretended, too, that there is a great confusion of ideas in this respect, and that this sort of mountain police, whose flower certainly has figured in brigandage, has sorry reminiscences. Its mere costume would suffice to maintain these: it is that of the famous " Fra Diavolo." I should not like to encounter such protectors of order in a gorge of the Apennines. However, the effect of the review was charming. Romans and foreigners of distinction flowed together under the oaks and parasol pines. The military bands played their finest airs, and I noted a hymn to the Pope by Gounod. The bishops thronged together, and applauded, either mingled with the crowd or on a terrace of the garden. Thus the two militias of the Pope were combined. The

fine sun, nevertheless, shone upon a fearful scandal,
for all who remembered that this armed force is in
the service of the pretended representative of Jesus
Christ. This very evening I heard a distinguished
French priest covertly express a feeling of regret,
which in his mouth meant much.

The Pontifical troops would be a very feeble barrier against revolution, but for the French army.
The Roman portion of the army, except some un-
mounted and mounted police, and the officers, who
are brave gentlemen, totally lacks solidity. It is
quite generally thought that in the day of battle they
would execute a fugue more brilliant than all those
of Bach. The Antibes legion, composed of Frenchmen, would doubtless bravely face fire; but as it is
recruited a little at hazard among our regiments, it
is not convenient in peace, and lacks discipline. De-
sertions from it are very frequent. As to the Zouaves, they possess bravery and conviction; they are
the elect. But most of these young gentlemen came
to Rome with chivalrous enthusiasm, in the hope of
combating the enemies of the Papacy. They had
often been told that the convocation of the Council
would bring on an outburst of bad passions, and then
there would be fine shooting.

The Council has come, and it is found that the
Knights of Malta will suffice to guard it. The Zouaves, then, find themselves reduced to the ordinary
service of a garrison troop; the military administration tends to confound them more and more with the
regular army. Many of them also begin to grow
very weary of their present position. As most of the
enlistments are for six months, it is to be believed that
large numbers will return to their homes, and that

gradually the corps of Zouaves will resemble troops
recruited by engagement bounties.   They will return
home, hardly edified by what they have seen at
Rome.   Their language is even imprinted with bitterness; they have retained the same enthusiasm for the
Holy Father, whose goodness to them is paternal; but
they know the interior chronicle of the Church; they
understand what cardinals' purple often covers.   They
have lifted the mantle of hypocrisy, which, under
decent and devout appearances, conceals the greatest
corruption in this Zion of Catholicism.   Their sojourn
at Rome changes, not their ideas, but rather their
judgments of men and things.   Yet they have not
come to the point which our soldiers reached when
in garrison at Rome.   They became such grumblers,
and so anti-Catholic, that their discourses shook
what their bayonets sustained.   And the authorities
preferred to send them to Città Vecchia, where they
can only speak ill of the Mediterranean, and where
they taste the most formidable listlessness that can be
imagined.   They are nevertheless the only efficient
props of the temporal Papacy, and the Emperor is
the true and efficacious chief of the Knights of Malta,
who guard the Council.   Truly, he gives proof of
rare goodness of heart, that would be more admirable
were it clear of political calculation.   It is true that
the calculation is radically wrong.   His Majesty
Napoleon III. alone makes an episcopal reunion
possible, where they are about to decree solemnly
the condemnation of the principles on which French
society reposes.   In recompense he only receives
benedictions for his soul and very real marks of ill-
will.   I have already related that the Roman curia
does all it can to thwart his desire of pursuing the

magnificent excavations of the Palace of Cæsar. Not
only is the convent of women, which arrests the work,
allowed to remain, but they have just laid the foundations of a new church in another part of the Mont
Palatine.   It is perfectly useless for the purpose of
worship, but it is a very ingenious means of putting
an insurmountable and sacred obstacle in the way of
the plans of the mighty protector whom they hate in
the depth of their souls.   This perfectly confirms the
remark of an Abbé after Mentana, who said of the
French, " Our ingratitude will cover our gratitude."
Let us be just. The Roman managers do not like archæological labors which they do not direct ; the most
fruitful excavations undertaken by a layman, who
does not belong to themselves, are under suspicion
with them, and they are pleased to chastise such impertinence.   They like only the science of which
they hold the key, and approve those discoveries
alone which have paid for their patent, and brevet
with an undivided submission.

The Council has confined itself, for a few days, to
nominating the Committees of which I have spoken.
The Committee of Conciliation was named Friday
the twelfth.   This is no doubt less needful with our
modern manners than in the rude sixteenth century.
The debates in the Council of Trent often assumed an
alarming turn. Sarpi relates that two theologians who
were opposed to each other on the question of justification by faith, seized one another by the beard so firmly
that they could not be separated.   Were beards as
long in Europe as in the sixteenth century, and manners as violent, the question of infallibility might
well lead to similar scandals ; but it all goes on in
the depths of the heart.   Besides, the Ultramontane

prelates know how to say every thing with neatness and grace; as one of our poets has said,

" E'en hate itself must use the tones of love."

They envelope the most odious theories in charming formulas. *These are the confectionery of Catholicism*, was the charming remark which I heard last night in a Roman drawing-room. They draw sugar from the vilest substances, as skillful confectioners can. Thanks to them, the Committee of Conciliation will be a sinecure. The other three, the Commissions on Faith, Discipline, and the Christian Orient, are to be named by ballot. Their influence, moreover, will be very potent; according to a regulation, which seems to me very ingenious, the propositions elaborated for several months by congregations appointed by the Pope will not be elaborated anew by committees. They are to be presented in the lump to the Council, which will decide at once all those which will not awaken too great discussion. You perceive how much this limits the leadership of the Council; opposition shows itself with much more difficulty in a large assembly than in a committee. The pressure of the majority is much stronger when encountered ever compact and ardent. The Papacy evidently has free play. The tradition of ancient Councils is invoked, but this important and delicate question of order will not be submitted to the deliberations of the Assembly. The Gallican bishops stand firm on the essential things; but it is to be feared that at the outset they may lack skill, and, perhaps, firmness. Yet there is talk about a very sharp altercation which was provoked by the method

of the ballot in the nomination of the Committee on
Faith. Naturally, it is impossible to know these
things in a precise way, on account of the obligation
of secrecy imposed on the bishops.

For the moment, social life is very brilliant at
Rome. A fashionable drawing-room here has now a
peculiar aspect, with which nothing else in Europe
can compare. Bishops and cardinals elbow fine
ladies in splendid toilets, and epaulets devoted to the
Holy See, and foreigners of all nations—they talk
only about the Council; the mystery surrounding it
excites curiosity. The great ladies side for given
opinions as in political life. One drawing-room
patronizes Papal infallibility, another is very much
opposed to it, and forms an opposition drawing-room.
People are naturally obliged to express themselves on
such delicate matters with rare prudence; yet passion
crops out. What strikes me is, that in all that I
hear about the Council, the course of its labors and
the result to be expected from it, they forget only
one thing, namely, that it is supposed to be presided
over and directed by the Holy Spirit. People speak
of it as we speak at Paris of our Corps Legislatif,
when we are calculating the chances of a law which
we have at heart. Hopes and fears are inappropri-
ate when people count on miraculous illumination;
but in reality they do not count upon it, and they
fall back constantly into petty calculations. I ought
also to acknowledge that people are very benevolent
in the higher society of Rome; that one is received
there with perfect good-will even when he follows
another flag, and that you encounter no bigoted exclu-
sion. Even here the spirit of the times has exerted
its enlarging influence, and I was able to satisfy

myself that very heretical books were there read and relished.

The great expenses which the Council imposes on the Holy Father will be partly paid by voluntary subscriptions. I was told yesterday that within ten years he had received near twenty millions of dollars for the expenses of his temporal power. A frightful figure when we reflect that it is taken from the spiritual necessities of the Church in a world where pagans are still in the majority. The present collection is, in itself, entirely legitimate. But it furnishes good souls, who burn to exhale their fanaticism, a very precious occasion to display it. The journal of M. Veuillot, *The Univers*, publishes a daily list of subscriptions, accompanied by the exclamations of the donors. At the pitch of his quarrel with Monseigneur Dupanloup, he registered with ill concealed satisfaction violent attacks on his adversary. Since the Council has begun he no longer publishes them, but he gives in full all the follies that can pass through the brain of a fervent bigot. Brave country curates, or convinced beadles, pay five francs for a reverberating exclamation in favor of the infallible Papacy, and imagine they have acquired immortal glory as soldiers of the faith. Among these subscriptions I have observed one which perfectly expresses the opinion current in the circles of ignorant piety. It runs about like this: " Holy Virgin, remember that Pius IX. proclaimed your Immaculate Conception, and cause his infallibility to be proclaimed." This simple man imagines that the Pope rendered the Virgin immaculate, and he demands the recompense of so great a service. However, it is impossible to conceive all the absurdities to which

Mariolatry can give birth in the ranks of the simple
and of the lower clergy.   One of my friends heard a
Capuchin preaching at Rome on the conversation of
the child Jesus with the doctors of the temple.   He
openly sided with Mary when she reproached him for
remaining behind, and taxed him with impertinence.
He dared to add, " Behold his punishment on the
cross."   I well know that this excess of stupidity
which turns to blasphemy, is a particular case ; but
I am persuaded that, should we presently examine all
the sermons delivered in honor of the Virgin, in convents and country parishes, we should be terrified at
the progress of idolatry.

God the Father and Jesus Christ are banished by
popular piety to that obscure distance, where the
Greeks placed the mysterious Saturn, concentrating
all their glances on the brilliant and charming divinities of Olympus.   Mary occupies the foreground in
Catholic piety, at least in its popular manifestations.
And I shall attach no importance to the negative
triumphs of Liberal Catholicism in the Council, should
it obtain them, so long as it shall not have repealed
the dogma of the Immaculate Conception of Mary.
While this dogma shall be recognized and accepted,
with itself it will maintain in fact the infallibility of
the Papacy and the good right of Mariolatry.   Were
Liberal Catholicism firm and courageous, it would
distinctly put the question on this ground ; it might
then hope to restore its Church, and inaugurate a
phase of religious renewal.   It would be needful also
to affirm the good done by modern liberty, and not
allow it to be treated as a disorder with which the
Church has, perforce, to make terms.   A Council under these conditions, without realizing all that we

believe conformable to the truth, would be a benefit, and would withdraw more than one advantage from the passionate enemies of the Gospel. But, if Liberal Catholicism is content with an equivocation—if it thinks to triumph because the dogma, practiced and triumphant, shall not be formulated—then it would lull itself in vain illusions; these very illusions would render it more timid; and while it should fall asleep over a chimerical victory, the papal usurpation would daily grow, and some new Encyclical, worthy of the preceding one, will come to teach the Church and the world that Jesuitism, like the reed in the fable, bends and does not break, but lifts up its head with the first favorable wind.

December 17.—Last evening I gathered up in a great and brilliant company much valuable information about the Council. It is not passing on so sweetly as may be thought; parties are coming to light. The adversaries of infallibility even appear quite irritated at the regulation which I have made known to you, and which gives from the outset a preponderating influence to the papal congregations. Further, the Holy Father has nominated a Committee of twenty-two members, to which every proposition must be submitted before being presented to the Council, and it makes no decision which has not been ratified by the Pope. He has also appointed five consulting theologians on the great question of infallibility, who are all quite pronounced in favor of the new dogma. These preliminary measures clearly reveal the firm intention of the Romish party to reach their ends by fair means or foul. The Liberals have also attempted to protest against this arrangement; they name a bishop who

on this point was thrice called to order by the Cardi-
nal-President. They even mention a much. graver
fact; a French cardinal will this very morning leave
Rome and the Council. He is said to have declared
that he would have nothing to do with a Council
destitute of freedom; probably he did not express
himself so clearly, but his step has been so understood; decidedly our French bishops appear better
than was anticipated beforehand; twenty are reckoned under the flag of Monseigneur Dupanloup.
This is because you can never foresee what men will
do gathered in a deliberative assembly. Napoleon
I. thought himself very sure of the National Council
which he assembled in 1811, to sustain him in his
difference with Pius VII. The regulation which he
had invented might be compared with a cord put
around a man's neck, and which on the least pressure
strangles him. And yet the Assembly turned out recalcitrant, and he was forced to cast certain prelates
into the dungeons of Vincennes, that the Council
might not turn in favor of the Pope whom it was
meant to combat. Surely the Castle of Saint Angelo
will not open before any of the bishops who sit here;
but what well-informed men most dread is the relaxing influence of this city, the moral malaria of
this world without frankness—with supple, caressing,
and false manners. The first concession of the Fathers was the acceptance of the Council at Rome;
the most recent tradition allowed them to demand
another city, where their independence would be
more assured. Nor should it be forgotten that the
Holy Father has a crushing majority in his favor,
and that if they are content to count votes without
weighing them, he is sure to conquer along the whole

line. To him a check would be irreparable, even though it might be a real advantage for the Church, as I have endeavored to show you. And he will move heaven and earth—I mean the heaven of which he is master; which is not that of life eternal, but that factitious heaven whence he causes anathemas and indulgences to rain at will. Whatever the Council may decide, the result of its decisions will be very grave, and will inaugurate a new phase in the history of Catholicism. Before leaving Rome, I hope to know the composition of the Committee on Faith, named by ballot.

This will disclose the number of voices belonging to the various parties. There is much animation in drawing-rooms, and passion breaks out. Last evening I met one of the chief of those called here the *non-infalliblists*, Cardinal Schwartzenberg. He shows himself very decided and energetic, and causes great scandal in the ante-chambers of the Papacy. Lord Acton, who has just been promoted to the peerage by Mr. Gladstone, and who belongs in the front rank of Liberal Catholicism, will not succeed in leading the English bishops back to a reasonable temper; they will remain the most fiery of the Ultramontanes.

I was told yesterday that Monseigneur Maret, the firmest of Gallicans, is lodged in the same house with M. Louis Veuillot. There is a curious approximation which forms a very marked antithesis.

December 19.—For a few days, Rome has adorned herself with her most enchanting grace. The heaven is resplendent and cloudless, and the moon envelops monuments and ruins in her silvery vail. Yesterday morning I walked for several hours along the abrupt hills that line the right bank of the Tiber. Nothing

more poetic and grand can be imagined than the
changing views obtained as we pass from hill to hill
athwart enormous reeds and thick brambles. Cattle
and sheep graze on the grassy slopes; rounded pines
and tall cypresses inclose the landscape in the most
picturesque fashion. The Tiber rolls its yellowish
waters under the severe arches of the Ponte Molle,
and breaks into a thousand. charming windings.
From the height of Monte Mario, we have on the left
the hills of ancient Etruria Soracte, that seems a
dome of verdure; the Apennines, whose snows glitter
in the sun; and finally, the enchanting curve of the
Sabine Mountains. The desert plain forms the foreground. In front rise the mountains of Latium; on
the right is the plain which goes to die on the shore of
the sea of Ostia; and then, Rome reveals its numberless domes. Every thing is silent and sublime in these
prospects, which become truly glorious under this
inflamed sky. Never did I better understand the
sovereign charm exercised by this land—fairer in its
majestic sadness than the most brilliant scenes of a
civilization in full activity. This morning—the last
Sunday before Christmas—Saint Peter's will be the
theater of the most pompous ceremonies of the Catholic worship. Beholding from my windows the splendid basilica bathed in the purple splendor of a fine
day, I imagine the little upper chamber in Jerusalem
where Jesus pronounced words that have created a
new moral world, and come resounding to the depths
of our souls, like his *Come forth!* in the depths of the
tomb of Lazarus; while the words of the Pontiff
awaken no other echo than that of the arches of his
temple. His are words of death, and not words of life.
He has just pronounced one which might well be

mortal to the Council. The *Unità Cattolica* published yesterday the Bull of Excommunication which is to accompany the opening of the great assizes of Catholicism. It was known that it had been read in the second session, but people did not think it would so soon be laid before the public. In reality it is a striking confirmation of the Syllabus, and an authoritative act of the Pope which decides from the first day some of the most important questions which were to be submitted to the Council; among others, all that bear on the relations of temporal power and spiritual power. Thus the Holy Father excommunicates formally all those who impose any restraint on the rights and liberties of the Church. Now these rights and liberties are perfectly defined in the last Encyclical and the Syllabus; they are the right of the Church to suppress all liberties except her own; beginning with freedom of conscience, of the press, and of education, which it calls pestilential, and which it has carefully set aside in all the Concordats which it has recently concluded. For her, liberty means the total subordination of the State to her dogmas and discipline; in a word, it is the Roman rule. Thus, whoever does not accept this odiously theocratic rule is excommunicated. She would do better to say, that she hurls her anathema at all Europe. Lest we should be mistaken here, the excommunication assaults one of the fundamental principles of modern law, namely, the equality of all citizens before the law and the unity of jurisdiction. Excommunicated are all who turn aside clergymen from the ecclesiastical tribunals. This is a thunderbolt which smites France, as well as England, Germany, Spain, and Italy. It is known that the German Catholics

had declared that they could not submit to the pro-
hibitions of the "Roman Index," because in times of
struggle and free knowledge they could not ignore
religious discussion. The recent bull takes good care
to declare outside the Church whoever shall read a
forbidden book. As the Pope addresses himself not
only to individuals, but also to governments, he thereby proscribes all States which do not abandon the
press to ecclesiastical, or rather Roman, censorship.
But you have not yet heard the grand peal of pontifical thunder. It is not about to smite impiety
blasphemy against God and his Christ :· no ! it con-
centrates all its avenging flames on those who have
laid profane hands on the possessions of the Church.
There is the sin which is forgiven neither in this
world nor in the next—for which there is no redemption. The bull makes no distinction between the
present and the past; it bears, then, on what was
done ages ago, as on the Italian law concerning
ecclesiastical estates. To touch the goods of the
saints of the Lord, is the abomination of desolation.
Thus you see at the outset that all modern princes are
put outside the gate of heaven ; it seems to me that
they acted sagely in not crossing the threshold of the
Council to be drubbed in solemn costume in the person of their embassadors. Excommunicated also are
all who shall not accept all the Encyclicals, and in
general all that shall emanate from the See of Rome.
It is declared that the excommunication can be raised
by no bishop, unless in the article of death, and only
for cases where the absolved shall not recover health ;
which is a very clear warning addressed to Victor
Emmanuel. This *motu proprio*, which withdraws
from the Council some of the gravest decisions which

were on its programme, seems to me a very suitable
opening of the opera got up by the Jesuits; it brings
back to monotonous forms the theme which should
be treated, and contains itself the idea of the work.
The liberal bishops are too good truly to lend themselves to this comedy of deliberation with the regulation collar on their necks, and under the constant
menace of more bulls of the same sort. Besides, how
can they resist the enormous mass of the bishops of
the Propaganda. The Apostolical Vicars coming from
the Orient, have the independence of our sub-pre-
fects toward the Papacy. Discouragement is also
succeeding irritation among the Gallican bishops; it
appears certain that on the first day of voting, Monseigneur Dupanloup made a sudden sally, to show his
indignation at the manner in which the deliberations
were conducted. To-day the phalanx of his sup-
porters is well defined. Cardinal Bonnechose, who
had some feeble wish of opposing the Ultramontane
movement, soon yielded. Probably the independent
bishops will seek to leave Rome as promptly as possible; at least, this is what I thought I divined from
the language of an Hungarian archbishop with whom
I spent the evening two days ago. He is lodged at
a hotel, so as to be like a bird on a branch, and
return to his country on the first pretext. On the
other hand, while the names of the Committee on
Faith are not exactly known, it is asserted that the
Ultramontane ticket was carried by a great majority.
For the moment every thing seems in preparation for
the triumph of Papal infallibility, more or less ex-
plicitly formulated. It is spiritedly said here that
the Holy Father, once elevated to this height, will
no longer be the Vicar of Jesus Christ, but that, com-

pared with him, Jesus Christ will fill only a secondary place.   Indeed, the Pope will be able at will to
modify the instruction of the world, and with even
greater boldness substitute his Missal for the Gospel.

December 20.—While Rome was inaugurating the
assizes of Catholic authority, Naples was celebrating
the saturnalia of atheistic demagogy.   It was announced with much noise that on the very day when
the Council should open, free thought would hold its
anti-Council, and in its turn fulminate anathemas..
The leadership of this fine enterprise belongs to a
member of the Italian Parliament, who sits in the
extreme left.   It was placed under the patronage of
Garibaldi, who is guilty of seeking to trench on the
prophet, and who might be content with having been
a hero.   An appeal was addressed to all the enemies
of religion; they hoped to have an Œcumenical
assembly.   They had only the most pitiful baccha
nalia.   The number of delegates was much inferior
to what had been expected.   They began by quarreling over the programme.   The President wished
them to be content with laying down certain general
principles—as the full freedom of conscience, the
separation of Church and State, and morality independent of all religion.   Had they been reasonable
they would have further reduced this programme
by excluding the last declaration, which, by entering
upon doctrinal subjects, would lead the assembly in its
own way to formulate dogmas; that is, to imitate the
Council while condemning it.   I could understand that
in presence of a solemn manifestation of the principle
of religious oppression, a grand manifestation of
the opposite principle should be invoked, and that
freedom of conscience should be strongly affirmed as

the sole condition of true progress, and, above all, as
the sole consecration of eternal right. But to try,
under the name of independent morality, to proclaim
the abdication of God, or at least of the religious
idea, in the bosom of a tumultuous assembly where
no free and many-sided discussion would be possible, was to trench on the Council, and oppose
violence of language to ecclesiastical authority. The
Assembly was so little disposed to enter reasonable
paths, that it thought the doctrinal programme submitted to it insufficient; another was proposed which
ventured much further into questions of principle;
they wished the anti-council to decree a full system
of psychology, or rather, an atheistic anthropology.
It was on this point that discussion arose in such
wordy vehemence as hindered any issue. On the
morrow it was to have been cheerfully resumed, when
the French delegates, who had been hindered
by a stormy passage, arrived. Hardly were they in
the hall, before they thought it their chief business
to indulge in such violent political assaults that no
theoretical discussion could be resumed. They cried,
Down with the Emperor Napoleon and long live the
Republic—a fine way of showing their gratitude to
the liberal monarchy that accorded them its hospitality. The Italian Government could not possibly
allow an allied power to be tranquilly insulted in a
great public assembly. I think they were perfectly
right, and that the deputies who invoked the great
principle of liberty in the Italian Parliament against
the measures determined on at Naples were entirely
mistaken. The anti-council closed amid tumult and
public laughter, to the great joy of its mighty rival
of the Vatican. If it was meant merely to produce

21

a caricature, it has succeeded; it is a *Punch* or *Charivari* success. Such follies comfort the authoritative powers, and fling into their arms, or at their feet, all timid souls who see freedom only in the hideous guise of license. Yet the cardinals and bishops would be wrong in laughing too much; the anti-council at Naples was, I grant, a completely absurd display; but there is another anti-council which will not be so easily dissolved, and which is held wherever men think, study, or love freedom; it is the anti-council of public opinion, which reverses the decrees of the Vatican, or rather, lets them fall to the ground like the dead leaves of an old tree which is soon to be dissolved in dust. This anti-council has an ardent and passionate left, which has flung itself into the extremes of incredulity through the exaggerations and follies of the Papacy. The Bull of Excommunication which I summed up for you yesterday, does much more harm to Catholicism than all the follies of the meeting at Naples to the cause of free thought. The Holy Father hastened to furnish the latter a consolation and an encouragement in his famous *motu proprio*, which only too clearly foreshadows the path in which the Council will pursue its labors. We may consider its opening phase terminated. I leave Rome to-day, rich in memories, and knowing better than ever what we are to expect of the religious form that has been elaborated here. The future will show whether I have been mistaken in my anticipations of the issue of the Council. I do not think so; the triumph of Ultramontanism may be more or less disguised, more or less equivocal; it is certain. How can we doubt this when we read the list of bishops named for the two great Committees on Faith and Discipline?

Though the Liberals are not excluded, the fanatics triumph. The curtain may fall on this first act of the comedy—its upshot is known.

It is in the capital of New Italy that I close these letters, which, written at Paris, would lose their true character, and no longer answer their design. I have witnessed a very interesting session of the Senate of the kingdom, in which the new ministry appealed to the confidence of the Parliament in demanding a provisional vote which would authorize them to collect the imposts until the reopening of the Chambers. Signor Lariza, the Premier, whose bearing is that of a simple and serious man, pronounced the truth of the situation in saying, " The discontent of Italy is not political, but administrative and financial." It is certain that the country is not tempted to surrender its reconstituted unity, and that it does not long for the humiliating yoke of foreigners. But it is succumbing under its deficit, arising as much from excessive expenses as, from bad administration, from the absence of regularity and uprightness in paying the taxes. The embarrassments of Italy fill the Monsignori of Rome with the liveliest joy; they do not percieve that the moral side of these difficulties comes from the education which Papal Catholicism has given this lively, supple, and intelligent nation, which, however, lacks that solidity which conscience alone communicates. For my part, I earnestly desire that the Italian government may undertake serious and radical measures of economy, which alone will prevent the shame of bankruptcy and save the national honor. To support these, it needs to find sustained devotion in the nation, and the abandonment of that carelessness, that fatal ease in deceiving the authorities and defrauding them of their due, as though they had not the same rights as an individual toward whom one is bound by a contract. You see that every thing, even finance, brings us round to the great aspect of things.

The information which I have received at Florence on the progress of evangelization does not differ from what I transmitted to you from Naples. The work of the Gospel proceeds calmly and with seriousness, but without noise, except at Venice, where it has in its favor the prestige of novelty. In Florence, the Vaudois Church has a truly magnificent establishment, which it owes, if I am not mistaken, to the generosity of the Free Church of Scotland. It occupies the Salveati Palace, formerly occupied by a cardinal, who surely did not dream of having such successors. There is found a theological faculty which has thirty students, and a church where a hundred persons assemble. The nets have evidently been flung faithfully into the sea, but the miraculous draught has not taken place. The movement has remained quite restricted; the Italian nation has not been really touched. Were it simply a matter of controversy— should we confine ourselves merely to provoking opposition to Rome—we might have great and prompt popularity, but the results would be purely negative. For myself, I remain convinced that, as I have already written you, Italy, as well as France and all the Latin races, will only awaken to true religious life under the breath of tempests; that the bitter experiment of the impossibility of dispensing with God must be carried through to the end, and that suffering and trial will alone prepare the way for the divine Healer. I think also that the reformatory movement must proceed from the very bosom of these nations, and bear no marks of foreign importation. No doubt it will be connected with the glorious movement of the sixteenth century, whose principles are immortal; but it will apply these principles in its own way, and according to the needs of the nations whence it shall emanate. What the Italy of to-day needs is a second Savonarola, more free from Catholic traditions, more lay without the frock, but with the same fire and intrepidity of speech.

This name of Savonarola now fills my heart and mind. He is certainly the purest glory of Florence. I experienced great and holy emotions in the Convent of San Marco, which is all permeated with his memory, after having been adorned as a mystic sanctuary by the brush of Fra Angelico, who has left on these immortal frescos the perfume of his prayers. Savonarola lives again under our eyes in the admirable portrait of Fra Bartolomeo, his beloved disciple, and at the same time one of the greatest artists of the Renaissance. The figure of the great Florentine Reformer is lean and sorrowful; we feel that he is consumed by inward fires—devoured by his desire of establishing the reign of Jesus Christ. A plaster cast of him produces perhaps a more puissant impression, such immense sadness and ardent faith does it express. It was in this little cell that he prepared his sublime harangues which moved the entire city, and which, for a moment, succeeded in throwing it into a species of ascetic fervor which could not endure: the reaction was terrible. A profound mystery hovers over the end of Savonarola; we have only the report

of the inquisitors who tortured him, and boasted of
having led him to a retraction. And yet he mounted
the pyre and died the death of John Huss. The Papacy was glad to have done with this inconvenient
John the Baptist, who scourged her brilliant vices
when she was heading the dissolute courts of Europe.
Savonarola has not the angelical sweetness of Saint
Francis; he is a man of conflict, an indomitable witness of the thrice holy God; it was needful that such
a man should be put to death, like all importunate
prophets who cannot bend to the proprieties of the
world and the Church. Let us hope that in our days
he will have a successor in this land which he so
greatly loved, and that, in presence of the excesses of
Romish idolatry, we shall see, not a simple tribune,
but a great servant of Jesus Christ arise and pronounce the word of life which shall resound in the
depths of the heart.

Atheistic declamations, like those which have just
given us the comedy at Naples—Rome might pay
for such, for they do but consolidate her power. She
will ever be right against impiety; but the true Christian, who asks no glory of the earth, who would only
serve the truth and combat error and sin, he is her
redoubtable adversary. Let such a Christian appear
with the gift to move the multitudes, and that art,
which is not to be learned, of pronouncing aloud the
word that is hidden in the heart of a generation, and
we shall see what the most sonorous anathemas can
do against him. The times of Luther and Calvin
would return, and the world would learn that the
Christian sap, far from being exhausted under the
bark of its century-old tree, is more generous and
vital than ever. Let us beseech God speedily to raise

up one of those great heroes of the faith called Reformers in the bosom of our old nationalities, which need a new inspiration. Let us hope that the Council, by its exaggerations in Ultramontanism, and the atheistic anti-council, which is held every-where, by its sad blasphemies may prepare the way for the blessed advent of this new era of evangelical liberty; but let us not forget that great servants of God speak in the name of all Churches, and that they are in some sort the children of their prayers. Who shall say how many sighs and tears shed in secret before God have preceded those glorious and fruitful hours of religious history which are fair as the morning dawn of the great day of the Lord !

E. DE PRESSENSÉ.

THE END.

I.

Jesus Christ: His Times, Life, and Work.

Translated by ANNIE HARWOOD. 12mo., pp. 496. $3 75.

One of the most valuable additions to Christian literature which the present generation has seen.—*Contemporary Review.*

M. de Pressensé is not only brilliant and epigrammatic, but his sentences flow on from page to page with a sustained eloquence which never wearies the reader. The life of Christ is more dramatically unfolded in this volume than in any other work with which we are acquainted.—*Spectator.*

The successive scenes and teachings of our Lord's life are told with a scholarly accuracy and a glowing and devout eloquence which are well presented to the English reader in Miss Harwood's admirable translation.—*British Quarterly Review.*

The work of an able and excellent author, whose appreciation of our Lord Jesus Christ, both in his person and in his work, is at once profound and discriminating, and whom no doubts or difficulties hinder from claiming the honor due to the Name that is above every name. In point of learning, intellectual power, and that charm of brilliancy of diction for which the French language is so remarkable when wielded by a master, the merit of this work is remarkably high.—*Sunday Magazine.*

Its arguments are sound, clear, and well illustrated. Of its learning there can be but one opinion, as its pages every-where abound with the results of thorough, well-digested, and extensive research.—*The Rock.*

It is a book eminently adapted to be useful.—*Christian Work.*

II.

The Mystery of Suffering, and Other Discourses.

New Edition.

In these sermons we recognize the same intellectual power, the same exquisite felicity of diction, the same sustained and dignified eloquence, and the same persuasive invigorating Christian thought which are conspicuous in that work—["Jesus Christ: His Times," etc.]—*British and Foreign Evangelical Review.*

. . . The tone of the discourses is so tenderly beautiful that a reader who did not believe one word of the Christian mysteries might be affected by it.—*London Review.*

Sermons brimming up and running over with truth and beauty.—*Weekly Review.*

These are very remarkable discourses. They are distinguished by all the nice analysis of thought and glow of feeling so characteristic of Dr. Pressensé's ministry and writings.—*Evangelical Magazine.*

A volume of beautiful and thoroughly Christian sermons.—*London Quarterly Review.*

They are not ordinary sermons, but replete with valuable thoughts, often beautifully expressed, and are characterized by true pathos and holy unction.—*United Methodist Free Church Magazine.*

III.

The Church and the French Revolution.

A History of the Relations of Church and State from 1789 to 1802. In crown 8vo.

M. de Pressensé is well known and deservedly respected as one of the leading divines of the Evangelical section of the French Protestant Church. He is a learned theologian, and a man of cultivated and liberal mind. In the present monograph he comes before us as the historian of a period which he rightly judges to have a more than local and temporary interest in the fortunes of the national Church of France. And, on the whole, he has done his work not only ably, but impartially. . . . We are not aware that any previous writer has treated the subject from the purely ecclesiastical point of view.—*Saturday Review.*

IV.

Early Years of Christianity.

Translated by ANNIE HARWOOD. 12mo.

This is a sequel to Dr. Pressensé's celebrated book on the "Life, Work, and Times of Jesus Christ." We may say at once that, to the bulk of liberal Christians, Dr. Pressensé's achievement will be very valuable.—*Athenæum.*

De Pressensé tells the glorious narrative with singular force and clearness of expression.—*British Quarterly Review.*

The great theme on which he has labored with the utmost earnestness and zeal suffers no loss of color or life. He holds his brilliant intellectual gifts and his profound learning subordinate to his fervent and absolute faith in the divinity of his Lord and Saviour; but he is well entitled to our credit when he declares that the feeling which has inspired the book has laid no fetters on his freedom of examination.—*Daily Telegraph.*

It is impossible to part from these graphic and learned representations of the purest ages of Christianity without a deep reverence for the ability of the author as a scholar, and his zealous advocacy of the truth as a Christian.—*The Rock.*

V.

The Land of the Gospel:

Notes of a Journey in the East.

He gives us his first and freshest impressions as entered in his journal upon the spot; and these will be found full of interest, especially to every thoughtful reader of the New Testament.—*Evangelical Christendom.*

www.ingramcontent.com/pod-product-compliance
Lightning Source LLC
Chambersburg PA
CBHW020946030726
47496CB00005B/1373